April
&
Oliver

April
&
Oliver

TESS CALLAHAN

GⅼC

GRAND CENTRAL
PUBLISHING

New York   Boston

Grand Central Publishing
Hachette Book Group
237 Park Avenue
New York, NY 10017

Visit our Web site at www.HachetteBookGroup.com.

Printed in the United States of America

First Edition: June 2009

10 9 8 7 6 5 4 3 2 1

Grand Central Publishing is a division of Hachette Book Group, Inc.
The Grand Central Publishing name and logo is a trademark of Hachette Book Group, Inc.

Library of Congress Cataloging-in-Publication Data

Callahan, Tess.
   April and Oliver / Tess Callahan.—1st ed.
      p. cm.
   Summary: "The story of April and Oliver, two inseparable childhood friends whose existences again collide with the sudden death of April's younger brother"—Provided by publisher.
   ISBN 978-0-446-54059-9
   I. Title.
   PS3603.A4436A87 2009
   813'.6—dc22   2008037861

Book design by Giorgetta Bell McRee

For my parents,
GRACE *and* JOHN

Acknowledgments

For sharing their perceptions regarding this book in particular or writing in general, I thank Meliset Abreu, Douglas Bauer, Sven Birkerts, Nicole Bokat, Anne Calcagno, Anne Callagy, Chris Callagy, Leonard Casper, Deirdre Day-MacLeod, Susan Dodd, Don Freas, Amy Hempel, David Lehman, Tom Lorenz, Jill McCorkle, Naomi Rand, Marly Swick, and especially Caprice Garvin. I am grateful to *Baltimore Sun* columnist David Steele for generous details about sportswriting. For musical inspiration, and for her insight into Beethoven's allegretto from Symphony No. 7, as expressed on NPR's *All Songs Considered,* I thank pianist extraordinaire Hélène Grimaud. I am grateful to painter Roy Kinzer for making me a better writer by teaching me how to see. Thank you to my old friend Andrea for bringing adventure to my childhood. I admire and appreciate my agent, Anne Edelstein, for her wisdom and radiance, and my editor, Deb Futter, for her keen, intuitive eye. Finally, I thank my family members and my husband, Vincent, for their faith and support.

I am especially grateful to my longtime friend and trusted reader Sasha Troyan, without whom this manuscript would still be in a drawer.

April
&
Oliver

Prologue

BUDDY HAS BEEN LOST FOR SOME TIME, his wipers whisking the thick Maine snow, when he spots a missed turn in his rearview and brakes. The car fishtails, rocketing into a spin. The faster it pivots, the slower time moves. Buddy is the fixed point, the world careening around him.

He takes a young maple with him into the gully. A few stubborn leaves cling to the branches that protrude through the windshield. Everything is abruptly quiet. He sees bits of sky. A lone heron. The car is resting on its side with Buddy somehow in the passenger seat, his back to the window and his foot beneath the crushed steering wheel. The angle is impossible; it appears to be someone else's leg. The dead engine ticks; he smells gasoline and sap, freshly split wood, his sister's griddlecakes.

He remembers being lost in the woods as a child with his sister, April, and their friend, Oliver, the scent of wet leaves and the downy chill of night descending. This is what comes to Buddy now. A brook gurgling and sloshing over scattered rocks. The three of them stepping from stone to stone. His small hands in their big hands. Water funneling down. The beginnings of a question he feels but can't say. It has the shape of a person bending over him, waiting.

The mangled sapling creaks. Buddy looks into the car and sees a young man with startled eyes wearing his parka. He can't imagine who it is. He looks down on the smoldering baby-blue Malibu dusted with drifting snow. The scene is oddly tranquil. Strapped to the sideways roof, the deer he shot this morning appears to stand upright, ready to bolt.

Specks of snow travel in. Buddy hears each flake as it touches his hair, the soft down on the buck's antlers. He remembers putting his hand on its side as it lay in the snow, feeling its heat. Those dark, gentle eyes. His sister's eyes, worried every time he skinned his knee. "I'm sorry, April," he used to say.

"It's okay, Budster," she replied, dabbing the gash gingerly. "We all fall sometimes." But her smile was pained; she hated when he got hurt.

He wishes he could let her know that what's happening now doesn't hurt at all. He's fine. A veil of snow shrouds the windshield. Buddy feels a growing pause between each breath, like a stride lengthening, an aperture opening by increments, until at last he slips through.

Chapter

1

LONG BEFORE DAWN on the morning of the funeral, a rogue wind enters April's apartment, clattering the shells of her wind chime, causing her to bolt upright in bed. Night air seizes her. Her mind hurtles through darkness, not wanting to remember, but the realization gaining on her. *It's today.* Papers fly off her nightstand. The curtains tangle and snap. She finds her way to the window, her long hair flaying, but just as she reaches the sill, the gust dies down. Against reason, her thoughts clamber for a passage back, a chance to say to him, *Don't take this trip. I have a bad feeling.* Instead, they said good-bye cheerfully, without the slightest premonition.

An aria rises from the street below. A familiar man with a bedraggled overcoat and unkempt beard wanders the train station across the way. When he has enough to drink, his voice carries clear across Sunrise Highway. The sad timbre of it reverberates inside her, echoing just beneath her sternum. She closes the window.

The stillness of the train station tells her it's not yet five in the morning. She doesn't bother to look at the date; she knows. Draped over the back of a chair lies the black dress she set out for herself.

Instead, she pulls on some jeans, gets in her car, and drives to the diner. It's a Sunday, after all.

The usual waitress with milkweed hair and creviced eyes raises her brow. "Aren't you about three hours early?" she asks, pouring two cups of coffee.

"Busy day," April says.

"He here yet?" she says, pointing to the second cup.

"I'll drink both. Thanks."

"Shoot yourself," says the waitress over her shoulder.

April shudders. *Suit yourself.* Of course that's what she said. *Jesus,* she thinks.

April draws the second mug over to her side of the table. The booth feels cold with no one else in it. An immense aquarium illuminates the storefront—an improbable place for a fish tank, but she's never seen an ounce of algae. Vibrant koi glide back and forth. Buddy loved to watch them. April has been taking him here for breakfast most Sundays since he was eight. Ten years already?

People pass by the storefront, heads bowed against the impulsive wind. April gives a start, thinking she sees Buddy dashing to the door—he's always late—but it's only a jogger sprinting by. She cups her hands around the coffee, still too hot to touch. Steam furls up in delicate ribbons—not an amorphous cloud, but a rhythmic swirl, a whirling dervish of mist. She feels the warmth on her face. The vapor lifts and circles with excruciating grace, frail and lithe as the beggar's notes. She cannot bear to watch it, or to stop. Gradually, the rising steam slows and dissipates into shallow wisps of breath. April thinks of many things—tying Buddy's shoelaces, cleaning gravel from a scraped knee, combing his hair before school, the cowlick that refused to flatten. And at the same time, she sees nothing but vapor.

For an instant she doesn't know where she is. The coffee is long cold, and the restaurant teems with people. Outside the window, sunlight bleaches the pavement. The deep-eyed waitress waits at the end of the booth, tapping her pen. "Oh, right," April says. "The check."

She glances into her purse for her wallet and sees that his is there, too, though she's not sure when she put it there. The leather is smooth and molded to the shape of his back pocket. He always asked to treat her, and she never let him. Not once. She takes a twenty from his wallet and leaves it on the table.

Back in her apartment, the wind has clustered papers up against the closet door—insurance forms, the accident report, the death notice. She doesn't pick them up, but leaves her jeans on the floor beside them. The slinky fabric of the dress chills her skin. Rather than wrestle a brush through her windswept hair, she lets it be.

The church doors are locked, so she sits on the cold stone steps and waits. Since the accident she has lost grasp of time. She asked that the hearse meet her here because she couldn't bear to go back to the funeral parlor. Finally, carloads of people arrive. They are teenagers mostly, with hip-hugging pants and thrice-pierced ears, yet their faces, shocked and raw, give the impression of children.

The funeral mass and the drive to the cemetery pass like someone else's dream. The only thing vivid is the past, those grimy fingernails April could never get him to scrub. The home run he hit on his ninth birthday.

The priest opens his prayer book and reads, his words falling like leaves into the open grave. April cannot register them, only the dull timbre of his voice and the barest whisk as he turns an onionskin page. She remembers the time she dropped Buddy in the upstairs hallway, near the top of the stairs. She tripped on something—her father's shoes, maybe; he was always leaving them out in the open—and the baby went flying. She can still hear the thud when he hit the floor, the stunned silence when he did not cry. She was sure she had killed him. When Buddy finally wailed, she was so relieved that she cried, too.

She glances right, feeling someone's stare, only to realize it is Buddy's car, its face turned toward her. She parked it haphazardly, uneven with the others. It is hers now, by default, but it feels wrong for her to inherit it from Buddy, eighteen, barely a driver himself.

From time to time, she feels Oliver look her way, his glance grazing her skin like a swatch of sun between clouds, a warmth so brief she shivers. She is intensely awake, yet cannot shake the sense that she is dreaming. She rubs the worn band of her wristwatch, thinking how time, too, has gone haywire, jumped its tracks, turning like a corkscrew instead of moving ahead, so that the three days since the accident have elapsed in seconds while this moment in the cemetery spans her entire lifetime.

April looks at the line of cars, wondering if T.J. will show, if he has even heard the news. It has been two weeks since the protection order, and the idiocy of missing him enrages her. Beyond the cars the sky is a fierce, crystalline blue, and against it the trees shed vibrant shades of ocher, rust, and red. A group of leaves rise on a current of air, the breeze moving the sleeves of April's dress so softly she holds a breath. If the brilliance of the day is God's idea of a joke, she isn't laughing. She wants thunder and hail. She thinks she can almost will it to happen.

When Buddy was a baby, the gentle smacking of his lips was enough to rouse her from sleep. She knew how to unlatch the crib rail and slide it down quietly so as not to disturb the dog, whose jangling tags in the dead of night could awaken their father, always grouchy when woken. She would give Buddy his bottle even before he cried for it. She remembers the milky scent of his skin, the down of his hair, and the tiny half-moon of his fingernails.

The group blesses themselves, following the priest, and April does the same, drawing a line from head to heart, shoulder to shoulder, father to son. The brakes were soft; April had noticed that. Week after week, she told herself to get them fixed with her next paycheck.

If her parents were alive, they would not survive this, she thinks. She imagines her father here, arms folded across his chest, silken white hair quivering in the breeze. *His only son,* April thinks, his fishing partner, his shortstop, his free safety. Buddy was the only person to bear their father's resemblance, with the same thick neck, enormous hat size, and surprisingly high-pitched laugh.

". . . and so we pray for the repose of the soul of Bede Simone Junior," the priest reads.

April bites the inside of her mouth. No one called him Bede; Buddy hated the name, short for Obedience. He said Bede is what water does on Scotchgard, or a notch in a rosary, not something you call a human being.

The name suited their father, though. April can't help but picture him here, and her mother, too. She would have been superbly dressed for the occasion, her coarse wheat-colored hair pulled back in a fancy clip, accentuating the fine lines of her face. April inherited that delicacy. She constantly has to prove to people, men especially, that she is not as fragile as she looks.

Buddy was just the opposite, tough on the outside only. In the winter of third grade, he had a bad case of strep throat. To pass the days home from school, April and Oliver, then sixteen, constructed a tent in his room out of blankets and chairs, and filled it with pillows, a lamp, and a step stool to act as a table. Inside, they took turns reading to Buddy from *King of the Wind*. When the boy was too tired to keep his eyes open, he asked Oliver to play piano on his back. "Bach," Buddy said, smiling at his own joke. "Beethoven will keep me awake." Finally, Oliver lay back on the floor. It had grown dark inside the tent. "He's out," he whispered. "What should we do now?"

"My dad's home by now," April said. "We could go to your music studio."

"Let's hang here for a while," Oliver said.

April slid over and lay down perpendicular to Oliver, with her head against his chest. It was a daring thing to do, but neither said anything. She heard Buddy's lengthening breaths, and the solid percussion of Oliver's heart sounding against his ribs.

April looks at the white of the coffin. She imagines the long screech ending in a crunch of metal. Then, silence. It was Oliver at his piano who taught her about measuring sounds, holding them in memory, but that was ages ago. He lived in California so long, she thought he was done with the East Coast, but two months ago she heard the news that he was back, and engaged. April glances at him, his head bowed, one hand covering his mouth as the priest reads the final blessing, the other gripping his fiancée's fingers so tightly his knuckles are white. On Bernadette's small hand, the ring looks big. April thinks she ought to feel something, but doesn't.

Bernadette wears a hound's-tooth blazer and matching calf-length skirt, her fair hair neatly French-braided, silk scarf around her neck. April compares this with her own dress—the black brocade, drop waist, and short, flouncy hemline—like something she might wear dancing. She touches the pleats with her fingertips, wondering what possessed her. It doesn't matter that her mother has been dead seventeen years; she would disapprove.

The priest closes his book, and people turn back to their cars. A group of Buddy's friends gathers in a spontaneous huddle, arms across one another's shoulders, foreheads touching. A boy with a shaved head lets out a sob. April pictures her dead parents walking separately toward a limousine, not looking at each other.

April thinks of her living grandmother at home in her kitchen peeling onions. No one has told her. It is too soon after last year's stroke, they decided. But April suspects they don't want to tell Nana because that would mean admitting it to themselves. In any event, the decision is made, and it is not the first lie April has conspired in.

She hears car doors open and close, and rummages through her purse for her keys, Buddy's keys, with the dangling pocketknife he used to gut fish and cut lines. The knife was a gift from their father when Buddy was twelve, and the Swiss Army logo is nearly worn off from his touch. She opens each blade and closes it again, then the can opener, nail file, scissors. He kept it immaculate.

The huddle of Buddy's friends breaks up. They walk arm in arm. Cars pull away. Small groups linger. Oliver and Bernadette stand close together, speaking softly. Bernadette glances over. April can almost read her lips. *Go on, Oliver. Talk to her.* Bernadette retreats to the cars as Oliver moves toward April. Her skin heats. She holds the keys tightly, hearing his steps in the grass.

The gravedigger switches a lever, and the mechanized pulley lowers the casket beside her parents' graves. *This is the part you're not supposed to see,* April thinks as the gleaming white hood descends into shadow. She steps closer to the edge, wondering if her parents are watching from wherever they are, if they are anywhere. It's hard to picture them together, let alone with Buddy. That would not be his paradise. So what *would* be Buddy's heaven? Here, she decides, back in his life.

"April," Oliver calls.

"I don't want to be buried here," she says.

"What?"

"I want to be cremated."

"Don't talk like that," he says.

The coffin, swallowed by shade, makes a small thud as it hits bottom. It's real now. Her whole family is in this cemetery. She wonders how long before they backfill. The grass is damp—at some point she slipped off her shoes—and she imagines the earthen walls of the grave, cool to the touch. Oliver takes her arm. She feels herself collapsing, yet she is still standing. She draws back from him. The gravedigger pulls up the straps, frowning at April to suggest she is too close.

"Hey," Oliver says to him. "Can't you see we're still here?"

The man raises his arms. He looks only bored. April turns her back to Oliver and blows her nose. He puts his hand on her shoulder. It feels heavy and warm. She moves away, certain that above all she must not fall apart, not with Oliver.

A horn sounds and his brother, Al, beckons from their father's station wagon, the motor running. Bernadette gathers her skirt and slips into the backseat. Oliver waves them on.

"There's no room in my car," April says quickly, her voice thicker than she wants. "Buddy's shit is everywhere." But Al is already pulling away.

"We could have picked you up," Oliver says. "You could have asked."

"When I go, I don't want a funeral. God forbid Nana feels she has to pay for it."

"April," he says tensely. "Why assume you'll die before an eighty-year-old woman?"

"I'm just saying that she's my only blood relative now. If anything were to happen . . ."

"Anything like what?"

She notices his perfectly pressed suit, the regimental tie. She says nothing.

The gravedigger walks to the backhoe some distance away and leans against one of the giant tires. April wonders what would happen if she waited him out, but Oliver leads her toward the car. "I heard you went to the police," he says, softening his voice.

"Hm?" she says, glancing back. She thinks of the day her parents brought Buddy home from the hospital, swaddled up like a spring roll, smelling of Desitin and her father's cigarettes, his pale eyes transfixed on the ceiling fan.

"The protection order," Oliver says. "My father told me."

She looks at him, the handsome way he has aged, the chisel of his jaw, those soulful eyes. No wonder he was Nana's favorite, even if he wasn't a true grandson. "What was I thinking?" she says. "If I croaked, no one would even tell Nana, would they? They'd say I was on extended vacation. Me, who's never taken a trip in my life."

He frowns.

"I have a passport, though," she says. "You never know when you might need to get out of the country."

"I see you haven't lost your knack for changing the subject," he says.

"Well, Oliver," she says, "I believe you've been known to do the same."

He looks down. "Let's go," he says.

"Fine," she says, turning abruptly. "I'll drive."

Oliver ignores this and gets behind the wheel. She wants to argue, but no words come. She clears off the passenger seat, tossing Buddy's cassette tapes and camping catalogs into the rear. Oliver moves his seat back and adjusts the mirrors.

"My father helped put up the money for this car, even before Buddy had his learner's permit," April says. "Can you imagine how he would feel to see me get my hands on it?"

Oliver's face is still. His Adam's apple rises and falls. When he doesn't know what to say, he doesn't say anything; that's one thing she admires about him. She notices his profile, the crook in his nose that she has always found attractive. His chin is more angular now, the contour of his face arresting. Yet something is missing. His hair, which in adolescence fell in a lovely, disheveled mass, is neatly slicked back, giving him a gangster look. His eyes alone are the same, the color of Caribbean shallows, so full of sincerity it is hard to look at them squarely. April's are just the opposite, so dark that the last time she was taken to the emergency room, the paramedic could not distinguish the pupil from the iris.

"I'm sorry I wasn't here for your father's funeral last year," he says.

She hears by the gravel in his voice that he means it. "It was two years ago," she answers. "And there's no need to apologize. California isn't exactly a subway stop."

"I sent a card, but I'm not sure if I had the right address."

"I got it. Thank you. You know I'm not much of a letter writer."

"Right, well, I left a voice mail, too."

"I'm sorry, Oliver. I wasn't in a frame of mind to talk. Please don't take it personally."

"Of course not," he says. "I'm sure it wasn't an easy time for you."

"It was hard on Buddy. I became his legal guardian, though I'm pretty sure the judge had his doubts. Buddy moved in to my apartment because I couldn't keep up the taxes on my father's house."

"Didn't you get some inheritance? Your father's bar must have been worth something."

Her father's portion of the bar—co-owned with his partner, Quincy—was willed to his stepbrother, Oliver's father, not April. Oliver would object, if he knew. "There were liens on the property," she says. "It wasn't worth much. Anyway, Buddy eventually got his own place near the university with friends. He was thrilled to start school." She looks down at her dress, smoothing out the pleats.

They park in the long, semicircular driveway of Oliver's father's home, behind the other cars. Oliver cuts the engine and holds the keys in his hand. "How long since we've seen each other?" he asks. "Five years?"

"Maybe," she says. "I'm bad with time."

Crisp oak leaves fall onto the windshield. It feels strange to be in a car with Oliver again, here in this once familiar driveway. It makes her want to feel like a teenager again, but instead she feels ancient.

"I ought to buy my dad a new plaque," Oliver says, nodding at the one over the front door. THE NIGHT FAMILY is carved in slightly crooked letters. "I can't believe he still has that one."

"It's beautiful," April says. "He loves it because you made it for him."

"Bernadette wants to know what happened to the *K*. It must have been dropped somewhere along the line, Ellis Island, I suppose. She says it's not too late to change it back."

"To Knight with a *K*? You're kidding, right?"

"I think the idea of being *Bernadette Night* creeps her out. *Bernadette Day* would be fine. *Bernadette Sunshine*—that would suit her."

"Oliver Knight, with a *K,* would be redundant. Forget chivalry. You need your darkness."

He gives her a wry look; he's missed that sort of remark. She avoids meeting his eye. In his lap he fingers the keys, noticing Buddy's pocketknife. "I hear Buddy was driving your car," he says, handing her the key chain.

She blinks.

"I hope you're not thinking that makes it your fault, because this car would have been even worse in the snow."

"You don't know what I drove."

"Anything would be better."

April shifts in her seat, feeling heat behind her eyes. "Let's eat," she says. "I'm starved."

Patterns of cold cuts, neatly arranged on doilies, adorn the table in the family room. April ignores the sandwiches and pastries but eats the olives one by one, spearing them with a toothpick until the bowl is empty. Beside her, Oliver spreads mustard on a roll as Bernadette arranges a dainty salad on her plate. April feels Oliver's eyes on her but doesn't look up. She's not afraid of breaking down anymore. Her insides are smooth and hollow as a carved-out canoe. She's floating. "Hey, Al, got a smoke?" she calls.

Al stands nearby, his back to them, scooping potato chips onto his plate. He is shorter and broader than his brother, Oliver, the lines in his face hard and mischievous. He glances at April over his shoulder. "Sorry," he says, patting his chest pocket.

"Smoking again?" Oliver asks tentatively.

"No." Al frowns. "She isn't."

April unscrews another container of olives, with pimientos this time, and eats them straight from the jar, licking the juice from her fingers. "Anyone got a cigarette?" she calls.

She gave up smoking years ago. No one answers. She doesn't really want to smoke, but a dull noise in her head is getting louder, like an insect she cannot swat. She sees the fold in Oliver's brow, knowing she has put it there. She can be kind to him one minute, cruel the next. She doesn't know why. It's more like reflex than choice. She glances at Bernadette. "Your fiancé is about to give me a lecture on smoking," April says. "Can I see the rock?"

Bernadette glances down at the ring, extending her hand with ballerina grace. "I suppose we ought to announce it," she says.

"We need good news."

"The timing." Oliver shakes his head.

"Anything to dilute this," April says, glancing around the room.

"April," Bernadette says. "Oliver's told me how close you and Buddy were. I want you to know how awful I feel."

"We fought a lot," April says. A stupid response, and not true. She shoots Oliver a glance, but he looks away.

"I love that old picture of the three of you," Bernadette says, "the one where you and Oliver are swinging Buddy by the arms and legs."

"I don't remember that one," she says. When Buddy wanted tips on stealing bases, he asked their father, but when he had trouble with his math homework, he went to Oliver.

"He'll make a good dad," April says to Bernadette. Then April glances at Oliver, catching his eye. "He loved you," she says, her fingers grazing his tie just below the knot. Then she steps back, arms folded, surprised to have touched him.

Oliver lowers his eyes. Bernadette caresses him, and he puts his arm around her in a gesture so natural it appears involuntary.

April backs away, taking the last few olives. She goes upstairs to an out-of-the-way bathroom that once belonged to Oliver and Al. Framed over the light switch hangs Oliver's Eagle Scout badge, right where she remembers it. In the medicine cabinet mirror April sees that her hair, which a grade school teacher once described as sable black, has turned overnight to dull soot, overly long and unkempt. She bunches it in her fist, a handheld ponytail, and wonders how she would look bald. Shaving it off would be easier than getting a comb through it. Better yet, let a mortician deal with it. They did wonders on Buddy. Except for the subtle waxiness of his skin, April might have thought he was only asleep, and would bolt upright at any moment to laugh at the mistake.

"April."

She jolts. Bernadette stands outside the bathroom. For a moment, April sees only the hound's-tooth, a pattern that plays tricks with her eyes.

"Oh," April says. "Were you waiting long?"

"No," Bernadette says.

April gathers her purse, glancing around for her brush. She feels completely scattered. Bernadette, on the other hand, strikes April as the kind of person who rarely misplaces anything. Even her face gives the impression of balance and harmony, no one feature dominating the rest. Her eyes are blue, like Oliver's, and full of sympathy. It is impossible to dislike her. "Sorry," April says, leaving the room. "All yours."

"April," Bernadette stammers. "Listen, I just want to say that I lost a sibling, too. My sister, I mean, when I was twelve. I don't mean to say that I know how you feel, just that I'm very sorry."

"Thank you," April says. "And I'm sorry about your sister."

Bernadette's eyes well up. "Fifteen years ago." She waves her hand dismissively.

April caresses her shoulder.

"This isn't what I meant to happen—you consoling me."

"It's okay," April says. "Do you have a picture of her?"

Bernadette hesitates, then opens her purse and shows April the only photo in her wallet. A young woman waves at the camera with stubby fingers. She has a wide, flat, freckly face; almond-shaped eyes that are deeply slanted; and almost no neck. Her tongue protrudes slightly from a goofy, affectionate grin. April is aware that Bernadette is studying her reaction.

"She looks very sweet," April says.

"All sweetness," says Bernadette.

"How did she die?"

"Congenital heart defect," Bernadette says, closing her wallet. "But she'd been doing so well. My parents had just found her a job bagging groceries. It happened so fast."

April gives her hand a squeeze. Bernadette moves into the bathroom, and April takes her leave.

Downstairs, the crowd has thinned. "Looking for a place to sit?" asks Oliver's father, Hal, patting an empty chair beside him. Oliver leans in the kitchen door frame, sipping a glass of water.

"No," April says. "Thanks."

"You're welcome to stay here tonight," Hal says.

"That's kind," she says. "But I'm fine."

"You're staying with a friend, then?"

"Right," April says, though it must be obvious there's no friend.

"April." Hal shifts awkwardly. "What about the rifle?"

"What?" she says.

"Buddy's gun, the one he hunted with."

"The Bangor police gave me everything that was in his car. It's still in my trunk, I guess. I haven't touched it. His duffel bag, too."

"I'll take it out for you," Hal says. "Leave it all here."

"Thanks." She looks at him, her father's stepbrother, with his patient, gentle eyes. He is as different from her father as a man could be. She kisses his cheek, smooth and smelling of soap, and remembers her own father's face, the texture of sandpaper. Aftershave and nicotine. It's crazy to miss her father more now with Buddy gone, but since when do things make sense? She steps back. Around her people are talking, laughing, whispering in cahoots, a discordant symphony. The room contracts, the air compressing. She heads for the back door.

Out on the deck, she finds Al lighting up. "Liar," she says, holding out her hand.

"Believe me," he says. "You don't want to start this filthy habit again."

"I just want to hold it," April says, hoping that will steady her.

"Mooch off someone else."

It is a relief to hear Al being himself.

"Where are you staying until this thing with T.J. is settled?" he asks, taking a drag.

"It's settled."

"You mean he packed up his things?"

"I brought everything to his friend's house."

"It's not settled."

"You said you would keep this a secret. How is it that your father found out? And now your brother?"

"You could come down to South Carolina with me," he says. "I've got two more weeks of training camp."

"Right. Me and the boys."

"They'd love you."

"Who would you say I was? A groupie?"

"A woman with legs like yours has no need to explain herself." He exhales smoke over his shoulder, but the breeze blows it back in her face.

"I'll pass," she says. "Besides, you need to concentrate on your work. An entire column last week on Ewing's legacy? That's ancient history, Al. What your readers really want to know is what Pat Riley uses on his hair. I know he's in Miami now, but surely you can still find out."

He raises an eyebrow. "Thought you didn't read my stuff."

"Win or lose, there's never a strand out of place. I'd like to know his secret."

"Riley's long retired. Sorry to disillusion you." He smiles—not wryly, as usual, but gently, in a way that makes her uncomfortable. "April," he says. It feels strange to hear him use her real name; normally he calls her Rose, his nickname for her since they were teenagers, when he used it to make fun of the awful dime-store perfume she wore. "What about Charleston?"

When she doesn't answer, Al drops his cigarette and crushes it.

April folds her arms in front of her, staring down at the lines in the deck. "If I hadn't gone to the police, none of this would have happened."

"How do you figure?"

"When Buddy asked to borrow my car, I thought: *Perfect, T.J. won't look for me in Buddy's car.*"

"If Buddy had electrocuted himself shaving, you'd find a way to blame yourself for that, too."

They stand in silence for a moment, leaning on the rail and staring through the screen door into the house. April sees someone pouring a scotch. She could go for a drink right now, a little Absolut to scorch her throat or a sweet, dark sherry to coat it.

Al sighs heavily. "No one's accusing you, Rose. If you want to blame yourself, that's up to you."

She nods.

"I'm serious about Charleston."

"I know you are."

"I've got a plane to catch." He frowns. "I'll see if I can't scrounge up an extra ticket for the season opener. That is, if you promise to use it."

April doesn't feel she can promise anything at the moment, nor imagine herself paying attention to basketball. "See you, Al."

He kisses her, on the lips as usual. It's not a sexual thing exactly, more like a provocation. The ash on his breath stirs her craving for a cigarette. "Try not to break too many hearts on the road," she says. He smirks and trots down the deck stairs.

She can leave, too, she thinks. Just slip away without saying good-bye, Al-style. Through the screen, she sees Oliver standing in the living room, his back to her, his posture tense. It's true that Buddy loved him, even though they hadn't seen each other in years. It's normal for lives to drift apart; April expected it. Even back then, when she and Oliver used to take Buddy down to the creek to catch frogs and let them go, April understood it wouldn't be forever.

April cannot think of any reason to stay. She goes down the steps. Wind stirs the dormant lilacs. The day has chilled, a swift cloud cover sealing off the sun. Dry leaves scramble across the gravel driveway, circling in eddies and scattering again. April has not worn a jacket.

The car's interior is cold. As she drives, darkness sets in with a sudden, stark desolation. She longs for the gradual, lingering dusks of summer, and shivers to think of the weeks ahead, days getting shorter, nights falling abruptly.

She parks in the train station lot next to her building. When she enters the apartment, she looks for signs of T.J. Since the protection order, she hasn't heard from him. Not even a phone call. She knows she should be relieved, but the apartment, though small, is cavernous with no one in it; she herself doesn't count.

She walks from one room to the other. There is a grating feeling in her stomach; she is being whittled out. The bookshelf is cluttered with remnants of T.J., electronic parts she cannot identify, nails and screws in open jars, drill bits in a coffee can, green rubber bands overflowing from a White Owl cigar box, held together with masking tape. On the floor beside the television is a friend's disemboweled VCR, dusty and piled with copies of the *New York Post*. She once made the mistake of throwing some away. Not twice. She considers taking T.J.'s discarded gadgets and tossing them out the window. She might actually do it if she could stay with the thought long enough.

She knows which taxi dispatcher is working downstairs by the volume of his radio. Today it is Henry, half deaf. She closes the kitchen window and goes to the rear of the apartment, out onto the fire escape where she cannot hear the voices. She takes a breath. A cigarette would do the trick. Or bourbon. But she doesn't really want either. The sky is heavy with rain, though none falls. She hears a distant ambulance, teenagers breaking bottles on the corner, an incessant car alarm, all gradually drowned out by the approach of the 6:42 lumbering into the station, screeching as it comes to a halt. She hears the air brakes release a breath, doors gliding open, and imagines the commuters pouring out.

April has always liked her apartment. She is accustomed to the cups rattling in the cabinets and the furniture inching around. The consistency of the schedule soothes her. While the front of the apartment faces the platform, the back is shrouded by scrawny elms, holdouts against disease. When in leaf, they partially conceal a McDonald's parking lot beyond.

As the sound of the train grows faint, April hears her wind chime stir in the cool night air. The chime is constructed of shells she and Oliver found on the beach. He made the mobile for her eighteenth birthday—to remind her, he said, of her dream to live by the sea. That was not a dream she thought about anymore. To get through each day was enough. Over the years, she stopped noticing the chime altogether. Until now. There is no room in April's brain for the fact that Oliver has moved back east. It seems as implausible as Buddy's death. Surely she will wake up tomorrow and find that no part of this day was real.

Chapter

2

OLIVER STANDS IN THE STREET, staring up at the darkened windows of April's apartment. The night is so quiet, he hears the rise and fall of his own breath. It makes him uneasy. Over the train platform, fog moves beneath greenish lights. A lone traveler leans against an advertisement for a Broadway play, the letters obscured by graffiti. Oliver pushes the buzzer again. The doorway of April's building is littered with crushed McDonald's wrappers and railroad tickets. He waits. From around the corner, a man ambles by unsteadily. He has muttonchop sideburns and smells of liquor. He gives Oliver a skeptical look before crossing the street and lying down on a bench beneath the trestle. Oliver glances up at April's window once more, hoping he has made a mistake. Maybe he copied the address incorrectly from his father's book. He doesn't want her to live here.

He retreats to his car. Perhaps she went to a bar, he thinks, the one where she works, or someplace to be alone. The traveler on the train platform opens an umbrella, useless against the mists that drift sideways and upward on currents of air. Oliver's shirt clings to his skin. The cemetery. He remembers the blank look on April's face. It was a relief to him when Bernadette wept, because he knew how to respond to tears—the squeezed hand, tissues. But April. When had he ever known how to react to her?

He gets back in his car and tries to think of the fastest route to the cemetery. He has been away so long, it takes him a minute to remember the Long Island roads. He doesn't expect April to be at the cemetery, but now that the idea has entered his mind, he has to try. He feels his pocket for his keys and touches something small and hard, the button he found after dropping his keys in his father's driveway. Black satin, the size of a pearl—he recognized it as belonging to April's dress.

As he pulls up to the east gate of the cemetery, he spots Buddy's car parked beneath a tree. He waits for a long moment, staring. As children, hide-and-seek was pointless; he and April always knew where the other would be. He felt her presence gravitationally, as when she would inch toward him from her end of the seesaw, letting him feel his own weight.

Light rain falls, drops beading on the hood. The car, glistening beneath a streetlamp, appears incandescent in the darkness. Oliver parks and gets out, the ground slick with decaying leaves, the aroma sweet and moldering. The car is unlocked. He reaches in and pops the trunk. No duffel bag, no rifle. He's not sure if he should feel relieved or worried. He glances into the cemetery. The gate is locked. He looks at the wrought-iron fence and regrets that he is still in dress shoes. He scales it, holding his breath as he swings one leg and then the other over the prongs. He jumps to the opposite side, landing on all fours in the sodden grass.

The graveyard is dark. He walks hesitantly, bumping into headstones, trying to recall the direction of the grave. Rain falls, bringing down leaves. A startled animal scurries in an overhead branch. Oliver hopes he will not come upon his mother's tombstone by accident. He doesn't want to see it, not in the dark.

He does not see April until he is upon her, her dark hair and dress almost invisible. She is kneeling beside Buddy's grave, her back to Oliver, ankles splayed. He runs his hand through his hair. "April," he says softly, not wanting to frighten her.

She does not answer, but continues to rock.

He squats beside her, her eyes glassy and unfocused. "April," he says hoarsely. "It's me, Oliver."

For an instant their eyes meet. "He was afraid of the dark," she says finally. "Remember? We used to read him to sleep."

Oliver bows his head. He touches her back, her dress damp. "Let's go," he says, feeling a catch in his throat. "You'll get pneumonia."

She gets to her feet in a slow, druggy way. He is surprised by her compliance. The way she looks, he thinks he can suggest anything and she will agree.

"When was the last time you slept?" he asks.

"I pace," she says. "It's a kind of sleep."

"Hardly."

"My body won't stay down. Like it's full of helium."

Ballast, Oliver thinks. "I'll follow you home."

They walk to the gate, and she tosses her shoes through. Oliver clasps his hands together to give her a leg up. It's an automatic gesture snatched from childhood. Her stockings are torn, her dress clinging to her thighs. When she is perched on top, he tells her to wait, fearing that the sidewalk will hurt her feet. He hoists himself up and leaps down.

"I can jump by myself," she says. "How do you think I got in?"

"It's cement on this side," he says, reaching up. "I've got you."

He takes hold of her waist and she slides down, her dress bunching up against his abdomen. It doesn't matter how many trees they scaled as kids, how familiar these gestures; she is completely alien. She gazes at him, her eyes black as volcanic ash. "Oliver," she says. "You shouldn't have come here."

He hesitates, and then lets go.

She tugs down her skirt and picks up her shoes. He watches. Nothing about what to do next occurs to him until he hears her ignition.

Oliver trails closely, April's taillights reflecting on the slick highway. She pushes eighty, exhaust billowing. He imagines the wheel vibrating in her hands. When they reach her building, Oliver follows her upstairs. The hallway is floored with dingy linoleum, the walls in need of paint.

"Your suit," she says.

"It's only rain," he says, draping his jacket over the back of a chair.

"Have you eaten?"

"The olives gave me indigestion," she says, opening the refrigerator.

Oliver glances at the stove clock to see that it is gaping from its socket, wires exposed, stopped dead. "What's his name?"

"Excuse me?"

"The protection order."

"History," she says. "That's his name."

"What if he comes back? Shouldn't you stay someplace else?"

"Here, have some salami before it goes bad. I don't eat it."

Oliver glances at the meat. "What did the police tell you?"

"To change the locks."

"And have you?"

"Here's some bread, but you probably don't eat white, do you?"

Oliver rolls a slice of meat with his fingers and puts it into his mouth. He is hungrier than he realized. "April." He swallows. "Locks?"

"He's got the protection order," she says. "He won't come here."

"So you're still sleeping here while he has a key?"

"Budweiser?"

"April."

"I haven't brushed my hair in three days," she says, exaggerating. "I need a shower. Can you let yourself out?"

"Do what you need to do," he says.

She slips out of her muddied heels and walks languidly on the hardwood floor, reaching behind her neck to release the top button of her dress. Oliver remembers the one in his pocket.

Once the bathroom door clicks shut, he starts opening cupboards. The existence of the rifle strikes him as a disastrous prospect. The apartment is small enough; he ought to be able to find it. He opens a cabinet stuffed with electronic parts, camera lenses, and various tools in no apparent order.

When Oliver hears the shower, he moves to the bedroom, glances under the furniture and into the closet. On her bed-side table is a plastic-coated library copy of Flannery O'Connor stories. More books line the bureau. He notices one about do-it-yourself plumbing repairs, and a travelogue on Patagonia. His heart quickening, he pulls open the heavy dresser drawer. Would a rifle even fit in here? He glides his hand beneath April's clothing. What he's doing is wrong; he knows that. The fabric is silky. He imagines the rifle layered beneath her slips. What if he feels it? He has never touched a gun in his life. What if he moves it and the thing goes off?

"It's not there," she says from the doorway.

Oliver looks up. He hears the shower running. Steam drifts from the room behind. Her dress is unbuttoned halfway down her back, loose across her shoulders.

"I left it in your father's garage."

"I'm sorry," he says. "I just thought . . ."

"There's a bottle of aspirin in the bathroom," she says, coming toward him. "Knives in the kitchen. A train platform across the street. You think I'd need a gun?"

She is so close he can see condensation on her skin, droplets of moisture in her hair. She smells like grass after heavy rain. "Just tell me you won't do anything stupid."

"If you trust me, Oliver, you'll go home." She closes the drawer with her hip and leans against it. He moves her aside and, to his own surprise, reopens the drawer.

Folded inside a satin slip is an envelope bulging with photographs. He leafs through them, grainy black-and-whites, mostly taken at a distance: April tending bar, buying a newspaper, filling her gas tank. Al is in one of them. Nana, another. Oliver looks at April. She takes the stack from him.

"Did *he* take these?"

"Before he knew me," she says. "Followed me for weeks. Creepy, right? But I was vain enough to be flattered." She tosses the pictures in a wastebasket. "It's time for you to go."

Oliver loosens his tie. "The sofa will do."

"The trains will keep you awake."

"I'll take my chances."

April sighs and turns back to the bathroom.

In the kitchen, Oliver eats a sandwich then makes another. His head swims with exhaustion. Beside the toaster is a dog-eared copy of *The Elegant Universe* by Brian Greene. He rolls up his sleeves, takes off his belt, anxious to get out of the damp clothing. The light blinks on April's answering machine. He wonders if she will listen in front of him.

She comes out of the bathroom wearing a long T-shirt and over-size gym shorts that he guesses are the boyfriend's. Her hair drips onto her shoulders, dampening the shirt. She tosses her dress over the back of the sofa and paces to the coffee table, the window, the bookshelf, then stops, confused.

"April."

She whirls around. "Jesus," she says. "You're still here?" She comes into the kitchen.

"Hungry?" he says, offering his sandwich.

She shakes her head, striding out of the room, then back again. She puts her hands over his on the sandwich, closes her eyes, and takes an enormous bite. Her hair smells of shampoo. Her shoulders are wet. "I'm starving," she says, wiping her mouth.

"You have a message."

"Did you have the Budweiser? I don't touch it."

"Has he called you?"

She takes the bottle out of the refrigerator, holds her T-shirt over the cap, and twists it off. She touches the cold bottle to her forehead, then hands it to Oliver.

He hasn't had a beer in years. He prefers wine now, quality labels because the cheap stuff gives him a headache. He takes the beer.

Kids' voices rise from the street below, a naughty shriek and a tangle of laughter. Oliver looks at April. He imagines their childhood selves bursting into the room, hot and sweaty, running to the refrigerator and filling glasses with iced tea. He sees April's braid speckled with bits of grass, his own tanned skin and backward Mets cap. He pictures them staring over the rims of their cups as they gulp thirstily. Who, they wonder, are these two somber and preoccupied adults standing in the corners of the room? Not their future selves, surely. They run out again and hop back onto their bikes.

"I see you still like to read," he says.

"We all have our escapes, right? You understand; you've got your piano."

He shifts uncomfortably, taking a swig of beer. It tastes better than he remembered. He takes another mouthful and passes it back to her. Her throat moves as she swallows. The fine hairs framing her face are beginning to dry, waving up, and he notices a strand of white amid the black. She hands the bottle back to him, pressing it to his chest, and walks off.

He glances at the moist impression left on his shirt, shivering as he unfastens the buttons. He finishes the beer alone, goes into the living room, and takes off his shoes. She left a blanket and some dry clothes on the sofa, pin-striped boxers and a Rangers T-shirt. Oliver does not like the idea of getting into another man's clothes, this guy's least of all. They are big on him. She has always gone for monstrous men. Oliver doesn't get it.

He sleeps restlessly, his body too long for the couch, the trains roaring through his dreams. After midnight the schedule slows, and the apartment is quiet for longer intervals.

At 3 AM, he awakens with a start. The room is faintly lit by the glow of the station. April paces in the dark, touching the walls, her hands moving like a mime testing imaginary confines. Oliver sits up, meaning to console her, but he feels tranquilized. April traces a crack in the wall with her fingertips. Oliver stands groggily, bumping the coffee table, and makes his way to her.

"Listen," she says. "There's a baby crying."

Oliver squeezes her shoulders. "You need sleep," he says, leading her to the bedroom. The bed is untouched. He pulls down the covers and guides her down, but when he straightens up, so does she.

Oliver does not think about what he does next. His body moves of its own accord, wanting only to anchor her, to coax her down. He lies beside her and drapes his arm over her arm, his leg over her leg, and his chest to her back, his weight securing her. Ballast. He has never felt so tired, so thoroughly leaden. He is vaguely aware of the snugness of her body, the light pressure against his groin, her breath deepening.

His mind drifts, yet he is awake. Or nearly so. A train whistles. Above the bed, a photograph clatters against the wall. Oliver cannot remember the image inside the frame. Past and future rattle the windows, powerless to enter. Through a fluke of physics, he and April are beyond the reaches of space and time. He holds her against him, wanting to restore her, himself, and Buddy missing between them.

"You're killing me," she says, though he can't be sure if he hears it or dreams it. He is falling hard into sleep, his mind struggling to find her, remember her; the person he was.

Oliver awakens alone and disoriented. Birds chirp outside an unfamiliar window, sunlight flooding the sheets. It takes him a moment to reconstruct the night.

In the living room, curtains billow, the window fully open. April sits on the fire escape. Oliver climbs out beside her. A light breeze moves her hair. Her eyes look calmer; she might actually have slept. She looks up into the elms, nearly bare. "When I first woke up," she says, "there was a second before I remembered."

He nods.

"Everything's unhinged," she says. "I need to do laundry, but it doesn't make sense. My mail's piling up in my box. The only place that feels normal is work. People ask for drinks and I get them, automatic pilot. But when it's time to come home, I have to get back into Buddy's car, and I can still smell the aftershave he wore on his last date."

Oliver thinks of things he might suggest: counseling, Prozac, a roommate. All ridiculous. "It'll wear off," he says. "The aftershave."

"That's what I'm afraid of."

He touches her hand, lacing his fingers between hers. She turns away and without looking returns the pressure.

"Oliver," she says later as he puts on his jacket, reaching for his keys on the table. "I like her."

He turns to her. April stands at a distance, arms crossed in front of her. He puts his hands in his pockets and feels the button there, silky and pearl-shaped. He almost forgot to return it.

"Bernadette suits you," she says. "I think you'll be happy."

"Thank you," he says hoarsely.

He waves at her, since it is apparent she is coming no closer, and lets himself out.

Chapter

3

OLIVER DRIVES IMPATIENTLY. If he wants to make his tax law class by nine, there is no chance of stopping home for a change of clothes. The expressway into the city is throttled; the traffic here is just as bad as in California. Why couldn't he and Bernadette have chosen someplace simpler for their graduate work? He turns off the traffic report; he has already passed all possible turnoffs for alternative routes. For better or worse, he is committed to the road he is on.

Buddy permeates Oliver's thoughts, not in distinct memories so much as a pervasive remembrance of his pigeon-toed walk and bashful smile. Gone, he is acutely present. Oliver feels off balance. In practical terms, Buddy has not been part of his life for years now, so why does he feel like an amputee? He glances at his watch; it is unlike him to be late. He has an irrational fear that this singular tardiness is the beginning of a permanent change, and he will never get to class on time again.

Maybe it was this disorientation that contributed to his lapse in judgment last night. On one hand, April needed someone with her, but did it have to be him? He could have taken her to his father's place, or Bernadette's. Then he would have nothing to explain to Bernadette or himself. As it is, he doesn't plan to mention anything; his second inconsistency of the day, and it's barely nine in the morning.

As traffic merges into the tunnel, Oliver becomes aware of a melody in his head. Has it been there since he first woke up? Haunting and hypnotic, it feels like a Beethoven piece, but it's not. Who, then? The car in front of him stops and Oliver brakes hard. *Oh, God,* he thinks, it's his own song, one of the last he composed at eighteen. As soon as he realizes this, the song strikes him as juvenile and repetitive. He does not want to remember it, but there it is, wrapping itself around his thoughts like roots circling in an overgrown pot.

Police lights whir at the mouth of the tunnel. A green Maverick lies crumpled against a guardrail. Cars inch by, straining for a view. Oliver catches a glimpse of two paramedics hunched over someone with skinny calves and gaudy shoes, a teenager, maybe. Then Oliver is inside the tunnel, its yellow tile walls arched around him.

April. He remembers one of the first awkward moments between them as adolescents. He was at his summer job, watering the Blue Star juniper, the hose snaking to life in his hand, when he caught sight of April under the nursery awning, bending to smell a gardenia. Perhaps it was because he did not recognize her at first that he was able to see her, the April Simone his friends saw, with her long legs and tanned shoulders, wearing cutoff shorts and a tank top that exposed the curve of her spine, the edge of her shoulder blade, the supple crease of her underarm. Her dark hair was pulled back in a makeshift knot, sweaty tendrils glued to the nape of her neck. Oliver didn't notice at first that the spray from his hose had veered onto the walkway. When April looked up, revealing her face, he turned away.

From the time they were fifteen until eighteen, April faithfully came by the music studio where Oliver practiced five nights a week, to listen to him. She came straight from her father's bar, where she spent the afternoons busing tables and running the dishwasher. Her father's partner, Quincy, tended to keep her late, and on those nights Oliver practiced longer than usual. Quincy worried him.

He remembers one of her visits. He doesn't know why it comes to him now, inside the tunnel. The studio was dark except for a single light illuminating a maze of sheet music scrawled in faint pencil, notes so quick and urgent they were indecipherable to anyone but him. His fingers ached from hours of playing, but he didn't stop. The composition was all but there when he heard the click of the door. He didn't know what time it was, only that she was late. It was always that way. The songs came in the pressured moments of waiting, his hands straining to keep pace with his mind.

When he heard April's footsteps behind him, he started the song from the top, eyes closed, mind awash. He felt himself rising up from the bench, dispossessed from his hands at the keys. The studio reverberated, guitars quivering on their hooks, flutes vibrating inside their cases. If April was breathing, Oliver could not hear it.

When it was over, he leaned on the piano. The room was silent but teeming; the walls retained the sound. April straddled the bench with her back to him, the coarse denim of her jacket whisking his shoulder. Her long hair was in disarray, scented with smoke from the bar.

"Quincy keep you?"

She did not answer. The dim halo of light reached the worn knee of her jeans, her fist resting on her thigh, thumbnail gnawed. She was the kind of girl he would expect to have long, frightening nails, a color called Cherry Vanilla or Fire Truck Red. Instead they were unpainted, bitten down to the flesh. Each time Oliver noticed this, it came as a surprise. Her Western boots were silver-tipped, imitation snakeskin, as if she were someone to contend with.

"Can you do it again?" she said. "Slower this time."

Oliver grazed his fingers over the keys without depressing them. He wanted to ask her something, but what? The question floated in his mind, just below articulation.

April got up and slid down along the side of the upright piano, her usual spot. On the floor, she pulled her knees to her chest and bowed her head. Oliver began the song with eyes opened this time. He noticed that her hands, now raked through her hair, were in fists. She sat with her back to the piano to hear the music with her body as well as her ears.

Oliver tried to concentrate on the song as he had the first time, but he kept thinking of April in the steamy, windowless back room of the bar, loading and unloading the dishwasher. He screwed up the last few notes and the song ended abruptly. "I wish you'd quit that place." He paused, waiting for the usual argument.

"It's your best song yet," she said. "You've turned a corner. Something's new."

He closed the piano lid and sat near her on the floor. "What about it? I could get you something at the nursery. The orchid lady just quit. Or you could take my job when I leave." He let the sentence trail off. She could have gotten into college, too, had she applied. She looked up, her face flushed. He smelled booze and wondered why he hadn't noticed before.

"They'd die," she said. "The orchids."

He thought of the creamy petals easily bruised, smooth as newborn skin. "I'm telling you, April, you don't need this job. You can do better."

"Remind me," she said. "How much is the scholarship for?"

"Don't," he said. "You know I turned it down."

She looked at him with dark, unblinking eyes. Oliver had called Juilliard on his own, declining their offer before discussing it with his teachers, his father, least of all April. "You could still enroll without the scholarship," she said. "Take out a loan."

"Listen," he said. "Stanford isn't exactly chopped liver."

"It is if you're Oliver Night."

"It's only a piano, April. It's not my life."

She was silent.

"At least I have plans," he said. "Which is more than you can say."

He thought this would provoke her, but she only sighed.

"Sure, Juilliard would be fun, but then what? If you're not Horowitz, you end up playing for tips in some sleazy bar. Or worse, teaching in high school."

"That's not it," she said. "You're afraid you'll like it too much, that it will swallow you whole."

He laughed unconvincingly.

April stood and walked toward the door. Her boots did not look comfortable. Neither did the jeans. Oliver shut off the light and took out his key. At the door, she accidentally backed up against him and then jerked away with a start.

"God, you're jumpy," he said.

She wrapped her jacket more tightly around her and slipped through the door. Outside, the air was cool and crisp, fragrant with lilac. Oliver thought of orchids, Dancing Girls and Lady's Slippers, too delicate to touch.

Along Sunrise Highway, traffic lights turned with no one to obey them. April and Oliver passed beneath the train trestle and took the shortcut, down along the creek where they used to play. He noticed litter and beer cans, a single high-heeled shoe, and a broken baby carriage turned on its head. April was walking unsteadily, wavering up and down the bank of the dry creek. She tripped on a root, landing on hands and knees.

He bent to help her up but instead she rolled onto her back. "I've got the spins," she said, covering her face with her hands. "Don't let Buddy see me."

"He's asleep by now. Come on. You can't stay here."

"You go ahead. I'll get it back in a minute."

Oliver sat down beside her. The half-eaten moon sifted in and out of low, fast-moving clouds. A breeze stirred the blossoming maples, luminous beneath a streetlamp. Across the road above them, house lights went out one by one. A great place to get mugged, Oliver thought, here where no one could see them. April laced her fingers through the sparse grass, her dark hair fanned out around her face, oddly pale in the moonlight.

"Oliver," she said. "I fucked up."

He leaned closer, wanting to hear more, but knowing that if he asked, she would clam up. He searched for the right thing to say, but all that came to mind was the song.

"Oliver," she said again. "Why don't you ask that girl Daisy to the prom?"

He cursed himself for waiting, allowing her to change the subject.

"She's sweet on you," she said.

"If I wanted to, I would."

"Scared?"

"No," he said, laughing.

"I think you are."

"If I need a shrink, I'll pay for one."

She sat up, her knee pressed to his thigh. She looked worse now. Shaky and hot. "You've never done it, have you, Oliver?"

"Jesus," he said.

"Free advice. The first time make sure you face her. A girl likes to know who's there."

"You're drunk."

"And don't kiss if you don't mean it," she said seriously. "There's nothing worse than obligatory foreplay."

"What makes you think I need your advice?"

"Because you went out with Maryellen Kowalski three times and never kissed her good night."

"First of all, that's none of your business, and second, maybe I didn't want to. Maybe it would have been one of your so-called token gestures."

"Or maybe you don't know how."

"Piss off," he said. Her knee on his thigh was creating heat. He was sure she felt it, too. "I'm out of here," he said.

She leaned forward on all fours, one hand on either side of him. Oliver smelled whiskey on her breath, salt in the air, the heady fragrance of buds. His gaze traveled the curve of her jeans, the sway of her back, the arc of moon-white flesh inside her blouse. Her eyes were steady, fixed on his. *What the hell,* he thought, *let her humiliate me. I'm in for the lesson of my life.* Her hair grazed his cheek, her breath so close he could almost taste the liquor. "Oliver," she said. "Go to Juilliard."

It took him a dazed minute to realize what she had said. April stood and walked precariously up toward the sidewalk. He waited for a long moment, praying for his hard-on to go down. He had half a mind to go after her, pin her to a tree. But she was right. He was afraid, not of sex, but of her.

He got up slowly and followed her down the street. They walked in silence until they had reached her house. Juilliard, he thought. And she was in a position to give him advice? April, the dishwasher?

"Go ahead," she said. "I know what you're thinking."

"Really," he said. "So now you're a psychic."

"Slut is more like it."

"Is that what you think of yourself?"

"A shot for every table I wipe down," she said.

"What's that supposed to mean?"

"Overtime pay."

Oliver blinked, confused.

"What was I supposed to do? Admit I'd never tasted whiskey? Me, who works in a bar?"

His skin went cold. *God,* he thought, *don't let her be talking about Quincy.*

She hugged herself, looking up at the dark window of her bedroom. "The first time was the worst because I didn't know how to drink yet. By the third round I couldn't find my way back to the bar stool." She laughed in a jittery way, like someone pulled out to sea. "Quincy was feeding me shots with his mouth and I was saying Oliver is waiting for me at the studio—it was the night before your tenth-grade recital and I wanted to hear you play the whole thing from start to finish—but I never made it to the practice or the performance because I was home in bed with what I told you was the flu, but really I was throwing up."

"April, that was two years ago."

"He was pissed because I was so far gone he had to drive me home and drop me off a block from the house in the hope that no one would see us and I'd be able to find my way to the back door. He wanted me to admit I'd brought it on, but I wouldn't, even though it was true I'd had a crush on him since I was twelve, but even then, all I ever wanted was a kiss, which is the one thing he's never done."

Oliver said nothing.

"See, I'm a fuckup."

"Someone should shoot him."

"I played my part."

"He's forty years old."

"He says being wet is the same thing as saying yes."

"I don't want to hear any more, okay?"

She looked down.

Oliver put his face in his hands. "This has been going on since you were fifteen?"

"For the next six months he didn't even look at me. Then it happened again. Then a month later. Now it's just what we do."

"Have you been to a doctor? Do you at least use protection?"

"It's not like that. He says I'm too young. All he wants is the smell on his hands so he can finish the job alone. But sometimes he can't wait. The line keeps changing. He says he hates himself. He says he's not the kind of guy who goes around sticking his hand up kids' skirts. He says if I were his daughter, he'd put a bag over my head and lock me in the basement. He tells me what a great guy my father is, and what a shit *he* is. Then he pours me another shot and tells me I'm fucking beautiful."

Oliver shook his head miserably.

"See," she said. "You thought I was someone better."

He dragged his fingers down his face. "You are."

"I shouldn't have told you."

"What kind of man would do this?"

"You act like I have nothing to do with it."

"Do you love him?"

She looked away.

"What happened to *Don't kiss if you don't mean it?*"

"We don't kiss."

"Ah, a great romance."

"I never said it was that."

"What, then?"

She continued to stare at the blackened house. "I'm drunk," she said. "You should tell me to go in."

"You don't need him," he said. "Walk away."

She turned to look him in the eye, her expression grave and uncertain. "One of these days I'm going to get fucked," she said. "All I want is for someone to kiss me first."

He looked at her blankly.

"Just once." Her voice wavered. "To know what it's like."

"What are you talking about?" he said harshly.

Her eyes brimmed. Oliver felt a stab of fear. He had never seen her cry, not when her dog died, not when she broke her arm. He was on the brink of a realization that refused to surface.

"You're right," she said. "It was a stupid idea." She hurried up the walk and disappeared into the darkened house.

Chapter
4

T.J.'s POWDER-BLUE PICKUP SITS ALONE in a far corner of the electronics shop parking lot. April gets in, knowing he always leaves the cab open, and settles into the passenger seat. The interior smells of cigarettes. She doesn't know what brought her here, except that it's the only place she can think of to clear her mind.

She sees one of her lipsticks on the dashboard, and feels comforted that he hasn't thrown it out. It's a familiar spot, this passenger seat, a place to let herself be idle, staring out the window while T.J. takes the turns. She likes to let her mind wander. He won't have his lunch break for another hour or two, so she's safe here, where no one can find her.

Nearly a year has passed since they first hooked up. He had been a regular at the bar for months before that, but they never spoke beyond what was necessary, Seagram's straight up. Always in Western boots and a shirt with the sleeves rolled up, he was a loner who disliked it when people sat next to him. April knew better than to try to make conversation. But she also knew that he watched her, pretending to stare at whatever game was on the tube while stealing glances in the mirror. She never let on that she saw. He looked like someone who had lived through more than the average person. For one thing, he had scars along one side of his face and down his neck. Also, he carried himself as though he bore more than his own weight—unlike the five o'clock suits who breezed in with their briefcases and big talk, bragging about contracts and closed deals. Those were the men, with their wedding bands and manicures, who usually hit on her. April was never interested in men who came on to her. It just wasn't attractive. She preferred the quiet ones who obviously had a story to tell, but who weren't about to tell it.

One night when she saw T.J. glancing at her in the mirror, she stopped what she was doing and stared back until he realized he'd been caught. He visibly tensed, bringing his shot glass up to his mouth and staring back at the game. She poured another and put it in front of him. "This one's on the house," she said.

He didn't thank her, but he looked her dead in the eye for the first time. She was right about the pain in his eyes.

He stayed until everyone else had gone.

She wiped down the bar until she reached the spot in front of him. "Nowhere to be?" she asked.

"No," he said steadily.

"Me, neither."

"That's hard to believe."

She shrugged. "My name's April."

"I know your name. I know lots of stuff about you."

She raised her eyebrows. "Such as?"

"You call cabs for your drunks. You feed a stray cat in the alley, and you've got a brother who adores you."

She hesitated.

"I've seen him come in."

"He's a good kid," she said uncertainly. "What else do you know?"

"You don't like men who piss in the corners. And this place is full of them."

"It's a commuter bar," she said. "We get all the hotshots and wannabes. Plus a few normal guys, like you."

He laughed. It was an odd laugh, more like a chortle; he wasn't used to humor. "I been called a lot of things, but I'm pretty sure that's the first time I ever been called normal."

"Sorry," she smirked. "I didn't mean to insult."

She closed out the register, turned out all the lights except the one behind the bar, and sat next to him on a stool.

"Ain't there some rule about mixing with the customers?" he said.

"Who says I'm mixing?"

He was well built, with a blunt, angular face and a dimpled chin, late thirties or early forties. He would have been routinely good looking if not for the pearly, translucent skin on the right side of his chin, cheek, and neck. She felt a desire to touch the milky, pellucid scar, but knew enough not to. She didn't ask about the fire. Instead, she let her knee graze his on the bar stool.

April saw herself, a twenty-six-year-old, weary-looking bartender, flirting with a forty-something man with broad, slumping shoulders and a wary eye. What was the point? She'd been through this before. It never ended well.

He stopped her abruptly, his massive hand encircling her knee. She felt a stab of fear, that old rush. And curiosity, too. If she waited long enough, what might he reveal to her? He touched her face, drawing his thumb firmly down along her jawbone, causing her to tremble. She shut her eyes and felt his lips press against hers, brief and tentative; nothing like what she had imagined. "Better for you if you don't mess with me," he said softly, and turned to leave. She didn't argue.

It was two weeks before she saw him again. She was unlocking her car in the parking lot, feeling for the keyhole, when someone appeared beside her. She gasped then, seeing it was him, laughed. "Hey," she said. "You scared me."

It was 3 AM, the lot empty. Only the neon light of a storefront across the street enabled her to see his face, the good side, which appeared in blinking reds and greens. He was perspiring despite the cold, a camera over his shoulder. "You remind me of someone," he said, his breath rising.

"Want to go for a cup of coffee?" she said, seeing the glaze in his eyes. "There's an all-night diner . . ."

He touched her hair, his breath warm and damp, saccharine with liquor.

"Do you need help getting home?" she said. "I can drive you."

"My wife, Denise," he said.

April hesitated.

"She died," he said. "She's dead. She looks like you. My wife."

He stared for a moment longer. April touched his face, the dark half, feeling the silkiness of the burnished skin. He closed his eyes, leaning his face against her hand, then turned away. He walked back to his pickup, head bowed, hands in his pockets. As he pulled away, a gust lifted an empty carton off the back of the truck. It rolled across the icy lot. April picked it up and saw the label: PULSAR CAMERA & VIDEO.

The following day when she stopped by, the store had just closed. She saw him through the glass sitting at a worktable behind the counter, patiently dismantling the electronic heart of someone's boom box. He arranged the components meticulously on the table. He knew how to be careful when he wanted to. He was wearing glasses and a shirt with TOMMY embroidered above the pocket.

April saw herself staring in through the shop window. It occurred to her that they'd all been in their forties, every one of them, since she was a teenager. Was it her fault she wasn't attracted to men her own age? *Attraction* wasn't the right word. It was more like curiosity. But she was getting tired of it. The script had grown stale. Maybe this time she would walk away. Maybe she didn't need it anymore.

At that moment, he looked up and saw her. He took off his glasses and hesitated before rising to let her in. *What the hell,* she told herself. *You're here, aren't you?*

"Your place?" she said, looking around.

"No," he said. "I'm just the repairman."

"At least now I know your name," she said, glancing at his shirt.

"No, no one calls me that. It's T.J."

"T.J.," she repeated. She leaned on the counter, picked up a screwdriver, and twirled it in her hand. "So," she said. "How did she die?"

"I don't want to talk about it."

She sat down. "What time do you get off?"

"I'm off."

"Hungry?"

"Listen," he said. "There are some things you should know. First of all, there hasn't been anyone since my wife."

"Second?"

He leaned back in his chair, observing her. Under fluorescent light, his scars looked more severe, the type children might run from. "She cheated on me."

April nodded slowly. "So," she said. "Pizza?"

"There's more," he said. "You won't like it." He shifted in his seat. "I've been following you."

April pursed her lips. "How long?"

"Long enough to know you work a lot, don't go out much, and help your little brother shop for clothes."

"He's color-blind."

"He's crazy about you."

She leaned back. "So, why me?"

"I told you," he said. "You're a ghost."

April got up and stood behind him. She touched his shoulder, sliding her fingers inside his shirt until she felt the waxiness of his collarbone, the ancient, indelible scars. "I think I can prove you wrong," she said.

"April."

She awakens with a jolt, her head thumping the window behind her. T.J. is standing with one hand on the open driver's door. "Get out."

"Huh?" She looks around, confused.

"God help you if someone sees us. What do you think you're doing?"

"I—"

"They served me the goddamn papers, all right? Right here in front of my boss. I'm lucky I still have a job. And now you're here, what, as a ploy to get me locked up?"

"I took it back."

"What?"

"I went to the police station this morning and rescinded the order. It's gone."

He shifts his jaw from one side of his mouth to the other, staring. "I see. So we're pals again, is that it?"

She looks out the window.

He gets in and slams the door. He rubs his hand over his mouth. "I'll drop you off," he says. "Where you headed?"

"Forget it," she says. "I'll walk."

"Not from here," he says. "Not looking like that. My boss gets one look at those red eyes and he'll only think one thing. Rescinding won't undo that."

"Buddy's dead," she says.

He looks at her. She feels uneasiness in her body, a hollow disequilibrium, because now that she has said it, it must be true.

He waits a moment. "Your brother?"

She snaps a stray string off her jacket and winds it tightly around her finger.

"How? When?"

She waves a hand, signaling that she doesn't want to say.

"Why didn't you tell me?" he says. "Never mind. That was a stupid question."

"I'm sorry about the protection order." She wipes her nose. "I got carried away."

He bristles. "Well, maybe I did, too. But if you would've just been straight with me . . ."

"I told you, T.J., there's nothing to be straight about. I was at a Knicks game with my cousin, we went out for a drink afterward, end of story."

"Right. You and Mr. Sportswriter. And don't call him your cousin. You're not related."

"I'm not getting into this again."

She starts to open her door, but he reaches across and holds it closed. "Why are you here?"

"I just want everything back the way it was. I want all this to go away."

He looks doubtfully across the empty parking lot. "I know what it's like to bury someone, April, and it don't happen that way."

"Just come home," she says, "and we'll figure everything out from there."

"It doesn't change things just because you took back some papers. I'm sorry about Buddy, I really am. But I got to tell you, April, I'd still like to tear your heart out. You'll have to give me some time on that one."

Before he can take his next breath, April kisses him, sinking her fingers into his neck and pulling him over to her side of the cab. "Go ahead," she says. "Tear it out." She smells the familiar scent of his skin, Marlboro and motor oil, like the first smoldering of an electrical fire.

"Crazy bitch," he says. "Your brother is barely in the ground and all you can think of . . ."

"Get a condom," she says.

He moves her back against the door and drives his tongue into her mouth until she almost gags. She gropes for the glove compartment until it pops open.

"Fine, fine," he says, reaching for the box. It's awkward in the pickup but it's never stopped them before. He finds his way into her with a minimum of undressing. She wedges her hands over her head to keep from being pounded into unconsciousness, though in her mind she lets herself free-fall backward, the way Oliver taught her to make snow angels, trusting the white blanket to catch her.

T.J. clenches his eyes, his rage pure and clean. She's too dry, but tells herself not to think about it. She's seen plenty of lovemaking on television where the man is tender and the woman enjoys it, the usual Hollywood bullshit. That kind of sex is as unreal to April as snow on Christmas, one of those things that, while theoretically possible, simply never happens.

"Harder," she says. "Make me cry." But no tears come, not one. She thinks of Buddy dying alone in her car. His last thoughts. She wants to know if he had a premonition. She wonders if she is having one now.

Chapter

5

THE TRAFFIC TO QUEENS is strangely light. April finds a parking space in front of Nana's duplex, though cars are double-parked everywhere. The spot would have been too tight for her old car, but Buddy's slips in on a single try. *Lucky,* she thinks, *now when it doesn't matter.*

She turns the rearview mirror to assess the circles under her eyes. It's hard to pull one over on her grandmother. She goes over her story again in her mind. She's driving Buddy's car because hers is in the shop. She couldn't make it last Tuesday because someone called in sick at work. Yes, she knows she looks like hell, but it's just that she's tired. None of it will work, April thinks. Her grandmother catches everything.

She gets out of the car. Dandelions sprout from cracks in the sidewalk, trees from squares of dirt. Above, the centers of sycamores are cut out for power lines. Curls of bark litter the sidewalk. Up and down the street duplexes hug one another for balance, like people overcrowded on a subway car.

Three boys play basketball in Nana's narrow driveway. They grow quiet when April approaches. The basketball net was Nana's idea, to give Buddy something to do during endless holiday visits. It has been years since he last used it. April waves to the boys, but they only stare at her.

Inside, she finds Nana in her bedroom, still wearing her night-gown, sifting through a drawer of nylons, her eyes raw and moist.

"Nana, what's wrong?" April tosses her purse on the bed. Her grandmother's hair is in disarray, half fallen from its bun. She leaves the drawer open, stocking legs hanging out, and goes into the parlor without her walker, lifting her leg like a piece of luggage.

"Nana?"

The secretary is open, contents sprawled, the coffee table stacked with yellowed copies of a Catholic newspaper. Couch cushions lie in a corner.

"Were you robbed?"

Nana moves her fingers through the pockets of a housedress draped on the back of the recliner. "I had it yesterday," she says.

"You've lost something?"

Nana skims her fingers along the mantel in and around the crowded picture frames. April notices one of Buddy, twelve years old, a dead pheasant raised in his fist, their father's hand on Buddy's shoulder, both squinting in the harsh sun. Nana smudges the glass with her fingertips. Has someone told her?

Nana reaches to the shelf, skin loose on her bones, biceps softly deflated. She removes a photograph and wipes the dust with the hem of her nightgown. It is a picture of her, taken in Spain some twenty-five years ago, her only trip back since emigrating as a teenager. In the photograph, Nana is in her early fifties, sitting on the edge of a fountain, her face radiant. Airborne droplets of water catch the glint of the sun. Her legs are crossed, accentuating the curve of her calf. Her hair, still black, is aloft in the breeze. Chin up, she grins at the photographer, daring him.

"Who took that picture?" April asks.

"Haven't you been listening?" Nana's eyes flash.

"I'm sorry. What did you lose?"

Nana looks into space, frightened. April follows her gaze but sees nothing. "Nana?"

"I can't remember," she says, bringing her hand to her chest. "As soon as you asked, it went out of my head."

"Don't get upset," April says. "It happens to me all the time. I walk into a room and forget what I came for."

"Don't let me go senile."

"You're not."

Nana blesses herself and touches the pendant hanging around her neck, a Christ the King crucifix. She kisses it and slips it inside her nightgown.

April picks up sofa cushions, frayed and pilly, and stuffs them back in place. She hears the basketball bouncing in the driveway, percussive as a heartbeat. She glances out the window. The hood of the car is strewn with bark.

Nana lifts the curtain. "Oh, my," she says. "Buddy's here."

"No." April's throat thickens. "We switched cars."

"Still? Isn't he home from that trip?"

"He promised to get the blood off my roof," April says, her voice higher than she wants. "I'm still waiting."

"So he got his deer," Nana says. "Tell him to bring some venison for Mr. Bergfalk. He used to be a chef, you know."

April presses her fingers to her temples. "If he's such a good cook, why don't you marry him? I bet he's asked."

"Don't be ridiculous. He comes to fix the pipes."

"Hm," April says. "Leaks spring like clockwork around here." April takes Nana's hand, small and bony, knuckles hard as acorns. "Come; let's do your hair while the faucet's still working."

"Smart aleck," she says. "Where did you get such a mouth?"

"Must be the genes," April says.

Nana touches her thin, silken hair, trying to see her image in the glass of a picture frame. Her eyes, once black and piercing, are filmy and translucent with age. April notices that, although forgetting to dress, Nana remembered to put on earrings. Silver and onyx, they hang almost to her shoulders, stretching the lobes.

"Where's your leg brace?" April asks as they move toward the kitchen.

"That ugly thing."

"How about your walker?"

"I use it when I need it."

"Suit yourself," April says. "Your hip is yours to break."

"Are you here to preach or set my hair?"

April stands beside Nana at the kitchen sink and pours warm cups of water over her scalp. Wet, her grandmother's hair is even more fine, the texture of corn silk. At the base of her neck, hidden beneath tufts of white, is the only remnant of her original color, the flagrant black she held on to well into her fifties. At twenty-seven, April already has strands of white just above her temple.

The window over the sink is spotted with water marks. Outside, barren tree limbs spring up and down like impatient horses shaking their manes. A swirling blanket of leaves obscures the garden, oddly centered in the tiny yard and framed with blue ceramic tiles Nana hand-carried from Spain. When April was a child, her father told her that the garden had once been a fishpond, narrow and deep as a well. Come autumn, he said, the carp sank to the bottom and settled into a trance-like, winter-long sleep. April would stare at the garden, mesmerized by the thought of the sleeping fish, their shiny orange heads nudging the surface in spring. Later, she found out he had made the whole thing up. There had been no well, no fish.

"How's that boyfriend of yours?" her grandmother asks.

"There's no boyfriend, Nana."

"Still taking the belt to you?"

"Don't be ridiculous."

"Don't *you* be ridiculous, missy. You think I didn't notice that shiner last month?"

April shivers as she pours shampoo in her palm and lathers. "Well?"

"I walked into a door frame. You know how clumsy I am."

"Sure do. Always bumping into the wrong type of men."

April smiles. "Keep talking and the soap will run into your mouth."

"Spencer never raised a hand to me. They don't make men like him anymore."

"What about the first one?" April asks. Nana rarely talks about Nick Simone, her first husband, who ran out on her when April's father was young. Judging by the pictures on the walls, he never existed. Spencer Night is everywhere.

"Your father looked just like him," Nana says. "Sometimes when he walked through the door, I thought it was Nicky back from the dead." She always speaks of him as dead, though no one knows what became of him.

"I'm going to rinse now," April says. "Close your eyes."

"Your father deserved better," she says.

"Don't cry, Nana. I have to rinse."

"Remember the time Spencer found that mongrel tied to the railroad tracks?"

April has heard the story before. She can almost recite it.

"Imagine someone doing that to his own pup!" Nana says. "If Spencer hadn't untied him, imagine! Poor thing, all skinny and beaten up. Spencer brought it home, nursed it back, taught it tricks. He loved that dog. But you know, whenever they went for a walk, the pup searched every face on the street, looking for his master. After all the love Spencer gave him, he still wanted the face he knew best, the one who tied him to the tracks."

April gathers Nana's hair in her fists and squeezes out the water. "We're done."

"Spencer loved your father like his own. Treated him no different from Hal. He wanted them to feel they were both his boys. But your father remembered his father. When the phone rang, he was always the first to answer. It was never the voice he hoped for."

April wraps Nana's head in a towel.

"Ay," Nana says, straightening. She holds her back, glancing at the photograph hanging above the table. April's father and Uncle Hal, nine and three, in matching children's sailor suits. Hal's smile is shy and impish, his legs swinging from his chair. April's father, standing behind him, has the stance of a little man, one hand on his hip, the other on his stepbrother's shoulder.

For part of her childhood, April believed that her father and uncle were half brothers. Nana concocted stories about Hal's birth and infancy that changed with each telling. One night he was born in a snowstorm; the next it was during an eclipse. "Her memory's gone to hell," April said to Oliver one spring afternoon when they were twelve. "I guess it's true what they say; you only remember the firstborn."

They were sitting on Nana's stoop, waiting for their parents to come out so they could go home.

"Sometimes it seems like she really believes those stories," Oliver said, nudging a loose brick. "I think she's convinced herself."

"Of what?"

"You know, about my father."

"What are you talking about?"

Oliver laughed, and when she did not join in, he stopped. "I wonder what's keeping them," he said quickly. "I'll go check."

She grabbed the leg of his jeans and stared up at him. Oliver sat down again. He rubbed his face in his hands and looked at her over his fingers. "Don't tell me no one told you."

She didn't speak. Blood drained from her face. She hated being the last to know.

"When Nana married Spencer, he was widowed, right?"

April nodded.

"And he had a son. Eighteen months old. My father."

April leaned away from him. She closed her arms across her chest. "Nana's not his mother?"

Oliver shook his head.

"So she's not really your grandmother?"

"Of course she is. Just not if you're talking blood."

"What does that make us?"

"Strangers, I guess." He laughed.

April stood, stone-faced.

"Stepcousins," he corrected himself.

"You're lying. My father would have told me."

"My father only found out when he got married and needed a birth certificate. Who knows? Maybe your father doesn't know."

"And when were you planning to tell me?"

"Tell you what? Nothing's changed. She's still my grandmother."

"I want to go home," she said. "What's keeping them?"

"I'll go see," Oliver said, rushing into the house.

They never spoke of it again.

April leads Nana to a chair. "They certainly don't look like brothers, do they," April says, nodding at the photo.

"The uniforms are adorable, aren't they?" Nana answers.

"It can be important to know who your blood relatives are," April says. "If you get sick, for instance, and need a kidney."

"Lucky we have such a big family."

"Hm," April says.

"You think I'm an old fool, don't you. You think I don't know what you're getting at."

"An old wizard is more like it."

"I had my reasons, let's leave it at that."

April sorts the curlers on the table, the back of her neck prickling. She didn't expect Nana to concede so quickly.

"If you think Hal is any less my son than your father was, you've got another think coming."

"I've never thought that," April says.

"Think of your father, all his life thinking *his* father deserted him. You think that did him an ounce of good?"

"Hal's mother didn't abandon him. She died."

"Do you think there's a difference to a one-year-old?"

"He's not one anymore."

"He knows."

"But you never talk about his real mother. Wouldn't she have wanted him to see a picture, hear stories about her, something?"

"His real mother?" Nana says, her voice rising. "I raised him from when he was a baby. Just who do you think his real mother is?" Nana has switched to Spanish, a sign of how upset she is, and although April's comprehension is generally spotty, this time she catches every word.

"Lo siento," April says, but Nana shoves the box of curlers across the table.

For an instant, April sees herself lifting Buddy from his crib, him giving her his shy, drowsy, through-his-fingers smile, his body warm and soft, conforming to hers, resting his head in the nook beneath her chin. She smells the milkiness of his skin, the down of his hair against her cheek.

"Just who do you think raised him?" Nana says.

"I'm sorry," April says. "You did a great job with both of them. Everyone knows that."

Nana glances at the photograph. She wipes the dampness from her face with a dishtowel. "It was easy with Hal," she says, switching back to English. "You praised him, and he was a sponge. Your father was made of something else. He craved attention, but it wouldn't soak in."

April collects the curlers and parts her grandmother's hair. She moves the comb gently. Nana's face is flushed. What an idiot April was for upsetting her.

"Your father turned out all right, didn't he?" Nana says.

"He was a good father."

"He must have been, the way Buddy adored him."

April feels woozy. "And me? Didn't I adore him?"

Nana looks up, her eyes more focused than they had been earlier. "Abrilita?" she says, using her childhood nickname. "What's wrong?"

April holds the table for balance and knocks over the rollers. "You want the usual?" she says, twirling a lock of hair. "Or something new?"

Nana turns in her seat to see April's face. "You're pale as a stone," she says.

"We could change the part," April says, guiding the comb. "Take advantage of your cowlick."

"You look like the devil," Nana says.

April smiles and puts a bobby pin between her teeth. "It's the only face I've got."

Nana stands, holding on to the back of the chair, and faces April. "Where's Oliver?" she demands.

"How do I know?"

"Have you seen him since he moved back?"

"What does that have to do with anything?" April feels lightheaded. A few bites of Oliver's sandwich last night; has she eaten since then? She remembers pangs of hunger during the night, but they passed. When she awoke, her body was calm, craving nothing. Now her vision is dark at the edges, the room wavering. No, she will not pass out. Not in front of Nana. She grabs hold of a chair and lowers herself into it. "Sit down," she says to Nana. "You haven't told me yet how you want your hair."

"What's his number?" Nana says, moving to the phone. "I think I have it on speed call in the bedroom. I put the new number in last week. I knew he'd come back eventually, didn't you, April?"

"It's temporary, Nana. Don't walk without your brace."

April lets her go, praying that she will make it to the bedroom without falling. She hears the creak of bedsprings as Nana sits down.

Thank God, April thinks. She lowers her head between her knees, hair whisking the floor. She counts backward, waiting for the dark spots to recede. She hears Nana's voice calling into Oliver's answering machine.

April straightens up, dizzy but steadier, her vision clearing. She stands, holding the table, and opens the refrigerator. She takes out the orange juice and forces herself to take a few sips, drinking straight from the carton. *Okay,* she decides, replacing it. *I'm all right.*

She finds Nana sitting on the edge of the bed, holding the telephone with two hands. April takes it from her, listening to the dead air on the other end. "Nana," she says, hanging up. "You're using up his tape."

When Nana looks up at her, April sees her fear. "I'm just tired," April says. "I'm sorry I scared you. Come; let's get you into some dry clothes." Nana's hair has dampened her shoulders. She allows April to help her.

"Where is he?" Nana says, taking a photograph from her night-stand. April shivers, thinking she means Buddy, then sees she is holding a picture of Oliver. For as long as April can remember, Nana has kept his picture closest to her, under the halo of light at her bedside. There are no priests in the family. Oliver, good-hearted and attentive, is the next best thing. For all these years, he has continued to call her every Sunday, and every Monday April has been subjected to a detailed installment of his life, often more than April cares to know. She wonders if Oliver ever asked about her, and if so, what Nana might have said. *Still working at that bar! Still dating hoodlums!*

"She's got no Spanish blood, that girl," Nana says with a sigh.

"Neither did Spencer, and look how he turned out," April says. "Bernadette's a good person, Nana. Don't worry about them."

Nana replaces the photograph, Oliver's college graduation picture, not one of April's favorites. His hair is overly coiffed, his smile stiff; perhaps the tie was constraining him.

Nana picks up the other photograph on the nightstand, taken on

Oliver's eighth birthday, the summer solstice, an evening warm and bright. April remembers the party, the endless game of keep-away, the neighbors' children one by one called home to dinner until only she and Oliver were left. When he thought the game was over, she stole his Boy Scout canteen, a birthday gift from his father. Deep in the yard he caught up with her, grabbed the canvas strap. They whirled in a circle, both holding on with two hands, spinning faster and faster, centrifugal force pulling them apart, their grip holding them together. The speed was terrifying, dizzying, like a tornado. They reeled until they could not stop, their momentum defying gravity. If either one released his hold, the other would go flying, but neither let go.

In the photograph, their image is blurred. It is hard to see where one begins and the other ends. "I don't know why you hold on to that," April says. "Whoever took it used the wrong shutter speed. And it's overexposed."

Nana moistens her sleeve with her tongue and rubs a fingerprint from the glass. "I took it," she says. "And it's perfect."

When April leaves, the boys are gone, the basketball silent in the driveway. An Eldorado has boxed her in, and she leans on the horn until someone comes out to move it. She is impatient, afraid that Oliver will show up, concerned by Nana's message. He would want to talk, and April has nothing to say.

Once the Eldorado has moved, she backs up, tapping the car behind her, which she recognizes in her rearview as an Audi. Not Oliver's. She pulls out abruptly, then slams on the brakes, nearly hitting an oncoming car. She didn't look. The nose of her car juts into the street unscathed. She catches her breath and blushes as if Oliver were watching.

Chapter
6

APRIL TIES HER APRON, glancing at the handful of customers sitting beneath stuffed mallards and mounted buffleheads, glass-eyed and dusty. The Duck Inn is quiet.

The daytime bartender looks at his watch; she is an hour early.

"Consider it a peace offering," she says, "for all the times I'm late."

He shrugs and takes off his apron. No one offers condolences because no one knows. This is one place Buddy rarely came, and where April isn't expecting to see him every time she lifts her head. She leaves a note for the boss that she's available for overtime. She wishes she could sleep here at night.

Nevertheless, things remind her. A conversation develops about car accidents, vehicle safety records, the pros and cons of anti-lock brakes. There's a man with a Giants shirt just like Buddy's. And laughter from across the room that could almost be his.

While mixing a screwdriver, she spots herself in the mirror, April the bartender. Maybe it doesn't matter anymore how she got here. She's been doing this job so long, it feels like who she is. The heavy sky makes the room darker than usual, the varnished wood without its usual gloss. She tells herself, for sanity's sake, not to think any-more about Buddy. Sleep deprivation gives her a queer buzz. Her mind keeps slipping into odd, disjointed memories.

She sees herself as a child walking to the bar with her father, hand in hand, April taking giant steps in an effort to match his stride. When they reached the tavern, her father would prop her on top of the bar.

"Check out that smile," he said once to a chinless man on a bar stool. "Is she going to be a knockout, or what?"

"Drop-dead gorgeous," the man answered.

From that height, April could see a tank of tropical fish behind the bar. There were angels, guppies, mollies, and swordtails, all bobbing to the vibration of the filter. A picture was taped to the back of the tank. At first April thought it was a landscape. Then she recognized the hills as hips, the river a seam between a woman's thighs. Her nipples were pink as pieces of coral, her hair lemon blond. The walls of the tank were stained with algae. An angel drifted, fins folded, kissing the surface for air. April wondered if fish could drown.

Her father fixed her a Shirley Temple with an extra-plump cherry and left her sitting in a booth with her multiplication tables and gumdrops while he checked inventory. The chinless man came over and slid in beside her. His face was flushed and leathery, breath sweet as licorice. His eyes were glassy and sentimental, like her dad's at the end of the day, and his sweat smelled familiar. He was taller than her father, older, with greasy hair combed back to keep it in place.

"Promise me you'll never cut your hair," he said, handling her ponytail. His fingers were swollen and creased with dirt.

April's father appeared and leaned on the table. "Yo," he said. "Sit any closer and you'll smother the kid."

"We were just talking," the man said. "She reminds me of mine when she was that age."

Her father pointed his thumb over his shoulder and the chinless man left, but April had not been afraid. She was acquainted with the thickness in his speech, the careful clumsy way he moved; he was like someone she had known a long time.

"Hey, pipsqueak," her father said, sitting down. "You flirting again?" She smiled. He tapped a cigarette on the tabletop. "So, who you gonna marry when you grow up?" he asked, lighting up. It was a ritual question.

"You, Daddy."

"Then you better save yourself." He smiled. "I'll be waiting."

It is one of the few memories she recalls from before Buddy was born.

April in the mirror appears haggard and small, but her father always looked confident behind the bar, in his element. She can still see the quiet, pleased expression on his face when he could make a girl blush with a simple compliment. If she lingered until his shift was over, he would invite her to play pool, stand behind her as she shot, brush against her lightly as he circled the table and took aim. Often her father forgot April was watching.

When their parents fought, Buddy would come to April and huddle against her. April rocked, listening to the rising crescendo of their voices, bracing herself.

Once when she was nine, she awoke in the night to the sound of her mother screaming. April's fingers iced over and her pulse throbbed in her ears. *He's killing her,* she thought. Halfway down the stairs, April stopped. In the dim, greenish glow of the fluorescent stove light, she saw her mother on the kitchen floor, nightgown shoved above her breasts, hands clutching her husband's back. He was moving against her like a boat docked in a storm, rocking helplessly against the pier. He kissed her, swallowing her sobs with his mouth, and for one shocking moment, April understood.

By midnight, the commuters are gone and the bar is sparsely filled with the after-dinner crowd, people escaping arguments or planning them. April eats pretzels to keep her awake and mops the floor behind the bar to give people the message.

The front door opens. She moves the mop and wrings it out, taking her time before acknowledging the customers who have seated themselves at the bar. She straightens up, wiping her hands on her apron, and sees Oliver's face, stark in the mirror, with Bernadette beside him. *Jesus,* April thinks with a jolt. How did they find out where she works? They look sleepy and rumpled, suggesting they were curled up in bed only moments before. She turns to them. "What'll it be?"

Oliver hesitates, startled by her tone. He has never done this before, not since they were teenagers and he would stop by her father's bar to bring her a sandwich for dinner. That was different. At fifteen, busing tables was nothing to be ashamed of.

"Last call," she shouts. Customers glance at their watches. She turns back to Oliver and Bernadette. He is wearing a UC Berkeley sweatshirt, she, a sizeable denim jacket, probably his. Without makeup, she looks pale and delicate, her thin, silken hair loose around her face. Oliver is unshaven, smelling faintly of breath mints and cologne. They have just made love, April concludes, and in the sweetness of the aftermath, decided to make her their mission. She turns her back and straightens up the bar. In the mirror, she sees Bernadette staring up at the stuffed merganser with cigarette holes in its wings, her forehead tense. Oliver puts a protective arm around her. "Have you made a decision?" April asks. "I'm trying to get out of here."

"Seltzer," Oliver says.

"You don't have tea, do you?" asks Bernadette.

"I can make some in the kitchen," April says. "It's the generic stuff. Nothing fancy."

"It's too much of a bother."

"No bother." April puts a seltzer on the bar in front of Oliver and twists it open. She makes the tea and closes out the cash register, draining the taps as the last customers leave. Bernadette takes a few sips of her tea and lets the rest go cold. Too strong, April supposes. She takes out her keys. "Are you leaving out the front or back?"

"Which way are you going?" Oliver asks.

"I've got another hour of cleanup," she says, turning off the neon lights.

"We can help you," Bernadette offers.

"Thanks, but it's a one-person job."

"April," Oliver says. "We came to see you home, so we'll do whatever it takes to get you out of here."

"It isn't necessary," April says. "And to be honest, I don't want you to."

"Too bad," Oliver says. "Because here we are."

April dead-bolts the front door and starts turning chairs upside down on tabletops. What the hell. Let him see her like this. She carries a rack of dirty glasses back to the dishwasher and begins loading it. Her apron is discolored, her hairline damp with perspiration. Oliver comes in behind her. "I'm going to clean the bathrooms next," she says. "Want to watch that, too?"

"Nana said you fainted today."

"I didn't."

"So she lied?"

"She misunderstood." She snaps on a pair of rubber gloves, canary yellow. "I work faster alone." She picks up a bottle of disinfectant.

"Bernadette wants to offer you her place, if you don't mind the smell of paint. You'll have it to yourself for a week."

April stops herself before asking where Bernadette will be. She wonders why they bother with separate apartments. "Thank you, but I like my own bed."

"If I thought you'd changed your locks today, I wouldn't be bothering you."

"What if I did?"

He raises a skeptical brow.

She brushes past him and heads for the men's room. He follows her inside, motioning for Bernadette to come after. The room is dingy, the wall behind the urinal spotted from men who missed their mark. Bernadette folds her arms across her chest, appraising the scene.

"So you're the janitor, too?" Oliver asks.

"The extra money buys me a tank of gas," April says. "Did you think I'd be too proud?"

April thinks of her grandmother at Our Lady of Perpetual Hope, cleaning priests' toilets for twenty-five years, hearing their complaints about paint chips in the bathtub. *"What was I supposed to do?"* Nana lamented. *"Stand there and catch them as they fell?"*

"I didn't come here to argue," Oliver says.

"Why are you here?" April asks.

"Appease me," he says.

She sighs, wiping her forehead with her arm. "First of all, I'm not going home. And second, I don't need an escort."

"Where are you going?"

"Nowhere if I don't get this bathroom done. Now will you excuse me, please?"

"I'll help you," he says, taking a scrub brush. "You do the sink. I've got the john."

"I'll do the mirror," Bernadette says. "I can handle that."

"Don't you think this makes me just a little uncomfortable?"

"We do our own every week," Oliver says. "A toilet is a toilet."

April shakes her head and wrings out the mop, like strangling a chicken. For a few moments, they work in silence. She pummels the sink until the bristles of her scouring brush are bent. When Oliver is done, he comes beside her and lathers his hands to his elbows. She notices the fine hair on his forearms, curly and wet.

"I've mopped us into a corner," April says.

She watches his back as he bends over the sink, his shoulders beneath his canvas shirt, sleeves rolled up. He has changed his clothing since leaving her apartment.

"It's strange," he says, prying loose a paper towel from its overstuffed bin. "My memories keep moving back; today all I can think of is the week he was born. I had poison ivy and wasn't allowed to touch him, remember?"

April doesn't answer. Bernadette wipes the glass, their faces streaky in the reflection.

"I picture him flying down the hill in his Big Wheel with that guinea pig, Ratsy, on his lap," Oliver says. "But I can hardly remember what we said to each other the last time we spoke. I keep trying to reconstruct his face. All the photographs feel wrong."

April stares blankly. She knows this is hurtful, but she wants to hurt him. Oliver looks at her in the mirror. The room smells of window cleaner, scouring powder, and, despite everything, urine. Bernadette fidgets uncomfortably.

Oliver shifts his weight, raising his arm to say something but then running his hand through his hair instead. April feels the air move. Warmth radiates from inside his shirt, the heat he generated cleaning.

Bernadette touches April's shoulder and she feels her skin flinch involuntarily, like a horse shooing a fly. She knows she ought to feel comforted, but she is ready to beg them to leave. "Let's get you home," Bernadette says. "We don't want you to have another night like last night."

April looks at Oliver, but he puts his hands in his pockets and stares at the drying floor. "Last night?" April says.

"I brought some herbal sleeping pills," Bernadette says softly. "Nothing addictive."

April looks at him again, but Oliver will not look back. She tosses the cleaning supplies into the bucket and pushes through the door.

Behind the bar, the phone is ringing. April snatches it.

"Change your mind?" T.J. says.

April stops, looks at her watch, and turns her back on Oliver. "No," she says quietly. "Just running late."

She feels Oliver step closer.

"Did you remember what I asked you to bring?"

April glances at a bottle of Seagram's. "I forgot to ring it up, and now the cash register is closed out."

"So pay for it tomorrow."

"It doesn't work that way."

"Who is it?" Oliver asks.

"Is someone with you?" T.J. says.

"No. I'm leaving now."

"Someone's there," he says.

"I'll be over in ten minutes."

"I'm coming to you."

"No. I've got my coat on." At this, Oliver catches her eye, glancing at her bare arms to acknowledge the lie. She hangs up. "My friend Carla," she says.

He bites his lip and nods. "Well, I guess we've done everything we can do here." He picks up Bernadette's coat.

"So you're staying with a girlfriend?" Bernadette says hopefully.

Oliver stares at April as he slips Bernadette's coat over her shoulders. She stares back. "That's right," he answers. "She's staying with Carla."

April sits on her hands while she waits for the idle to settle down. In her rearview mirror she sees Oliver's taillights swing out of the parking lot. She can relax now, because he will not be back. He saw what a waste of time the evening had been. He will go home and press himself upon Bernadette before they are even inside the vestibule. He will think over and over again how lucky he is to have someone so sane and benign.

She pulls out of the lot and drives toward the rented room where T.J. is staying. She isn't worried about getting to sleep because they won't, at least not until drink and exhaustion overtake them. She will climb the stairs to his windowless room with its slanted ceiling and chipping paint and listen to the desperate cot creak beneath the weight of their forgetting.

W I N T E R

~~~~~⌒

Chapter

7

PARCHEESI LIES OPEN on Nana's kitchen table, the playing board strewn with pistachio shells, crimson as rose petals. Beside it a Rock-'n'-roll Santa with blue suede shoes gyrates its hips, the battery so drained the jingle is more like a drone. Oliver turns it off with a smile, but Nana is oblivious. "I see Mr. Bergfalk was here," he says, kissing her cheek. She smells of cold cream and Dippity-do, her hair recently set.

"Freesia again." Nana points vaguely to a vase on the counter, not bringing herself to look at it. "He knows I'm allergic."

"And mistletoe, I see," says Oliver.

Nana waves her hand to suggest he is being foolish. Oliver slips Bernadette an amused glance. Nana has a string of gentleman friends, all eager to please, none succeeding. He has no idea how she meets them. "You remember my fiancée, don't you?"

"Imagine April working on Christmas Eve. Did you ever hear of such a thing?" Nana asks.

"Bernadette," he reminds her. "You met at Thanksgiving."

"Air traffic controllers, okay. Police officers. Telephone operators. But bartenders? Can't people live without a gin and tonic for one night?"

"Not everyone's Christian," Oliver says.

"Exactly. Couldn't she have found a nice Jewish fellow to fill in?"

"Maybe she wanted to work," Bernadette says.

Nana looks at her directly for the first time, scrutinizing. "How did you two meet, anyway?"

"Oliver came to my rescue," Bernadette says. "He saved one of my kids from drowning."

"She's exaggerating. The kid wasn't even close to the river."

"He slipped on the rocks. He could have fallen in."

"Excuse me," Nana says. "You have children?"

"Not my own. I work with special-needs kids. We were doing a cleanup in the park. Oliver was jogging by when one of the kids took a spill. I never could have picked him up myself."

"Picked up Oliver, you mean?" Nana asks.

Bernadette blushes. "The boy," she says.

"Believe me," Oliver says with a smirk, "I was the one who picked up Bernadette. I'd seen her before. She's amazing with these kids. They light up when she's around."

Nana studies her. "You must have a lot of patience to do that kind of work."

"I try."

"Patience isn't always what Oliver needs," Nana says, raising a brow. "Sometimes he needs a good kick in the pants."

"I'm good at that, too." She grins, glancing at Oliver.

Nana appraises her. "What kind of special needs? Do you work with mongoloids?"

"Nana," Oliver says gently. "They're not called that anymore."

"Mentally retarded, then? I'm sorry if I can't keep up with the lingo."

"Yes," Bernadette says. "Kids with mental and physical disabilities, everything under the sun."

"You must be a strong person, then," says Nana.

"I love the kids," Bernadette says. "Some days it doesn't feel like work at all."

"And other days?" says Nana.

"There are heartbreaks, of course. It can be hard."

"On those days, you'll have Oliver here to listen to all your sad stories at the end of the day. He's good at that."

"Yes, I know," she says softly, looking at Oliver with affection.

"Give me your hand," Nana says.

Bernadette extends it reluctantly. "Do you read palms, Mrs. Night?"

"Don't be ridiculous. It doesn't take an astrologer to see that you don't do much housework."

"Nana!" Oliver says.

But Bernadette only smiles. "My secret is cold cream."

"Hm," Nana says wryly, relinquishing Bernadette's hand. "Mine, too." She studies her for a moment. "You realize, don't you, that Oliver is not your ordinary man."

"If he were, I wouldn't be marrying him."

"He's not going to give you a conventional life."

"What's that supposed to mean?" Oliver says, but the women ignore him.

Bernadette smiles gently. "Well, Mrs. Night, I was under the impression that I give *myself* my life."

"Those are pretty words," Nana says. "But don't underestimate the influence of marriage. After all, here you are living in New York because of Oliver."

"Actually, it's the opposite, Nana. I found a law school here because Bernadette is doing her doctorate at Columbia."

"You'd be back anyway," Nana says. "You have unfinished business here."

"Really?" Oliver laughs uncomfortably. "And what might that be?"

"You remind me of Oliver's mother," Nana says to Bernadette. "Don't you think so, Oliver?"

"It hadn't occurred to me."

"Yes," Bernadette says. "His father says so, too."

"Not the eyes," Nana says, "but something about the chin, and that small, triangular face. Oh, she was a lady, wasn't she, Oliver?" She turns to Bernadette. "Oliver was the apple of her eye. He got all her good manners and common sense. How could he do otherwise, with his big brother keeping her up worrying all night?" She laughs. "That Al, he liked to party, didn't he, Oliver."

"Still does." He sighs.

"Oh, Al had them biting their fingernails," she says to Bernadette. "The problem was that Al got all of his mother's charm and none of the logic." She pats Oliver's arm. "I understand what it's like. My oldest sister in Malaga, she was a harlot. I had no choice but to be good."

"I hate to break it to you, Nana," says Oliver. "But I've got my vices."

"Well, I certainly hope so," she says, giving him a wink. "A man who goes through life without burning a piece of toast will never get what he wants."

Bernadette grins. "If that's the case, Oliver, I think you've got some catching up to do."

He smirks.

"Now, my granddaughter, April, she's another story," says Nana. "Can't put a slice in the toaster without burning down the house."

"Well," Oliver says wisely. "I'll try not to go that far."

"Unless that's what it takes," Nana says.

Oliver smiles back weakly, unsure what she means.

Nana sighs, glancing out the window. "April, working on Christmas Eve." She frowns. "Do you know that when her father was a teenager, he used to disappear every Christmas? Just take off for God-knows-where and reappear a week later? He was mad at *his* father, of course. He liked having the power to disappear, too. Spencer and I were sick until he came home. And it scared Hal. When Bede meandered back, he never would say where he'd been."

Oliver touches Nana's hair gently. "We'll all be together tomorrow. April, too." But as soon as he says this, he realizes it is a lie. No one has told her about Buddy. "Come," he says. "We'll be late for dinner."

As Oliver goes to the closet for Nana's coat, he notices a picture on the mantel, April in her crisply starched Holy Cross uniform, fourth grade, eyes sparkling, teeth sweetly crooked. Her face is framed by a nebulous backdrop, a blue ethereal haze. In the two months since their clash in the bar, he has not spoken to her.

In the kitchen, he helps Nana with her coat.

"Are these your sons?" Bernadette says, looking at the sailor-suit picture.

"Sometimes a lie is more like the truth," Nana says. "The truth isn't always the way it happens."

Oliver thinks of Buddy. How long can they deceive her?

"I thought of him as my boy," Nana says. "No less than that."

Oliver smooths her lapels.

"It was a car accident," Nana says. "Who can explain that?"

Oliver gives Bernadette a furtive look. Has someone told Nana?

"Stone drunk," Nana says. "And he was driving that Packard like a race car. The poor woman never saw it coming. The carriage was mangled, but Hal landed in the grass without a scratch." Nana touches the image beneath the glass. "God caught him in the palm of his hand." She looks up at Oliver and strokes the side of his face.

Oliver shivers, glancing at Bernadette. He takes Nana's hand. "I haven't heard that story before. Did you ever tell my father?"

"I wanted us to be a family," Nana says.

"Of course," he says. "We are." He brushes lint from the shoulder of her coat. Nana reaches for the frame and takes off the back. A second photo slips out. "Your grandmother was a beautiful woman," she says. "I suppose she would have wanted you to know that."

It is a studio shot, the kind women sent to their boyfriends during war. The woman is attractive in a nondescript way, but Oliver sees no resemblance to his father or himself. "Thank you, Nana," he says gently. "But bloodlines don't matter to me. I consider you my grandmother."

They start down the stairs. Nana holds tightly to Oliver's elbow.

"Have you met Buddy?" she asks Bernadette.

"Once," she answers, which is half true, if you count the funeral.

"The baby of the family gets away with murder," Nana says. "Buddy says he wants to go skiing for Christmas, and everyone says sure. Just like that. Poof, and he's in the White Mountains."

Oliver and Bernadette exchange a disconsolate glance. It's wrong to withhold the truth this way, but since her stroke happened shortly after Bede Sr.'s death, no one is willing to take another chance.

During the lengthy drive east, Oliver turns off the radio when the carols begin to annoy him. For as long as he can remember, Christmas revolved around Buddy. After Al, Oliver, and April grew wise, Santa was perpetuated for Buddy alone. The family held a collective breath on Christmas morning; they lived the magic through him. Who knows how long he pretended to believe for the sake of everyone else?

Oliver remembers wrapping presents with April one night on the living room rug while his parents made tea in the kitchen.

"How do we wrap *this* one?" Oliver asked, holding up a basketball.

April grinned. "Just wait until we get to the junior lacrosse sticks."

"You're spoiling him. Even your dad doesn't give him this much stuff."

"My father"—she shook her head—"got him a giant stuffed Pooh Bear. He's in another world. The kid is seven years old!"

"A young seven," Oliver said. "He'll be sleeping with Pooh till he's twelve."

She smiled with one corner of her mouth. "You just like disagreeing with me."

"Not true."

"There you go again." She jabbed his ribs and he snatched her wrist. With her free hand, she lightly slapped his cheek.

"Fresh," he said, snatching that hand, too. She giggled, pulling away.

"I just don't get it," his mother's voice rose from the kitchen.

Oliver let go at once.

"Journalism, fine," his mother said. "But why sports?"

Oliver pictured them flipping through the day's mail, more college catalogs for Al.

"Because it's what he loves," his father answered.

"Oliver loves the piano," she said. "But he's not foolish enough to make it his life."

April's eyes darkened. He felt her staring at him.

"We don't know that yet," his father said gently.

Normally his father would challenge her more, but it had been a few weeks since the diagnosis. Everyone was still hopeful, but careful, too.

"Anyway," he continued. "It doesn't matter what we think. You know Al. He'll do what he wants."

Oliver could hear her resignation all the way from where he sat. "Well," she said. "At least we have one reasonable son."

April gave Oliver a pained, inquisitive look. Her lips parted; there was something she wanted to say.

"I say we don't wrap it at all," Oliver said, tossing her the basketball. "Just stick it under the tree."

"Is that what Santa would do?"

"Buddy doesn't believe anymore. And if he does, he shouldn't."

"That's not what you really think."

"I don't know what I think," he said, rubbing his face. "Except that you can't believe in magic forever." He felt her hand on his knee.

"I'm tired of wrapping," she said. "Play me something."

"Not now," he said, glancing at the kitchen door.

She stood and pulled him to his feet. "Let's go for a drive then. Let's go to the beach."

"The beach?" He laughed. "With what? My learner's permit?"

"A walk, then. To the high school. We can shoot some hoops. We can climb the water tower. It doesn't matter. Let's go."

"It's eleven o'clock at night. It's thirty degrees out."

She pulled their coats from the front closet. "Good night, Uncle Hal, Aunt Avila," she called. "Oliver's walking me home."

"Good night, honey," his father called.

"Be careful, Oliver," his mother said.

Outside it was raining. "Perfect," she said brightly. "We'll ride our bikes."

"Our bikes?" He grinned. "You mean my bike?"

"And Al's."

"He'll kill you."

She headed for the garage. "I'll race you."

He pulled his hood over his head. The rain was cold and sharp. "Where are we headed?"

"Anyplace," she called over her shoulder. "As long as it's unreasonable."

Oliver smiles to himself. In the backseat, Nana snores. He turns off the highway. The road winds through wooded lots. They pass a burned-out barn, a pony grazing in a garden, nibbling the shorn-off stubble of last year's corn. Sea smoke drifts from a passing pond. The high school appears, low and sprawling, the baseball diamond empty and dark.

Oliver remembers a conversation with Buddy six weeks or so before the accident, the start of Buddy's freshman semester in college. He called to ask Oliver's advice on choosing a major. It had become clear that an athletic scholarship was not in the picture.

"Do what you love," Oliver had said. "Do what you can't not do."

"Is that how it is with you?" Buddy asked. "With law?"

Oliver was silent for a moment.

"Trust yourself," he said finally. "You'll know if it feels right."

Chapter
8

THE HOUSE IS DARK except for a string of lights neatly framing each window. Snow whirls slowly through the bare branches of sugar maples, the first white Christmas in years. April finds the key in the mailbox where Hal said it would be. Buddy's car ticks behind her, its tracks fresh. The other cars are blanketed, giving the impression they have been there for years. She stands for a moment at the front door and looks up at the NIGHT FAMILY plaque Oliver carved in high school. She loves the beautiful irregularity of the letters, each one filling with white. The world is so quiet she can hear the snow.

She had not wanted to come, but Hal insisted they keep up the tradition in memory of Buddy. What could she say to that? "I'll come in the morning," she offered, but he said his Christmas Day waffles were meant to be eaten in pajamas. She was told to come straight from work.

She slips off her boots without turning on a light. A note on the side table is barely legible in the dark. "Take Oliver's old room," Hal wrote. "He's on the roll-away in Al's room."

She hangs up her coat. The fire is nearly out. She can't blame Hal for wanting everyone here. It is the one night each year when the house is full. It has been a decade since Avila's death. Surely he could have remarried if he wanted to, but as far as April knows, he has never gone on a date.

She sits on the rug in front of the sofa and watches the dying fire. It feels so strange to be in this house without Buddy. His absence hits her physically, a hollowness inside. Yet she is glad to be here, away from her apartment. T.J. has not moved back. He waits for her to go to him.

He has taken to photographing her again at odd moments when she is not watching, scraping ice off her windshield, setting out a saucer of milk for a stray cat behind the bar. If he is looking for evidence, he won't find it. He slips the unmarked black-and-whites into the mail, and when she receives them, she tosses them in the trash. In most of them, she doesn't recognize herself. She appears smaller than she remembers, lost inside her clothes. In every shot, she looks out of place.

On the coffee table is a plate of shucked oyster shells and lemon rinds, stemware filmy with eggnog, Hal's reading glasses, and a tie she figures for Oliver's; Al almost never wears one, and the regimental stripes are not Hal's style. She picks it up and smooths it over the arm of the chair. The crackling of the wood makes her feel quiet inside, the aroma musky and sweet. She slumps back against the foot of the chair. The room chills as the fire languishes. This house has not changed much, with its endless bookshelves and cozy hearth. What impressed her most as a kid was the absence of a liquor cabinet.

The ashy fragrance of the fireplace makes her eyelids heavy. She remembers the time her father caught her stealing from his liquor cabinet. A junior in high school, she had been invited to a party with seniors and wasn't about to show up empty-handed. It wasn't really that she liked to drink, but as a social skill, it proved useful. She had gotten to the point where she could down three shots without feeling drunk, which impressed the kids she hung out with, particularly boys.

Her father came into the room silently. She jolted when she spotted him, wondering how long he'd been watching her. She closed the liquor cabinet and folded her hands in front of her.

"Little bitch," he said quietly.

She tried to think of a plausible explanation for standing there, but there was none. "I always replace what I take," she said. "If that's what you're worried about."

He lunged for her. She ducked, but instead of striking, he took her by the shoulders and hurled her back against the wall. Buddy's first-grade picture clattered down, the glass shattering on the hardwood floor. A shadowy fog invaded the room. She felt the coolness of the floor against her cheek.

"April, sweetheart." Her father pulled her arm until she straightened into a sitting position. She felt there was an ax in the back of her head, and she laughed aloud, picturing it.

"Jesus, April," her father said, pulling her up. "Why do you have to do this? Why can't you just be good?"

She pictured her dead mother appearing in the doorway, covering her mouth with the sleeve of her bathrobe and vanishing again. April prayed Buddy wouldn't wake up. "I'm sorry, Daddy," she said.

"You're impossible," he said. "Stand up now. Show me you're all right."

"I'm all right."

"Jesus, how did I get a daughter like this?"

"Go back down to your poker game. I'll clean up," she said. "I'll buy another frame."

He kissed the top of her head. "Behave yourself, April. I see a bottle missing later, I'll break your legs."

She couldn't help it; she pictured the ax in her head and her legs in casts. She knew it was sick to laugh, that it could cost her. As soon as her father descended the stairs and the rec room door clicked shut, she cracked, her laughter so hard she could barely breathe, nor see the shards of glass she was trying to sweep, so fast and hot were her tears.

"Screw the party," she thought to herself, and instead walked to Oliver's studio. It was late, but he was there. She was still dressed in her stupid, tight clothes, but it didn't matter. It was only Oliver.

He stood up from the piano, looking surprised. "Thought you had a date," he said. Then, "God, you look like hell."

"It must be the ax in my head." She laughed so sharply it came out as a sob, which made her laugh even harder.

"Are you drunk?" he asked.

"No," she said, touching her head. "That's the problem."

He touched her neck, parting her hair to look at the back of her head. The gentleness of his touch combined with the tenderness of the pain was excruciating. "Jesus," he said. "You've got a goose egg. I'm calling my father."

"No. A bump is good. It means the swelling went out instead of in."

"You should at least take some aspirin."

"I'd probably throw it up."

"Nausea is a sign of concussion."

"Just play me a song. That's all I need."

"Tell me what happened, and don't give me the slipping-on-the-staircase story."

She sat down wearily. "I'm a pathological wiseass, that's what happened."

"Are you giving him an excuse?"

"No, but if I hadn't been doing something wrong—"

"You don't deserve this."

"How do you know?"

"I know."

"Believe me, Oliver. There are things about me you wouldn't want to know."

"What things?"

"Why don't *you* make some mistakes once in a while so I don't have to?"

"I make mistakes."

"Name one."

"You're trying to change the subject. You should see a doctor."

"You don't always have to be good, you know. You're allowed to screw up."

"I do, all the time."

"Have you ever smoked a cigarette? Did you ever get drunk?"

"I've had a beer or two. Why should I get drunk if I don't want to?"

"Okay, you name it, then. What's something you secretly want to do, but know you shouldn't?"

He blushed, averting his eyes. She saw his gaze fall to her bulky, high-heeled shoes, too heavy for her feet. Even she could see that now. How stupid, her clothes! Her skirt had inched up, revealing the place where her stocking ended, the suggestion of a garter, and a narrow swatch of exposed skin shockingly white against the dark nylon. Oliver got up abruptly and went to the piano, running his finger clamorously up the scale. "I want to be a musician," he said.

She leaned forward in her seat, pulling down her skirt. "And that's bad?"

"It's impractical."

"What if Mozart thought that way?"

"I'm not Mozart. Besides, it's a different world now."

"Yo-Yo Ma? Midori?"

"I don't need to be famous. I just want to play."

"So?"

"You don't understand. You're a girl. Guys are supposed to make a living."

"Is that what your father says?"

"You're only asking that because you know the answer."

"He loved books, so he became a professor. Maybe his parents thought *that* was impractical."

"It's a hell of a lot safer than trying to make it in music."

"Safe?" She went over and stood near him at the piano. "Look, if your *dad* wants you to be happy, why don't you?"

"I do. I am. I will be."

She sat on the bench, looking up at him. "What if your mother weren't sick?"

He turned sharply and stared down at her. "What does that have to do with anything?"

"Oliver," she said gently. "Just because she's dying doesn't mean you have to follow her advice."

"No one says she's dying," he said harshly. "Would you stop it? I don't want to talk about this anymore."

She took his elbow and pulled him down beside her on the bench. She slid her arm around his waist and leaned her head on his shoulder. "I'm sorry," she said.

He leaned his head on hers. She felt his breath through her hair. Told herself to keep breathing. "April," he whispered. "I want to go away somewhere. Far away. With you."

As soon as the words were out, he stood nervously. He went over and inspected a cello that had hung in the same spot for years. She took her cue and stood to leave, pretending not to have heard.

Someone touches her arm. She flinches, opening her eyes. Oliver slides down beside her. It takes her a moment to place herself back in Hal's living room. The fire crackles; Oliver must have added another log.

"Just get here?" he asks, though it must be obvious she was dozing. His voice sounds deliberately casual. His hair has grown a bit since the funeral, and he is unshaven. Her fingers and toes tingle, adjusting to the warmth of the fire. She glances behind her at the window. The shade is not drawn, but the room is dark enough that she decides not to worry. She takes the tie from the armrest and coils it around her hands like a strangle cord, which she drapes across the back of her neck, chin resting on her fists. She stares at the fire, listening to the sizzle and snap.

"Well, hello, Oliver," he says to himself. "Nice to see you, too."

She smiles at him despite herself.

He leans over and kisses her cheek. The abrasion of his skin against hers gives her a start, the prickly stubble, the warmth of his lips. He smells faintly of dinner wine and his brother's cigarettes. She brings her knees to her chest and folds her arms around them.

"Why don't you take your old room," she says. "I'll be fine here on the sofa."

He waves a hand and settles back. "It was ridiculous here tonight," he says. "All of us putting on a show for Nana."

"Thank God my parents aren't here. They would never have gotten through it."

"And you?"

She sighs. "Buddy's mail gets forwarded to me. You'd be amazed how many bills a dead person can get. I pay them and throw out the catalogs." An ember falls from the log, glows, and vanishes. "There's a girl in Kingston who thinks she's in love with him. She doesn't understand why he won't answer her letters."

"How awful."

"So last night I wrote her a love letter and signed his name. I plan to send it along with his obituary, explaining that I just came across the unmailed letter in his knapsack. What do you think?"

"You're kidding, right?"

"Why?"

"It's cruel."

"I thought the opposite."

"What if they hardly knew each other?"

"She's crazy about him."

"It's a lie, April. What if you got some detail wrong? What if he wrote to her before, and she sees the handwriting is different?"

"She'll believe because she'll want to."

"You're playing with someone's deepest emotions."

"Am I?" She looks at him.

He turns toward the window.

"Would it be better to tell her that there's no record of his feelings, and that for most of the time she's been in love with him, he's been dead?"

"It's honest."

"Sometimes you have to think about the purpose of *honest*."

"No you don't."

"I'm going to mail it."

"Do what you like."

"I think Buddy would want me to."

"I can't argue with that."

They fall into silence.

"How are you?" he says finally. "I mean, really."

A few glib answers pass through her mind; she lets them go. "Well, I got myself here tonight," she says. "Snow and all."

He nods appreciatively, glancing toward the window. "It's lovely, isn't it?"

"It never snows on Christmas," she says. "Sleet, hail, freezing rain, okay. But this? It's a goddamn Hallmark card out there."

"No," he says. "A card could never capture this. Nothing could."

"Nothing?" she says. "Winslow Homer? Robert Frost?"

He smiles. "You just like disagreeing with me."

"George Winston's *Winter*," she says. "Don't tell me he didn't capture snow."

"Snow, yes. But *this* snow, here and now?" He turns to look at her. His eyes look different in this light, not the usual crystalline blue, but a deep, smoky indigo. Her face warms.

"What do you think it means?" she asks, nodding toward the window.

"The snow?" He tilts his head curiously. "It means itself."

"Don't go getting all Zen on me." She elbows him. "I'm a girl who needs answers." She realizes immediately that it was a mistake to touch him. He hasn't moved, yet he feels much closer now.

"Answers, eh? So, what's the question?"

She looks back toward the window. *The question.* She is still staring at the snow when she feels Oliver lift her hair out from behind the tie. She shudders, surprised by his touch. He begins to braid her hair, the way he used to when they were children.

April closes her eyes. For a moment she allows herself to feel his closeness. Her scalp tingles. Grains of ice beat upon the windowpane. Oliver's breath moves in and out of his lungs. She feels it on her neck. She is in a trance. She tells herself not to move and then to move quickly to break the spell.

"How's Bernadette?"

"At her parents'," he says, but that wasn't what she asked.

"Have you set a date?"

He pauses, finishing the braid and pulling it snug. "December seventh," he says.

"You're kidding, right? Pearl Harbor?"

"The place she wants is booked till then."

Oliver sifts his hands through the braid, loosening it. Her skin prickles, electrified. His fingers are cool as water. She feels his hand on her shoulder. He slides the tie slowly from around her neck. The silk against her skin makes her shiver. What Oliver fails to understand is the range of possibilities; that people can destroy themselves and one another and the whole planet with nothing stepping in to stop them; that she can destroy him without even trying. It wouldn't take much, she thinks, to let her thigh relax against his, blood rising to the surface of her skin, until they began to consider the harmlessness of a moment longer. And another.

April remembers Oliver's high school graduation party, nearly a decade ago, when she pulled him from his chair for a slow dance, leaning her body into his. Their cheeks pressed, she felt him stiffen against her, his blush warming her face. "Jesus, April," he breathed.

She laughed, pulled back, and left him there. She went to Al and sat on his lap. Still flushed, Oliver picked up his soda can and took a gulp. He tried to joke with a friend, pretend he wasn't watching, but she knew he was. She giggled, stabbing Al's chest with her finger, and he, his breath ripe with Heineken, moved his palm over her knee, playing with the hem of her skirt.

After a moment, they announced that they were going to buy more beer and needed Oliver's car to do it.

Oliver stood before them. "You're in no shape to drive, Al," he said. April couldn't look at him.

"Relax, Oliver," Al said, grabbing the keys from the table. "April's driving. We'll be right back."

April was sure Oliver would stop them, but he didn't. They never returned to the party. None of it was planned. She danced with him as a joke, to embarrass him, and was caught off guard by the warm rush deep in her own body. He was so close she could almost hear the movement of his thoughts, the roll of the tide; she had slipped inside his skin.

But she could never defile Oliver. He was too good. Too pure. So she had to make it look heedless, as though one brother were as good as another.

April looks at him, not the high school boy anymore, but a man she barely knows wearing a fancy watch and a five o'clock shadow. Almost nothing about him feels familiar, except the eyes. Those eyes. April gets up suddenly. Oliver doesn't object. He draws his hand down the side of his face and across his mouth, a gesture of deep consideration she has seen many times on his father.

"You know what they say." She nods toward the fireplace. "If you stay awake, he'll never come."

He doesn't smile, but only looks at her with a troubled, thoughtful expression. "Good night, April."

It is nearly dawn when she has the dream. Buddy is at the top of the stairs looking down at her. He has put on a little weight and looks ruddy, having just come in from the cold. He smiles at her, his eyes serene the way they sometimes looked after he spent long hours out on the lake alone. He opens the window at the top of the stairs and begins to climb out. It is a two-story drop. April screams, runs to him, but by the time she reaches the landing, he is gone.

She awakens in front of the half-open window, snow drifting in. She has never walked in her sleep before. She looks down at the undisturbed lawn laden with snow. The sky is dark except for a pale glow on the eastern horizon, diffused by the dark silhouettes of barren trees. In the thicket, a deer moves in a slow high-step, lifting its legs in and out of the deepening snow.

Her breath fogs the glass, and the deer vanishes. Wind groans against the side of the house, and Oliver's rondos rise in her mind, circling there as they have all night. She remembers sitting beside him a few hours ago, the roughness of his cheek, the crackle of embers, and the smell of ash. After they said good night, she felt different in her body, gentler toward herself. Even now she feels the afterglow of his nearness, the way she once felt as a kid after receiving communion, saturated by presence. Why can't she feel Buddy's presence that way? Her dream of him does not answer the question she still can't fathom: *Where is he?* She shuts the snow-laden window and heads back to her room.

Chapter

9

OLIVER WAKES to the smell of waffles and coffee, his neck stiff from the cot. The door to his old room is closed. He thinks of April on the other side, asleep in his childhood bed.

The bathroom is damp and steamy, fragrant with someone's shampoo. His grandmother's slippers lie atop the scale, registering nothing. He sees the impression of her feet, supine in the worn terry-cloth insoles. Al's travel kit sits open on the counter beside their father's aftershave. Oliver looks around, but nothing belongs to April.

Downstairs, Christmas carols are turned on high. Nana chatters to Oliver's father at the stove, correcting him on his cooking, while the dog lies at his feet, waiting for something to fall.

"Goddamn it," Al says, leaning on the Formica with the newspaper spread in front of him. "They screwed with my lead again. Dumb-ass night editor—"

"Al," his father scolds.

Al folds the paper. The phone rings and he grabs it.

Oliver looks at his watch. Bernadette is supposed to arrive in fifteen minutes; he doesn't have much time to get ready.

Al hangs up. "Same idiot," he says.

Their father frowns. "Someone keeps calling and hanging up," he explains to Oliver.

"Where is April, anyway?" Al asks.

"Go wake her," his father says. "This is almost ready."

Before Oliver can make a move, Al is taking the stairs two at a time. "Rose," he yells. "Haul your lazy ass out of bed."

"Honestly," Nana says to Hal. "To think you raised him."

"He's hopeless," Hal says. He glances at the photograph of Oliver's mother beside the phone; they often shared the same affectionate lament, Oliver recalls. Who would expect a son like Al from such quiet and serious parents? Oliver was studious and obedient to make up for his brother, but in retrospect he can see it was Al who baffled and delighted them.

He fills a mug with coffee and glances at his brother's byline. The lead is fine, probably improved. Al isn't good at accepting criticism, unlike Oliver, who is, he knows, too willing.

The doorbell rings and the dog springs up. Bernadette is early. "Shit," Oliver says, and the dog sits.

He goes to the door, tying his robe, and Cricket follows. April's cowboy boots are in the foyer, black imitation snakeskin, not meant for snow. Her silver barrette is on the side table, and he remembers that when he saw her during the night, her hair had been loose. He imagines Al waking her, entering her room without knocking. The dog paws at the door.

"Shit," Oliver commands, and the dog sits. He grins and opens the door.

"Oh, no," Bernadette says, seeing him. "Am I that early?"

"I'm late." He kisses her. "Don't worry."

"Bernadette," his father says, a spatula in his hand. "Merry Christmas, sweetheart."

Oliver takes her coat. She is wearing pearls and a green silk dress that the dog eagerly sniffs.

"Cricket," Hal admonishes.

The retriever flattens her ears.

Al comes bounding down the stairs. "Bernadette." Seeing her outfit, he whistles—not genuinely, Oliver thinks, but gratuitously, as one might for a child playing dress-up. Bernadette blushes.

"Tell the truth," Al says, kissing her cheek. "What's a classy woman like you doing with a slob like my brother?"

"He cleans up nice," she says, patting Oliver's cheek.

"He's got you fooled," Al says.

The dog runs to April, who is coming downstairs, wearing Al's sweatpants and a flannel shirt that looks slept in. Al whistles again, facetiously this time, though it sounds more like he means it. April is without makeup, in formless clothes, her hair disheveled from sleep; Oliver prefers her this way. Cricket rises on her haunches and places her big paws on April's shoulders. "Oh, God, Cricket." She laughs, pushing the dog away. "Your breath could sink a battleship." The dog wags her tail, flattered.

The telephone rings again and Hal reaches for it. "Eat," he tells everyone, pointing at the table.

Cricket rolls onto her back, limbs akimbo, and April rubs her stomach. Odd, Oliver thinks. Pets were always Buddy's department.

"Listen you—" Hal says sternly into the telephone, then looks at the receiver and hangs up. "Kids playing pranks," he says shaking his head, though Oliver is sure his father thinks otherwise.

April looks at the telephone and folds her arms. She appears fatigued and wary. Her hair is pulled back in a lopsided ponytail. Sheet marks crease her cheek. "Morning," she says to no one in particular. "Nice to see you, Bernadette," she says, kissing her cheek. She pats Nana's shoulder and sits down.

"That's it?" Al asks. "No kisses for the rest of us?"

April blows him a tired kiss. "This looks great, Uncle Hal. I'm starved."

A lie, Oliver thinks.

During the meal, she eats sparingly, like someone rationing food during war. Beside her, Nana talks nonstop. Occasionally April nods, but her eyes keep drifting to the window, snow shielding the pane.

The phone rings and she stands.

"Let me," Hal says, but she waves him away. She says hello and turns her back to the dining room. The table is noisy with conversation. Oliver leans back in his chair to see her in the kitchen. She looks out the window again, her eyes cast to the sky. She does not say anything, but stays on the line for a long moment, listening.

Oliver casts Bernadette a glance, but she only looks at him quizzically.

"Who's she talking to?" Nana asks.

Hal shrugs. "Have another waffle, Mom."

April turns her back again before bowing her head and hanging up. Hal catches Oliver's eye from across the table; they have the same thought.

"Was it Buddy?" Nana asks when April returns.

"Yes," April answers. "He said he wished he could be here."

The phone does not ring again.

When people finish eating, Hal comes around with more coffee and Bernadette carries leftovers to the kitchen. Oliver stands, collecting dishes.

"Oliver," Nana says. "Play us that new piece of yours."

April looks up from her plate. The room goes silent.

"Nana." He laughs. "There hasn't been a new piece in ten years." He gathers dirty forks in his fist.

"You know the one I mean," she persists. "Tra la la, ta dee te da."

April hums along. Nana stops, and April continues. The song comes back to Oliver in a whoosh, closing over him like an ocean wave. How is it possible they remembered?

"What song?" Bernadette asks.

He looks at her in a panic.

"Something Oliver composed," Hal says. "I remember it, too, now that I hear it. It was one of the last ones, wasn't it?"

Oliver doesn't answer. April stops humming and looks at him.

"*You* composed things?" Bernadette laughs. "On what, a harmonica?"

April's lips part with astonishment. It is nearly impossible to surprise her, but now Oliver feels the bewilderment of the entire family.

His father laughs uncomfortably. "You mean Oliver hasn't told you? He could have been a concert—"

"It's not a big deal," Oliver says abruptly. "For God's sake, you'd think it was a previous marriage." As he gets up, he bangs his knee on his chair, which hits the table, causing several cups of coffee to spill into their saucers. So what if he hadn't told Bernadette? Wasn't it a relief to know that she loved him for who he was, not for some talent he may or may not have possessed? He flexes his fingers. The chords are lost. His body holds no memory. "I'd better get ready for your parents," he says, handing his plate to Bernadette, who looks at him with her jaw open.

"Whoa," Al says as Oliver climbs the stairs. "Someone's touchy."

In the shower, Oliver feels the burn in his face. Bernadette once asked him about the piano in his apartment, dusty and out of tune, and he explained that it had been his mother's, and he kept it for sentimental reasons though he didn't play. It wasn't, strictly speaking, a lie. Still, Bernadette will take this to heart. She will want to know why Oliver did not tell her, and she will want a suitably complex answer.

He dresses in Al's room, and hears April go in to the shower. He buttons his shirt, white and starchy, abrasive against his skin, and knots the tie, bold stripes to match the suit. He pats his pocket and realizes he left his comb in the bathroom. The shower is off. She ought to be done by now. He knocks.

After a moment, April opens the door. Her hair is wet. She is wearing his robe, which he left on the door. "I need something," he says.

She nods in agreement and lets him in. He is irritated by her calm. Who is she to accuse him, with all she's given up? Compared with her decisions, his are at least sane. He dries an oval in the mirror and combs back his hair. April leans against the tile and folds her arms in front of her. She probably dislikes the way he looks, his hair too neat, his clothes, standard. She prefers gold teeth and MOTHER tattoos, not men who mousse their hair. He looks at her in the misty reflection. "I would have told her eventually," he says. "It's ancient history. It's not relevant."

April says nothing, which fuels him further. He closes the door and holds it shut. "What about those phone calls? You expect us to believe you're not seeing him again?"

"No one's judging you, Oliver. We all have choices. Einstein could have been a carpenter."

"Oh, sure. And that's not a judgment?" He slaps the door. The sound is louder than he expects. April takes a step back. For an instant he understands how men can do her harm. April barely breathes; she has come upon a snake in the woods and is determined to stay perfectly still. She knows how to handle herself, he thinks. She has been in this spot before. This is her specialty. Wouldn't she love it if he struck her? Wouldn't it confirm everything she believes?

"Oliver," she says evenly. "It wouldn't matter what profession you went into if you would just live the way you play."

"Played." He feels his body clench up, hands balled. "And how is that, April? What is it you think you understand about me? No, don't answer. Why should I ask *you*?"

She blinks but keeps her eyes on his. She doesn't move.

"I'm leaving," he says. "You're wearing my robe."

She stares. "You want it now?"

He glances at his watch. "Bernadette's family is waiting."

"Turn around," she says.

He hesitates and then obeys, though it must be obvious he can see her in the mirror. She takes off the robe. Underneath, she is wearing a black slip with spaghetti-strap shoulders and a short, scalloped hem, which ends where her stockings begin. She takes a midnight-blue dress from the towel rack and pulls it over her head.

"Make yourself useful if you're going to stare," she says, lifting her hair. He turns slowly and touches the velvety fabric at her waist. He centers the dress on her hips then moves the zipper up her back. She lets her hair fall but keeps her back to him. He shoves his hands quickly in his pockets.

"Look," he says quietly. "What's wrong with moving on with my life?"

She looks at him in the mirror. "I had a dream about a man who shut up all the doors and windows of his house, not realizing that the tiger he was trying to keep out was in his own basement."

"I don't understand dreams."

"It was getting hungry down there."

"They frustrate me. That's why I don't remember them."

"If you don't remember them, how do you know they frustrate you?"

"I have to go."

She nods.

He picks up his robe and opens the door to leave. He turns back to look at her. "So what happens in the dream?" he demands.

"Oliver," Bernadette calls from the bottom of the stairs. "It's time, honey."

"Either the tiger starves," Oliver says. "Or the man gets eaten. It can't end well for both of them."

"Maybe the man made the mistake on purpose," April says. "Maybe he wants to be consumed."

Oliver pauses, trying to take this in.

"Oliver?" Bernadette calls again, her voice worried.

He doesn't understand, but it feels harder to leave now. He hears Bernadette's steps on the stairs, and though he is sure he has nothing to hide, he closes the door on April.

When he sees Bernadette halfway up the steps, with her trim, silken hair framing her anxious face, he thinks of Daisy, a girl he dated in high school. The memory is enormous and startling, like a whale surfacing beneath a skiff.

The summer was one of the driest on record. In the west, thick smog smudged the Manhattan skyline. Out east, trees burned in the Hamptons. In between, lawns across the island turned brown. The roses Oliver had planted in his father's new yard suffered. Although he had read the gardening books, he lacked his mother's intuitive sense of how to keep the flowers alive.

Late in August, shortly before Oliver was to leave for college, he lay on Daisy's sofa with his shirt off, a revolving fan propped on a chair across from him. Her parents had rented the small apartment for her near the train station because it was cheaper than campus housing, and because they didn't want her living in Manhattan anyway. The condition was that she share the rent with a roommate, preferably a girl from her high school class. A known entity. She found April, who had never been more eager to move out of her father's house.

It was hard to say if Oliver would have asked Daisy out had she not been April's roommate. In any event, he had no regrets. She was a flutist, preppie and trim, with carrot-red hair. She drank five glasses of milk a day and had a passion for ice-skating. She was, in every way, an unlikely friend for April.

Oliver had determined he would not go to college a virgin, and once he gave himself over to it, he could not get enough of Daisy. Having recently given up piano, he had plenty of time on his hands. They spent night after night in the apartment while April worked at the bar. Most nights she wasn't home by the time Oliver left at one or two in the morning. He would see traces of her, an ashtray out on the fire escape or coffee grounds in the sink, and he knew she saw evidence of him, a forgotten jacket on the back of a chair, a box of condoms brazenly left in the vanity.

On one occasion Daisy had caught Oliver snooping through April's closet, and he had to confess that he was looking for his mother's jewelry box, the one she had given to April on her deathbed, but he was also just looking.

A few weeks after his mother's funeral, he had found April in his parents' room, helping to sort clothes for the Salvation Army. April was standing in front of his mother's antique dressing mirror, holding a hanger to her chin. It was a dress his mother had worn to one of his recitals, high-collared and elegant, with a dozen lace-covered buttons down the back, unlike anything April would wear. In the failing light, it looked to Oliver like a wedding gown.

April was still, one hand at her throat and the other on her waist. The dress had suited his mother, streamlined and subtle. She had disliked primary colors, dressed only in pastels, whites, and the occasional gray. April, on the other hand, tended toward electric pinks and neon yellows.

She smoothed her hand down along the fabric. Oliver went in and sat on the bed. She looked at him in the mirror, her eyes shiny in the dusky light. "Try it on," he said.

"It wouldn't fit," she answered.

Everything about the room bore his mother's imprint, the pale pink walls and lace curtains, cherrywood furniture with curvaceous legs, and the lavender fragrance lingering in her clothes. It was the inner sanctum of the house, a room free of televisions and radios, a place meant for reading, undressing, slipping into cool, clean sheets. The place where his mother had died.

During the last weeks, April had visited the house regularly to bathe his mother and change her bedpan while his father was at work. She assumed the role of daughter.

Early one morning, on his way to the shower, Oliver paused outside the door to listen to the quiet exchange of female voices he had never heard growing up. He could not make out what they were saying, only the tone, so different from the way his parents spoke to each other. His father's voice was gentle but baritone. Even his questions sounded resolute. April and his mother, on the other hand, spoke in a soft, meandering cadence, searching for something.

He glanced through a crack in the door and saw that his mother was giving April a lacquered box. Later April swore it was only a common jewelry box, a sentimental keepsake, but Oliver felt sure there had been something inside.

He was ashamed when Daisy caught him snooping for it, but Daisy surprised him by offering to help. The two of them picked through April's things like crows through trash. Oliver went for the carton of papers at the back of the closet while Daisy sorted through lingerie and cosmetics. Soon he forgot about his mother's box. He didn't know what he was looking for, but he was sure it was there.

"Look at this," Daisy said. "Seventeen shades of nail polish. I've never seen her wear any."

Oliver wasn't looking at the nail polish but at the white cotton underwear that lay in the open drawer. Somehow he had expected something satiny and dark.

He went back to the closet, where he found the oddest things: a book about growing orchids, her brother's preschool drawings, and an envelope of news clippings about Oliver's recitals.

"What's that?" Daisy asked, taking one from his hand. "Young Talent Outshines the Rest. What a headline!"

"It's the *Glenport Gazette*," he said. "Not exactly the *New York Times*."

"At seventeen years old, Oliver Night mesmerized his audience." She laughed.

"Please."

"During a spellbinding rendition of Beethoven's Sonata in F Minor, opus fifty-seven, Appassionato, Night's fingers became a fury of simmering emotion, sweetened by its own restraint. His interpretation was edgy, looming on the brink of chaos, yet soulful and soaring. In the extended, sometimes anguished first movement, he plunged the audience into—"

"Enough."

"Modesty's not going to help your career."

"I don't have one, remember?"

She slipped the clipping back into the envelope. "Come over here," she said. "You'll never guess what I found."

In the bottom drawer of April's dresser, beneath a layer of clothes, was a hardbound notebook. Oliver could not imagine April keeping a journal, but there it was. Daisy picked it up and smoothed her hand over the surface. The binding was covered with olive-green fabric, tattered and used. "What do you think she writes about?" she asked, holding the book to her chest.

"How should I know?"

"Well, we can't look, can we. That's going too far." She handed it to him.

He didn't want to take it, but it felt warm in his hands, alive. He felt the edges of the pages with his fingertips. Daisy was watching him.

"Which way did it go?" he asked, placing it back in the drawer.

"The spine facing right," she said.

"Are you sure? I thought it was this way."

"I'm sure," she said. "With the blue shirt on top."

He closed the drawer and exhaled. "Let's clean up," he said. "My mother's box isn't here."

Later, they lay clean and naked on Daisy's futon. It was the only bedroom, with twin-size futons head-to-head in an L shape, flush against the walls. Daisy fell asleep, lips parted and eyelids fluttering. Oliver dozed on and off, knowing he ought to go home.

At one thirty he was awakened by the sound of an idling car. He heard voices but could not make out the words. He stood up from the futon, careful not to disturb Daisy, and looked out the window.

Two stories below, April was standing on the curb beside the car. The driver was holding her arm through the passenger window, re-peating something in a plaintive voice. She pulled away, but he held on to the sleeve of her cardigan, stretching it. April slipped out of the sweater, leaving it in his hands. *Quincy?* Oliver wondered.

When he heard April's key in the door, he slipped back into bed. He tried to remember where he had left his clothes. He couldn't imagine why he had been so careless. Somehow Daisy and he had left the bedroom door ajar. He heard April dead-bolt the front door and go to the window. She was panting, having run up the stairs.

The car slowly pulled away. There was a dull, beeping tone in the next room, and he realized April had taken the phone off the hook. She went into the bathroom and ran the tap. Oliver felt the foot of the bed for his clothes, but could not find them.

"Hm?" Daisy said groggily.

"Sh," he said. "It's her."

April's futon was directly beneath the window, awash in a pool of streetlight. Oliver recognized his jeans and underwear strewn over the bedspread. He reached across Daisy and snatched the clothing just as the bathroom door unlocked. He froze. April came into the room, barefoot but still in her clothes, walking with exaggerated caution; she had been drinking. He was sure she must have seen him, but she sat cross-legged on her futon with her head in her hands, facing the opposite wall.

Daisy touched his chest beneath the sheet. He put his finger to her lips. They would just have to wait it out. Once April was asleep, he would slip into his clothes and leave.

April sat for a long while, holding her middle, rocking. Oliver was in an uncomfortable position, supporting himself on his elbows with Daisy beneath him, his jeans still in his fist. Daisy's breathing grew deep and regular, her head lolling on the pillow. Finally, April lay back. For a moment Oliver saw her face, eyes fixed on the ceiling. Her lips moved silently, and she covered her face with her hands.

Lines of light from the blinds curved along her body. She rolled onto her side, her back to him. His eyes traveled the curl of her waist, the rise of her hip, the downward slope of her thigh. Her pants were taut across her backside; he wondered how she could sleep in them. But gradually her fist on the pillow opened one finger at a time, like one of his mother's roses.

He looked down to find that Daisy was awake, staring at him blankly. He had the cold sense that they had been waiting for this moment. There was no hesitation. He sank down, his groan loud enough to wake the dead.

April did not stir, but he imagined he could feel the seizure in her muscles, the suspension of breath. Daisy and Oliver looked at each other without surprise, the pretense gone. They had known all along what they were about, each other's door to *her*. Then, to be sure April had heard, Oliver closed his eyes and whispered to Daisy how desperately he loved her.

Chapter
10

THE MIDDAY SUN reflects sharply off newly fallen snow. April puts on her sunglasses, which fog from the inside. She lets the motor run while she moves a broom across the car's windshield, then plows the roof. Al comes out of the house with his jacket half on and gets a scraper from the back of his Jeep. He lifts up her wiper and chisels away.

"What's your rush?" he says.

"I'm working at four. Have to change first."

"What are you doing after work?"

"You mean at two in the morning?"

"That's right."

"I don't know. I thought I might go roller-skating."

He smirks. "Hop on a train. I'll meet you at Penn Station."

"For what?"

"Nightcap. Breakfast. It doesn't matter."

"Don't you have somewhere to fly to?"

"Not until Thursday." He folds down the wiper and walks to the other side. "How about it?"

"There *is* something called sleep."

"You won't be sleeping," he says. "Come on. I want you to say yes."

"I can't."

He lets the wiper pop down. "You're seeing him again, aren't you."

She goes to the back of the car and sweeps snow off the taillights.

"Not answering is the same as answering."

"If you already know, why ask?"

"I could get you a date with Keith Van Horn, but you want the slob at the end of the bar."

"He's married." She gives him a look. "Besides, if all I wanted was a bang buddy, I wouldn't have to look as far as the NBA."

"Darling, if that's all you're after . . ." He opens his arms, grinning.

She rolls her eyes, gets into the car, and turns up the defroster.

Al gets in beside her. "Oh, Jesus," he says, flicking Buddy's graduation tassel with his finger. "You've got to get out of this death trap."

"Are you offering me another set of wheels?"

"Take mine," he says, holding out his keys. "I'd rather drive this myself than see you in it."

"Don't you have an ounce of sentimentality?"

"Yes, but I'm not much for morbidity. It's time to rejoin the living, Rosie."

"Hey, I got myself here last night, didn't I?"

"And tonight?"

"I don't think it's any of your business."

He hooks his hand around the back of her neck and pulls her toward him. "The hell with Van Horn," he says. She smells cigarettes and bubble gum, which he wedges into his cheek in order to kiss her. She slaps him away and he laughs. "Call me on my cell phone if you change your mind," he says, getting out of the car. "I can be at the station by three."

She nods.

He circles around to her door and raps on the window, which squeaks as she rolls it down. "Rose," he says. "Dump the cowboy."

He kisses her, softly this time, then puts his hand on his chest and sighs dramatically.

"Get out of here." She laughs, rolling up her window, and watches him trot to the house.

By the time April climbs the steps to T.J.'s room, it is a quarter past three in the morning. She lets herself in. The lights are out, and she makes her way quietly to the cot, which she finds empty. She hears the door close and turns around to find T.J. behind her. She goes to him, slides her arms around his neck, but he keeps himself rigid.

"I was expecting you last night."

She steps back. "I told you I was going to my uncle's house."

"Straight from work? In the middle of the night?"

"Yes. That's exactly what I said."

He nods, unconvinced. "How's your so-called cousin?"

"Fine," she says. "Wonderful. They've set a date."

"I'm talking about Razzle Dazzle," he says. "Mister NBA."

A draft chills her from within. "He's fine, too, I guess. We didn't really talk."

"No, huh."

"I told you to come along, T.J. I told you it was wrong to spend Christmas alone."

"I wasn't alone."

She doesn't touch this. "Look, if you want me to leave—"

He takes her purse and drops it on the floor. Then her jacket. Her scarf. He lifts her blouse over her head rather than waste time with buttons. He turns on the light, a stark overhead bulb, and examines her body.

"Not everyone leaves marks." It's a dangerous thing to say, but he doesn't seem to hear. He stares at her bare arms, her collarbone, her ribs. She's cold but keeps from shivering.

"Turn around," he says. "Bend over."

She does, not because she wants to, but because it doesn't matter. He moves his big hands down her back. "God, I'm starting to forget how Denise was different."

"I need a drink first," she says.

"I look at you, and I swear sometimes I see her staring back."

"I'm her," she says. "And I need a drink."

He kneels down and moves his hands around her waist. "Five years," he says, "and the longer she's gone, the more I keep expecting her." He leans his face against the small of her back.

April looks at the room's only window, small and painted shut. Rain pelts softly. Bits of ice slide down the glass. She can't see a thing. She thinks of Buddy's girl in Kingston, the letter in April's purse, sure now that she will mail it. The girl needs an answer. Any answer.

T.J. leans back, sits on the cot, and hides his face in his hands. April turns and sits beside him. She touches his back, but he's unaware. "If only she hadn't lied to me," he says.

April withdraws her hand. "Forget that."

"I saw them together," he says. "I saw how she looked at him."

"Stop," April says.

Out on the street a dog howls.

T.J. takes the pillow and hugs it to his chest. He stares deeply at the wall. "When I was a kid, one of the places they put me had a puppy, a little beagle named Keeper. Real happy and cute. Used to sleep with me at night."

April isn't following, but knows better than to ask. She pulls the bedspread and wraps it around her. It occurs to her that she could have been with Al right now, watching a movie or sleeping in his armchair. He once offered to take her to an all-night bowling alley. Why did she say no? She's an idiot, that's why. But it's too late for her. It's always been too late.

"It wasn't the old lady's dog," T.J. continues. "She got it from her son after he died. Poor guy just wasted away till there was nothing left of him. He must have been fifty, but he looked as old as she did. Used to come to the house every Wednesday night and shoot up after the old lady was in bed. Left needles everywhere, but she never caught on." He laughs softly—that throaty chuckle of his. "She was real innocent-like. He used to take her money, too. He was all she talked about. She thought he was Christ back on earth. God, if she ever knew the stuff he gave us. Anyway, he died and we got the dog."

April doesn't know what to say. She feels dazed, trying to understand. Foster care, is that it?

"Damn, that dog was cute. Slept every night curled up right here," he says, hugging the pillow more tightly. "But another kid, Cory, he was older than me, he wanted the dog with him. Every night he'd try to steal him away, and every night Keeper would come back to my room. Finally, he told me if the dog slept in my room one more night, he was going to bash my brains in. I said the dog sleeps where it wants. That night he locked it in his room. I heard it pawing at the door half the night, then, I didn't hear it no more. Not a sound." T.J. goes silent, staring at the wall.

" 'No goddamn shitty-assed dog disrespects Cory Vanderwert,' that's what he said in the morning. I went out looking, 'cause I knew he couldn't have gone far with it. Found it in the Dumpster with its head turned the wrong way and its legs pointing out stiff like it was on a fucking rotisserie." He laughs his strange, hoarse chortle. "All it needed was a goddamn apple in its mouth." He buries his face in his hands. "Fuck," he says miserably. "Fuck, fuck, fuck."

April lifts her hand to touch him, but instead folds it back in her lap.

"On my way back to the apartment, I was planning how to kill him. I pictured the old lady's frying pan. It was heavy and black, like it was made of wrought iron. But when I got there, I saw two cops in the living room. It was so weird, like they'd read my mind and came to arrest me before I'd even done it. But they were there for something else. The littlest kid—I can't remember his name 'cause he was always so quiet—had been doing dive bombs off the couch like he always did when the old lady was sleeping. Only this time he broke his neck." He draws a breath, still staring into some corner of the wall April cannot see. "He looked so tiny on that stretcher. I could tell by the way the EMS guys looked at each other that it wasn't good. He wasn't a bad kid, neither, not like some of them. Just loved doing dive bombs.

"Anyhow, the rest of us got reassigned right away. Lucky for Cory that information was sealed because I would have gone after him if I could have." He sighs. "I don't know how the old lady survived after that, 'cause I'm pretty sure the agency was her only income. I can't picture her face no more, but I still see the dog lots of times when I get into bed. I can almost feel him snuggled up right here."

April touches his arm, and he looks at her for the first time. She doesn't know what he sees in her face, but he grins. "So surprised, babe? That's you, isn't it. You've got your prissy little life, your mom and dad to take care of you, a brother you grew up with in the same house all those years. One house. Real brother. And those make-believe cousins of yours. You must think it's a dandy world, don't you. You think life's a candy walk. Well, I hope it stays that way for you. I really do." His eyes move from her face down to her breasts.

"What happened to your parents?" she asks, but it's too late. He gathers her hair in one hand and unzips his pants with the other. She glances at the bottle of vodka, but she's lost her chance.

He frees himself from his jeans and groans like he'd been bound up in there for half his life. "C'mon, baby. Take me away." He lies back, closing his eyes, and she understands what's expected. She watches herself dimly, through painted glass. She's barely in the room. Mentally she takes inventory of the bar, clears the drain under the sink, stocks the supply room, anything but this. After a while T.J.'s back arches. He catches his breath, and then stands suddenly, turning her around.

"Where's the condom?" she says.

He pushes her back against the desk, shoving the black denim down over her hips.

"Stick it in without a condom and I'll cut it off," she says.

"Christ," he says, reaching in his pocket. "If it's true you've never done it without one then you haven't been properly fucked yet."

"Fine, call me a virgin but put on the goddamn rubber."

He gets it on and rams himself in. She is as dry as he is hard. She thinks of the round steel brush that hangs in the basement of the bar, the way her father used to curse, jamming it down the stubborn pipes. She bites her lip until she tastes blood. Bizarrely the desk clock reads nine thirty; six hours fast, she wonders, or six hours slow? She pictures Al in the city glancing at his watch, understanding by now that she will not call. She tells herself she chose this. This was her choice. Her nails sink into the desk. T.J. quickens, a human jack-hammer. Her flesh joggles on her bones. If it takes much longer, she thinks, she's going to lose a filling.

A searing pain erupts inside. Has he split her cervix? April swallows her scream, which rings out inside her body, brittle as ice chipped from a windshield. With just the right blow the whole length of her will shatter and slide away.

T.J. lets out a small whimper, piling his weight onto her back and panting heavily. She turns toward him but he straightens and heads for the bathroom.

"T.J.?"

He doesn't answer. She hears a sob.

She pulls up her pants and looks for the vodka beside the bed. She takes a long swallow, then another. She slips on her shirt and stuffs her bra into the pocket of her coat, her hands too shaky for the clasp. She pulls on her scarf and catches her reflection in the dim, tarnished mirror over the bureau. Her face is sallow except for the shadowy moons under her eyes. She tells herself she wasn't drunk enough, that's all.

She opens the bureau drawer to look for a brush, but finds it empty. She opens all the drawers, seeing nothing but hairballs and dust. She goes to the closet, where she finds a row of empty hangers and a tightly packed duffel bag. The relief hits her before she even understands what she is looking at.

T.J. comes up behind her and slides his arms around her waist, buries his face in her hair. "Don't think for a minute I won't be back."

She turns to face him. "Where are you going?"

"To find a better town for us. In the Midwest, maybe. Or Texas. Someplace where people will leave us the hell alone."

"Jesus, T.J., how much more alone could we be?"

"I'm doing this for me and you."

"There's no you and me. There's only you and her."

"Don't bring Denise into this."

"She's here. She's us."

He pushes her and she falls back into the closet, clattering the hangers.

"Why did you do that?" he says. "Why did you have to piss me off?"

She straightens, rubbing her shoulder, and ducks under his arm. She heads for the door but he cuts her off and holds it shut. "Wait," he says. "Did you hurt yourself?"

"No, I didn't hurt myself. *You* hurt me."

"April—"

"I'm not moving to Texas."

"You don't have to promise anything. We can talk about it when I get back."

"I promise I'm not moving."

"It's the sportswriter, isn't it."

"For God's sake."

"I saw you today," he said. "So don't make a liar out of yourself."

"There was nothing to see."

"A fuck is one thing. But a kiss is something else."

"Look," she says. "I'm sorry about what happened to you as a kid." She puts her palms on the sides of her temples, pressing. "I can't imagine what it was like for you. All I know is I've got to get out of this room. Move to Texas if you want to. I'm going home."

"Wait for me, that's all I'm saying."

"No."

"What, then? You think some other guy's going to want you? Good luck."

Her eyes fill. "If that's what you think, why are you so goddamn uptight about every guy I talk to?"

"What they're thinking of don't take more than fifteen minutes, and it ain't a walk down the aisle."

Her cheeks burn.

He reaches into his pocket and pulls out a ring, not diamond but pearl, with sapphires on either side. "My mother's," he says.

"No, no. I don't want it."

"She gave it to Denise when we got married, but Denise only wore it for a few months. I thought that was an insult to Mom."

"T.J., are you listening? I'm not putting that on."

"Sure you are, honey. You absolutely are."

She stiffens as he slips it over her knuckle. The pearl is shriveled and discolored like a piece of dried-up garlic. April tells herself to keep breathing. Don't panic. Once home she can lather it off, use a wire snip if she needs to. Surely he's left one of those lying around her apartment. She looks him in the eye. "When are you ever going to tell me how Denise died?"

He turns away and lifts his duffel bag from the closet.

"T.J.," she says.

He turns and looks at her. "A hundred aspirin and a bowl of Cheerios," he says. "Didn't bother with a note. Any more questions?"

Chapter
11

THE HEAT IN BUDDY'S CAR is slow to kick in. April cranks it up, though clearly she'll be home by the time the car is warm. She shivers, trying not to think of T.J.'s story, the tiny bones snapping in the little boy's neck, the puppy stiff in the Dumpster, its suede fur stained by coffee grounds and eggshells. Will she ever be able to wash these pictures from her mind? Yet this was just *one day* from T.J.'s childhood. Not the worst, either. There are his scars, after all. If only she had gone into the city to meet Al instead. Where would she be now? Drinking bitter coffee in some greasy diner and laughing at Al's bad jokes. But really it's Buddy she misses. He was the one who could take her mind off herself. She spent so much time going to his games, helping him shop for clothes, going over his term papers with him and, later, college applications. They talked about friends and girls and college. He always wanted to know her opinion, and she inevitably turned the question back on him. What do *you* think you should do, Buddy? Which shirt do *you* like? What major appeals to *you*? And it worked. Over time, he was gaining confidence; he was on his way.

Only now, two months later, does it dawn on her. If she stops in the coffee shop where they used to meet on Sunday mornings, he will never be there. When the phone rings, it will never be him. People say the dead linger, that you feel their love in quiet, intangible ways. But it's not true. April feels nothing but the absolute nature of his absence. When Buddy was alive there had never been time for the kind of empty space that now exists in her mind. She wants him back. She wants him now, sitting beside her in the car.

Instead, she is going home to her empty apartment. For an instant she wonders if she should have stayed with T.J. No, she decides, better if she hadn't gone at all. The dog! The boy! But not knowing it wouldn't change the fact of it. There it was. Here she is, still trying to take it in, still trying to shake it. The weight is overwhelming. She wants to confide in someone. Oliver. But even as the thought enters her mind, she feels the impossibility of it.

As April sits shivering, waiting for the traffic light to turn, Oliver, miles away, is startled awake by Bernadette's cool hand on his arm. He fell asleep in the recliner with the lamp blazing.

"Tax law at four in the morning?" Bernadette says, rubbing her eyes.

He sits up stiffly, groaning. "I figured if anything would get me back to sleep, this would."

"Insomnia again?" she says, slipping into the chair with him, draping her legs over his.

"Just overtired, I think," he says, caressing her arm.

"Oliver," she says after a moment. "We still haven't talked about it."

For an instant he has no idea what she means. "Oh, that," he says, glancing at the piano.

"Well?"

He shifts in the chair, moving her weight off his thigh. This is the last thing he wants to talk about, but he owes it to her. "My mother told me to get a good profession, that my music would always be there," he says, running his fingers across his closed eyes.

"That sounds like good advice."

"Except the piano was a jealous lover," he says, nodding toward the instrument. "I chose law and she dumped me."

"Cute." Bernadette smiles. "But now tell me what really happened."

"It was a practical decision."

"But why go cold turkey? Either you never loved it as much as your family thinks, or you had some drastic reason for giving it up."

"Don't overanalyze, Bernadette. I was a busy college student."

"Fine. Then play me something now. 'Mary Had a Little Lamb.' Anything."

He shifts uncomfortably. "It's out of tune."

"That's not the reason," she says. "You're a terrible liar, Oliver. Why don't you just tell me the truth?"

"Because I don't know," he says. "All right?"

"You don't know why you won't play?"

"I don't know why I can't."

"But it was a decision. You see that, don't you?"

"Bernadette, you're pushing this."

"Maybe your parents pressured you too much. That happens a lot."

"No. It was just the opposite. They couldn't get me to stop playing. They worried that I didn't sleep enough. My mother was terrified that I'd try to make a career out of it."

"Was that a thought?"

"I'm too realistic."

"But now you miss it."

"No. Why does everyone think that?"

Bernadette simply stares. He turns his face toward the window. He can almost feel the light pressure of April's back against his shoulder as he played in the darkened studio. The scent of her hair. The piano was like a secret door. When he stepped through, he felt released from who he was supposed to be. April understood. Oliver looks at Bernadette, her beautiful, worried face, and feels the impossibility of explaining. Yet she needs an answer, something with logic behind it. "You had the talent, but not the desire, is that it?"

"No, just the opposite."

She eyes him skeptically. "When I was a kid, I took ballet for eleven years. When I closed my eyes at night, I saw myself onstage. Whenever someone asked what I wanted to be when I grew up, the answer was the same. But as it turned out, I couldn't even make it into a local production of *The Nutcracker*. For all those years, I dreamed the wrong dream, Oliver. I know what that feels like, and it's not what you're talking about. You walked away from something that was yours, didn't you."

He reaches across and touches her hand. "There are no wrong dreams, Bernadette. You should dance if you want to. It may not be a career, but you can still . . ."

"But I can be more useful working with kids. It's what I know how to do."

"Still, if it was such a big part of you . . ."

"I'm over it, Oliver. We're talking about you here."

"Well, I'm over it, too."

"Are you sure?"

"Jesus," he says.

"What was the dream?" she says. "Concert pianist?"

He looks at her carefully and puffs out a breath. "I liked to compose," he says in a croaky voice.

"Ah," she says, eyebrows arched. "Who was your idol? Bernstein, Ives, Lennon?"

"Cage," he says.

She lets out a surprised laugh, then covers her mouth. "I'm sorry," she says quickly.

"It's not that I composed like him, but I admired his nerve."

She narrows her eyes and taps her index finger against her cheek the way she does when she's thinking. "So is that what you feel you're lacking? Balls?"

He studies her.

She smiles, slipping back onto his lap. "Oliver," she whispers, sliding her hand down to his lap. "I'm sure you've got more than you think."

He grins, pulling her face to his.

As Oliver one by one unbuttons the flannel top of Bernadette's pajamas, April parks. She shudders, cursing the drafty car. As she walks to her door, a patrol car cruising the train station pulls up beside her. He rolls down his window and she bends to talk to him. His face reminds her instantly of her father, a sober version, minus twenty years or so. "No trains for the next hour, darling," he says.

"I live here." She nods at the building.

"Ah, heard about the muggings, then?"

She frowns, shaking her head.

"Three this month. Two at this station, one at the next. He carries a knife and he's not afraid to use it."

"What does he look like?"

"No ID yet. He strikes from behind. Knows how to avoid the station cameras. He likes the wee hours, so you'd better watch your back."

"Right."

"I'll watch you go in."

Once inside her apartment April glances at the clock. Nearly five, and the winter sky shows no suggestion of dawn. She goes to the sink before taking off her coat and begins lathering her hand. She works the soap in and around the ring and, after several minutes, nudges it over her knuckle. The pearl that must have been beautiful once is gnarled and grotesque. Garlic and sapphires, hadn't she read that in a poem recently? The *Four Quartets*? She takes off her coat, sits on the sofa with a blanket, and examines the band.

She thinks of the women who wore it, T.J.'s troubled mother and young wife. With the ring in her hand, April can almost hear the dead women's thoughts, especially Denise—her want of direction, her vague aspirations, her passivity. She imagines an all-around capable person who lacked any particular talent, someone who would gladly have sacrificed adequacy in one area of her life for the chance at greatness in another.

T.J. was her departure. Or arrival. She floated through life like a twig in a stream, happening upon a job here, a boyfriend there, always looking for signs that it all made sense, that it was destined. She was waiting for life to find her.

When they met, T.J. was so certain they were meant for each other that she had to believe him. It was his decisiveness that won her over. What she felt was not so much love as relief, because finally someone appeared who was willing to be her rudder. Yes, that was it. She was far better at reacting to situations than creating them. *That* was her genius, and with T.J. she found a way to exercise it.

April awakens to loud knocking. Although it is 9 AM, snow-shrouded windows darken the apartment. She has slept about two hours, which is worse than not having slept at all. She looks through the peephole and is startled to see the detective with whom she filed the protection order. She runs her hand through her hair, but there is no point trying to salvage her appearance. She opens the door.

"Miss Simone," he says. "Perhaps you remember me, Detective Arredondo. This is my partner, Detective O'Hara."

"This can't be good news," she says.

"Don't be alarmed," says Arredondo. "We just came to talk about your case."

"What case? I rescinded the order."

"May we come in?"

They sit at the small, linoleum kitchen table, a hand-me-down from Nana.

"We came by last night with a search warrant," says O'Hara. "The landlord let us in."

She looks around and sees that they have rifled through her things. How had she failed to notice last night? Had she even bothered to turn on a light?

"Sorry," says Arredondo. "We tried to straighten up."

April's hands are clammy. She folds them under her arms.

"We were under the impression from his boss that Mr. Desole still lived at this address."

"What has he done?" asks April.

"It's like this," says Arredondo. "We're updating our computer system down at the precinct, and some enterprising data-entry gal turns up your file in a stack of misplaced papers. And not knowing any better, she enters your protection order as new, and boom, a cross-check turns up from a precinct in Salt Lake City."

"I'm not following."

"If we'd had this system in place when you came in, it would have turned up then. It's only dumb luck that it showed up now."

"We believe the man you filed against, Timmy Desole, is wanted in Utah," says O'Hara.

"Tommy," she says. "Thomas John."

"Timothy Jason." O'Hara slides a photograph across the table. "Is this him?"

April sees what must be a younger T.J., grinning. Beside him is a woman, dark-haired and young, with a scant, fragile smile.

April shakes her head.

"Is that a yes or a no?" says O'Hara. He is the sterner of the two, tall, with a fortyish face to contrast his snowy hair.

"It looks like him," she says.

"We stopped by his employer's house yesterday," says Arredondo. "Not something you want to do on Christmas night. But you can understand how we might have been concerned for your safety. He gave us this address, but it looks to us like he's moved out."

"He's been renting a room near the wharf in Freeport, but he's gone now. He left at four this morning."

O'Hara stabs his pencil on the tabletop.

"Can you give us that address?" Arredondo slides her a pad.

"You haven't told me what he's wanted for," she says, writing.

O'Hara gives her a look. "Not everyone rescinds their charges," he says. "Not everyone has the opportunity."

Her skin goes cold. She glances back at the photo, the girl's edgy smile. "He told me she committed suicide."

Arredondo leans closer. He has mink-dark hair, olive skin, and a hideous leopard-print tie. "We think she had a little help."

April's stomach sours. She pops up and paces around. "Are you sure?" She faces him. "Could there be some mistake?"

Arredondo takes her in, his warm brown eyes contrasting with O'Hara's cool impatience. *They probably get a lot of people to cooperate this way,* she thinks. "Are you really so surprised?" O'Hara says. "Given the way he treated you?"

April folds her arms around her middle. She was upset because her grandmother noticed the black eye. She had to miss a day of work, not because it hurt but because she was embarrassed. You can cover bruises with makeup, but swelling is another story. So she filed the protection order. It was a knee-jerk reaction. It wasn't like she thought he was actually dangerous.

When she doesn't answer, O'Hara shakes his head incredulously.

"You see, April," Arredondo says, "your silence makes it look like you're protecting him."

She looks at the picture. "He said he loved her."

Arredondo picks up the small writing pad and slaps it against his palm. "Apparently a little too much."

April sighs. "He said he was headed to the Midwest or Texas. That was as specific as he got."

Arredondo glances at his watch, and she sees him thinking, Route 80 West, 95 South, there were a dozen or more possibilities. "Still driving the same blue pickup?"

"He was yesterday."

"We figure if he's going to contact anyone, it will be you. Did he say anything to that effect?"

"He said he would be back for me. I told him not to."

She notices O'Hara glance at the knot in her robe; it's true what T.J. said about the fifteen minutes. Quincy taught her as much.

"I'll help," she says. "I don't want anyone else to get hurt."

"Including you," says Arredondo.

"I don't think he'll be back," she says.

Arredondo hands her his business card and folds her fingers over it. "Don't be so sure."

SPRING

Chapter
12

THE AWNING ABOVE TATTERS FRANTICALLY, making it difficult for Oliver to hear what Bernadette is saying; something about lilies versus daisies. The notion of seafood under the stars had seemed right for this first day of spring warmth, but not long after they arrived at The Blue Marlin the wind shifted, bringing sharp salt air off the ocean and wildly flipping the pages of the florist catalog between them.

"I'll get your sweater from the car," Oliver suggests, folding the book. "We can look at this in bed tonight."

"Should I order you dessert?"

"Just coffee. You look too cold to sit here much longer."

She nods, rubbing her arms, and stares at the raucous ships moored in the harbor, clanging and bucking like tethered colts.

Oliver tosses the bouquet book into the backseat and grabs Bernadette's cardigan. As he locks the car, he notices a white Camaro in the next row. He goes over, though it is out of his way, and glances in the window. Buddy's high school tassel hangs from the rearview. He straightens abruptly and stares back at the restaurant. Cool air sifts through his hair, rippling his shirt. He stands for a moment without knowing what he is thinking.

He has not seen April since Christmas, when they fought in his father's bathroom, an argument he has since put out of his mind. What comes back to him now is not the words they spoke, which he can't recall, but rather the way her presence charged the room, the threat of her nearness. He decides not to look for her.

Inside, he glances around. He sees a table of college kids writing on the back of a place mat, a young man patting a woman's pregnant belly, and an older woman tittering at an old man's joke. Oliver feels removed from these people so engaged in the moment. He wonders what has happened to him that his mind is always elsewhere.

Someone yells to him. It is the old woman, waving her cane and calling his name. He tells himself she looks amazingly like Nana, but cannot accept it is she until he reaches the table and she kisses his cheek.

"Oliver, it was like a vision. I was just telling Mr. Bergfalk about you, and in you walked. I thought I was dreaming."

The man stands and shakes Oliver's hand. He is a good fifteen years younger than Nana, well dressed and smart looking. "To tell you the truth," he says, "she talks about you all the time, so it's not such a coincidence."

"I see." Oliver smiles. "So you're sick of me already."

"Not at all. But I probably know more about you than your fiancée does."

Oliver glances at the back veranda, remembering the sweater in his hand.

"Bring her here," says Nana. "You can get Mr. Bergfalk's approval."

"Don't worry," he says, handing the waiter his credit card. "I already like her from the photographs."

Oliver smiles uncertainly. "I saw April's car in the lot."

"What a doll," says Mr. Bergfalk. "This was her idea, you know, a once-a-month date night with her as chauffeur. Last time it was an Italian place."

"Mr. Bergfalk can't drive on account of his prosthesis," says Nana.

"Well, I could if I had the right kind of vehicle, with all the expensive doohickeys. I've gotten used to buses."

"She's in the bar," says Nana. "Go tell her we're ready to leave."

"Okay. I'll meet you out front."

When Oliver reaches Bernadette, she has his suit jacket over her shoulders. "I was just going to look for you," she says.

"My grandmother and her gentleman friend are here. Why don't you go say hello while I pay up."

"Do you think she'll remember me this time?"

"She adores you. Go on. I'll be right there."

After she leaves, Oliver steps into the bar, swarming with Knicks fans. A play-off game is on, causing thunderous eruptions. It takes Oliver a moment to spot April at the end of the bar; he must have walked right by her. He sees the predictable dark lipstick, dangling earrings, clingy sweater, but something gives him pause. She rolls a glass of club soda between her palms, staring at the television. Beneath her vague expression of interest, Oliver sees something else. He stares until all at once it appears like an inverse image in an optical illusion. Her expression has not changed, yet the same lines that drew a picture of indifference now spell bone-crushing grief; she has been carved out, marauded from within.

He raises his hand to his chest. It feels like spying to catch her so unguarded, yet he cannot stop.

A man beside her is talking, leaning close in an effort to get her attention. Finally, he puts his hand on her back, and the ruin on her face sinks out of sight like a fish in a muddy stream. She nudges away and pulls from her purse a tip for the bartender. She glances at her watch, starting to stand, when all at once she stops. She lifts her eyes and looks directly at Oliver across the bar. Did she feel him there? They stare for a moment, acknowledging that he has slipped, uninvited, into her space.

She looks down and buttons her coat.

Someone touches his shoulder. He smells Mr. Bergfalk's cigar breath. "Can't find her? Well there she is, right over there."

She comes over, smiling. "Who bumped into whom?"

"We spotted Oliver," says Mr. Bergfalk. "Had to shout him down, he was so oblivious." He chuckles. "I remember those pre-wedding days."

"There is a lot to think about," says Oliver, glancing at April. "You've lost weight."

"Have I?"

"Pretzels for dinner." Mr. Bergfalk nods at the bar. "It's no wonder."

"Well, thanks, I guess," she says.

"It wasn't a compliment," says Oliver.

Mr. Bergfalk raises his eyebrows. April laughs, then wedges through the crowd in the direction of Nana and Bernadette.

"I only meant that you should take care of yourself," calls Oliver.

"Son," says Mr. Bergfalk quietly, shaking his head. "Quit while you're ahead."

As the others chat in the entrance, April plays with her keys, looking toward the door. "How about the diner for dessert?" asks Oliver.

"It's up to our chaperone," says Nana, giving April a wink.

The diner is crowded. They take the only open booth, though it means squeezing three on one side. April gets in first to give Bernadette the middle and Oliver the aisle for his long legs. But after a few minutes Bernadette leaves for the restroom, and when she returns, Oliver slides into the middle. He feels his hip meet April's.

"Can you breathe?" he laughs, trying to make light.

"Good thing I lost weight." She smiles, but her eyes flash. He has cornered her.

Nana is talking nonstop about a childhood trip to Italy, where her father had relatives. "In Venice we saw the Bridge of Sighs," she says, "where prisoners could look back at the floating city one last time before their execution. Everyone should stand there once in his life. Did you hear me, Oliver?"

"The Bridge of Sighs. I'll put it on my list."

"Lists are for people who don't do what they want," she says. "Just go."

"Right now?" He laughs.

"If that's what it takes."

"Well," he glances at his watch. "Who's coming?"

"Italy wouldn't be a bad honeymoon spot," says Bernadette.

"On the Bridge of Sighs, you've got to be alone," says Nana. "Even if you're with someone, you're not. April, you should go."

"To tell you the truth, Nana, it doesn't sound tempting."

"That's what everyone thinks until he stands there. You'd be surprised what a little solitude can work in your soul."

"A little companionship don't hurt, neither," says Mr. Bergfalk. "These are young people, Reina. What they need is to be in love, not standing on some lonely bridge."

"You think there's a difference?" says Nana.

Oliver's skin prickles. He feels April fidget, the scruff of her jeans rubbing his. Warmth radiates from her thigh. He takes a sip of water, not daring to look at her.

"If you don't mind me saying so," says Mr. Bergfalk to April, "you ought to devote less time to me and your grandma's social life and more to your own."

"The men she picks," says Nana, "she's better off sitting here with us."

April rolls her eyes. "I need to use the bathroom," she says to Oliver. "Excuse me."

"You must know some nice fellows in law school," says Nana.

"What about Jeff?" says Bernadette. "We could invite him next week."

"I need to get out of here," April says, but no one moves.

"We're having a barbecue on the twenty-fourth," says Bernadette. "Why don't you come?"

"No," April says. "I mean, thanks for the invitation, but can you please let me out so I can use the bathroom?"

Bernadette and Oliver stand, letting April slip by.

Oliver runs his hand down his face. Trying to push April always backfired. In that way, she has not changed at all.

She takes her time coming back. Oliver spots her at the counter, watching the last minutes of the Knicks game. He gets up to take the check to the register and goes to her.

"They're losing in overtime," she says. "I just saw Al in the press box."

Oliver gives her shoulder the faintest touch. "April," he whispers. "It's only been six months. You can't expect to feel better already."

Her eyes flash. "Why do you think everything has to do with Buddy? This has nothing to do with him. For God's sake, I go out for a few drinks and everyone worries that I'm going out for drinks. I stay home, everyone worries that I'm staying home."

"Come on the twenty-fourth," he says. "No hidden agendas."

"If I do, I'll bring my *own* date."

"Good," he says. "Do that."

Chapter

13

KENNY TAKES A HARD LEFT, forcing April against the door. He looks at her and laughs. She slaps his arm in mock indignation. He likes the car's power, driving with one hand on the wheel, the other draped out the window. His fingers are stubby, arms covered with pale, fleecy hair. He is clean-shaven, his silken red hair cropped to his skull. He has the face of a boy, round and soft, squinty-eyed, always smiling. Seeing him there, chin cocked, April feels her stomach quiver.

"So will there be anything good at this party?" he asks.

"I'll be there." She smiles.

"You know what I mean."

"I told you, they're not exactly the wild type. We'll just stay a few minutes."

"Ashamed of me?" He raises an eyebrow.

She laughs, though she isn't sure.

They pull into the town house complex. A neat row of boxwood lines the drive, and urns of periwinkle announce each doorway. Beyond the tennis court glints the shimmering surface of a pool. A cyclist crosses in front of them wearing a lime-green jersey and a torpedo-shaped helmet. The bike, April supposes, is worth more than her car.

"Tell me he's a student and he lives here," Ken says.

"He works, too. Number thirty-three. Over there."

"Jesus Christ," Kenny says, parking.

April knows she must be out of her mind. Oliver left another message on her machine asking her to come, saying she was isolating herself and that she needed the family. Family, she thinks. She and Oliver aren't even from the same planet.

She freshens her lipstick, glancing in the mirror on the visor. Kenny opens her door, smiling as she stands. "You look hot," he says.

She flushes, unsure if it is a compliment or threat. "Let's skip the party," she says.

A muscle twitches at the base of Kenny's jaw. A swift, almost imperceptible shadow crosses his pale gray eyes. "One beer," he says. "So I can check out your folks."

They walk around to the back patio of the town house. The grass is lush and uniform, without a single weed. "Kenny." She puts her hand on his arm. "Let's split. I'm not feeling well."

"Nice try." He smirks and enters the yard.

The air smells of hamburgers and lighter fluid. There are two dozen or so people standing around, some sitting in lawn chairs. They all look young and collegial, casually but expensively dressed. She wants to die.

When she spots Oliver at the grill, he looks at her with astonishment, skewer in hand. Clearly, he didn't expect her to show. His eyes go to her skirt, which is short, the color of cantaloupe. God, what was she thinking? Oliver comes directly over, wiping his hands on his apron.

"Ken," she says, reaching for a potato chip. "This is my cousin Oliver."

"Oliver?" Ken says. "For real?"

She elbows him.

"Can I call you Ollie?"

"No," April says firmly.

Oliver glances at April, more amazed than insulted.

"Like them puppets," Ken says. "Kukla, Fran, and Ollie. Wasn't Ollie the snake?"

"His name is Oliver, and wasn't that before your time?"

"I watch a lot of late-night television, babe. Nice to meet you, *Ol-iv-er*," he says, exaggerating each syllable.

"You, too, *Ken-neth*." Oliver smiles.

"See that?" Ken grins, poking April. "Ollie here's joshing around with me. Hey, got any brew?"

Oliver ignores the question and kisses her cheek. "April," he says, squeezing her arm too tightly. "I'm glad you decided to come." His clothing smells of hickory from smoking the meat. "Honey," he calls. "Come meet April's friend."

"How do you do." Bernadette's eyes graze Ken's massive arms, then April's legs. Seeing her horror, April feels queasy. She is aware that everyone is staring at them. *What the hell,* she thinks. She's here now. This is happening. She may as well play the part. "Got any beer, Oliver?" She keeps her sunglasses on.

"In the cooler."

April walks away briskly, leaving them alone. It won't do any good to stand around and finesse things. Whatever is going to happen will happen whether or not she tries to control it; that's one thing she's learned.

She goes inside to use the bathroom and pauses in Oliver's living room. She kicks off her sandals so as not to dirty the creamy carpet, which feels thick beneath her feet. She takes a deep breath and tries to steady her pulse. Except for his childhood home, she's never been in a place that belonged to Oliver. Although Bernadette has not officially moved in, April sees her influence: gingham curtains, the lavender smell of potpourri, and cheerful artwork colored by children—butterflies and rainbows. She looks around for the portrait of Oliver's mother, but it's not here.

April always loved that portrait, painted when her aunt Avila was in her twenties. It made her look elegant, kind, like Princess Grace. When she died and Hal offered it to the boys, they flipped a coin for it. Al lost. But where is it now?

After using the bathroom, April enters Oliver's room. She knows it is the wrong thing to do, but she's so deep in mistakes now, what does it matter? As a teenager, Oliver kept a photograph on his bureau of the four stepcousins. It was taken on the water flume at Great Adventure when they were children. They were sitting in a pseudo-log, tightly packed in size order. Buddy was four, April and Oliver twelve, and Al fifteen.

As the photograph was taken, the log was careering down a precipice, water hurling at the children. Buddy was wide-eyed, holding on with elbows locked. Al was howling, fist in the air. April had both arms flung skyward, half out of her seat, laughing with her mouth open as Oliver, taking a gush of water in his face, held on to the back of her belt to keep her from going overboard.

The photograph is not here. Instead April sees a picture of Oliver and Bernadette standing under a blooming dogwood, a posed shot. His arm is firmly around her waist, their smiles wide. April touches it, wondering where it was taken, and what backdrop was cut away to make it fit in the oval frame.

She hears voices and quickly leaves. Outside, she heads for a beer.

"Hey, Rose," Al says as she bends over the cooler. "That's one hell of a skirt you almost have on."

"Better watch yourself, Al. My guy is here."

"I can see that," he says, signaling for her to pass him a cold one.

She sits next to Al on top of the picnic table. Oliver and Kenny are still talking; Bernadette has drifted away. Kenny is standing with his sunglasses on, hands folded over his chest, shaking his head at something Oliver said. April cannot imagine what they are talking about.

"Pretty gutsy of you, Rose," Al says.

"Ken's just a friend."

"Right."

"Don't you believe in platonic relationships?"

"No."

"What about us?"

"Case in point."

She laughs, wiping the bottle of Amstel on her sleeve. She takes a sip.

"Rose, do me a favor. Tell me this new guy of yours is a teddy bear."

"He is."

"Wouldn't raise a hand to you if his life depended on it."

"Damn right."

"Does he work?"

She takes another sip.

"Don't tell me," Al says. "Just checked out of Riker's Island."

"He's a debt collector."

"What?"

"A repossessor."

"Oh, God."

"Hey, at least he pays his bills."

"And yours, too?"

She looks at him sharply.

"Listen, Rose, if you need cash I'd be more than happy—"

"I don't, and no one pays my bills but me."

"T.J. leave you with some debt?"

"It's fine, Al."

"Rose, you should let us help you out."

"I got myself into this, I'll get myself out. I just don't want to lose Buddy's car."

"Your car," he says. "And frankly, you could do better."

The bottle is cold and wet in her hand. She holds it between her knees, feeling goose bumps on her thighs. Al slides closer, glancing back at Kenny. "You know, Rose, I've seen hockey players with no teeth, linebackers with necks like tree trunks, but your guy there has got to be the ugliest son of a bitch I ever laid eyes on."

She laughs. "I'll take that as a compliment." She takes another swig, tilting her head back, and feels her skin go warm all at once. Someone has come up close behind her. "Besides," she says. "It's never the mean-looking ones who are dangerous. It's the clean-cut guys you got to look out for. Right, Oliver?" She feels his breath.

"You're the expert," Oliver answers.

She turns to look at him, her skin tingling. "Where's Ken?"

"Taking a piss."

"Like my skirt?"

"If it were any shorter, it would be around your neck," Oliver says. Al laughs, but Oliver does not.

"Oops," she says. "Have I embarrassed you?"

"No," he says. "Only yourself."

"Get off it, Oliver," Al says. "A woman with legs like that has a responsibility to show them."

April laughs nervously. As someone goes into the house, she catches her reflection in the sliding glass door. It is true; the skirt is short, even by her standards. She remembers as a teenager trying on her mother's lingerie, which she found in an attic trunk—garters that took forever to snap, a crotchless teddy with the tits cut out. She caught her breath as she saw her reflection: The lingerie made her look curvaceous, seductive, cheap; more grown-up than she ever imagined she would be. But her face in the mirror was stark. She felt ashamed of her mother for the futile, demeaning measures she had taken to keep her husband home.

Ken comes out of the house. "Time to go, baby cakes," he says. "Ollie doesn't want us here."

Oliver straightens.

"Is that true?" April says. "Are you asking us to leave?"

"No," Oliver says. "I never said that."

"Let's go," Ken says.

She picks up her purse.

"April," Oliver says. "I wish you'd stay."

"Ken and I are together," she says. "I thought you understood that."

As they walk away, she hears Al say, "Good going, Oliver."

When April gets into the passenger seat, she feels an ache like someone's fingers pressing the back of her eyes. Why is she such a fucking dramatist? Why can't she be a normal person? Ken lets the tires screech as he lunges out of the parking space. She leans her face in her hand.

"I don't believe for a minute they're your family," Ken says. "You don't even look like them."

"I take after my father," she says without looking up.

"I think Ollie has a thing for you."

"Don't be ridiculous."

"I'm going to take you for a little drive," he says. "I know a special place."

"No," she says. "Not now."

"You're going to enjoy it," he says. "Trust me."

"I'm not in the mood."

"No? You're sure dressed like you are. Or is that for your cousin, too?"

She feels herself go numb all at once, submerged.

"I was married once," she says. "Did I ever tell you that?"

Ken glances at her. They are stopped at a light.

"My husband died."

"Oh, yeah?" Ken says. "How's that?"

"I slit his throat," she says. "He fucked with me and I slit his throat." It feels like the truth.

The light turns but Ken doesn't move. "You're crazy, lady. You've got a cuckoo family, and you're the biggest nut of them all."

"Get out," she says.

Ken laughs.

"Get out of my car before I kill you."

Ken stares for a moment, dazed. He puts his hand on the door handle. April holds a breath. There is a ringing in her head, like when she worked in a factory one summer and the deafening machines would come to a halt all at once, that mesmerizing quiet, the startling ability to hear her own thoughts. If he gets out of the car, she thinks, her life will change.

A car honks and April flinches. Ken stares at her, a smile growing on his face. He accelerates. "You'll kill me? Is that what you said?"

He turns into the parking lot of a boarded-up grocery store, drives around to the back where the Dumpsters are. April opens her door; Ken reaches across her and slams it shut. She feels a buzz in her brain like a distant chain saw.

Ken cuts the engine and lets the car roll to a quiet stop. It is dusk. She can hear sparrows clamoring in foliage beyond the chain-link fence.

April did not notice the clouds massing, but now isolated drops splatter the windshield. Ken moves his palm down the length of her hair and coils it around his fist like a rope. She thinks of Bernadette and Oliver rushing to bring the food indoors, the ruined potato chips, laughter, the coals going out, the smell of wet clothing and her own panicky perspiration as they hurtled down the water flume.

A frenzy of rain bombards the car, hammering the roof like fists, cascading in a thick, rapid blur down the windshield. April's hair is twisted in Kenny's fist, but she tells herself he won't strike. The big talkers never do. It's the scrawny, inferior guys who turn on you. Or the big dumb ones who never had a date in high school. Or the psychotics who can't stop thinking about their dead wives. Ken doesn't fit into any of those categories. All he really wants is a blow job.

"Fuck off," April tells him.

"That's exactly what I had in mind." Ken smiles.

But April is incapable of it. Maybe two years ago, maybe yesterday she could have, just to get him off her back, but something has turned, like the day tequila—her drink of choice for years—suddenly became repulsive to her. "Not a chance," she says.

"Come on," he says, pulling her hair in a menacing tease. "You didn't wear that skirt for nothing." He opens his fly.

April sinks her fingernails into his wrist. Ken howls and lets go. "Bitch," he cries. She grabs her keys from the ignition and holds Buddy's pocketknife, unopened, in her fist.

"Maniac," he says, examining the fingernail marks on his wrist. "I bet you did kill your old man."

For a fraction of a second April catches a glimpse of someone standing beside Ken's window. She closes her eyes and hears the explosive shattering of glass, pieces flying through the car, onto her clothing, into her hair. Rain wetting her face. Blood trickling down the back of Kenny's neck, blotting his shirt. The person outside the car drops whatever it was he used to break the window.

Ken is breathing in a quick, shallow panic, hyperventilating. He stares at the glass, the tiny cuts on his arms, and sees that his fly is still open. Tears well in his eyes as he flicks a shard of glass from his lap and zips.

The man opens the door and reaches in. His right hand is covered with small dark hairs, speckled with blood; the left is hairless, pearly and smooth. He hauls Kenny out onto the pavement.

April gets out, feeling rain drill against her skin, saturating her clothing all at once. She can barely see.

By the time she reaches the other side of the car, Kenny is rolling on the ground, holding his side. T.J. stands beside him wearing drenched blue jeans and heavy Western boots, his face knotted. He shifts his weight, poised to kick.

"No," April shouts, lunging at him. She aims to shove him off balance, but T.J. stands his ground like a monument. He snatches her arm.

"You want to defend him?" he says.

Be calm, she thinks. Trying to push him was a mistake. "T.J.," she says. "It's not worth it. Let him go."

He takes her other arm, gripping tightly. She tries not to wince. *Don't concede anything,* she thinks. T.J.'s face is clenched like a baby about to wail, eyes narrowed to slits, shining with frustration. He looks helpless and desolate, yet buoyant with rage, intensely awake. April averts her eyes. She can almost feel the weight of his misery, a cinder block on her chest. She struggles for breath. Behind him, Ken stands up and takes a few steps. He stumbles on the demolished camera T.J. used to break the window, gets to his feet again, and hobbles toward the far end of the lot.

T.J. doesn't look. He stares at April, holding her arms. Her knees shake. Water glistening down the sides of his face makes his scars blur together. "I thought you were different," he says. "But you're not."

Keep breathing, she thinks.

"Look at you," he says. "Playing the bitch in heat."

She almost laughs at the cliché, his lack of imagination. She remembers the time she was caught in a riptide and no one knew because in her panic all she could do was giggle.

"Act like a slut and you'll be treated like one," he says, shaking her a little. "Didn't your mother ever teach you that?"

April licks her lips, clothes clinging to her. She feels his eyes moving over her body.

T.J. smiles painfully. April's fingers are numb. She remembers the keys in her hand, the pocketknife. Can she open it one-handed? "He might call the police," she says, looking in the direction Kenny ran. "You don't have much time to get away."

T.J. releases her. She catches her breath. *Don't rub your arms,* she thinks; *don't give him the satisfaction.* She holds the keys in front of her with both hands, fingering the knife. T.J. glances in the direction Ken went. There is no sign of him. Just behind the car is T.J.'s powder-blue pickup.

"Always were an easy liar," he says. "I'll give you that." He lets go of her face, runs his hand through his dripping hair, staring at her from head to toe. His chin quivers. She sees a flash of desire in his eyes. Or hatred. "I loved you," he says. "But you didn't deserve it."

"You loved Denise," she says, maneuvering the knife. "You never saw me."

T.J.'s reflex is instantaneous, his hand flying from his side to her face in a perfect arc. No thought, no decision, just reflex. It is a kind of kinetic brilliance, physical perfection, pure efficacy inside a second. April never sees it. She is on the ground, tasting blood in her mouth.

He points at her, his finger trembling.

As she gets to her knees, she sees herself arguing with her father, knowing it would end badly for her, but unable to stop.

She reaches for the fallen keys, but T.J. steps on them, staring down at her. He picks up the key chain and, seeing the pocketknife, opens it. He tests the blade against his thumb, closes it again, and tosses it at her. "You should have thought to carry some proper protection." Reaching into his denim jacket, he pulls out a revolver. "Like this."

April sways on her feet. She hears rain hissing on asphalt, pinging the hood of the car, thunder rumbling in the distance like her father's voice, her own breath. The gun is silver, slick and wet, small in T.J.'s hand. The regrets come at once, countless and simultaneous—that the police, finding her body here, will likely assume her a prostitute; that even if it is deemed murder, her family will construe it as a kind of suicide; and that Oliver's last memory of her will be in this absurd skirt, her face smug and cold, concealing everything.

T.J. places the revolver in April's hands. She stares at it, confused.

He steps closer, positioning it with the barrel pointed at his chest. He caresses her fingers to stop them from shaking.

"No," she says.

He leans into her, pressing her back against the car. His hand moves over hers on the gun, searching for the trigger. April can't breathe, terror sparking through her like an electrical current. With his free hand, T.J. touches her hip, her waist, her breast, his face calm for the first time. Then he kisses her, crushing her against the car, the gun wedged between them. She feels his tongue in her mouth, the taste of blood and rain, the handle of the pistol cutting into her rib, the tip pressed to his sternum. He lifts her skirt.

"No."

"Do it," he says. "No one will blame you."

But April doesn't touch the trigger. She tries to splay her fingers, work them free of the weapon. Her voice is raspy, barely there. "I won't," she says.

He lowers her skirt, smooths it down over her thigh, and stands back to see her. His face is different. Still pained, but not twisted up like before. His eyes are more open, lips parted, expectant, like a boy. The rain is letting up. He runs his fingers down her face, over her nose, the bruised lip. "I been to Kansas," he says. "There's work out there, and the living's so cheap, lots of people have their own horses." He hesitates. "I remember you said when you were a kid, that's all you ever wanted."

She swallows, clutching the car behind her.

"We could leave tonight. Be in Wichita by Thursday. All we need is gas."

"T.J., put the gun away."

He lowers it, holding it in his palm like a dead bird. "What's the matter?" he says. "Don't like horses anymore?"

April's teeth chatter. She has never felt so cold. T.J. stuffs the revolver in his pocket and touches her face again with the flat of his hand, feeling her like a blind person. "Should have pulled the trigger when you had the chance," he says and walks to his truck.

As he pulls away, April's skin convulses in shivers, hands shaking as she reaches for her keys. The interior of the car is covered with glass. She takes a blanket from the trunk and drapes it over the seat, tosses the demolished camera in the back, and gets in. She drives home checking her rearview every few seconds, hands rattling on the wheel, rain stinging her face from the shattered window.

Once in her apartment, she double-locks the door, closes the shades, stands over the garbage and shakes glass from her hair. She throws out her skirt and runs a hot shower. Finally, when she is almost too weak to stand, she turns off the water, wraps herself in her robe, and goes to the phone. She checks the number twice before punching the buttons. As she listens to the endless pause between each ring, she thinks how easy it would be to hang up. Then the sound of a human voice on the other end startles her. "Yes," she hears herself say. "Detective Arredondo, please."

Chapter
14

APRIL LOOKS IN THE MIRROR, gliding her finger over the temporary cap in the side of her mouth. The color does not match her real teeth; she wonders if it is noticeable when she smiles. The dentist was suspicious, of course, but everyone buys her clumsy stories eventually; they don't want to think otherwise. Next she examines the bruise, patting it gently with concealing cream. It's important not to use too much or the caking is a giveaway.

Hoping to catch a three o'clock bus to the collision shop, she glances at her watch. It was cheaper to replace the whole door with one from a junkyard than to have a new window installed. With luck they found a white one to match the car, or she's in for a lot of questions. She opens the refrigerator, stares, and closes it again; she hasn't been able to eat more than a piece of toast for two days.

April pushes the button on her answering machine and replays Oliver's message: "Hey, April, it's Oliver. I, uh, just wanted to say I'm sorry about yesterday. Do me a favor and give me a ring so I know you got home okay."

She ought to have called back yesterday, but she wanted to wait until now, when she figures he's not home. His machine picks up.

"It's April," she says, trying to sound cheerful, but it's not in her. "I'm sorry for putting a damper on your party. And yes, I got home fine."

When April arrives at her grandmother's the next day for her weekly hair setting, Nana is in the alcove off the living room, scrounging through a pile of pictures. The nook was an addition, built as a cantilever off the face of the house, overlooking the busy street. The floor sags, and April wonders how long before the whole thing collapses. Nana is wearing a pink shower cap pulled down over her ears.

"Expecting rain?" April asks.

Nana turns to look at her. "Oh you," she says, recognizing April. "Don't you know anything? They always make you wear this for surgery."

"Surgery?" April says. "What's the trouble?"

"My heart," Nana says, turning back to her pictures.

April steps closer, caressing Nana's back with the tips of her fingers. "Broken?" she says.

Nana nods. "Triple bypass. Detours everywhere."

April looks down at the table covered with pictures of Buddy. She swallows. "What are you up to here?"

"Buddy asked me to find his high school graduation picture, but I don't think your parents gave one to me. Isn't that odd?"

April feels a shiver skip across her skin. "Oh, did Buddy stop by?"

"Don't be ridiculous," Nana says. "He's in the White Mountains. He called this morning."

April sits down, drawing her hands down her face. "How did he sound?"

"Concerned. He needs to find this picture. Oh, he said to tell you he was sorry about your car."

April holds a breath. "My car?"

"The accident with your car." Nana turns to face her. "Well don't act so surprised. Why else would you be driving his?"

April glances out the window at the white car in the street. She lets out a breath. "Take that thing off your head," she says. "I'll make some lunch."

April lifts the shower cap from Nana's head, noticing the earrings beneath. They are long, turquoise, Indian looking. Nana stares, touching April's lip where it is swollen. Then she touches her own lip and cheek. "Nicky was here last night," she says.

"Nana, Nick left fifty years ago. Then you married Spencer, remember?"

"Nicky used to hit your father," she says. "And I was too scared to protect him. Imagine that."

"It's okay, Nana. He's long gone."

"No," she says. "He lives in the basement. He'll outlive us all."

April shivers. "Come on. Lunch."

"You know," Nana says as they move toward the kitchen. "You look a lot like I did when I was your age."

April smiles. "I'm lucky, then."

"It won't last. Then what?"

"You tell me."

"Find yourself a good man, April. Someone like my Spencer."

"No, Nana. That's not the answer for me."

"The one you live with is a bum."

"I told you, he's gone. We went our separate ways. Besides," April says, filling the kettle, "if I could change anything, I wouldn't want a guy. I'd want to live alone somewhere in a small town where no one knows me. All by myself. Doesn't that sound nice?"

"Hmpf," Nana says. "Sounds preposterous. Who would take care of you when you're old?"

April smiles wryly. Planning ahead has never been her strong suit. "Look, I bought some marigolds for your garden."

"I don't like marigolds. Everyone has them."

"They're the giant kind." When April sees that's not working, she adds, "Oliver picked them out."

"Oliver." Nana's face lights up. "Let me see them."

"They aren't blooming yet. There's not much to see."

"I'll call to thank him."

"I'll let him know."

"He has a good heart."

"Yes," April says, "he does."

After lunch, April brings the flat of marigolds out to the small garden where the phantom carp once lived. She unwittingly chose flowers as gold as the fish, to make the story come true.

Her father spun so many tales; April listened with relish and adoration. Later she realized that he told those stories to girls at the bar, too. They would sit there in their snug clothing and styled hair, listening. April could almost hear their squeamish giggles. She thought of the picture taped to the back of the aquarium, the way the naked lady smiled to suggest she enjoyed being there even though the neglected tank was grimy with scum and the scavengers sucked at its sides.

The pond April imagined in her grandmother's yard was clear as the tropics, the fish healthy and silken, their fins rippling like kites on a summer sky.

Along with the marigolds, April has a bag each of peat moss and manure, a watering can of fertilizer, a hand shovel, a hoe, and a dandelion fork. She is wearing an oversize T-shirt and baggy pants, her hair pulled back in a loose ponytail. The sun is warm on her back. She likes turning the soil, pulling weeds. She learned to garden from Oliver when they were in high school and he worked at the nursery.

April pauses to look at the sky, her capped tooth throbbing. The maple above her, too big for the yard, is covered with half-size leaves a tender shade of yellow-green. The branches swish and frolic. As a child, she loved to climb trees on blustery days to be closer to the wind, loved how it felt inside her clothes, in her hair, the wild energy of it. Who needed food and sleep?

A stab of pain in her tooth interrupts her thoughts. Somewhere along the way, she screwed up. The girl she was at nine did not survive adolescence. Last month she turned twenty-eight, still living the same gimmick, an impostor in her own life. But there is no going back. All she has is the April she's made of herself. Besides, despite a smattering of courses at a community college, she doesn't know how to do anything but tend bar. And garden.

"April?"

She turns. Because he is standing in front of the sun, she cannot see his face, but she knows the voice. "Hey, Oliver."

He sits down beside her.

"Shouldn't you be in class?"

"Semester's over. I start my internship next week. What about you?"

"Off today." She wedges a plant from its container, placing it in the hole. She is grateful he doesn't stare at her lip. Maybe he doesn't notice. "Nana call you?"

He nods. "To thank me for your marigolds."

April glances at the house to see if Nana is watching. She is, of course. April waves with the shovel. "She wouldn't have liked them if I didn't tell her they were from you." She dusts dirt off her knees, embarrassed by how she must look, but Oliver smiles gently.

"Did you hear the latest?" April continues, nodding toward the house. "Nick Simone's living in the basement."

"Oh, no. Why doesn't she have delusions about Spencer? At least they'd be more pleasant."

April starts on a new hole. "Your party get rained out?"

"We moved inside. Need some help?"

"If you want." She hands him a flat.

"April, I'm sorry for—"

"Me, too. Let's forget it."

"I didn't want you to leave."

"Just pass the watering can."

"I was an idiot."

"Fine." She smiles. "You were an idiot."

He smiles, too, filling his hands with peat, packing it loosely around the roots of a marigold. He handles the plant gingerly, the way she has seen him touch Bernadette's hair, the nape of her neck, fingers like butterflies. When he glances up, April looks away. "What happened to your mother's portrait?" she asks. "The one your father gave you?"

"Oh, that. I finally gave it to Al."

She looks at him questioningly.

"I don't know." He smiles. "Maybe I didn't want it staring at me all the time."

April sits back on her ankles. "I'm surprised you still hold on to the piano."

"Have you ever tried to move one?"

"I'm sure if you sold it, someone would be glad to come and get it."

"Are you offering?"

"I'd take it if I could. There's so much crap in my apartment, there's barely room for me."

"T.J.'s stuff, you mean."

She tries to separate two immature plants, but the roots are fragile and intertwined, so she puts them into the ground as one.

"What about your lip?" he asks finally.

She thinks of the usual excuses, missed steps and falling bookshelves. She trims a broken bud off a damaged plant, saying nothing.

"Help me out here," he says. "I'm trying to square the girl who reads Stephen Hawking with the one I saw at the party. Will the real April please stand up?"

"It was Brian Greene," she says. "I couldn't get through Hawking."

"You didn't answer my question."

"You don't get it," she says. "I read not to think."

"You think," he says. "You think a lot."

"Yes, but I'd rather think about wormholes in time than a fat lip I can't do anything about."

He touches his own lip, studying her. She feels suddenly nervous. "Can I ask you something?" he says. "If it's too personal, you don't have to answer."

"Uh-oh."

"It's about Quincy."

Her insides go cold, like fog freezing on asphalt.

"I just wonder if you ever look back on that, I mean—"

"No," she says. "I don't."

"Don't get upset. I just wonder if it wouldn't be useful to—"

"It's not."

"I mean, I'm just curious about how you see it now."

"I don't. I don't see it."

"April, that's not reasonable."

"So you're telling me you go home at night and talk to Bernadette about the things you did in high school?"

"Well, if statutory rape was on the list, I might."

"God, you're always exaggerating. Why are we talking about this?"

"Because we never have."

She closes her eyes tightly.

"Look, you don't have to talk to *me* about this. Just tell me I'm not the only one who knows. Tell me you've confided in a girlfriend, a customer at the bar, anyone."

She looks down at the grass.

"A forty-year-old man and a fourteen-year-old girl," he says, lowering his voice. "At least tell me you see what's wrong with that."

"You want me to say I made a mistake? Yes, I fucked up. Happy?"

"April, don't you see? He wanted you to believe it was your fault, and you did."

"Fine. He had a dick for a brain. Can we stop now?"

"He gave liquor to a child, that alone—"

"He didn't pour it down my throat."

"He was your boss."

"Stop. I'm not talking about this." She covers her ears.

"And your father. He didn't help matters, did he. Why did he have you work there to begin with? To save a few bucks on a dishwasher?"

She stands abruptly, knocking over the watering can, drenching her sneaker.

"April, please." He looks up at her. "I'm only trying to—"

"Look, Oliver. I've gotten over these things. Why haven't you?"

"Pretending they never happened isn't the same as getting over them."

"Why now, Oliver? Because I screwed up at your party? I'm sorry I can't be as perfect as you." She glares down, breathless. "Just don't invite me next time."

He stands slowly. His eyes fall to her mouth. Maybe it looks worse than she thought. He cups his fingers under the line of her jaw and runs his thumb lightly over the swollen lip. She steps back as calmly as she can.

"I'm sorry," he says, stuffing his hands in his pockets. "I'm just worried, April."

"It's my business."

"If it's me who has to ID you in the morgue one day, I'm going to take it pretty damn personally."

"How do you get from a fat lip to the morgue?"

"Faster than you think."

"You're such an alarmist."

"And you have no sense of alarm, do you. Not an ounce. Except once. Something made you go to the police."

"T.J. is gone. Will you get over it?"

"He's not gone, April, not as long as you're living this way. He's here now. He's in your head. Him or someone like him."

"Living what way?"

"You're an intelligent woman. You can break this."

The dandelion fork trembles in her grip. "God, you're infuriating. If I were a killer, you're the one I'd kill."

He looks stunned only for an instant. Then he can't help it. He laughs. Her cheeks blaze because she's not sure if he's making fun of her.

"I'm sorry," he says, holding his stomach. "But I think that's the best compliment I've ever gotten."

She tries not to smile, but it's no good. "Bastard," she says, hating him more now because he's made her laugh. "You make me crazy." She smacks his shoulder and he snatches her arm in the familiar way they did as kids. But it's different now. The pressure of his fingers sends a warm rush up her arm. Her heart quickens.

He steps closer until the prongs of the dandelion fork in her free hand touch his chest. "How would you do it?" he asks. "Poison? Stabbing? How about strangulation? Wouldn't that be satisfying?"

For the first time in years, she looks him dead in the eye. So blue and clear. Luminous as glacial ice, those radiant cobalt crevices lit from within. Her voice comes out in a rasp. "I'd hit you with a bolt of lightning."

His smile fades. She sees now that they are not just one shade of blue, but a thousand, pale and oceanic near the pupil, dark indigo around the rim, with flecks of sea green and gold. She feels a light shimmering sensation; she is no longer in her body, yet is intensely aware of the way his fingers have loosened around her wrist. It takes her a moment to realize she has stopped breathing.

There is a wild knocking at the window. They turn to see Nana holding the curtain open, flailing her arm.

"Oh," Oliver says, releasing April's arm. He runs his hand through his hair and tucks his shirt though it has not been disturbed. April drops the dandelion fork. Her skin tingles from the soles of her feet to the base of her neck.

"Oh, my," Nana says.

April whirls around to see Nana standing on the top step by the side door. She has her shower cap back on, inside out this time. "Jesus, Mary, and Joseph," she says, touching the medal on her necklace.

"Nana." April rushes toward her. "Where's your walker? You could hurt yourself out here."

"So you finally brought him by," she says, "the infamous boyfriend."

"No, Nana. That's Oliver."

"Listen, you." Nana shakes her finger at him. "You're not welcome here. I saw what you did."

"Nana, please."

Oliver steps closer, holding out his palms. "Look, Nana. It's me."

"Get away from me, Nicky," she says, voice shaking. "Bede doesn't want your toys. You're not his father anymore. You've done enough."

Oliver doesn't move.

"Bede was just a little boy," Nana says, her eyes filling. "I should have protected him." She touches the cross again, bringing it to her lips.

April caresses her back, nodding for Oliver to leave. "It's okay, Nana. Nicky's gone. He left years ago."

"Where's my Bede?" she says. "Why doesn't he come to see me anymore?"

April bites her lip, opening the door and helping Nana inside. Oliver puts his fists in his pockets. "I'll call you," April says. He nods, though she sees that he does not believe her.

SUMMER

Chapter
15

THE TABLES ARE SET with gold-trimmed Lenox china and long-stemmed crystal. Oliver handles the utensils carefully, conscious of Bernadette's mother beside him and her father across from him. He measures his sips of the dry, oak Merlot, drinking just enough to be sociable. He needs to keep his mind sharp.

The place is crackling with conversation, the doors of the great room open to the radiant June day. Seven PM, and still the sun shines brilliantly on the rows of lavender and baby's breath just outside. The heady fragrance drifts in to Oliver, along with the sound of children's laughter. Bernadette has invited the kids she works with and their families. Most of the children are outside adoring the family dog. One girl, short and round with hooded eyes, trots over to Bernadette. Her heavy, flat-footed gait causes people to look up from their meals. Bernadette extends her arms even before the girl is near, and she comes faster, landing upon Bernadette with a cumbersome hug. They giggle.

"Miss Bernadette, watch my split," she says, demonstrating her uncanny flexibility. Bernadette cheers as if it were the first time the girl has ever shown her. Oliver squeezes Bernadette's hand under the table and leans over to give her an admiring kiss. The little girl frowns.

Bernadette is wearing a cream-colored, sleeveless dress, stained now by the chocolate hands of children. She is unconcerned. Her golden tan shoulders shake with laughter at something the little girl says. Oliver feels hot and constrained in his suit; the day is made for shorts. He looks at the gift table piled with presents and fidgets in his chair. Neither he nor Bernadette believes in engagement parties, but her parents were insistent.

Oliver's father catches his eye, smiling at the pigtailed girl, now doing cartwheels for Bernadette. Oliver smiles, glad for his father's presence at the table. The other seats are occupied by Bernadette's family, except April's and Al's, which are vacant. He has a game, and said he would drop by late, if at all. No one knows about April.

The dessert plates are served at last, and Oliver feels relieved that it will soon be over. The pigtailed girl trots back, her dress covered with grass stains. "Miss Bernadette, can I have more cake?"

"Here," Bernadette says, pulling up a chair. "Have mine."

The girl sits down gleefully, her short fingers around her fork, and digs in. Between bites, she hums a monotone version of "My Fair Lady." A mustache of blue icing appears on her lip. Bernadette's mother smiles affectionately from across the table, but her brother, rocking his chair back on two legs, winces at the girl. Brad is in his early thirties, Oliver guesses, with a blunt-cut ponytail. He's a computer geek, too successful for his own good, according to Bernadette. His hair is as blond as Bernadette's and even sleeker. He wears an Armani suit jacket, narrow leather tie, and Levi's with holes in the knees. He glances at his watch listlessly and signals the server for coffee, making no effort to hide his boredom.

At first, Oliver was disappointed that April didn't show, but now he is glad. He can't picture her here. Just as he thinks this, his father waves at the doorway. Oliver turns to see Al and April standing together in the long, slanting light. Sunshine pours through the open

French doors horizontally, and their shadows stretch to the opposite wall. Oliver waves to them, but they don't see. Brad lifts his coffee cup almost to his lips and stops to put the cup down.

April and Al catch sight of Hal and cross the room. They stop at the gift table, where April places a box covered with satiny lilac wrapping and a large bow. Al tosses an envelope.

"There's my other son now," Hal says, smiling at Bernadette's parents. "A sportswriter," he adds. "Always leaving early or arriving late."

"And his wife?" Brad says.

"No, no. My goddaughter, April."

Brad wipes his mouth with his napkin and buttons his suit coat. Oliver feels his throat constrict. April wears a charcoal dress, calf-length, with long, narrow sleeves and a high, classic neckline; pearls that she must have borrowed from Nana, with matching earrings; black heels, dark stockings, hair pulled back in a bun.

Oliver has never seen her like this. He thinks he ought to like it, but doesn't. She looks beautiful, but wrong. He prefers her in blue jeans with her hair disheveled, laughing inappropriately. She holds herself with quiet reserve, formal and remote. She chose everything perfectly in an effort to blend in, but Oliver can't keep from staring. He takes a drink of water, wishing he could loosen his tie.

Bernadette's father stands as they come over. "Allen?" he says, extending a hand. "Such interesting names in your family. Allen Ignatius, Oliver Jonah. Who knows what we can expect for our grandchildren? Dmitry, perhaps? Antonia?" He laughs heartily.

"Call me Al," he says coolly. "This is Rose."

"April," Hal corrects. "Come, have a seat."

"We can't stay," Al says. "I have a deadline tonight."

"What about April?" Bernadette's father says admiringly.

"We came in one car," she explains. She still has not looked at Oliver. Not even a glance.

"We'll find you a ride home," Brad says.

Oliver looks at him. Brad is leaning forward in his seat, hand over his mouth, studying her openly. April's face flushes. "I've got some things to get back to," she says. "We just came to say a quick hello." She looks at Al for support.

"Stay," Al says. "It'll do you good." He squeezes her hand.

After a few moments, she walks Al outside and they stand for a moment beside the open door of his Jeep. Through the window, Oliver sees her dress move in the breeze. Both in dark formal clothes, standing together in the slanting light, she and Al look like figures in a painting, their closeness suggesting an aura of intimacy. Oliver's stomach feels queasy.

The little girl beside Bernadette lifts her plate to lick it.

"Eh, eh," says Bernadette gently. "I know the icing is good, but use your fork."

"Is there more?"

"Not now," Bernadette says, stroking her hair. "You go run and play."

"Who's the lady?" says the girl, pointing.

"That's April. She and Oliver were friends when they were your age."

"Who's Oliver?"

"You remember him," says Bernadette, patting Oliver's hand. "He's the lucky guy who gets to marry me." She winks.

"But he doesn't have blond hair."

"You don't have to marry someone with your hair color, silly," says Bernadette.

The girl looks at Oliver and frowns. "He should have blond hair," she declares and trots heavily out the door.

"Hm," says Oliver gravely. "I'll dye it, if that's what it takes."

"You'd look hideous." Bernadette grins.

Oliver hears the noisy idle of Al's Jeep as he pulls away. No sooner is he gone than Brad is out of his seat, meeting April at the door. He motions toward the kitchen. April touches her pearls, shaking her head. Not hungry. Brad touches her back lightly and directs her in a gesture she cannot politely refuse.

Hal catches Oliver's eye and raises a brow. April and Brad disappear into the kitchen.

Bernadette frowns, taking a sip. "He didn't waste any time, did he."

Oliver clears his throat. He wants to ask something.

"He doesn't like my kids being here," Bernadette says. "You'd think growing up with a sister like ours, he'd be a little more tolerant. He can be a real dick sometimes."

"Hm." Oliver says no more, and waits for April and Brad to come out of the kitchen. They don't.

After the guests have gone home, Oliver and Bernadette sit on the deck and open gifts in the cool night air. Hours before, Brad took April home in his black Porsche with the top down. She looked wan and subdued, a bit apprehensive, but at the same time serene and polite. She kissed Bernadette and Oliver good night, thanking them for the party. "Safe home," Oliver said, squeezing her elbow. She smelled dusky and sweet, like burning fields, and he wished he could be alone with her, for just a moment, to be sure she was all right. He imagines Brad speeding along the winding north shore roads, narrow and canopied with trees, April's hair coming undone in the wind. Better Brad than T.J., Oliver tells himself. He tries to shift his thoughts.

"Your parents enjoyed the day."

"They love a party," she says, checking over her thank-you list.

"Your dad's quite gregarious."

"He can be."

Oliver watches her, waiting for something more. When she doesn't say anything, he picks up the last gift, wrapped in lilac paper. "What do you think about April and Brad?" he asks hesitantly.

"He's just looking for a good time," she says, running her finger down the list. "Who knows?"

Oliver tenses, holding the package.

"I told him he'd better watch out, though," she says, erasing something. "That she has a hell of a boyfriend. That Ken guy, I mean."

"I don't think that's a steady thing."

Bernadette shrugs. "Are you going to open it?"

"You don't think it's a possibility, April and Brad?"

"He won't do her any harm, if that's what you're worried about. But if he can charm the dress off her, he will."

"Right."

"Don't worry. If there's anything April isn't, it's naive. She's got his number." She caresses his arm. "She did look pretty tonight, didn't she."

Oliver hands her the package. "Let's open this so we can get out of here."

Bernadette puts her pen in her mouth, tears open the lilac wrapping, and shoves it in the trash. She puts the box on the floor between her ankles and pulls out a delicately carved, antique hourglass. The pen drops from her mouth. "Wow," she says. "My dad will be impressed." Her father collects antiques, especially clocks, sundials, odometers, anything that registers time and distance. "Who's this from?" she says, glancing at the list.

"April."

"God, how could she afford this?" She turns it over carefully and lets the sand flow. The wood is intricately carved, the glass tinged with age, and the sand white as the vast, unruined beaches they played on as children.

"Oliver?"

"Hm?"

Bernadette puts the hourglass back into its box to empty out in darkness and then sits on Oliver's lap. "Sometimes you get this look in your eye." She runs her fingertip over his eyebrow. "Where were you just then?"

Oliver feels her weight on his thigh. The dress is taut over her backside. "Are your parents asleep?" he asks.

She nods.

"I'd like to do it in your father's Studebaker."

She laughs, covering her mouth. "He'd kill us."

"Where is it?"

"In the storage garage, the old stable."

He grasps her hand and leads her down the deck steps. When they are some distance from the house, they begin to run, hand in hand, Bernadette holding her shoes. The grass is dense and moist, black in the darkness.

They enter the converted barn, breathless, and close the door behind them. It is dark. Startled birds flutter in the rafters. Though it has not been used as a stable for decades, Oliver swears he can smell hay and leather, the heat of animals. He pulls the cover off the car and moves his palm along the gleaming, curvaceous chassis, a 1950 Champion with a split windshield and bulbous headlights.

"Don't knock anything over," Bernadette says, breathing hard. "He knows exactly where everything is."

Oliver opens the car and helps her in. He feels removed from himself, as in a dream. "We have to be careful," she says. He guides her onto his lap, straddling him, and moves his hands over her elegant neck and shoulders, the delicate collarbone. He unzips the dress. Her eyes are dark and dilated, her mouth open. He kisses her hungrily, without tenderness. He feels detached from himself, gripped by a sudden, bleak desolation.

He closes his eyes, and without wanting to sees the gray dress, her fingertips grazing the luminous pearls, the hourglass running out in darkness. Bernadette cries out, tears moving down her cheeks. He holds her against him, caressing her hair. "I'm sorry," he says. "Did I hurt you?"

She laughs, clutching his shirt. Normally he handles her carefully, like something that could break. "Bernadette, are you all right?"

She glides her hand down his chest, inside his shirt, and leans her head on his shoulder. "Finally," she says, "I know you mean it."

Chapter
16

BRAD CUTS THE ENGINE in front of April's building and looks up at the grim windows, sluggish pigeons patrolling the ledge. "You're kidding, right?"

She rolls her eyes and opens the car door. "Thanks for the lift."

"I get it," he says, taking her hand. "You don't want me to know where you live, so you're grabbing a cab."

"I live here," she says, pulling her hand away.

He gets out of the car and walks with her to the door. She sees his intrigue deepen as he stares up at the building. "Let me come in," he says. "I won't pressure you. I just want to see what it's like."

"No."

"Two minutes."

"Good night."

"Okay, okay. It's too soon. Come out with me on my boat tomorrow. I'll show you the Sound."

"I'm sorry."

"The Met, then. I have tickets for Saturday."

"Brad, you've been awfully sweet, but I'm going in now."

"Your phone number, at least."

"You're not used to being turned down, are you?"

He licks his lips. "You're attracted to me. Admit it."

She smiles and gives his cheek a pat. "You'll be over this in ten minutes."

"You're throwing away a hell of a time."

She lets the door close and hears the Porsche roar as she climbs the stairs. By the time she reaches her apartment, he is gone.

April unlocks her door and instantly knows that someone has been there. The smell of a cigarette lingers. She enters slowly, leaving the door open behind her, and turns on a lamp. Smoke rises from an ashtray on the table. T.J.'s brand. She hears the door close behind her.

She listens for the sound of his breathing, telling herself not to panic. "How did you get in?" she says.

"You left the window open by the fire escape," he says. "When did you change the locks?"

She turns to face him. He stands just beyond the reach of the light, his figure tall and shadowy. She knows she ought to be frightened, but all she feels is rage. "You broke my goddamn tooth. Do you have any idea what a crown costs?"

"I'm sorry."

"And Kenny's rib. It takes a real man to kick someone who's lying on the ground. Yes, that was gutsy of you, T.J."

He stiffens at the mention of the other man's name. She tells herself to shut up, remember Arredondo's advice.

T.J. rubs his hands together. "I came to tell you I'm clean."

She sighs miserably. "I've got to call work," she says, moving away. "They asked me to fill in tomorrow." She picks up the receiver and punches in Arredondo's number, which he had compelled her to repeat back to him until he was assured she knew it by heart. She's halfway through when T.J. takes the phone from her and gently cradles it back into place. He smells of soap and apricots; he used her shower.

"Wichita," he says.

"No."

He swallows, squeezing her hand. He is wearing a sleeveless muscle shirt, denim jeans, and the same heavy boots she has seen him in a thousand times. "April, no one's sorrier than me. You've got to believe I didn't mean to hurt you."

"Just like you didn't mean to hurt your wife?" Even as the words leave her mouth, she knows it's a mistake, exactly the kind of provocation Arredondo told her to avoid.

T.J. flinches. She can almost feel the spasm pass through his body. He steps back, balling his fists. "What've you been hearing?" he demands.

"I think you know."

"It's a lie, April. They thought it was me, but I didn't do nothing. That's why I came out east. I didn't stand a chance there. Nice, pretty girl like Denise. A man like me, with scars. It was her family who got the DA thinking it was me. But I swear to God, April. She done it to herself. You've got to believe me."

"Then turn yourself in, T.J. Tell the truth. Things will work out if you're honest."

"Jesus." He laughs sadly. "You actually believe that, don't you."

"What else can you do?"

"Come with me. We can start fresh. Things can be different for us, you'll see."

"There's no *us*, T.J. There never was."

"You're wrong. You and me are the same. You know it, too." He reaches for her face. She remembers the first time he touched her, how surprised she was that those large, calloused hands could be so warm and soft. She feels a glimmer of hesitation before pulling away.

"Go," she says. "I'm calling the police as soon as you leave. Don't come back again."

"How will I get your answer?"

"You already have it."

Once he has left, she waits a few moments before picking up the phone, relieved when she gets only Arredondo's voice mail. "It's April Simone," she says. "He's back. But he's not your man."

Chapter

17

THE COALS ARE RED AS RISING SUNS. Oliver prods them with a skewer, sweat dampening the back of his neck. The surface of his father's pool glints with light filtered through young foliage. A plunge would be invigorating right now, but he keeps his post by the grill.

Beside the pool, Al lies collapsed in a lawn chair, sleepy from sun and beer. Though it is far from nightfall, distant fireworks rattle like machine guns. The dog cowers, resting her chin on Oliver's foot. "Not your favorite holiday?"

The retriever looks up at him.

"Mine, neither," says Oliver.

Bernadette hums to herself, setting out napkins and paper plates. Her fine silken hair is tied in a bun, and her white swimsuit shows her tan.

"Hey." He winks when she comes within earshot. "You look like a goddess."

"Damn," she says over her shoulder. "I was aiming for genius."

"That, too," he calls.

Oliver hears a car door slam in front of the house and waits for

April to appear in the yard. As usual, she is the last to arrive. But when the gate opens, he sees instead a tall, lean man with a lopsided stride. It takes Oliver a moment to recognize him.

"Quincy," Oliver's father calls from the back door. "You made it."

Oliver backs away from the grill, wiping his forehead. *Quincy?* A surreal feeling creeps over him. It's been nearly a decade since he's seen the man. He's graying at the temples now, with crow's-feet that radiate into his hairline when he smiles. Still, he looks younger than his age, which must be past fifty by now. He greets Oliver's father with a two-handed shake. He has a kind face, which Oliver has always found hard to square with the facts.

"Quince," Al says, standing from his chair. "You old fox. Still pool sharking?"

"Never lose," he says. "Well, almost never."

"I brought some friends by the bar, what was it—five years ago? And this guy cleaned us out," Al says admiringly.

"You asked for it," Quincy says. He has the look of a lumberjack, with pleasant, rugged features and, despite the heat, a flannel shirt rolled to his elbows. He eyes Oliver uncertainly. "Is this Oliver?" he says. "My, you're all grown up."

Oliver bristles. He wonders if Quincy has any idea how much he knows. They shake hands but say nothing.

Al sits backward on a patio chair, draping his arms on the back-rest. "So what brings you around?"

"I've finally stashed away enough cash to buy out your dad's half of the bar."

Oliver and Al turn to their father in unison, eyebrows raised.

"Your uncle willed it to me," he says sheepishly. "I guess he thought April and Buddy were still too young. Of course I'll give the money to April when it's sold. I was planning to tell her about it next month, once things are settled, so please don't mention it yet."

"You're not planning to hand the cash over to her right away, are you?" Al asks.

"What else would I do? It's hers. She could use it to go to college or get a better apartment."

"Or buy a Harley for her next dude," Al says. "You need to wait, Dad. She's not in a good place right now."

"Give her some credit," their father says.

Al raises an eyebrow.

Their father glances at Oliver for support.

Oliver shrugs, casting a look at Bernadette. "How would I know?"

Oliver's father and brother knit their foreheads in precisely the same way. Oliver frowns. So what if he and April were inseparable as kids? Clearly, the adult April is someone they know far better than he does.

"I think she'll do fine with the money," Quincy interjects. "She was always a responsible kid. And besides, it's not exactly like winning the lottery. She won't be retiring to Tahiti."

Oliver studies him, those soft eyes and drowsy smile. It's hard to imagine him winning at pool, no less the other things Oliver knows but shouldn't.

One night in Oliver's studio, when April came in smelling of liquor, she admitted what was going on with more detail than Oliver was prepared for. Apparently Quincy had a set of rules in which he was allowed to touch April but she was not allowed to touch him. Every night his clothes stayed intact while he reached inside hers. He did everything he could to get a response from her—aside from kissing, which would have implied love—and once he got the reaction he was looking for, usually something audible, he asked her to leave so he could finish the job alone. This restraint on his part, he claimed, was out of respect for her age.

Over time, she said, she learned to fake it, but in reverse, holding the ecstatic unraveling of her body inside the small, tight bubble of her mind, then smothering it just before it took hold, the way she'd once seen a senile neighbor snip all the buds off a rosebush.

Only once did she wait too long. She was drunker than usual. He lay on his back behind the bar and told her to straddle him. She said no. They'd never done anything like that before. He said there was nothing to worry about, he was fully clothed. "Come on," he said. "Life is dreary. Let's have a little fun." As soon as she got on top of him she realized it was a mistake. His smile vanished. His face clenched up. "Oh, Christ," he said, digging his fingers into her backside.

All at once her hips began to gyrate, her body turning inside out like petals bursting. He grimaced, letting out a prolonged moan, a blend of pleasure and regret. For a moment there was no sound but their ragged breath tearing open the air. And then, April's sob.

"Shit," he said, pushing her off, examining his pants. He stood and went to the men's room.

After that, he didn't touch her for months, and she ignored him. Then he started in again with the free drinks, casually at first, then insistently. He waited until he could work her up to three shots before he made a move. She let him do what he wanted, but this time she gave up nothing, not an ache in her face, not a sigh, not a shiver. Quincy went to greater lengths to elicit a response, but April had taught herself how to extinguish pleasure. By the age of seventeen, she had already determined that sex was just something to get through.

"Shall we get down to it?" Oliver's father says, opening his notebook on the wrought-iron table.

Quincy sits with him, scraping his chair on the cement patio.

"How are Pam and the kids?" Oliver's father asks.

Quincy opens a worn leather wallet. "Eight and five already," he says, taking out a photo. "I'm too old to have such sweet little girls."

Indeed, Oliver thinks.

Al walks to the edge of the pool and dives in, shattering the placid surface. Another car pulls noisily into the driveway.

"Must be April," Hal says. "I told her to get that muffler looked at."

Oliver hears the rough idle of her car die abruptly, then the slam of the door. The gate swings open and the dog rushes at her.

"Cricket," April says, dropping to her knees. The dog licks her neck and she laughs, pushing her away. April's hair is braided. She wears a roomy, sleeveless T-shirt, shapeless shorts, and dangling earrings. She is holding a bag of pretzels and a bottle of mineral water.

"Hi, folks," she says. Al pauses and hangs on the side of the pool. Seeing Quincy's back, she stops.

"Sweetheart," Oliver's father says, rising.

Quincy remains seated. He turns and waves sheepishly, then slips the photo of his children back into his wallet.

Oliver tries to read April, but can't. She kisses everyone's cheek except Quincy's, and when she gets to Oliver he thinks he may as well be a tree, she is in such a state of distraction.

Once she sits down, Quincy goes over and sits on the end of her lawn chair. She draws her knees up to her chest. "I'm sorry I didn't come to the funeral," he says quietly. "We were in Toronto that week visiting Pam's parents."

"It's okay," April says.

"I always meant to call you afterward, but I didn't know what to say, just like I don't now."

"I'm all right," she says, not looking at him. "Thank you."

He reaches for her hand but she doesn't offer it. Quincy returns to where Oliver's father is sitting and snaps open a beer. April blows out a long, discreet breath. Oliver tries to catch her eye, but it's no good.

Bernadette approaches. "Thanks for the hourglass," she says, touching April's arm. "You were way too generous. We're taking it as a wedding gift, okay? Nothing more from you!"

"It wasn't expensive," April says. "I got lucky, if you can believe that." Her voice is croaky. She looks everywhere except at Quincy.

"Hey," Al calls from the pool. "How about *my* kiss?"

She waves a hand, dismissing him, and opens her bottle of water. Bernadette goes into the house to get more ice.

"She's lovely," Quincy says to Oliver, nodding after Bernadette.

"Isn't she," Oliver says.

"Have you set a date?"

"December something," Oliver says. "I have a mental block about the day. Drives Bernadette mad."

"The seventh," April says.

"There you go." Quincy smiles. "Your friends will get you there on time."

The men resume their discussion, and Oliver returns to the grill. April summons the dog by kissing the air, then leans forward, pigeon-toed, and holds up a pretzel. Cricket's ears spring up. "Catch," April commands, dropping the morsel. The dog snatches and swallows in one motion. "Good dog," she says, nuzzling her ear.

There is something familiar about April's posture. The gesture and tone of voice register deeply in Oliver's memory. Buddy. He was the one who taught the dog to catch, who nuzzled her in exactly that way. Oliver watches, mesmerized.

Bernadette appears with ice. "Did Brad get you home all right the other night?" she asks, touching April's back.

April nods without looking up.

"He didn't harass you, I hope."

"Nope."

"He asked me if you were seeing anyone, and I said I wasn't sure."

"Pardon?" April rubs the dog's chin.

"The guy you brought to our barbecue."

Oliver looks up from the grill. April stops petting the dog, and for Oliver the spell is broken, Buddy gone. "No," she says. "Is there anything that needs doing around here?"

"We're all set," Bernadette answers.

"Rose," Al calls, beckoning her with his finger. "Ten bucks says I can beat you at ten laps, even though I'm winded."

April has her arms around her middle, a bit hunched. "I'm not in the mood, Al."

"Turning me down? Don't break my heart."

She kicks off her sandals and sits at the edge of the pool with her feet in the water. Al swims over and puts his hands on her knees.

They speak more softly now. Oliver cannot hear. He sees April put her index finger against her temple, and with an exasperated laugh pull an imaginary trigger.

Oliver leaves the coals to kindle on their own and lies in a lawn chair. He puts his sunglasses on and looks at the pool where April is undressing. Beneath her clothes, she wears a sky-blue one-piece swimsuit, surprisingly conservative. He glances at Quincy and sees that he is also watching. She dives in.

Al gets a jump on her. He has the stronger stroke, but April is quicker at the turnarounds. The turbulence in the pool attracts everyone's attention. Oliver's father folds his arms across his chest, smiling at the race. Bernadette watches in silence.

When April wins, she raises her fist.

Al comes up behind her, puts his arms around her neck, and pulls her under. Oliver's father laughs, waving his hand, and then turns back to Quincy. Oliver continues to watch. Al tries to force April under, but she has his hair in her fist. If Oliver didn't know better, he might think they were trying to kill each other. Al lifts April across his shoulders and she shrieks. At that moment the dog leaps to her feet and rushes to the side gate.

April and Al stop and look at the dog, who is barking savagely at the gate. Holding a bag of hamburger buns, Bernadette comes out of the house and looks around at the commotion. April hauls herself out of the pool and grabs a towel.

"Is someone here?" Oliver's father calls.

On the opposite side of the gate stands a large man with his palms up in surrender to the dog. Oliver's father grasps Cricket's collar and pats the back of her neck where the fur stands on end. "Sh," he says. "You're okay, girl." The dog crouches reluctantly, flattening her ears. "Don't worry about her," Hal says to the man. "She's all bark." He reaches for the latch. "You must be here for the estimate. I didn't expect you until Monday."

The man takes off his Mets hat and crushes it in his hands. "No, actually. I'm a friend of April's."

Oliver sees the surprise register on his father's face. He stops, hand on the latch.

"Name's T.J.," the man says, extending his hand. Hal hesitates, then shakes it with a backward glance at April, who stands cocooned inside her towel, a puddle of water forming at her feet.

No, Dad, Oliver thinks, watching his father. But the gate swings open and T.J. enters the yard. Cricket sniffs at his pant leg with a low growl. As T.J. gets down on his knee to pet her, Oliver feels queasy. But Cricket, always a sucker, is already on her back.

April stands in front of him, glaring down.

He glances up at her, squinting, then straightens to his full height so that she has to tilt her head back to look him in the face. "Well," he says meekly. "You always said you wanted me to meet your folks."

She puts her hand on her forehead, shaking her head incredulously.

"I'm here to show you I don't have nothing to hide. I won't stay long, but go ahead, call if you want. I'm not about to go running."

April turns and strides into the house.

T.J. looks after her doubtfully, then turns his attention to the others, who stare back in awkward astonishment. Oliver thinks T.J. will follow April inside, but instead he makes his way cautiously to a lawn chair and sits down beside Quincy. Al comes over and pulls up a chair directly in front of him, so that their knees nearly touch.

"Hey there, big guy," he says. "Name's Al."

"Allen Night." T.J. smirks. "I read your stuff."

"Not a fan, I take it."

"You're okay," T.J. says. "But you focus too much on the coaching."

Al lets out a snort of a laugh. "Well, thanks for the tip."

April steps out of the house. She looks at T.J. and Quincy sitting beside each other, Al in T.J.'s face, and hesitates.

"Come on, Rosie," Al says, pulling a chair beside him and patting the seat. "Join the stimulating conversation."

Instead, April sits down beside Oliver. He feels oddly gratified. She shivers hard beneath her towel. He resists the urge to touch her arm.

"So, T.J., what do you do for a living?" Al asks. "A sports critic, perhaps?"

"Repairman," T.J. says. "Electronics mostly, but I can fix almost anything. Vacuums, lawn mowers. Always loved broken stuff, especially the ones people say can't be fixed."

"That must make you a popular guy."

"I can always find a job, if that's what you mean."

Al nods. "So, Mister Fix-it, where you from?"

"Born in the Bronx," T.J. says evenly. "Moved out to Utah when I was seventeen."

"Ah. How'd you fare out there, with all those scrub-faced Mormons?"

TJ stiffens. "You talking about my face?" he says, touching his ear.

"I wasn't," Al says, surprised. "But we can."

"No." April leans forward in her seat to let Al know he's going too far.

"It's all right," T.J. says. "You want to know what happened to my face?"

The group stares in silence. Quincy laughs nervously. "Well, this has been entertaining," he says, standing. "But Pam is expecting me for dinner."

Hal gets up to walk out with Quincy, who waves without turning back to look.

"Don't stop now," Al says to T.J.

"My old man was drunk, like usual," T.J. says. "He got it into his head that my mom had someone on the side, but it wasn't true. I knew because she spent every free minute with me." His voice wavers, nearly breaking, and in that instant April gets out of her seat and slips into the one vacated by Quincy, right beside T.J. In the four steps it takes for her to move from one seat to another, Oliver feels miles elapse, years pass. All at once she is impossibly far from him.

"My dad, he wanted to teach my mom a lesson," T.J. continues. "So he set fire to what she loved best."

Al studies T.J., deciding something. "So, he burned the house down, is that it?"

"No. He took me out to the alley and put a lighter to my pajamas. Didn't take but a second." When no one says anything, he adds, "I guess he didn't want to wreck the furniture."

Al runs his hand over his mouth and chin thoughtfully. "Quite a story."

"He was madder than hell, too, 'cause he'd won the Trifecta the day before and never got to cash in his ticket, seeing as how he was arrested."

April is leaning forward, elbows on knees, her face hidden in her hands.

"And your mom?" Al manages.

"Died of an overdose four months later," he says. "She missed him, if you can believe that."

April drags her fingers down her face and puffs out a long breath. "Okay, T.J. Time to go." She stands.

T.J. stands and so does Al. "Tough breaks," Al says, hands on his hips.

"Stuff happens to all of us," T.J. answers. "I just got mine early on."

"I hope things get better for you."

"They have."

"And by the way, you come around looking for April again, my brother and I are going to break your legs."

T.J. studies Al, then gives Oliver a cursory glance. "I think she's old enough to decide for herself."

"She goes back to you one more time, we're going to break hers, too," Al says.

"Gee," T.J. says. "That's real touching."

"Stop it, Al," April says, slapping his shoulder. "Go on, T.J."

They walk toward the gate. "Let's have a beer somewhere," T.J. says to her.

"No."

"Look," he says more quietly. "I don't care what happens. I just want you to believe me." T.J. is still talking as they pass out of view.

Oliver stares at the gate, listening as T.J.'s pickup roars to life. He feels Bernadette looking at him. He reaches for her hand, shaking his head. Her face softens then. She pats his hand. Al claps his hands loudly, looking after the closed gate. "That's our girl," he says.

"Do you think she called the police when she went inside?" Oliver asks.

"April? Defend herself?" Al says. "Besides, they'd be here by now."

"Maybe we should call."

"If there's no protection order anymore, he hasn't done anything wrong."

A moment later, April reappears alone. She rushes through the gate and slaps it closed behind her, ignoring the dog prancing beside her.

"Sure can pick 'em, Rose," Al calls.

April casts him a savage look and disappears into the house.

Al gets up to follow her.

"No," Hal says firmly. "This is hard enough for her without you making it worse. Bernadette, why don't you go? See if she's all right."

Bernadette rises uncertainly and slips into the house. Oliver stares after her. Not until he feels his father's hand on his shoulder does he realize how tense his muscles are. "She'll be okay," his father says, but Oliver hears the worry in his voice.

"She doesn't know how to take care of herself," Al says. "Of all the men she could choose, she picks *this* dude?"

"It's pretty clear to me that it's over," Hal says. "She knows it even if T.J. doesn't."

"There will be another one," Al says. "You'll see."

"Give her a chance," Hal says.

Oliver glances in through the back door. Bernadette's arm is around April's shoulder, the bay window before them. April blows her nose. Bernadette runs her hand down the long, dark sheath of April's hair, saying things he cannot hear. Then they hug.

Oliver stares, transfixed. It's a long embrace. He thinks he ought to be moved, but instead feels unsettled. Finally, April pulls back, wiping her eyes. She nods at something Bernadette has said and picks up her things to leave.

"Where are you off to, sweetheart?" Hal says as she enters the yard.

"I told some friends from the bar I'd go see the fireworks with them," she says. "Uncle Hal, I'm sorry about this. I had no idea."

"You've got nothing to apologize for."

"Another scene. I'm two for two."

"It wasn't a scene. We're only worried about you, April. What about reinstating the protection order?"

"I think he understands now," she says. "But yeah, I'll do it in the morning."

Hal hugs her. "Promise?"

"Promise."

She waves good-bye to Al and Oliver in a general way without looking at them. Once she's gone, Al says to his father, "What do you think that promise is worth?"

Hal turns to him. "Do you forget that she helped take care of your mother when she was dying?" He lowers his voice. "Do you forget that she was cooking dinner for her family when she was nine years old? Can you show me a more responsible person than that?"

"I'm not saying she's not a good person, Dad. I'm saying she has no common sense."

"No, you're saying she's not good for her word, and I'm saying she is."

"Even if she goes to the police in the morning," Oliver says. "What about between now and then?"

"She said she'll be with friends," Hal says. "Didn't she?"

Oliver folds his arms and decides not to comment. There's no point in further worrying his father, though it's pretty clear to Oliver that April isn't headed for fireworks.

Chapter
18

OLIVER PARKS IN FRONT of Bernadette's apartment building, motor running.

"You were preoccupied today," Bernadette says, touching his arm.

"It was a weird day, wasn't it," he says, shaking his head.

"I mean even before T.J. showed up."

He looks at her.

"What's your problem with Quincy?"

He raises his eyebrows, hesitating.

She smiles. "Veiled in Saran Wrap, that's you."

He laughs uncertainly.

"Don't worry. It's a virtue. Now what about Quincy?"

"Well, what do you see?"

"You're cold toward him."

He looks out the driver's-side window. "I never liked him, even as a kid. I can't explain it."

"I didn't know there was anyone you didn't like."

"If I don't care for someone, I try to keep it to myself, apparently not very well." He turns to look at her. "What else does the Saran Wrap show?"

"You're worried about April."

He sighs. "Aren't we all?"

"But you, especially."

He rubs his eyes. "I don't know. Maybe it's a spillover from my father. He's always felt responsible for April and Buddy. Their parents, well, they weren't bad people, they just never checked in when it came to parenting."

"Why don't you give April a call? She's welcome to stay with me tonight."

"She's out with friends, at least she said so."

"You know, Oliver, I didn't get the feeling that T.J. was an imminent threat. This may sound strange, but I was impressed by his honesty."

He looks at her to see if she is serious.

"Well, he's not self-pitying. You've got to give him that."

"Before Buddy died, she got a protection order against T.J. Whatever he did to prompt that is enough for me. I'm sorry about his childhood, but not that sorry."

"You're right, of course," she says. They stare out the window.

"Oliver, you know you can't fill the gap her brother left. No one can."

"Who says I'm trying?"

Bernadette purses her lips, appraising him, working out calculus, he the apparent equation. He looks at her for a long moment. If he were more of a man, he thinks, he would ask her what she was thinking. Instead, he glides his fingers over the silk of her blouse and kisses her. He moves his hand down her waist, hip, calf, then circling her ankle, narrow as a colt's.

"Sure you don't want to come upstairs?" She winks.

"Mm," he says, kissing her again. "Next time. I need to get up early tomorrow to catch up on work."

"On a Saturday?" she says. "I'm taking a few kids to a petting farm. I was hoping you could join us."

"Another time," he says. "You know how I love llamas and goats."

She smiles with disappointment.

"Tomorrow night," he says. "I'll want to hear all about your kids. And the ducks and bunnies, too."

He watches her skip up the steps to her building. After a moment a light goes on in her apartment. From the third-floor window she waves to him with her scarf. Not her usual enthusiastic wave, he thinks.

He stops at an intersection, the traffic light reflecting bloodily on the hood of the car. He imagines his future with Bernadette: a cedar-shingled Colonial in Connecticut from which he will commute to a law firm in Manhattan, she to her private practice; an au pair for the children, blond like their mother; racquetball on Thursday nights; sailboating on the Sound.

The light turns, luxuriant night air pouring in the car window, ruffling his hair, awakening his skin. It rained earlier in the day, and the air is clean. He smells the heaviness of summer, hears the song of crickets and the swish of dense trees illuminated by moonlight. The breeze traveling through his shirt caresses him. He flips his directional, and knows without having to decide that he is going to look for April.

It is after eleven when he reaches her building. Most firework shows are over, but a single rocket soars above a rooftop, explodes in all directions, and dissipates. The windows of April's apartment blaze with light, but she does not answer the buzzer. Her car is not in the station lot.

Oliver returns to his car. As he flips on his directional to pull away, he notices a police barricade under the train trestle. Yellow police tape flaps in the wind. He pulls up alongside an idling cab. "Excuse me," Oliver calls to the driver. "Do you know what happened here?"

"Shooting or stabbing," the man calls casually.

Oliver cuts the engine though he's right in the middle of the street. "Someone was killed?" he says.

"Well, they weren't rushing the person to the hospital, let's put it that way. Police photographer took a good two rolls. You should've seen the crowd when the nine fifty-two let out. Something to talk about over dinner, I guess."

"So the victim was a man?" Oliver asks, hardly breathing.

"Couldn't say. Take a look in the morning paper."

Oliver remembers to restart his engine only after a cab behind him honks. He thinks the logical thing is to stop at the police station and ask. Instead, he goes to the bar where she works. When she's not there, he thinks of one more place he can try.

Twenty minutes later, he pulls up in front of his grandmother's duplex. The bluish glow of the television flickers in the front room. April's car is in the street. He lets out a long breath, pressing his palm to his chest. He ought to go home, he tells himself, now that he knows she is safe. He gets out slowly, touching the hood of her car as he passes. It's still warm. An old confidence surges up in him. He may not understand her, but he still knows how to find her.

The front door is unlocked. He lets himself in quietly, so as not to disturb Nana if she is asleep. Except for the glow of the television, the living room is dark. He sees them huddled on the sofa, Nana's head on April's shoulder. The muscles in his back ease. He didn't realize how tense he had been. They don't hear him, and for a moment he considers leaving; they look so peaceful.

He walks around quietly to face them. Nana is asleep, her head slumped against April, who holds a pillow over her own stomach. Although he is standing right beside her, she is not aware of him. On the screen, a television evangelist pounds his fist on a pulpit and speaks of the fires of hell. April watches with eyes glazed, and Oliver sees she is elsewhere. He kneels beside her.

"April," he says. She blinks, turning to him glassy-eyed. His skin chills; he wonders if she is stoned. "Hey, are you okay?"

April draws a breath with some effort. "The fireworks freak her out," she says. "Reminds her of the war."

Oliver isn't sure which war she means, but he nods.

"She's asleep now. Shall we put her to bed?"

April nods, and this, too, is labored. Oliver kneels on the floor by Nana's feet, peels open the Velcro on her orthopedic shoes, and slips them off. He puts her leg brace beside the coffee table. Nana is breathing deeply, mouth open. "Her dentures out?" Oliver asks. April nods. Oliver puts one arm behind Nana's back, the other under her knees, and lifts her. He is alarmed by how light she is—ninety pounds at the most. Her skin, damp and cool, has the texture of cellophane. He carries her to the bedroom and sets her down.

When he comes back, he switches off the set, turns on a lamp, and is relieved to see no marks on April's face or arms.

"She hates Independence Day," she says, staring at the dead screen.

Oliver sits on the sofa beside her, the cushion warm from Nana. "April, what's going on?"

She turns to him unsteadily, licking her lips. "She shouldn't be living alone anymore. I offered to move in with her, but she's right: Who knows who might show up at the door? We've got to convince her to move in with your father."

"He's been trying for years. But I'm talking about you, April."

"What kind of world is it where a man can set fire to his son?"

Oliver's blood chills. "A free one." There is a faint aroma in the room he cannot identify. Something warm and redolent and unsettling.

"Six foster homes in ten years. Who was looking out for him?"

"April, you aren't well."

"Then he joined the army, straightened himself out, and learned to be a mechanic. When he got out, he met a girl who actually loved him, and he felt his whole life would change. When they made love he thought how easy it would be to snap her little bones with his hands, and he prayed never to do that, prayed to be free of the need to set fire to everything that made sense. But his prayers weren't good enough."

Oliver sighs, running his hand through his hair. "Did you see him again today, after he left my father's house?"

April turns to him, her eyes more focused now. "Imagine a boy who grows up without a single person who loves him. Imagine if I had grown up without you, Oliver? Who's to say I wouldn't have killed by now? Who's to say I haven't?"

Oliver swallows, still unsure if she is high. Her voice is thick, her eyes shiny.

"Look, you're full of shrapnel," she says. "I've discharged everything on you."

"You're not making sense."

"Debris," she says. "I've been trying to tell you."

He hesitates.

"Al says I'm a junkie, addicted to abuse."

"Don't believe that."

"T.J.'s hooked on bourbon. What's the difference?"

He hesitates.

"This is what I think. Addiction is just a way of trying to get at something else. Something bigger. Call it transcendence if you want, but it's a fucked-up way, like a rat in a maze. We all want the same thing. We all have this hole. The thing you want offers relief, but it's a trap. Same with my father. Every shot of whiskey, a promise."

Oliver touches her hand on the pillow and finds it cold. He cups his fingers over hers.

"I want to get up," she says. "Just walk away and leave myself behind."

Oliver trembles. "April, tell me what you took."

She closes her eyes for a second, and when she opens them they appear to have rolled back in her head. She refocuses, her head nodding, and Oliver feels his skin prickle with fear. He touches her face and finds that it is searing. She leans back and closes her eyes.

The scent is stronger now, more familiar. Oliver remembers the time Al almost cut off his finger with their father's saw. A chill sweeps down his spine.

"Oliver," she says. "It might be worse than I thought."

He lifts the pillow from her stomach, and sees that it is soaked with blood. He gasps, but no breath comes. For an instant his lungs lock. April does not stir. Her shirt is torn and saturated. Her teeth chatter.

The room transfigures; Oliver is passing through a portal, one element to another. Colors appear as in a film that switches from black-and-white. He sees the bluishness of her lips, the paleness of her face, the bracken-like shape of blood on her shirt. Sounds come to him in a magnified way, like music played at the wrong speed. The raggedness of her breathing, and the distant sound of his grandmother's snores. He feels the air in the room touching his skin, the undulation of space, the fluidity of things he thought fixed.

Even as his perception slows and warps and heightens, he works quickly, pressing the pillow over the wound, lifting her in his arms, running. He hardly recognizes himself, this other Oliver, who knows what to do.

He moves faster than seems possible, hears his own pulse roar in his ears, yet everything feels slow. "Hold on," he tells her. "Stay with me." He maneuvers her into the car, straps the seat belt over the pillow to keep pressure on the wound. "Do you hear me? Stay awake."

Her eyes flutter, attempting to obey, but as he drives, her head slumps against the window. Her hand lies across the emergency brake, fingers limp. He leans on the horn and speeds through lights. He feels the presence of the hospital just seven blocks away, the car hurling in a trajectory toward it. He glances over to see if she is breathing, but he cannot tell. He forces himself to take breaths, resist panic. He can keep her alive through the force of his will. "April," he shouts, but there is no response.

Outside the ER, Oliver runs around to her side of the car and reaches in for her.

"Whoa, there." A man wearing medical garb stamps out a cigarette before trotting over to them. "We got it from here," he says, shouting to someone inside. He takes his time checking her vitals. To Oliver, everything is taking much too long. Finally someone appears with a gurney.

The waiting room is full. An elderly drunk lays passed out in a chair. A little girl vomits into a plastic plant.

The nurse at the triage desk waves to Oliver, telephone in the crook of her neck. "Trauma code," she says into the phone. "Gun-shot?" she asks, hanging up.

"I don't know," Oliver says.

"How long has she been out?"

"Five minutes. I'm not sure."

"What's your name, sir?"

"Night," he says absently. "Oliver."

A pock-faced orderly in blue medical garb pushes through the double doors. He moves quickly in a kind of dance, shoes squishy on the waxed floor. He hums under his breath as he takes hold of the gurney. Oliver holds the door open for him.

"You can't go in there," the nurse calls.

Oliver ignores her, his hand gripping the cool metal of the stretcher. The orderly doesn't care. April lies still. In the hallway, people are hurrying. They jostle one another in the entrance to the trauma room.

April is wheeled in, three nurses appearing at her side, a curtain pulled hastily around them. In the next bed, Oliver sees the white knuckles of a teenage boy gripping a bed rail as his forehead is su-tured. One nurse checks April's breathing, another her pulse, a third applies pressure to the wound with a mountain of gauze that goes in-stantly red. They call numbers to one another in calm, urgent voices and cut the clothing from April's body.

A doctor slips through the curtain, snapping a pair of latex gloves over his thin, graceful hands. "Are you hurt?" he says to Oliver.

Oliver is startled to be noticed. He feels absent, observing a dream.

He looks down at his shirt, saturated with blood, and wavers. "No," he answers. "It's hers."

"Then you'll have to wait in the lobby."

Oliver steps back but continues to stare through a gap in the curtain.

"What do we have here?" the doctor says, looking at April. A face mask and hair cap reveal only his eyes, pinched and exhausted. "Stabbing?" he asks, prying the wound with his fingers.

"Looks that way. Pressure's down," says a nurse.

"Prep the OR," he says, holding down a bandage. "We'll need blood. Do we know her type?"

"O positive," Oliver says. The universal donor. He knows because his is the same.

"Look, you'll have to leave," says one of the nurses.

"But wait outside," the doctor says. "We'll need to talk."

Oliver doesn't move. April is coming to, eyes fluttering.

"Good," says the doctor, taking her hand with his bloody, gloved fingers. "Tell us what happened." The orderly tries halfheartedly to escort Oliver from the room. "What happened?" repeats the doctor.

Oliver moves inside the curtain, and April appears to see him. She opens her mouth to speak. Licks her lips. He imagines she will call out to him, ask him not to leave her, but instead she says, "I'm fine, really," and closes her eyes.

Chapter
19

W HEN BERNADETTE FINDS APRIL'S ROOM, she pauses outside the door. Oliver's call startled her from sleep. In her
dream she had been tumbling inside the arc of a wave, overpowered
but strangely free. Now, as she stands outside the door, the atmo-
sphere of the dream lingers. She did not recognize his voice, gravelly
and wan. He launched into particulars, twenty-eight stitches, blood
transfusion, concussion. It took her a moment to realize he was talking about April. Bernadette rushed over, though he said it wasn't
necessary, April was stable and he would meet Bernadette for dinner
with the details. Still, Bernadette wants to see for herself.

She pushes open the door. The blinds are drawn, the room
shrouded in dusky light. Everything is still except for the drip of the
IV. Oliver sits beside the bed, head cradled in his arms on the mat-
tress. His elbow touches April's upper arm. They are asleep.

Bernadette brings her hand to her mouth. What she can see of
Oliver's face is ashen, his hair disheveled. Though sleeping, there is
tension around his eye. Crumpled atop the hazardous-waste bin lies
his bloodstained shirt, a yellow polo she gave him for his birthday.
Against the lemon fabric the blood is shockingly dark, almost black.
Oliver wears a blue hospital gown over his jeans like an expectant

dad in a maternity ward. April's face is turned away, her dark hair fanned out across the pillow. Bernadette's gaze circles back to his elbow, April's arm, the meeting of bare skin.

Bernadette considers the right thing to do. Her hand on his shoulder might be enough to rouse him. She imagines him jumping from his chair, embracing her. She pictures him saying, *Oh, Bernadette, thank God you're here.* She knows Oliver, guileless and candid. Yet if she leaves now, continues on her way to the petting zoo, he will spend all day in that chair without a thought of her. She knows him. She knows Oliver.

It is April she's not sure about. Bernadette has discussed it many times now with her mother over tea, April's coyness at the funeral, Oliver's sleeping at her place, the scene at the picnic. "Can't you see the obvious?" her mother said, setting down her teacup.

"Apparently not," Bernadette said flatly.

"He needs someone to rescue."

"I'm not sure, Mom. This April, she may have problems, but she's no Fay Wray."

"All the better because she doesn't want to be helped. That makes for a powerful chemistry. You'll have to play this right, Bernadette."

"It's not like they're flirting, Mom. Just the opposite. They're downright snappy to each other."

She frowned, dabbing her mouth with a napkin. "They have something to work out, Bernadette. If you bad-mouth her, he'll only feel protective. If you criticize him, you'll make him defensive. Just ride it out, sweetheart. Be her friend. Who knows? The worst may already be over."

Bernadette stares at them sleeping. *No,* she thinks, *not by a long shot.*

The room is quiet. It takes her a moment to notice that their breathing is synchronized. Bernadette's eyes brim. She wants to hate the tranquil beauty of the room. Instead, she is entranced. *It's going to be okay,* she tells herself. *Oliver is a good person. Nothing bad will happen.*

If she doesn't leave soon, she'll be late for the kids. What's the point of waking him? Bernadette goes over, caresses Oliver's shoulder and back, and when that doesn't work gives him a solid shake.

Chapter
20

WHEN APRIL TRIES TO OPEN HER EYES, white-hot light pours into her skull. She hears voices, first Oliver's, then others she does not recognize. Latex fingers lift the sheet, poking around at her side. She feels a stab of pain and looks down at where she's being prodded. Her vision blurs. There's something pinching her skin. Stitches? Then she notices she's wearing a blue gown. She tries to focus on the person touching her, a nurse.

"Hard to believe she drove a car like that," a voice says.

"Can I talk to her now?" says another.

"I'd rather not disturb her," says the nurse.

April opens her eyes, blinking at the painful light. "I'm awake," she says. Her throat is parched. The sound of her voice sends reverberations through her skull. "What hospital is this?"

"Jamaica," says the nurse. "Not yet, darlin'." She puts her hand on April's shoulder. "The doctor will let you know when you can sit up."

"April," Oliver says, bending close. The cadence of his voice is deeply familiar, comforting in its nearness, yet faraway; she is trapped in a well, his words floating down to her. "Just relax. You don't have to talk to anyone until you're ready."

"I'll talk," she says, struggling to focus. Oliver's face is pale, eyes ridged with exhaustion, his hair tousled as when they were kids. *What have I done to him?* she thinks. He backs away, fists balled, and gives someone his seat.

"I don't understand why you need to question her," Oliver says. "We know who did this."

"Do we?" the man answers.

Squinting, April sees the familiar dimpled chin, olive skin. He's lost the leopard-print tie and is wearing a tan chamois shirt. "Arredondo," she says, licking her dry lips. "You're out of your precinct."

"Thought I'd pay you a visit," he says, patting her hand.

"How did you know I was here?"

"Give me some credit. I'm a detective." He smiles. "So how you feeling, doll?"

"Never better."

Arredondo smirks at Oliver. "A regular Joan of Arc."

Oliver doesn't return the smile.

"So, want to tell us what happened last night?" Arredondo says.

"I'd just gotten out of my car. He came up from behind me," she says, trying to shift in the bed. It feels like she weighs a thousand pounds. "Do you mind if I keep my eyes closed?"

"Suit yourself. I'll do the listening."

"He put his arm around me like we were old chums, pressed the knife against my ribs so I could feel it, and said, *'Give me your purse or I'll cut you in half.'* I thought that was a strange way to put it, like he'd actually take the time to saw all the way through. Houdini, the mugger. I almost laughed. It's a bad habit of mine, laughing when I shouldn't."

"Did you see what he looked like?"

"Dirty-blond, short, mid-thirties. He smelled like anisette."

"Okay, keep going."

"I told him he could have the money but I needed the purse."

Arredondo frowns. "Didn't anyone ever tell you that's the wrong answer?"

"I have a picture of my brother in there, his First Communion. There are no other copies."

"Go on."

"He called me a crazy bitch and started pulling the purse. Then I realized someone had come up behind us. It was T.J. He had a gun, the same one as before, small and silver. He told the guy to drop the knife. '*Idiot,*' the guy said. '*Now I need to kill you both.*'" She blinks open her eyes but the light still hurts. "I'm not sure what happened next. I heard the shot. I guess the guy came down on top of me between the parked cars, because that's where I was when I woke up. I don't know how long I was out. I came to when the car next to me started up. The driver never saw us. I thought he was going to run right over me, but I rolled out of the way in time. He crushed the dead guy's hand, though. Never stopped to see what he'd run over. When I got up the first thing I did was throw up. I don't know why. I thought I'd better call an ambulance, even though I could see the guy was dead. I called from the pay phone at the station, and then I just got in my car and drove. I saw the ambulance pull in as I was pulling out. I knew I'd have to talk to the police, but I figured I could do it in the morning. I wasn't thinking. I felt so bad. I just wanted to be with my grandmother."

"It didn't occur to you that you might need some medical help?"

"I didn't know I was hurt. I mean I felt the pain, but I thought it was from the fall. When I was in the phone booth some people walking by stared at me. That's when I saw the blood, but I thought it was his. Once I was at my grandmother's house, I realized I was bleeding, but by then I wasn't sure I could get up off the couch, and besides, I didn't want to scare her."

Arredondo raps his fingers on the metal bed rail.

"She was in shock," the nurse puts in. "It's not unusual."

"What about Desole?" Arredondo asks.

"I told you, I passed out."

"And he didn't call you an ambulance, a gentleman like him?"

April opens her eyes and looks up at the ceiling, which appears to pulsate. "I don't know," she says. "Maybe he thought I was dead."

"Sure," Arredondo says, raising his eyebrow. "Did he contact you again since you called me last week?"

She glances behind Arredondo to where Oliver stands against the wall, his arms folded tightly in front of him. "He showed up at my uncle's house yesterday. I was going to call you in the morning, it being a holiday and all."

He shakes his head.

"Look, T.J. didn't do this."

Arredondo glances back at Oliver. They exchange a dismayed look.

"I'm not defending him," she says. "I'm just saying it was the other guy who stuck me."

Arredondo says, "Where do you think he is now?"

April looks to the window, Oliver staring out, hands clenched in his pockets. The subdued light framing his silhouette trans-fixes her.

"April?" says Arredondo.

"I don't know. Like I said, he wanted to go to Wichita."

"Until we find him, I want you to have someone with you all the time, understand?"

She nods, which only makes her headache worse.

"You get any more out of her, give me a call." He hands Oliver his card. "He may not have done this, but he's still wanted for murder."

"He didn't do that," April says. "It was a suicide."

"Still a true believer, eh, sweetheart?"

"What he needs is detox," April says, "counseling, rehab, a different set of parents, a single foster home instead of a dozen. Not jail."

"Boo-hoo," says Arredondo. He extends his business card between his fingers like a cigarette. "Hold on to it this time," he says. "You hear from him, I expect a call."

She takes the card.

Once the detective is gone, Oliver sits beside April, his eyes narrow and pained. "I don't understand," he says. "How could you defend him?"

She doesn't answer because nothing she could say would satisfy him. Instead, she closes her eyes, turning her face away. "Oliver, I'd like to be alone for a while."

"Oh, well," he says, standing. "By all means."

She looks at him. His skin is sallow, his eyes dark. Sleeves rolled up. A bandage in the crook of his right arm. April jolts, wondering if Oliver has given her blood.

"You can have all the solitude you want," he says.

He starts to leave then turns back suddenly. "You knew, didn't you, about the dead wife."

She turns her face away.

"It's a sickness, April. Only a deranged person would date a murderer."

She doesn't argue.

"What is it, the melodrama? Adrenaline? What do you get off on? Maybe you want him to kill you so you don't have to deal with your screwed-up life. Then we can remember you with pity and say *poor girl,* instead of seeing you alive and saying, *what a mess.*"

She closes her eyes, trying to sandbag the rush of emotion.

"It wasn't your date who gave you that lip after the barbecue, was it."

She looks out the window, mentally folding herself up like a seedling in reverse, curling back into the shell, underground, where his voice can't reach her.

"You couldn't have told someone he was back? What kind of idiocy is that?"

She tries to sink deeper, insulate herself, but it's not working. What Oliver doesn't understand is that she doesn't fear T.J. because he can't hurt her. Only Oliver can do that.

"The sicker they are, the more you love them, is that it? And this won't be the end of it, either. There will be another one out there—

the most vicious, pathetic, hard-luck case in all of New York, and by God you'll find him. You'll love him until he breaks every little bone in your body." Oliver's chest heaves, his eyes wide and startled. "I'm washing my hands, April. I can't take it anymore."

He leaves the room.

April clenches the sheet. She hears a roar in her head, a river breaking its banks. The pain tears at her stitches. It hurts not because she is a failure, but because he finally sees so.

Chapter

21

T.J.'S FIRST AWARENESS IS OF THE PAIN in his neck. Next, his need to urinate. He has fallen asleep in his truck. He sits up stiffly and blinks at the unfamiliar scene. Skyscrapers appear to shoot straight up, piston-like, out of the river before him.

It is an hour or so before daybreak, the blackness of the sky just beginning to thin. He makes out the shapes of the Chrysler, Empire State, and the wedge-roofed Citicorp. Closer still is Battery Park, the Woolworth building, and the empty space where the Trade Towers stood. He has never seen Manhattan from this side, which he figures for Jersey.

He gets out to pee and the wind hits him like an unblocked punch. He holds on to the car door for balance, hears the loud clanking of flagpoles, and looks around to see that he is in a huge, desolate place, littered with blowing trash. The air smells like last night's fireworks.

He looks for somewhere to take a piss, but there is nothing except grass and gravel and distant buildings he does not want to go near. He walks to the river, lined by a wide cement walkway and heart-shaped viewing binoculars rocking in their stands. He tries to pee into the river, but the wind blows it who-knows-where. His hand shakes as he zips. He wonders if there's anything left in the bottle under his seat in the truck.

As he turns back, he sees a shape rising up out of the river, taller than possible, the green folds of her cloak cemented in the hard wind. He sees the sharp prongs of her crown, the raised torch. Her back is to him, her face turned toward open water.

He saw the statue in person once before, he must have been five or six, aloft on his father's big shoulders, his father's hands circling his ankles to keep him from falling. Together they climbed the narrow stairs to the top and looked out at the world through the windows of her crown.

The wind causes his eyes to water. He stands until color begins to spread on the water beneath the far-off expanse of the Verrazano. Ferries rock in their berths. He remembers the Lady Liberty key chain he kept through his twenties, finally lost in a sewer drain.

Once he is back inside the truck, he notices the steering wheel. Then his hands. His shirt. He cannot tell in the darkness what the stains are. He turns over the ignition but the truck bucks and stalls. The gas gauge is below E; he drove here on fumes. He leans back, looking out at the last stars fading.

Clear as yesterday, he gazes through the drugstore window at Denise standing in line. The man behind her was asking her something. She giggled, head cocked, looking up into his long face. She shifted her weight like a nervous horse, fidgeting with her ring. Their arms brushed and neither backed away. T.J. stepped out of sight as they left the store. The man's Firebird was at the curb. He motioned to it. She shook her head, glancing at her watch. He opened the door, insisting. She glanced around, perhaps feeling T.J.'s eyes though he was supposed to be at work, miles away. When she walked away from the car, T.J. was almost disappointed; the rage he had been brewing was so sweet. The man pulled out of his spot and intercepted her at the next corner. They talked for a moment through the car window, and then, in one swift motion, she looked over her shoulder and slipped in.

T.J.'s blood surged, drunk with the power of certainty, which must have been how his father felt when he dragged T.J., seven years old, out of the kitchen—the clear knowledge that there was no other choice. His mother's screams were far away, inside glass. *You want me to admit to something I didn't do? Fine, I fucked the mailman. But don't hurt my baby or I'll kill you.* Oddly, T.J. was not afraid. His father was so calm, he was sure nothing bad could happen. Not until they were in the alley and his father pulled T.J.'s pajamas taut did he see he was reaching for his lighter. What impresses T.J. now is how his father had the presence of mind to do it outdoors, so as not to damage the color TV.

T.J. does not remember getting out of his truck again, but he is knee-deep on a steep embankment, the Hudson frothing over stones. He washes his face, hands, and sleeves. He takes off the shirt and lets it float away. The stains have soaked his arms like tattoos. He cannot remember whose blood it is, or where he's been living, or how long since his mother died. He wants to take off his skin, to douse the crackle of flesh and the smell of burned hair. He'll swallow the river if that's what it takes to wash the ash from his breath.

He feels the chill of water inside his clothes, over his shoulders, the current nudging him off the embankment. He sees his father lift him over the waves, waiting until the last minute before hauling him up by his hands, the two of them laughing, his father's grin clamping a Camel.

He remembers in one of his foster homes sleeping each night with a spotted beagle, the milky warm puppy curled against T.J.'s stomach.

He remembers when April once kissed him like she actually meant it; he feels the warmth of her skin, the heat of sun on his hair. The water turns pink. A drop of fire forms on the liquid horizon, earth and sky tearing in two. He remembers her last words, not the sound but the feel of them.

He sees what he has done. April in his arms on the ground. He holds her for a few seconds, but it might as well be his whole life. She is dead, or maybe it's him. He feels their thoughts running through each other like a school of fish that splits and merges. They are two, then one, and then two again. He applies pressure to the wound, but the blood moves through his fingers. Her closed eyes look calm; she is up in the crown and can see for hundreds of miles. Thousands of years. Oceans forming. The universe floating out like the hem of his mother's dress when she and his father danced.

He only has to relax his resistance slightly for the current to take him. He can't swim but knows how to float. His buoyancy and the river's speed surprise him. The water sways and rolls him the way it had before he was born, turning in the womb, whole and without scars.

Chapter

22

A GRAY CAR PULLS UP. Is it by coincidence that Oliver arrives
now, or did he leave word with the nurses to call if April was
released? Her cab is late. She stands outside the hospital holding on
to an awning pole.

Oliver slams his door and comes around to her. His arms and legs
move rigidly, without cadence, an instrument strung too taut. He
stands before her with hands on his hips.

"This isn't a prison," she says.

The sun appears through a tear in the gauzy sky, and though she
is wearing sunglasses, the sensation is like a hot coal leaning on the
inside of her skull.

He folds his tanned arms across his chest. "Who brought your
clothes?" he asks.

"Does it matter?"

"It does if it was T.J."

"It was Al, okay?"

"Al," he says. "And you told him it was because you hated the hospital gowns, not because you were planning to check out, right?"

The ground undulates like the deck of a boat; she nearly loses her balance. Oliver grabs her arm. "Come on," he says. "We're going back in."

She jerks her elbow away. "Oliver, I've been here for three days with no health insurance. Do you know what that adds up to?"

"Now's not the time to worry about money."

She laughs, pain shooting up the sides of her face. The taxi turns into the lot and she starts for it. Oliver takes her arm. "If you're going to be stubborn about this, at least let me drive you."

"No."

"Miss Simone?" A nurse with thick white hair and a young face hurries from the hospital entrance. "I just reached your doctor. She says she knows she can't make you stay, but please don't do anything that's going to open those stitches. Are you taking her?" she asks Oliver.

"Yes."

"Make sure she stays in bed. A few days at least. That's a serious wound. You need to let it heal, Miss Simone. Same with the skull fracture. Are you listening to me?"

"Thanks," April says. "I'll be careful."

The taxi honks. April and Oliver raise their hands in unison, April beckoning the cab and Oliver waving it on.

"Call with the name of her pharmacy," the nurse says. "She'll need some painkillers."

"No drugs," she says, eyeing the cabbie evilly as he pulls away.

"She needs to keep still," the nurse says, addressing Oliver.

He nods, opening the passenger door of his car. He waits. "If I had my way, I'd drag you back inside."

"How comforting," she says.

"Why don't you get in the car before you fall down."

She winces as she maneuvers into the seat and sees her pain register on his face. He circles around and gets behind the wheel. They drive for a few minutes in tense silence. She notices a large dark stain on the passenger seat. When the realization hits her, she sucks in air more loudly than she means to.

"Don't worry," he says. "It will wash out."

"Blood on tan leather?" She covers her mouth with her hand. "I'll pay for it to be detailed," she says, "and if that doesn't work—"

"You're not getting it, are you." He glances over at her. "You're alive, April. A car is a car."

She bites her lip, looking out the window. "What about washing your hands?"

He glances in his rearview, shifting lanes. "I was tired." He drives with one hand on the wheel, the other draped on the door, tapping.

"How much blood did you give me?" she asks.

"A pint is all they allow."

She looks down at her hands.

"You would have done the same for me if I were in trouble."

"But you never are."

The blur of northbound cars across the median makes her head ache. She massages her temple. Oliver glances over. She wants to thank him, to apologize for everything, but she has no way of talking to him except the old way. "You missed the exit," she snaps.

"Don't tell me you were planning to stay at your place. What, so he can come back and finish you off?"

She clamps her hands together, staring out the window. "Arredondo called me this morning. They found his truck in Jersey."

"Oh?"

"I think he may have killed himself."

"Were there signs of that in the car?"

"No, it's just a feeling."

"Forgive me if I need more evidence."

April wakes in the middle of the night blind with pain. There is a stabbing sensation on the inside of her skull like a bird pecking its way out. The air-conditioning is high and a comforter lies across her. Not the hospital. The pillow smells vaguely of sandalwood; Oliver gave her his bed. She remembers now that he went out with Bernadette, saying he might not be home till morning, which April appreciates.

She sits up, feeling the equilibrium shift in her head like a yolk in a shell. He left two Tylenol on the nightstand—not the whole bottle, she notices. Beside the pills, the digital clock glows 3:53. She takes the tablets, fingers trembling, and makes her way to the kitchen for water. As she reaches for a glass, she feels a pang in her stomach. The wound would be more painful if not for the headache. She manages to fill the glass with water, but as she brings it to her mouth, her hands shake so violently she cannot sip.

"April?" Oliver flips the switch. She gasps, light piercing her eyes. "Sorry," he says, turning it off. She did not hear him come in. She is leaning against the sink, holding the glass with two hands, water spilling over the edge. She sets it down.

He comes up behind her, touches her neck and forehead. "You're on fire," he says. "Did you take the antibiotics?"

"Yes," she says, but her voice is so weak, she regrets speaking.

Oliver reaches for the tablets on the counter, his chest to her back, hand on her waist. He smells of cognac, sweat, and Bernadette's perfume. He places one tablet in her mouth, squarely centered on her tongue, his fingers salty. She shivers. He positions his hands over hers on the glass, guiding it to her lips. She swallows, feeling him lean into her. She takes another sip. The water is cool in her throat. As she tilts her head back, she feels his breath in her hair.

He lowers the glass and brings the other tablet to her lips. Her eyes fill as he leans into her. "Come on," he says. "One more."

She parts her lips, head tilted back. He slips the pill into her mouth. A tear moves down her temple into her hair. He guides the glass to her mouth. She drinks, swallowing until the glass is empty. *Don't turn around,* she tells herself. *Don't look at him.*

He takes ice chips from the freezer, wraps them in a dishcloth, and guides April to the living room. He props cushions against the arm of the sofa and leans against them, feet up, and draws April in front of him, her back to his chest, a human pillow. He places the ice pack on her forehead.

She glances at the piano, cluttered with textbooks and law journals. "Oliver," she says, "play me something."

He is silent for a moment. "It's out of tune."

"I don't care what it sounds like."

"Trust me, it's unplayable."

She touches his fingers, long and graceful. His hands are one thing about him that hasn't changed. When they were young, she used to tease him that he had an old man's hands. *He's growing into them,* she thinks. "Oliver." She turns to one side so she can look up at him. "I'm sorry."

It is the first time she can remember saying those words to him. She feels him pause for a beat, go perfectly still.

"For what?" he asks.

"Everything. From the beginning."

He moves his arms around her waist, careful of her wound, and closes his eyes. "April," he says. "I'm not."

April is awakened by the sound of a car door. Her headache has cleared; the room is bright. She guesses it is past nine. In sleep she has rolled over and is lying with her cheek to Oliver's chest. His hand rests on her shoulder blade, inside her sleeveless nightshirt. She can't remember him putting it there. They fell asleep, and now, as she awakens, she feels a jolt of panic. She sits up. Oliver stirs, blinking at her, emerging from a dream. "April," he says. She hears footsteps on the front walk. Oliver's eyes fly open. April stands and rushes into the bedroom just as the front door opens.

"Honey?" Bernadette calls.

"Hey," Oliver says.

"I brought some eggs and bacon. How is she?"

"I don't know," he says, sitting up.

"You slept in your clothes?"

He looks down at himself. "I didn't want to wake her. My pajamas are in the bedroom."

Bernadette laughs. "Since when do you wear pajamas?"

"Since I have a guest."

"Ah."

April groans silently, ashamed. Lying is unnatural for him, and he's terrible at it. She heads for the shower.

As the water stings her wound, she remembers that she is not supposed to shower until the stitches come out. She turns and lets the water massage her back. The pain fades. Her head clears under the warm deluge. She uses Oliver's shampoo, which carries the sandalwood aroma she associates with him. When the hot stream runs between her legs she leans back against the tile. It was a mistake to stay here.

She dresses, makes the bed, and calls a taxi from the bedroom phone. Her headache is starting in again, but she wills it off. She smells bacon and coffee.

April finds them in the kitchen, Bernadette flipping an omelet, Oliver stirring sugar into his Jamaican blend. "Morning," she says, and they turn to her at once. She is struck again by how right they look together.

"Oh, God," Bernadette says. "You look awful."

"I was just thinking how I felt better," April answers, taking a piece of bacon. "Oliver, on the other hand, looks like he could use some more sleep. That couch isn't long enough for you, is it."

"I slept fine," Oliver says, looking at her.

"Oliver's pale," Bernadette says. "You're green."

April smiles.

"Sit down and eat," Bernadette says. "Food does wonders."

"Thanks, but I have to go."

Oliver looks up. "I hope you're kidding."

"We won't let you go," Bernadette says. "If you could see yourself, you'd understand why."

April looks in the mirror over the piano. "Don't I always look like this?"

"Sit down," Oliver says.

"My cab's here already. See?"

"Where do you think you're going?"

"Where else?"

Oliver drops his spoon into his coffee, shaking his head.

Bernadette puts her hands on April's shoulders tightly. "If I felt crummy, I'd want to be in the comfort of my own place, too. But didn't the police tell you not to stay there until he's caught?"

April wraps her sweatshirt around her middle and folds her arms. "He's dead," she says. "They told me as much."

"That is not what they said," Oliver says firmly.

"Look," Bernadette says. "It's hard to think straight when you feel lousy. Just stay with me tonight. Tomorrow we'll leave you alone. Promise."

April's head is throbbing again. She wants to get out of here before she starts shaking.

Bernadette puts her arm around April's shoulder and gives an insistent squeeze. "One night," she says.

"Okay, fine," April says, if only so she'll let go. "But I still have to go back to my place for a few hours. I've got bills to pay, and laundry. Who knows where they put the mail once the box was full."

"Good," says Bernadette. "I'll write down my address."

As Bernadette goes back to the kitchen for a pen, Oliver meets April's eye. She wants to be angry at him, but he looks so worried.

"Oliver," she says. "I appreciate everything you've done."

"You are the most stubborn person I've ever—"

"*Me?*" she says in a shrill whisper.

Bernadette reappears. April and Oliver turn away from each other in unison. Bernadette looks at Oliver questioningly before handing April the address.

"Thank you," April says. "I'll be there after dinner, nine or so, if that's okay."

"Fine," Bernadette says. "But you're welcome sooner."

April kisses Bernadette's cheek but only waves at Oliver. How could she be so stupid? The last thing she wants is to stay at yet another person's place. She wants her own bed. She wants her life back the way it was before, before what? Before the mugging? Before Buddy died? Before she met T.J.? Her mind keeps reaching back. What is it? Before what? Then it hits her. Quincy. She wants her life back the way it was before Quincy.

How absurd. Half her life ago. And why is this taxi so damn quiet? "Hey." She taps impatiently on the bulletproof partition separating her from the driver. "Don't you have a radio?"

After paying, April walks to the parking lot to see where she left her car. Wedged between the steep embankment of the train tracks and Sunrise Highway, the lot is narrow and endless. She has no idea where she parked; it seems so long ago. Then it occurs to her that she left the car at Nana's house. "Shit," she says aloud. Alternate-side-of-the-street parking; she's probably got three tickets by now. As she turns back toward her apartment, she notices police tape stuck beneath the wheel of a car. Was it here, so close to the station office? A large stain darkens the asphalt. The shape reminds her of a map. She sees Florida, Maine, even Texas; only the West Coast is wrong, with an extra rivulet suggesting the earthquake had already happened.

She doesn't know any more about the dead man than what she read in the newspaper: He worked the meat counter at a local grocery store, but had lost his job six months ago; drug paraphernalia was found in his apartment, which was above the Irish pub just across Sunrise. If not for the trestle between them, April could see his window from hers.

Once inside she wanders through the apartment and sits on the bed. On her night table sits a collection of Mirabai poems, four days overdue. A pigeon struts at the open window, its ebony eyes watchful and pert. It pecks the sill. Beneath the window lie T.J.'s boots, dirty and enormous. When did he leave them here? Why hadn't she moved them? She slips into them, takes a few awkward steps, and feels once more the weight of his existence, the burden he carried every day of his life. She is tired of patterns and probabilities, cycles that won't quit. She steps out of the boots, takes them downstairs, and leaves them at the curb. When the next train pulls in, one of the commuters will take them home, wash away their past with saddle soap, and make them like new again.

April awakes with a start and sits upright in the strange bed. The sudden movement sends shrill pain from her right temple up to the crown of her head. She hears herself cry out, holds her head in her hands, and slowly opens her eyes. Pink floral sheets, a pull-out bed. The room smells powerfully of roses. Dim light seeps into the apartment from behind the shades; it must be just before dawn. Then, focusing, she sees that someone is sitting in an armchair on the other side of the coffee table, her legs tucked up under her bathrobe, a mug of tea cupped in her hands.

"Do you need some aspirin?" Bernadette asks with concern.

April blinks. "Uh, no, it's okay now. It's just when I first sit up. What time is it?"

"I'm not sure," Bernadette says. "Early."

April sits cross-legged on the bed, gathering the sheets around her. On the coffee table between them stands a vase of scarlet roses, just past their peak. Some are spread wide; others droop, their heads bent toward the chessboard beneath them. Petals litter the black and white squares. "Have you been up long?" April asks.

"A little while," she says. "Couldn't sleep."

"Oh, I hope it wasn't because of me."

"Not at all."

Colorful children's art fills the walls, handprints, stick figures, and lollipop trees. Faces beam out of photographs of Halloween parties and wheelchair races. It's a happy apartment, April thinks. Beneath the lamp stands a photograph of Bernadette as a child, cheek-to-cheek with an enormous, round-faced young woman with a gleeful smile. "Your sister?" April asks.

"Yes," Bernadette says affectionately. "She was my best teacher. She made unconditional love look easy."

"You're like that, too," April says.

"Not always," says Bernadette. "I have conditions." She sips her tea, then picks up a bishop from the chessboard and rolls it between her palms. "Do you play?"

April wants to go back to sleep. It's so early. She doesn't understand why they're talking at this hour. "Uh, no. Not really. Buddy liked to, though."

"It's a shame Oliver won't play with me more. He says it's too embarrassing." She smiles. "For an intelligent man, he's terribly gullible. What he thinks I'm going to do is never what I have in mind. He protects the pieces I have no intention of taking and leaves the ones I'm after."

"You must be a good player."

"My mother taught me." She takes another sip, then places her teacup gently on the board. "She's a great lady. She's lived through a lot, raising my sister and then losing her. She's very strong."

April glances around for a clock. She would do almost anything to go back to sleep.

"She told me this amazing story just the other day about my dad when they were first engaged. Would you like to hear it?"

"Uh, sure." April takes her pillow and bunches it up in her lap. She wants to lie down but knows it would be rude.

"He was a good catch, my father: attentive, faithful, hardworking. He was an immigrant and had that do-or-die attitude. He and my mother were happy together. Then one day they went on a double date with a friend of his. The girl his friend brought, it turns out, was from my dad's village in Wales. They didn't remember each other—

he was a few years older than she was—but they knew each other's family names and where their farms were. They talked for hours. My dad was all lit up. It wasn't until that night that my mother realized how much he missed home, and how nothing in Brooklyn would ever compare."

April pulls her knees up to her chest, listening.

"Something in him changed after that. He was distracted. Whenever he saw this girl, he got tongue-tied and clumsy. Then strange things started happening. Her car broke down when her fiancé was out of town, so my dad went to help. Then she fell on some ice. A series of little calamities. My mom thought it was to get my father's attention, even if the girl was only doing it subconsciously. It wasn't that she was a real threat. She was plain looking with dowdy clothes, and hadn't been to college. My dad, by that age, was already quite cultured, and not bad looking. Still, there was something different about the way he laughed with her, a kind of abandon that made my mother nervous. On the other hand, anyone could see they didn't belong together. My mother knew full well it wasn't this woman he loved, but the place she represented, his homeland and his youth."

April studies Bernadette, saying nothing.

"My father's distraction got worse. My mother knew he would never break off the engagement; he wasn't that kind of man. The worst thing that could happen, my mother thought, would be for him to marry her while believing he was in love with this other girl. My mother couldn't talk to him about it because she knew he would genuinely deny everything; he hadn't admitted it to himself yet. So she decided to confront the girl. She said, *'Lucy, if you're going to have a go at it with George, I want you to do it now, before the wedding. I give you my permission. In fact, I want you to get it over and done with. But if it happens after we're married, God help you both.'*" Bernadette laughs. "She was gutsy, my mother. I wish I had her nerve."

April puts her fingertips together lightly in the form of a steeple and touches them to her lips. They gaze at each other awkwardly for a moment. Bernadette looks back to her teacup. "So, how do you think the story ends?"

April laces her fingers together in her lap. "Obviously your parents got married. As for the other part, I'm sure permission alone was enough to prevent it from happening."

"No." Bernadette smiles painfully. "It had to happen. My mother understood that even before my father did. You see, for men it's all about the conquest. He had to have her in order to forget her." She puts down the bishop and picks up the queen. "It's just the way men are."

April doesn't answer, but pulls the blanket more tightly around her. "Bernadette," she says finally. "You don't strike me as someone prone to generalities. No offense, but I wonder if what you said is what you really think."

"I don't know what I think anymore," she says, her voice thickening. "Anyway, it wasn't going to happen on its own. My dad wasn't the philandering type. So my mother planned a trip to visit her sister in Ohio, and while she was gone she asked him to look in on Lucy's furnace." She sets her teacup down. "It was like clockwork."

April looks at her gravely.

"She could tell as soon as she got home that it had worked. He was guilty and attentive. Remorse fosters devotion," she says. "It's the foundation of most religions."

"And the girl?" April asks.

"He realized on his own that she was part of his past, not his destiny, just like my mom knew he would."

April considers this, lightly pulsing her fingertips together. "Your mother must be very sure of herself."

"She had confidence in him, in their love."

April nods slowly.

Bernadette is perfectly still. Early morning light filters slowly into the room. As Bernadette lifts her teacup to her mouth, her hand trembles. Tears stream down her cheeks, hanging from her chin, spotting her silken bathrobe. "The problem is I don't think I'm as strong as my mother."

April slides down to the end of the bed. "Bernadette," she says softly. "Wouldn't it have been enough for this other girl to lay low for a while?"

"Apparently not."

April sits back. "Well, if it wasn't in your father's nature to do something like that, he must have felt awful afterward. I mean, it must have done some damage to how he saw himself. I'm sure neither your mother nor this other girl wanted that for him."

"Of course no one wanted to hurt him." Bernadette looks at her hopelessly. "But my mother didn't know any other way."

"Don't you think your father may simply have felt sorry for that girl? Responsible, somehow, to help her out? Maybe there was some nostalgia, too. Her accent must have felt so familiar to him, so tied to his past. Naturally it stirred him up. But those are passing feelings, Bernadette, not the same as love."

"How do you know?"

April stands and touches her shoulder. "I just do," she says quietly. She heads to the bathroom to change and be on her way. The tiles are icy beneath her feet. She glances back to see Bernadette reaching for her sister's photograph. She wipes the glass with the silken sleeve of her robe.

Chapter

23

O VER THE YEARS, the fence withstood three hurricanes before finally being taken down by an ordinary summer storm.

"I should have replaced it last year," Oliver's father says, hammering plywood to a post. "I saw it going." The dog sniffs at the box of nails, and he shoos her away.

Oliver takes a broken picket and places it on the cutting block. He raises the ax over his head and brings it down, splitting the wood. He likes the clear, clean sound of the crack, likes seeing what he can do with one blow. He has his shirt off, sweat running down his back. It is one of the hottest Julys on record.

"I appreciate your coming over," his father says. "They're installing the new fence next week, but in the meantime I don't want to lose the dog."

Oliver nods, brings the ax down again, and sees the picket fall in two.

His father sits back, resting. After a moment, he lowers his hammer. "You seem preoccupied, son."

Oliver shrugs. "Any more to be cut?"

His father looks around. "Looks like you got it all."

Oliver wipes his brow with the T-shirt he tossed on the grass.

He remembers the day after April left his apartment, when he came back after an early morning run. He was still sweating and wanted to cool off before getting into the shower. He looked around for something to read. The newspaper was not on the piano where he thought he had left it. Something looked different. The stacks of books atop the instrument were more orderly than before; someone had tried to make them look undisturbed. The light slanting through the window illuminated patterns in the dust. A clean rectangle on the varnished wood revealed where a stack had been removed to open the ledge. A cold wave passed through Oliver. He was sure he hadn't touched these piles since school let out. He noticed long streaky lines running through the dust, and moved this own fingers in the same pattern until they came to the knob. He hesitated for a moment before opening the lid. The keys did not have their usual inert aura. A powerful, inexplicable sensation came over him, prickling his skin. She had been here. She had touched the keys.

He placed his fingers on the ivory where he imagined her hands had been. Ever since Nana had hummed one of his songs at Christmas, he'd felt these peculiar moments seeping back into his life, a kind of undertow. He grazed his finger over the keys without depressing them. He heard notes in his mind, felt the presence of an entire song just on the other side of it.

He closed the lid.

Oliver balls up the T-shirt and runs it around his neck to soak up the sweat. His father looks up at him curiously. "How's Bernadette?" he asks.

Oliver sits on the cutting block. "Roman or Gothic, she's trying to decide the font for the invitations."

His father nods, squinting in the sun. "Any nerves?"

"You know her. Forever calm."

"I meant you."

Oliver shrugs. "People get married all the time, right?"

"Not you." His father winks, placing a nail against the wood. He sinks it in with three taps. He pauses, then, noticing Oliver's stillness.

Oliver cups his hands together. "April stayed over one night last week."

His father lowers his hammer.

"The night she left the hospital. I didn't think it was a good idea for her to go back to her place."

His father nods.

Oliver looks at his own hands, dirty from the wood. "Al thinks she brings on her own troubles, that chaos is what feels normal to her."

"If so, then it's her choice, isn't it."

"I'd hardly call it choice."

"We all have habits we'd like to break."

"Coffee and cigarettes, that's one thing. Men who beat you up is another."

"You're assuming a lot."

Oliver bows his head in his hands. "It's weird having someone back in your life after so long. Not that she is," he adds quickly, "back in my life."

His father says nothing.

"All the time we spent together as kids, that feels like a dream now, like someone else's past."

His father looks at him carefully, drawing his hand down the side of his face in that thoughtful way of his. "Come on," he says, standing. "Let's go inside and cool off."

Oliver follows, sure now that he has blurted out too much without having any idea what he means.

He sits in his father's kitchen at the same table where he ate many breakfasts as a child. On the wall near the telephone is a photograph of his parents taken during their honeymoon, outside a rented cabin in Vermont. It appears they are having a leaf fight, laughing, their hair and sweaters covered. His mother's hair was long then, auburn like the leaves. His father hands him a glass of iced tea. Oliver sees that his father is trying to formulate a question, but Oliver isn't sure he wants to hear it.

"Why did you give us Mom's portrait?" Oliver interjects. "You could have kept it yourself."

"It's too perfect," his father says. "This is more like her—her hair tangled, slightly off balance, laughing."

"She always was perfect to me."

"No one is, Oliver."

Oliver stands and looks out the window. "Did you have any doubts when you got married?"

"None."

"What about later?"

"Not me."

"But even when you're married to someone you love, you're bound to be attracted to other people, right?"

His father licks his lips, glancing at Oliver uncertainly.

"I'm speaking hypothetically," Oliver adds.

"The world is full of attractive people."

"So?"

His father straightens in his chair. "I suppose I enjoyed a bit of flirtation, conversation. Sure, I admired other women, but I drew the line. For your mother, it wasn't so easy."

Oliver blinks.

His father looks out the window. "Maybe she ought to have dated more before we got married. I was only her second boyfriend."

Oliver feels confused. Perhaps he shouldn't have brought this up.

His father turns to him. "Oliver, if you have any doubts, work them out now before you wed, because infidelity can devastate a marriage. Even if you resolve it, forgive her, turn the page, it's the trust that's destroyed. You never get her back completely, not the way it was before."

Oliver's mind clamors to make sense of what he has just heard. "Dad, I'm sorry."

His father waves a hand. "Over twenty years ago." He takes a sip, wiping his wet palm on his shorts, but Oliver sees that his father's hand is trembling.

Oliver wants to ask questions, but doesn't. The dog comes into the kitchen, laps water messily, then sits panting at Hal's feet. Hal rubs her ear and Cricket leans into him.

"She wanted to be a singer, you know, but her parents steered her toward secretarial school. After we got married, I always encouraged her to sing, but she was afraid she wasn't good enough." He sighs. "I never thought it was a good idea to start a family so soon, but she didn't want to wait. Those were hard years for her. I was preoccupied with my dissertation. I didn't pay enough attention to her." He puts his head in his hands.

Oliver reaches out to touch his father's shoulder.

His father straightens up, rubbing his face. "It was a onetime thing, not something she planned on. Someone took advantage of her loneliness, and I wasn't around to stop it."

"Dad," Oliver says. "Don't be too hard on yourself."

"I never wanted to hear the details. I was glad she gave her journal away before she died; I never wanted to read it."

"Journal?" Oliver says.

"It was her confidante."

"Where is it now?"

"I told her to give it to someone she trusted. It wouldn't have been right for me to read it."

Oliver thinks for a moment. All at once the hair rises on the back of his neck. "April."

His father doesn't answer, which Oliver takes for affirmation.

"But she was a kid."

"You remember how close they were at the end. She was like a daughter."

"April," Oliver says quietly. Then he sees it, the green fabric cover shiny and tattered, Daisy's arms folded around it and the empty space in the drawer where he had lifted it from April's belongings a decade ago. "Oh, God, it was Mom's."

His father touches his arm. "Don't think less of her, Oliver. I never did."

"I'm going to ask April to give it to me."

"I don't think that's a good idea. For all I know, she asked April to destroy it."

"I'm the son," Oliver says. "April's not even related."

"Mom couldn't have loved you more, but if she chose to give the journal to April, she had a reason."

Oliver stands from the table, suddenly restless.

"I'm sorry, Oliver. I shouldn't have told you this just as you're about to get married. You know I would marry your mother over again in a minute."

"It was obvious you loved her, Dad."

"Bernadette's a good woman."

"I know that," Oliver says. He looks at the photograph next to the phone. He can almost hear his parents' laughter, the crunching of leaves as they fall into them. Then the sudden descent of dusk and the first frigid gust of night.

Chapter

24

A N HOUR AGO, APRIL CALLED NANA to remind her to dress
for the trip, but when she arrives, her grandmother is in her
bathrobe, sifting through a paper bag of birthday cards collected over
the years. They are yellowed and sentimental. Nana is separating
them into piles. Those from Nick, Spencer, Hal and Avila, Bede and
Faith, the grandchildren.

"Nana, what are you doing?"

"It's my birthday," she says. "See?" Using lipstick, Nana has drawn
a vertical red line on her stomach, similar to April's scar. "I'm having
another child," she says.

"No, it's your neighbor downstairs who's pregnant. I told you
yesterday."

"Two husbands, two wombs," she says. "Two wounds."

April shivers. "Let's wash that off. They're waiting for us at the
beach house."

"Whose house?"

"Hal's time-share. Remember we went there last year, and the
year before?" April leads her to the bathroom, Nana unsteady without her leg brace. April soaps up a washcloth and gently wipes the
lipstick from her grandmother's slack abdomen.

"You never replaced my pillow," Nana says.

"I've bought you three new pillows."

"None of them is the same."

"The old pillow is ruined, Nana. What can I say?" She pats her dry.

"Is that boyfriend of yours coming?"

"There's no boyfriend, Nana. No husband, nothing. Got it?"

"I saw him kissing you by the side of the house. I saw him stick you with the dandelion fork, and you bled all over my pillow."

"You've got it all mixed up, Nana. Come on, let's get dressed." She moves her toward the bedroom.

Out on the street, a group of boys laughs and shouts. Nana looks in the direction of the voices. "Buddy dropped by yesterday."

"Really," April says, suddenly drained. She sits on the bed. "What did he have to say?"

"That you killed him."

April's head goes light.

"Never let him win a single game of basketball, even though he was so much younger. Shame on you," Nana says. "Just because Al did the same to you."

April puts her face in her hands and exhales. "I was playing honest," she says. "Improving his game."

Why haven't they told Nana about Buddy? Is it idiocy or cowardice? Honoring the dead is important to her. She still visits Spencer's grave once a month with a single sprig of bougainvillea from a plant flourishing in the dusty sunlight of her alcove. April glances at the plant, wondering how Nana manages to keep it in bloom amid so much forgotten clutter.

On the side table, behind a vase of plastic flowers, April notices a teakettle. She picks it up to find the bottom blackened. "What's this doing here?"

"I pulled it out of the trash. Can you imagine that nurse threw it out?"

"It's burned, Nana."

"Nothing a little elbow grease won't cure."

"How did it happen?"

No answer.

"Nana?"

"She must have turned it on before she left and forgot to tell me."

"But it whistles."

"What does she mean, throwing it out? Am I supposed to go without tea for a week?"

April sighs deeply. "Nana, how would you feel about a roommate?"

"Good grief." Nana turns to face her. "I hope you're not referring to Mr. Bergfalk."

April smirks. "Actually, I was thinking of me."

"You? Live here? Ha!"

"Ha? Why ha?"

"You think I want your crazy boyfriends traipsing through here?"

"No." April flushes. "There wouldn't be any of that."

"You think I need taking care of, is that it? Just because a nurse burned out my teapot, you think I can't cook my own peppers and eggs anymore?"

"Fine, I just thought you might be able to help me out."

"Do you know Hal wants me to move in with him, leave my own house? That will be the day." She pauses. "Help *you* out?"

"My lease is up at the end of October, and the landlord is jacking up the rent."

Nana eyes her wisely.

"Forget it," April says. "I'll just look for a roommate to cut my cost. In fact, there's a guy at the bar who's been looking—"

"Okay," Nana says. "I'll find room for you."

"Well, I wouldn't want to impose."

"Don't worry, missy. I'll make sure you earn your keep."

April grins. "C'mon. They'll be waiting for us at the beach house."

"Will Buddy be there?" Nana asks.

"If we don't hurry, they'll all be gone," April says.

"What about Oliver?"

"Oliver will be there."

"Then why are you dawdling?"

April rolls her eyes.

She enjoys the long drive to the Hamptons, despite the traffic out of Queens. The sky is aquamarine, the breeze warm and salty. In the passenger seat, Nana looks short as a child. One by one she takes out her hairpins and leans against the door, letting her silken hair rise in the wind. "When I was a girl, I used to take the train out here with my friends. I hardly spoke English then."

April smiles.

"In Malaga, my parents' house was half a mile from the beach. On clear days, I thought I could see Africa. My father worked near the Rock of Gibraltar, and I used to carry his lunch to him. The Mediterranean is nothing like the Atlantic. The water there is blue as sapphires."

She gazes out the window.

"As it turned out my sister, the one who stayed, married a rich man from Barcelona. And me? I got Nicky from Staten Island. He looked Spanish, but he wasn't. Acted like he had money, but it went through his fingers like rice."

They ride for a moment in silence. Nana looks over at her. "You were supposed to be Mae, you know. June if you were late. No one expected April. Such an impatient baby. That's how I knew you'd turn out the way you did."

"And how's that?"

"My first April in America I had to walk home from school in a thunder-snowstorm. Ruined my new shoes."

April smiles. "So that's me? Thunder and snow?"

Nana closes her eyes to the breeze. "When I was pregnant, I prayed for a son. But once Bede and Hal were grown, I wished I'd had at least one girl." She opens her eyes, glancing at April. "Someone to talk to."

April has seen pictures of Nana in her twenties, so much like April they could be the same person. There is a difference, though. When Nana smiles with her head tossed back, squinted eyes sparkling, she radiates brilliance and composure April could never hope to match.

"All my life it took me two tries to get anything right," Nana says. "And all of a sudden I'm old."

April takes her hand, chapped and ropy with veins, and holds it.

"I'm not sad," Nana says. "Just the opposite. Everything good in life has been sweeter because it took me twice as long to find it. You're like that."

April smiles. "So you think there's still a chance I might get something right?"

"No one's hopeless," Nana says. "Not even you."

"Thanks." April laughs. "I think."

Nana touches her cross, brings it to her lips, and kisses it. "Here," she says, pulling it over her head. "You need this more than I do." The necklace has been around Nana's neck as long as April can remember. She has never seen her take it off.

"What are you doing?" April says. "Put it back before it gets lost."

"I'm giving you something precious. Are you going to be ungracious about it?"

"Please," April says. "It belongs with you."

Nana opens April's purse on the seat beside her and slips the chain inside.

"Nana, I can't wear that. Spencer gave it to you."

"Actually, no."

"What do you mean?"

"I mean it wasn't Spencer," Nana says, looking down her blouse, adjusting the buttons.

"Well?"

"Did I ever tell you about the time I lost twenty pounds from a kiss? Couldn't eat for months."

"Wait a minute. I thought we were talking about the necklace."

"It wasn't long after I came here from Spain. I had a waitressing job even though I really should have been in school. One day this boy came in. He didn't look much older than me, but he was in a soldier's uniform and had a duffel bag. He was sweet and shy and did a lot of staring out the window, playing with the sugar packages. He hardly ate his eggs. I asked if they tasted okay and he said fine, just fine. He asked my name. Said his was Johnny. He sat there for a long time with his cold cup of coffee and even though the place got busy, I didn't give him his check until he asked for it; he seemed like he was thinking something important.

"When I came out of the kitchen with platters in my hands and noticed his booth was finally empty, I felt disappointed. Then I realized he was standing right in front of me in the aisle between the tables. Before I knew what was happening, he put the chain over my head. I felt the cross go down inside my blouse, warm against my bosom. Heaven above, it was a miracle I didn't drop those plates right then. He cupped his hands around my face and kissed me. I stood there trying to balance an omelet in my right hand and pancakes in my left. It wasn't a long kiss but it wasn't short, either. He took his time. His mouth smelled like coffee and butterscotch. The whole restaurant went completely still. People stared at us like the breath had been snatched out of them. He stepped back, looking at me, and said my name. I can still hear just the way he said it. Then he picked up his duffel bag and left.

"I stood there for what must have been a full minute before I had the presence of mind to put down the plates and follow him out. I was a madwoman. Imagine all those people staring at us, my boss included! What if I had been married? Or had a boyfriend? What right did he have, a perfect stranger? So I ran out into the parking lot. A bus was pulling away from the bus stop, and I chased it. I never ran harder in my life. My lungs burned. Finally the bus turned a corner and I couldn't see it. I fell down and tore my white stockings. Ruined my makeup, too. I'd never been kissed like that in my life, before or since."

"Well," April says finally, clearing her throat. "I'm sure I haven't, either."

"You're still young."

"You don't understand." April chuckles. "Guys today don't waste time with kisses, not the kind you're talking about."

"You mean *your* guys." Nana eyes her. "Keep the cross before I change my mind."

"Nana, I can't. Honestly."

"Why? Because you're afraid to change your life? Fine, live from one black eye to the next."

"What are you talking about?"

"You need to start doing what's uncomfortable for you, April. Because your idea of what feels right took a left turn somewhere."

April looks out the window, feeling the breeze lash through her hair.

"I know you're afraid to lose the necklace," Nana says. "But take the chance. It has no meaning in a box. I want you to wear it."

"All right," April says finally. "But why don't you keep it until Christmas?"

"That's you," Nana says. "Always looking for an out. No, April. The time is now."

Chapter
25

OLIVER POKES AT THE FIRE, causing sparks to rise. The night is cool and sumptuous, the turbulent surf resounding in the darkness. Stars rise over the ocean, the Milky Way teeming into the spray. There are no clouds, yet the air smells of rain.

April draws shapes in the sand, light flickering on her face. Oliver finds it hard to believe only two months have passed since the assault. She appears wholly recovered, radiant, in fact. She smiles at Al as they listen to the chortling snores of Nana, who is stretched out on a lounge chair, mouth agape. April covers her with a beach towel.

"It's all right," Hal says. "I'll bring her up to the house in a minute. It's late for her."

"Come on." Al stands. "Let's go for a dip."

"It's too cold," April says.

"The water's warmer than the air. Once you're under, you'll think you're in heaven." He turns to Oliver and Bernadette. "How about it?"

"Not a chance," Bernadette says, cozying up to Oliver. "I'm in heaven already."

Al rolls his eyes and Bernadette laughs. "No takers?" he says.

"All right," April says. "Why not."

They start down toward the surf. The wind picks up and April's hair whips behind her. It is dark, but Oliver sees her lift her shirt over her head and wade into the ocean. Al lunges ahead of her, diving into a wave. Oliver has never swum at night. The idea spooks him. At times he has waded in up to his knees or hips, felt the cool sensuality of the dark water, but he could never bring himself to dive in.

"They ought to be careful," Bernadette says. "It's about to rain."

The eastern sky flashes. Hal folds his beach chair and rouses Nana. Bernadette picks up empty bottles while Oliver pushes sand onto the fire, trying to smother it. He thinks back to earlier in the day, when he slipped into April's room while she was unpacking.

"Did you bring it?" he asked.

"Oliver," she said, closing her bag. "I think you should wait and think about this."

"Did you bring it?" he asked again.

"I'm not sure what your mother would have wanted. She never explained."

"April. I'll ask you once more."

"No," she said. "Look, I haven't read it myself. I don't feel right."

He bit his lip. "I realize you're trying to do the best thing here, but this is my mother we're talking about. I think I have rights."

"I'm not saying you don't."

"When we get home then," he said. "You'll bring it to me?"

"All right," she said.

April and Al swim out beyond the breakers until Oliver can no longer see them. The surf pounds and wind sucks spray from the waves into Oliver's face. His heart races; he doesn't know why. He places his hand on his chest, feels the blood coursing through him.

"Oliver," Bernadette says. "The fire's out already. Let's go." He looks up at her. She stands shivering, wide-eyed and expectant. His father and grandmother have gone up to the house. "Hurry," Bernadette says. "Before it pours."

He looks at the ocean but it is impossible to see them. He feels random drops sting his face. The rain is cold. He takes Bernadette's arm and pulls her toward him. He kisses her before she can speak. "Oliver," she says. "This is romantic, but I'm freezing." The rain falls harder, soaking his sweatshirt. He pulls it off, draws her down, and lowers himself over her. "You're kidding, right?" she says.

"Tell me you're not tempted," he says.

"Yes, but we're two minutes from a warm, dry bed."

"I want you here."

She looks at him for a moment, then rolls over, straddling him. "Okay, cowboy," she says. "Be careful what you wish for."

The skies open, saturating them, the deluge pummeling Oliver's skin.

When they return to the house, the rain has let up. Most of the lights are out. Giddy, Bernadette kisses Oliver on the stairs and goes up to shower. Oliver pops his head in his father's room. Hal is in bed with a book on his lap. "Should I lock up?" Oliver asks.

"April's out walking," he says. "She'll close up."

Oliver nods. He is wet and sandy. It must be obvious what he and Bernadette were doing out there, but his father pretends not to notice.

"Good night, then," Oliver says.

He paces, waiting for Bernadette to finish. After a moment, the light goes out in his father's room. He hears his grandmother snoring at the end of the hall. The door to April's room is ajar. He hesitates and then enters. Her knapsack is open on the bed. He quickly runs his hands through it, but finds nothing. He is about to leave when it occurs to him to check under the bed pillow. He feels something hard, and pulls out the diary. She lied.

Oliver does not hesitate. He takes the book to his room and slips it into the night table drawer.

The next morning, a few minutes after Bernadette leaves for her morning jog, the door to Oliver's bedroom opens. He supposes she has forgotten something, her water bottle, probably, and doesn't bother to open his eyes. "It's on the dresser," he mumbles.

The door closes again and he feels a whack on his arm. He bolts up.

"Bastard," April says in a fierce whisper. "What is this? Blackmail? Take your mother's goddamn journal. Just give me back mine."

"What?" Oliver says.

She hits him again with the book. "Where is it?"

He is bare-chested, in his boxers. He gets out of bed, disoriented. "What are you talking about?"

She enunciates each word with exaggerated pauses. "Where— is—my—journal?"

"Yours?"

"Don't act like you haven't read it. You were up all night, weren't you."

"Think what you like. I never turned a page." He pulls open the drawer. "Here."

She grabs it, and autumn leaves slip from the pages. They are dry and fragile, perhaps years old. She kneels on the floor, collecting them. Oliver crouches beside her and picks up a blood-red maple leaf, large as a human hand. He gives it to her.

She leaves, slamming the door behind her, and Oliver stands alone in the sun-bleached room. There, tossed on the rumpled sheets is an olive-green book, threadbare and old, the same diary he lifted from April's drawer years before. He picks it up and runs his hand over the binding, feeling the coarse, frayed fabric. He opens to a random page, and sees the familiar loops and curves of his mother's careful handwriting.

When Bernadette returns, overheated and exuberant from her run, Oliver explains that he needs to go into town to find a fax machine; there is an important memo he forgot to leave on his boss's desk the day before. It is an elaborate and outright lie, not something Oliver is accustomed to, yet it flows from him without effort.

He drives some distance before finding a coffee shop where he orders a cup, strong and black, and begins reading his mother's diary.

It is a disappointment at first. She wrote it much earlier than Oliver imagined, when he was a toddler, and it is full of mundane details about his and Al's development, his first steps, his fall from a bed. As they progress, the entries become less frequent, and her handwriting harder to decipher. Oliver is ready to give up and return home when he skips ahead and notices something unusual.

There is a description of thoroughbreds, or photographs of them, Man O'War, Citation, Whirlaway, and the layout of a room with knotty-pine paneling, a desk and vinyl sofa. The place is familiar to Oliver, yet he cannot place it. Then the description moves to something else, a man's touch, someone she refers to as "S."

There is no way of telling who "S" is, except for the setting. Oliver looks back at the dates. The affair occurred when Oliver was three, his brother five. "Oh, God," Oliver says aloud, closing the book. Several people look up from their coffee. He stands to leave.

It occurs to him halfway home that he forgot to pay for his coffee. He considers turning around, driving an extra fifteen minutes to make an honest man out of himself, but it is starting to rain, and that is reason enough to keep going.

As he drives, he keeps seeing the framed horses, their tense musculature, ears alert, oiled coats gleaming behind glass. It comes to him when he stops at a light. Once he remembers, there is no mistaking. The place his mother described was the back room of his uncle Bede's tavern. *S*, he thinks. Bede Simone.

Cars honk. The light has turned, but Oliver is frozen, idling in the intersection. His sternum aches, kicked in, his body inverting itself. The light goes red again, and he relaxes his grip on the steering wheel, covering his face. Without wanting to, he imagines his uncle's calloused hands in his mother's fine-spun hair, his repulsive swagger as he cajoled and wheedled her. He probably asked her to come by on the pretense of needing help. Oliver imagines him sitting next to her on the vinyl sofa, fabricating a tale of desperate unhappiness and luring her into some gesture of consolation. Uncle Bede, the consummate ladies' man. How could he help but go after his stepbrother's beautiful wife?

Chapter

26

THE CORN IS YOUNG, the husks tight as immature buds. April feels the stiff, squeaky resistance as she peels back each layer, exposing the kernels to light. Bernadette sits beside her on the front porch. Together they have shucked a dozen ears.

"He must have had to go halfway back to the city to find a fax machine," Bernadette says as Oliver pulls into the driveway.

April watches him, her hands yanking back a stubborn hull. He slips on his sunglasses and gets out.

"Did you find a fax?" Bernadette asks.

He nods. "Where are the others?"

"Sitting out back," Bernadette says, brushing silken threads from her hands. "We're done here. Let's join them."

Out on the beach Al tries to light a cigarette, cupping the flame against the breeze. April kicks off her sandals and follows Oliver and Bernadette across the damp sand.

"We thought you'd gotten lost," Nana says.

"I did," Oliver says distractedly.

April touches Nana's cheek with the back of her hand. "You're getting too much sun. How about some lotion?"

"Take me to the water, Bede," Nana says. "I want to get my feet wet."

Hal caresses her hand. "It's Hal, Mom," he says gently. "Sure, let's go for a walk." He helps her to stand.

April takes Nana's other arm, and the three of them walk down to the surf. The breeze is steady.

"Hold up your dress," April says as they step in. April watches Nana's face as she closes her eyes and inhales. She imagines her soaring back across the decades, wading gingerly into the sapphire waters of her youth.

Nana licks her lips, touching her neck to kiss the absent cross. April tries to think of how she might give it back.

"You're looking a lot better," Hal says to April.

"I am better."

"Are the stitches out?"

"For a few weeks now."

"I'm glad he's gone, sweetheart. I'm glad you're through with that."

April looks into the water. *Through,* she thinks. But there had been no body, no funeral. And even if there had been, who would have gone? If there was no one on earth to pray for T.J. except herself, what hope did he have?

"You know, don't you, that no one's to blame for Buddy's death."

April looks at him.

"For whatever reasons, it was his time."

"I wish I felt that way, Uncle Hal, but it wasn't his time. Not by sixty years or so."

"It happened."

"You think it was God? I think it was brake pads."

He sighs. "We still have you, April. We haven't forgotten that."

She looks down at the water. Nana has let go of her dress, the hem swaying in the froth. April wonders how much of the conversation she heard.

"Enough," Nana says, opening her eyes. "Do you want me to catch my death of cold?"

April and Hal smile at each other. Together they help Nana turn around and start up the beach.

After dinner, April circles the table, setting a bowl of fruit before each person. The doors are propped open, the fan on, but the house will not cool. Al has his shirt off, his skin sunburned and salty. He starts eating the berries before everyone is served, scooping spoonfuls into his mouth. April slaps his shoulder, his skin hot to the touch.

"Ouch," he says.

"She's right." Hal smiles, giving April a wink. "Who brought you up, anyway?"

April places a serving in front of Bernadette, who fans herself vigorously, adjusting the bowl.

Oliver is talking to Bernadette, complimenting her on the roast, refilling her wineglass and then his. April reaches over his shoulder, setting down a bowl of fruit just as he reaches for his glass. Their arms brush and the wine teeters. "Sorry," she says.

Without looking up, Oliver raises his hand dismissively.

"Bernadette and I have an announcement to make," he says. April moves toward the kitchen door.

"We've changed the wedding date," Bernadette says. "To October."

April stops in the doorway and turns to face the table. Oliver stares directly at her, and then averts his eyes.

"So soon?" Hal says.

"We just decided this morning," Bernadette says. "Crazy, isn't it? But the reception hall had a cancellation, and since they knew we wanted October originally, they called us first. I checked with the church this morning, and it looks good."

April turns and pushes through the swinging door to the kitchen. She drags a raspberry through the cream sauce and puts it in her mouth. Then a blueberry. She can hear bits of conversation through the door. "What's the date?" Nana asks.

"The fifteenth," Bernadette says. "The feast of Saint Teresa of Avila, in honor of Oliver's mother."

October fifteenth. Buddy was buried on the twelfth. Why should that matter? April eats another raspberry and hears the kitchen door open. Al places his empty bowl in the sink. "Seconds?" he asks.

April stands facing the counter, not looking at him. He leans on the Formica next to her. "Hey, Rose," he says, trying to catch her eye. "You've always got me." He pops a strawberry in his mouth.

"What's that supposed to mean?"

"You knew he'd get married someday, didn't you?"

"You think this upsets me? I'm not upset. Why should I be upset?"

Al smiles and eats another berry.

"What about you? When will you get married?" she asks, running a finger through the cream.

"Never," Al says. "I'd make a hell of a husband."

"You'd do okay."

He shakes his head. "There's not a woman alive who deserves me."

She laughs just as Oliver walks into the kitchen. "Hey," she says. "Congratulations." She licks the cream from her finger.

"They want coffee," Oliver says.

"It's on," she says. "Two minutes."

He walks out of the room.

Al rolls his eyes. "Does that look like a man headed for marital bliss?"

"He's just having a bad day," April says.

Chapter
27

CROSS-LEGGED ON THE PORCH SWING, April listens to the chant of crickets. It is late. She likes being the only one awake in a house of sleepers. She hears a tattering in the breeze and looks out at her car, Buddy's car, white under the stars. Someone touches her from behind and she gasps.

"Come on," Oliver says. "We have to talk."

April's heart quickens. She thought he had gone to bed hours ago. She stands and follows him. He takes long, uneven steps, his gait strangely loose. She wonders if she should let him drive, then lets the thought go.

The car smells of Bernadette's coconut sun lotion. Oliver coasts down the gravel drive in neutral, without lights, before turning the engine over some distance from the house. He takes a hard right and accelerates down the narrow road leading to the cove.

"How long have you known?" he asks without looking at her.

"If you're talking about your mother's diary, I haven't read it."

"But you knew about the affair."

"Excuse me?"

He puffs up his cheeks and lets out a long, slow breath, flexing then clenching his hands on the wheel. There is heat in his face, his chin set. April's stomach feels volatile. He turns off the road and stops the car abruptly near a deserted beach. The rim of an inky cloud glows faintly, cloaking the moon. Whitecaps froth luminously on the water's surface. Oliver cuts the engine.

"You could have told me," he says. "It would have changed things."

"Told you what?"

"I don't know how to think of her anymore. Or you, for that matter."

"Me?"

"We should have talked," he says. "Something happened, and we pretended it didn't."

"Let's go back. We'll talk when you're sober."

"Come on, April. With all the conversations we had when you were half-cocked, you owe me this one."

She folds her arms in front of her.

"And don't try to tell me you're on the wagon. How else would you hook up with the men you do? Or maybe you just like the scary ones."

Her jaw tightens. "I was never in love with T.J., but I cared for him. Maybe that's worth more."

"Sure. Why let a little skull fracture get in the way of friendship?"

"What's it to you, Oliver? You've got your life."

"I did."

She looks at him hard. "If you've got news, you'd better share it."

"Your father, my mother, that's the news, baby."

Confusion sears through her, then indignation.

"Oh, but it's true," he says. "And what's more, she liked it." From the glove compartment he pulls a flask, which April recognizes as her father's.

"Where did you get that?"

"My dad's got a box of your father's things in the attic. Stuff you didn't want, I guess. I thought it would make an interesting keepsake; you know, a reminder of the good old days." He takes a swallow and squints; it's painful to get down. "I know this isn't my usual style, but I've been thinking, April, if your father and my mother could screw in the back room of the bar while we were home in our high chairs, what's the big deal about you and me getting it out of the way?"

April bolts out of the car.

He goes after her and takes her arm. "Come on," he says, pulling her toward the dunes. "Let's take the scenic route back." He has the flask with him. He takes another swig, gagging, and offers it to her. "I filled it with something from Al's cabinet. I have no idea what it is, but I'm sure you do. Come on, April. Have a drink with me. In all these years, that's something we've never done."

She hates the sight of her father's flask, but takes it. The more she can down, the less for him.

"Ah," Oliver says, grabbing it back. "The family poison."

"So you want to fuck me, Oliver?" she says, wiping her mouth. "You've decided you hate me enough for that?"

He looks at her, letting his eyes roam freely.

A spark of terror skips down her spine. She keeps walking. On her right, the ocean pounds beyond the dunes. On the left, the lights of distant houses glow above the cliff. Oliver's steps quicken behind her. He grabs the back of her belt and she whirls around to face him. "I'll need more than just brandy for this," she says.

"No excuses," he says, handing her the flask. "This is all we've got."

She takes another swallow. "These are the rules," she says. "I can touch you, but you can't . . ."

"No rules."

"No rules, no game."

"Fine. I'm all yours."

"And keep your mouth to yourself."

"Sorry to disappoint you," he says. "But kissing wasn't what I had in mind."

"Go to hell." She yanks the hem of his T-shirt out of his shorts, her head light and aching like she just came in from the cold, whirling on a water flume, careering down, the momentum hair raising and unstoppable. She is more despicable than even she thought possible; more like her father than her father himself.

Oliver raises his hand to pull his shirt off and she ducks, shielding her face, the reflex instantaneous.

"Whoa," he says.

She backs away.

"Did you think I was going to hit you?"

"Why don't you? Wouldn't that be more satisfying?"

"For you, maybe."

"Piss off."

She starts walking again, the sand cool and dry. She shivers.

He takes her arm and pulls her toward him. He has left his shirt in the sand.

"You don't want this, Oliver. You think you do, but you don't."

"Wanna bet?"

"Think of tomorrow. Think of Bernadette."

"Now," he says. "I'm thinking now."

"The rules," she says.

"Fuck the rules." He moves his hand around the back of her neck, beneath her hair. It's the gentleness that shocks her. Even in his anger, he cannot keep it out of his touch. He moves his face to hers.

She knees him in the groin. He yells out, falling to his knees. April runs. She sprints fast and hard through the dunes and down a slope and over a rise until her heart drums and she is winded. She looks back. There is no sign of him. Her pulse races. She has no idea where she is, if she has overshot the beach house or has a mile to go. She looks up at the cottages on the ridge, trying to identify them. Hands on her knees, she catches her breath. The surf charges up the beach and recedes. Suddenly she hits the ground hard, sand in her mouth. Oliver pins her down, hands on her wrists, knees on her thighs. "What you need is a dick," he says. "So you can know how that felt."

"I warned you no kissing."

"Fine. Let's dispense with formalities." He holds her wrists with one hand. "You don't think I'm capable of this, do you."

"You are," she says. "But you won't."

"You underestimate me."

He eases down, letting her feel his weight, his eyes fixed on hers; he doesn't know any other way to do this. It's his gaze that's killing her, contemptuous but steady, gauging her response. She gathers sand in her fist, meaning to throw it, but she can't get her hand free. "I hate you," she says.

"Well," he says. "Something we finally agree on."

Through their clothing, she feels his groin press against hers. She wants to die.

"April," he breathes. There's an ache in his voice, a softness she cannot bear. "April, I—"

"Stop." She winces, turning her face away. She can almost remember that brief time in her infancy when the world was calm and she rested in her father's arms while her mother stood at the stove, warming a stew. *I love you, April.* Funny, but she can't remember anyone saying that to her. Or had her father whispered it in her ear in that ancient time when the world was calm? Whispered it with his honeyed, mellifluous voice. *I love you, April. Now put down the goddamn phone before I—*

"Get it over with," she says.

He lets go of her wrists. "What's that?" He runs his fingers along her temple, around the curve of her ear, down to her neck, his touch so light she experiences it as pain. "You're bleeding," he says in his normal voice. "You've got blood in your hair."

She touches her forehead, and her fingers come away wet.

"You must have hit a shell."

"It's nothing."

"We'd better get you home." He gets to his feet.

"I'll rinse it off."

"In the ocean?"

"Where else?"

"Do you think that's a good idea?"

She walks down to the water and wades in to her thighs, wetting the hem of her shorts. She is surprised to see him beside her. "It's just a scratch," she says.

"It's trickling down. Maybe you need stitches."

She cups water in her trembling hand and runs it through her hair, over her forehead, down her shoulder. It stings.

"I'm sorry," he says.

"It's nothing," she says, but her voice wavers. The bottom is molten beneath her feet.

A wave appears from nowhere, dousing them to their shoulders. Oliver gasps at the impact, glancing into the shifting black water; he has no idea how he got here.

"What is it, up to a mile that a shark smells blood?" she says.

"That's not funny."

"Come on, Oliver. Why not here?" She takes his hands and with the next swell they lose their footing. They tread, buoyant in the salt water.

"This isn't a good idea," he says. "There's an undertow."

"Go back if you want."

His chin quivers. The moon slips in and out of clouds. Oliver appears mesmerized by the dark current pulling him seaward, yet terrified, barely able to move. She imagines herself slipping her arms around his neck, floating. But Bernadette enters her mind.

"Let's go," April says, and takes the next wave in. As they reach the shore, Oliver stumbles. April takes his arm. "Dizzy?"

He holds his head. "I need to sit." He wanders over to a rowboat and sits down in it. She puts her hands on her hips, observing him. He slouches, elbows to knees, and puts his head in his hands. She gets in and sits gingerly on the bench beside him. The incoming surf laps the wooden sides of the boat. Oliver lies back, his head propped against a life preserver, and covers his eyes. "If this is what drunk is, I don't get the appeal."

"You're coming out of it now, that's the problem," she says, looking down at him.

"I feel like there's an earthquake inside my head."

"Ride it out," she says. "That, or get drunker."

"I think we've lost your father's flask."

"Have we? Then it is a big day."

"I'm freezing cold," he says. "Is that normal, too?"

"We could go back."

"No," he says. "Stay here with me for a while."

She finds the other life preserver and lies down, propping her head against it. She makes herself small so as not to brush against him. A wave whacks the boat broadside, spraying them with salt water. They're quiet, looking up at the stars as the incoming surf rocks the rowboat, now and then lifting it and setting it down again. She braces herself, not knowing when the next jolt will come.

"April," he says, shivering. "I don't know what I'm doing with my life."

"Yes you do."

"Why law?"

"You came to it somehow."

"By chance," he says.

"Everything's chance. That doesn't mean it's bad."

"No, not chance," he says. "Lack of imagination."

"You'll find your way, Oliver."

"I'm engaged to someone I don't even deserve."

"Yes you do. You're a good person."

"Am I? Then why did I do what I did just now? People go to jail for less."

"Stop it," she says.

"Attempted rape is what they call it. And look, there's plenty of forensic evidence. It's not too late to press charges." He glances at her.

"I hope you're joking."

"April, I don't know what's happening to me."

"You drank too much, that's all."

"No, it's more than that."

"I know your problem, Oliver. In your head is a girl who doesn't exist. You went to college. You must have read Jung."

"No. Freud, maybe. Something about cigars and hysterical women."

"It's called projection. Ask Bernadette. She's taking psychology, isn't she?"

"Sure. *Hey, Bernadette, why am I preoccupied with a girl I can't have, when I have a woman who's way beyond anyone I could ever hope for?*"

"You're not preoccupied. You're exaggerating."

"You'd make a lousy analyst. Don't you know you're supposed to affirm what the person says, not contradict it?"

"Unless he's full of shit."

"Fine, I'm not preoccupied."

"If you are, it's with the girl in your head, and believe me, she's not the one sitting next to you."

"So, who's next to me, then?"

"April Simone," she says. "The same girl who beat you in the fifty-yard dash on field day in fifth grade."

"You did not," he objects soundly.

She gives him a satisfied smile. "You never did get over that."

The boat lifts again, and this time stays aloft, bobbing on the waves.

"We're anchored, aren't we?" she says.

"Sure. All rowboats come equipped with anchors."

"You're such a wiseass."

"Don't worry. We're not headed out to sea, yet."

Wave after wave laps against the boat. The sky lilts. She feels the sea arcing and rolling. She thinks she has never heard any sound so precisely, so presently, as she does the creak and roll of the boat.

A warm breeze crosses over them.

"What about me and Bernadette, then. Projection?"

"No," she says. "That's real."

"You're awfully sure for someone who doesn't know the facts."

"It's obvious."

"What's obvious? That we're in love?"

"I don't like that expression. Imagine if instead of falling in love, people fell into courtesy? What if making a commitment to someone meant promising to be kind and polite?"

"Doesn't it?"

"For you and Bernadette, maybe. Not for everyone."

"So courtesy is the gold standard? How about passion? Does that enter the equation?"

The boat sways and turns. She starts to feel dizzy. "It's overrated," she says. "The stuff of wars."

He looks at her curiously.

"Except for artistic passion," she adds quickly. "Scientific, scholarly, architectural passion, that's what makes us human. Music, most of all."

"You're talking to a law student here. Surely you see the holes in your argument."

"For mystics, maybe, sex can be a kind of transfiguring experience. But let's be real. For most people it's just a question of getting off."

"I see, so you've had it with sex. Been there, done that."

"Basically."

"Wait a minute. Something else is coming back to me from Freud. I remember it now. Have you heard of the term *defense mechanism*?"

"Piss off," she says.

He smiles, happy to have stung her.

"Let's go back," she says.

"I'll make you a deal," he says, sitting up with a groan. "I'll read Jung if you read the letters of Heloise and Abelard."

"I've read them," she says. *"'Even if I could be queen to the emperor and have all the power and riches in the world, I'd rather be your whore.'"*

He laughs. "You're always ahead of me."

They've floated quite a distance from shore. There's no graceful way out of the boat. They splash over the sides and haul it in behind them. The moment they emerge onto the sand, shivering and wet, the awkwardness sets in. Oliver walks with his head down, ship-wrecked. The way to the car seems endless.

In the dim light inside the house she sees that his eyes are narrow and pained, the hangover taking hold. At the bottom of the stairs he stops her, placing his hand over hers on the banister. His fingers are clammy and cold. "April," he says. "What now?"

"Go to bed," she says. "Nothing's changed."

He looks at her blankly.

She slips her hand out from under his and ascends the stairs. He doesn't follow. After a moment, she hears him go back outside.

In her room, the first thing she does is empty her purse on the bed to find Nana's cross. She puts it on, not because she feels worthy, but because she needs it. She stands at the window, holding the chain. After a moment, she spots Oliver wading into the surf. The moon is exposed now, casting a brilliant lane on the heaving sea. He swims out beyond the combers until his image grows faint and is gone.

Chapter

28

THE SOUND OF A CAR DOOR startles Oliver from sleep. Beside him, Bernadette's forehead tenses in dream. He notices his shorts draped over the back of a chair and remembers his T-shirt left in the dunes.

He sits up. Curtains billow from the open window. His mouth is cottony, his head full of static. He hears voices outside and rises, looks out the window, squinting. The trunk of April's car is open, Oliver's father and brother standing nearby.

He dresses hurriedly, noticing scratch marks on his upper arm, a bruise on his shoulder. He puts on a clean T-shirt and goes downstairs. "April's leaving?" he asks his father, seeing her bag in the trunk.

Hal shrugs. "Says she has to work today."

Al bounces his basketball. "She had a mishap last night," he says. "Did you hear?"

Oliver's throat goes dry.

"A wave took her," Al says. "Dragged her along the bottom. Must have hit a rock, because she's got a nice little gash on her head."

"Is she all right?" Oliver asks.

"You know her," Hal says. "Not even fazed."

Oliver runs his hand through his hair. "Where is she?"

"She'll be right out."

"I could have sworn she said she was staying till tomorrow," Al says, tossing the ball against the side of the house.

The screen door opens. April comes out, taking the porch steps two at a time.

"Aren't you warm in that?" Al asks. Her sweatshirt is baggy, covering her wrists, Oliver notices.

"I like the air-conditioning high," she says.

He notices the cut along her hairline and looks away.

Al twirls the ball in his hand and catches Oliver's eye; he's on to him. Has April said something? No, Oliver decides. Al has always been able to read the guilt on his face.

She says good-bye to Hal and Nana, then goes to Al, who aims to plant one on her lips.

"Quit it," she says, shielding herself.

"Aw, Rose," he says, pulling her.

"I mean it," she says, pushing away.

Al moves back, raising his hands like a criminal. "Fine," he says. "Blame *me*." He lifts a dirty tennis ball from the grass and bounces it hard against the porch step.

April turns to Oliver. She smiles, glancing at his uncombed hair. "Nice do."

Oliver hates this ability in her. He doesn't break even the slightest smile, but stares at his haggard reflection in her glasses.

"Gee whiz," she says, turning away. "Everyone's so serious. I think you'll find a way to survive without me." She gets into the car and flings her purse on the passenger seat. He goes over and leans on the car door.

"I said good-bye to Bernadette earlier," she says, fishing in the pocket of her sweatshirt for her keys. "She sounds excited about your new date." She draws out the key chain with Buddy's pocketknife attached.

"April," he says quietly. She moves her glasses to her forehead. The gesture heartens him. He sees sincerity in her eyes. "Please stay," he says.

She studies him sympathetically. Just as she parts her lips to say something, there is a thud against the windshield. They both flinch.

"Sorry." Al grins, picking up the tennis ball.

April pulls her glasses down. "I'm broke," she says to Oliver. "Not working isn't an option." She turns over the engine.

He leans heavily on the car, dropping his head. She pats his hand. Not until she puts the car in drive does he back up. April pulls away, tooting her horn and waving.

Hal goes into the house. Oliver follows, glancing out through the screen door. Al is still in the driveway watching the car as it rounds the bend. He tosses the tennis ball away and helps Nana up the porch steps. "Hey there, darling," Al says to her. "Aren't you supposed to be using your walker?"

Nana doesn't answer but looks up at him squarely. "A wave," she says, frowning. "What do you think of that explanation?"

"Well," he says. "You know April. If there's danger out there, she'll be the first to dive in."

Just as Al reaches for the doorknob to help Nana inside, her palm catches the side of his face with a loud clap. Oliver winces. Given her frailty, the force was impressive.

Nana comes inside with surprising speed and hobbles by Oliver without comment.

Al touches his cheek. He strikes a match, and Oliver glances at him through the screen. "I believe you owe me one, Boy Wonder," he says, taking a drag.

All his life, something about Oliver has prevented people from accusing him; he was incapable of harm. Perhaps he almost believed it himself.

He goes upstairs. Bernadette stirs at the sound of the door. She opens her eyes and blinks. The bed is draped with sunlight streaming from the window. Light glows on the pillow and the silk of her hair. Oliver feels weak.

Bernadette sits up in bed, brushing hair from her eyes. "Lord," she says. "You look like a truck hit you."

He sinks into a chair at the foot of the bed. "I drank too much last night."

"Apparently."

Oliver clasps his hands in his lap to steady them. "I need to talk to you."

Bernadette brings the sheet to her chest. A chill passes through her gaze, and for a moment he thinks she knows.

Oliver stands, goes to the window, and taps the sill with his fist. "April left this morning," he says.

"Yes, I saw her in the bathroom. She said she had to work."

"You spoke with her?"

"I asked her opinion about the wedding favors. There's not much time now."

Oliver touches his forehead. "Bernadette, something's happened." He turns to look at her, her eyes tense.

"Are you still obsessing over that diary? So what, Oliver. Your mother made a mistake. People slip. It happens."

He stares at her. "That's it? People slip?"

She looks at him carefully. "Come on," she says with a purposeful laugh. "You act like it happened yesterday."

"Right," he says uncomfortably.

"Don't worry. We're all disappointed by our parents at some point. It's part of life." She slips on her robe, punching her arms through the sleeves. "I'm going to shower before the hot water is gone."

"Bernadette, I'm not finished."

She sighs, gazing at him, her eyes sad and frustrated. "Let go of it, Oliver." She kisses him lightly, her hand on his cheek. "Go scramble some eggs," she says. "You need to shut off your brain."

Chapter

29

THE COFFEE SHOP is a few blocks from April's apartment. Eight o'clock on a Saturday morning doesn't seem like her usual style. He was the one who asked to meet; she chose the place and time. Oliver is early. He stares into the enormous fish tank in the storefront. Calico koi with impressive whiskers scour the gravel for morsels. He's seen this place before, but when?

After standing outside for a few minutes, he glances in to see that she is already there, sitting alone in a booth with what looks like an untouched cup of coffee. He slides in across from her. She's wearing sunglasses.

"Hey, there," she says, her fingers fidgeting with a sugar package. "I didn't order you anything. I don't know what you drink." There's an edge to her voice. It's unlike her to show nervousness.

"Just coffee," he tells the waitress.

She glances around the shop. "This place never changes," she says. "Same wallpaper, same waitress."

"You're a regular, then?"

"Used to be." She looks out the window.

"Look," he says finally. "I'm sorry about . . ."

"You were drunk. Let's forget it happened."

"Right," he says quickly.

The waitress, a blue-haired woman with basset hound eyes, raises her brows as she sets down his coffee. He waits for her to step away before he continues.

"Look, I think you need to let me make a real apology. What I did was completely—"

"Excuse me, but I think I did as much to you as you did to me."

"Whatever you did back, I deserved."

"Oliver, I know you're hard on yourself, but what you think you tried to do, and what you actually tried to do, are not the same thing."

"You're making excuses for me."

"I'd be happiest if we could just let this go. Besides, I liked the rowboat."

"I liked that, too," he says quietly.

April goes back to the sugar package, turning it edge-to-edge on the tabletop. "So, are we done?" she asks.

He considers this for a moment. "No, I don't think so," he says. "Let's get out of here." He pushes away the coffee. "Let's go for a walk."

"A walk?"

"Why not?"

"I don't think it's a good idea."

"What's the harm?"

"Where to?" she says skeptically.

"Let's do something impractical," he says. "Let's look at dogs in the dog pound."

"That's insane."

"Exactly," he says, reaching for the check.

The pound smells of urine and bleach. The sound of barking is deafening.

"I'm not getting a dog," she says.

"Be open-minded. Think of the protection."

"What about protection from my landlord? He'd kill me."

"You're planning to move anyway, right?"

"Let's get out of here. It's too depressing."

"How about this cutie?" he says. A Doberman mix with ears like spears barks at them shrilly. Its tail wags furiously, but April walks away, glancing into the other cages.

"I live in an apartment. I work crazy hours. A dog isn't an option."

"So, we're window-shopping. How about this one?" He points to a rottweiler who bares his teeth. "Well, maybe not."

April keeps walking. "I don't even like dogs. Pets were Buddy's thing." She bends down beside the cage of the straggliest, most sorry-looking dog Oliver has ever seen.

"What about this one back here," Oliver calls. "Looks like a pure-bred chocolate Lab."

April ignores him. She is talking through the bars to the mutt. One of his ears stands precariously upright while the other, torn, hangs down. Dark and wiry, it's impossible to say what combination of breeds he could be. His thin tail wraps between his legs. He doesn't approach the bars while April talks to him sweetly. "You see that?" Oliver says. "His body language is not good."

"I hear him," April says. "He's saying, 'Why the hell should I trust you?' And given his circumstances, isn't he right?" She puts her hand tentatively through the bars.

"No reaching in," says the attendant, a potbellied man wearing earplugs.

April pretends not to hear, which isn't hard to do given the volume. This dog appears to be the only one not barking. He dips his head, sniffs cautiously, and takes a tiny step toward April. She looks up at Oliver and smiles at this achievement.

"How old is he?" Oliver asks the attendant. "He looks ancient."

"Anyone's guess," says the man.

"Is he healthy?" Oliver asks skeptically. "What's with the bald spots?"

"Look," says the man. "It's forty bucks to adopt. The rest you find out from a vet."

"We'll come back another day," Oliver says.

"He's not going to be here tomorrow," the man says. "His three weeks are up. No one's claimed him, and we have a slew of puppies sitting in crates in the lobby. If you don't believe me, take a look yourself."

"You mean he's going to be put down?" April says.

"We can't save them all, lady. That's just how it goes."

"I'll take him," she says.

"You'll have to fill out an application. You got a fenced yard?"

"I'll be moving in with my grandmother soon. She's got one."

"Hold on, April," Oliver says. "I thought we were window-shopping."

"You're right. I could use the protection."

"There are always ads in the paper. I saw one recently for schnauzer pups."

"You heard what the guy said."

"April, that's a ploy. He just wants to unload the dog."

"Sure, so he can free up the kennel for a more adoptable one. What's wrong with that?" She heads to the office with her wallet in hand.

Oliver follows her. "Look, April. Maybe this wasn't a good idea after all. If you ask me, this dog is dubious."

"Fine, then I'll call him Dubious."

"You're not planning to bring him home right now, are you? We don't even have a leash."

"You're right," she says, handing him a twenty. "Go find one for me. And some dog food, too. I'll meet you outside."

The dog is no more than thirty pounds, but he hauls April all the way down the street to her apartment.

"Well," says Oliver. "So much for leash manners."

"He'll learn."

"It looks like he's training you."

"It's only the first day."

"What about a bath? What if he has fleas?"

"Right," she says, opening her wallet again. "Run back and buy some soap."

When they reach April's building, the mongrel stops dead at the bottom of the stairs. "Let's go," April says, preceding him. The dog splays out, petrified.

"Never seen stairs?" Oliver asks.

"Open the dog food," she says. They place one piece of kibble on each step. The dog cranes his neck and gets the first three easily. He takes a step for the fourth, another for the fifth, and once he realizes he is on the steps, he makes a reckless dash to the top. Upon reaching the landing, he pees in terror. Oliver covers his eyes.

"I'll grab some paper towels," April says. "You carry him the rest of the way up."

Oliver carries the squirming dog into April's apartment and directly into the bathtub. Panicked, the dog flies out at once. They shut the door in time. April kicks off her sandals and stands in the tub. "Come on, Dubious," she says, turning on the tap. "It's fun."

Somehow the dog manages to squeeze himself behind the toilet bowl.

"I can already see what a great watchdog he's going to be," Oliver says.

"He doesn't have to earn his keep," April says. "He's a family member now."

"Great," Oliver says.

Within ten minutes, April and Oliver are soaked, while the dog, giving one more shake, appears basically dry. After another ten minutes he is lathered and foamy, appearing skinny beneath his flattened coat. He hangs his head, trembling and showing the whites of his eyes.

"He thinks we're trying to kill him," Oliver says. He holds the collar while April rinses with a three-quart pot.

"I knew these pots and pans would come in handy one day." She smiles. When they finish, there is a gritty ring about the tub. Oliver spits dog hair out of his mouth. April towels off the dog, who is no longer gray but tan with black markings. "Very handsome," she announces. "And younger than we thought. Look at those white teeth."

"April," Oliver says carefully. She is bending down in the tub, scooping mucky hair out of the drain. "I know I led you into this, but sometimes it's best to recognize early when something is a mistake."

She glances up at him. He is standing over her with his hands on his hips. "Is that what you do?" she asks.

He hesitates. "Sure, I make mistakes."

"I mean the recognition part." She stands in front of him now in the tiny bathroom, hands on her hips in a mirror image of him. Her face looks flushed and overheated. Even her hair is wet. The whimpering dog makes figure eights around their feet. "Three hours with me on a Saturday morning. Surely you have better things to do."

He doesn't know what to say.

She opens the bathroom door. The dog bolts. The cool air clearly feels good on his skin. "Look at how smart he is," April says, observing the dog at the front door. "He's telling us he wants to go out."

"That, or he never wants to see us again."

April gets the leash but Oliver pauses in front of the coffee table to see what she's checked out of the library: *An Interrupted Life* by Etty Hillesum and *A Brief History of Time* by Stephen Hawking. "Giving it another go?" Oliver asks, holding up the Hawking.

"I'm a glutton for punishment."

"Forget string theory," he says, putting down the book. "What you need is *Dog Training 101*."

The dog has no trouble going downstairs. He nearly pulls April down the stairwell. He looks clean now, though April and Oliver are damp and bedraggled.

"He'll need a lot of exercise, you know. Not to mention obedience classes, shots. These things add up."

She eyes him. "Don't you have somewhere to be by now?" They walk for more than a mile before finally stretching out on a park bench, letting themselves dry in the sun. The dog curls up in the shade beneath the bench, panting.

"He needs water," she says.

"He's scared out of his wits," Oliver answers. "Probably longing for his cage in the pound."

"He'll be fine after a few weeks."

"Let me help you with the vet bill," he says. "Since this was my harebrained idea."

"It's not joint custody." She smiles. "I'll be fine."

He bends over to pat the dog between their legs. "Hey, Dubious," he says gently. The dog leans toward his caressing hand. "I wonder what happened to his ear," Oliver says.

"They all have scars. His just happens to be visible," she says. "Now you'd better get to wherever you're going."

"Right," he says. He leans over and kisses her cheek carefully. She smells like flea soap and strawberries. She blushes, glancing away.

"You're not going directly to Bernadette's, are you?" she asks as he stands.

"Why?"

"You smell like a wet dog."

"Well, you're no perfume princess yourself."

"Beat it," she says.

He turns to leave.

"Hey, Oliver," she calls.

He looks back.

"Thanks," she says.

"Right," he says. "See you around."

AUTUMN

~

Chapter

30

THE CUBICLE IS POORLY LIT with a fluorescent bulb that whines and flickers. Unopened books cover the battered desktop. The stacks are strangely silent, the basement air fusty and inert. Oliver can't concentrate.

He thinks of Bernadette, her silken hair, her easy smile. Oliver was smitten with her from the instant he met her. He loved her confident laugh, her melodic voice, and the soft look in her eye when she applauded a child's scribbles. He'd never known a more good-hearted person.

The library is without windows. He wonders if the sun has set. If he pays attention, he can hear the dull drone of the city outside: traffic grinding, street vendors mongering, sidewalks straining under the weight of pedestrians. The trees in Washington Square Park have begun to turn, but just barely, the deep summer green yielding to an amber tinge. Oliver has always thought autumn New York's best season, with its crisp air and splashes of color, but this year it feels like a harbinger.

In the three weeks since Labor Day, Oliver has spent long hours in the library doing little. He tries to work, but his mind does not engage. He has attempted to tell Bernadette what happened, or rather almost happened, at the beach house, but each time the conversation takes a turn, and he never gets it out.

As Bernadette makes plans for the wedding, Oliver looks for signs of anxiety in her, but sees none. She smiles not in the giddy, exuberant way he might expect of a bride, but sagaciously, like someone celebrating the twenty-fifth anniversary of a strong, weathered marriage.

Oliver decides, at last, not to tell her. Although he would like to unburden himself, Bernadette does not wish to hear.

He thinks of his mother. It just doesn't add up. She was a straight arrow. She didn't even allow herself simple pleasures, chocolates or bubble baths. Everything she did had to pass the test of logic and usefulness. If it didn't make sense, she didn't do it. Camping trips, amusement parks, Oliver and his brother always had to persuade her of their practical purpose. She was the last person anyone would expect to have an affair.

But his mother had changed over time, particularly once she took up gardening. She started out with a tidy English garden, and within a few years it took over the yard, wild and lush. She had an exquisite eye for color. Oliver had always likened her landscaping to Mozart's Serenade in B Flat Minor, amazing for its absence of transitions. He admired that lack of compunction. Hydrangea, boom, delphinium.

The garden, somehow, makes him think of April. He remembers the night before a dance when she gave him advice on how to kiss a girl. "Ask her if she minds," she said. "Look in her eyes. Go slow. Keep your lips soft. Let her want it first."

"Where do I put my hands?" he said awkwardly. They had been sitting on the piano bench, fifteen or sixteen years old. He was way behind his friends, many of whom had already had sex, or claimed to. He wasn't about to admit to them that he'd never kissed a girl, no less ask their advice.

April stood up to demonstrate, taking a bite of her half-eaten apple. "Some guys are octopuses," she said, chewing. "They think the more they rub your back, the better. It's distracting. Just put your hands here," she said, placing his hands on her waist. "Keep them there, low and firm, and concentrate on the kiss. Hopefully she'll put her arms around your neck," she said, demonstrating. He smelled the apple, sweet and tart.

"How about the noses?"

"Don't worry about noses," she said. "So what if they bang? It's okay to laugh. All you need to do is tilt your head one way, and she'll know what to do, like this." She tore off a piece of the apple with her teeth. He heard the crisp snap, felt a spray of juice on his neck. April held the slice of apple between her teeth and leaned into him, reaching her face to his. He felt her go up on her tiptoes before it occurred to him to bend his face to hers. He took the apple in his teeth. There was an awkward moment when he thought it would fall. He groped for it with his mouth, felt the barest brush of her lips against his.

She sat down abruptly and took another noisy bite of the apple. He sat down, too, angling away from her. In his mouth, the fleshy fruit was cool and succulent. He turned it over with his tongue, too embarrassed to chew. He let it dissolve.

He heard her take one last snap off the apple and toss the core noisily into a trash can. "By the way," she said, gnawing. "I've never been kissed, either. I just watch a lot of movies, mostly old black-and-whites."

"I don't believe you," he said, swallowing at last.

She picked up her backpack. "Have fun tonight," she said, without looking back.

"Yeah," he said. "Thanks."

Oliver covers his eyes for a moment. His face is warm in his hands. Is this productive? Isn't this precisely the kind of reverie he's been trying so hard to avoid?

I'm thinking of withdrawing from classes, he imagines himself saying to Bernadette. *Taking a semester off. I can't concentrate on anything.* He runs his hands through his hair, feeling perspiration on his forehead. Would she understand? If only school didn't take so long. If only he weren't doing it here, in the East. Maybe he and Bernadette should simply elope. They could do it this month, move back to California. He could study law out there. None of these things is logical, of course. Bernadette, in her beautiful, clearheaded way, would point that out to him. The best thing to do was to stay the course.

Oliver swings his knapsack over his shoulder, the books leaden. He glances at his watch. Already ten minutes late, but it doesn't matter. Al is never on time. He descends the steps to the subway, which smells of curry, urine, and incense, and catches the express just before the doors close.

His heart beats quickly. He likes just making the train; something in him is finally in sync. The wheels churn rhythmically against the tracks, the car swaying. Beyond the windows, nothing is visible in the black tunnel. Oliver's reflection in the glass is cool and composed, not like someone whose life is coming apart. Marriage, graduation, a new job, new city; everything ahead of him. In time, life will feel normal again.

Three quick stops to Penn Station. Oliver hopes the Knicks have not gone into overtime or he'll be waiting forever. But Al is already at their designated spot, under the mammoth Amtrak information board, among the hordes of disheveled travelers and sleeping homeless.

"Just get here?" Oliver asks.

Al nods.

More good timing. His luck is changing. "I thought you'd be late," Oliver says.

"They gave the interview to Schmidt. I didn't even get into the locker room. Ask me why they have two of us covering the same goddamn game." He takes a drag of his cigarette, ignoring the NO SMOKING signs. "He won't get anything out of them anyway. They lost by one point in the last three seconds of play. The players are not going to be in a chatty mood." He snuffs out his cigarette. "I hate this job."

"Thought you loved it."

"I need a new paper. Someplace where I'm not the kid fresh out of the minors. Boston would be nice. Going from *Newsday* to the *Globe*, I'd be respected there. Here I'm dogshit."

"Do you need to call in?"

"I faxed them my copy. They can screw with it all they want. I've yet to recognize a sentence I've written."

"Come on," Oliver says. "Let's get a beer."

"This way," Al says. "I know a good sports bar on Eighth."

Oliver smiles. "Don't you ever get enough?"

"Hey, we're all addicted to something."

At the bar, Al stares at the screen, sipping beer. "Pray the Bills don't go all the way," he says.

Oliver breaks a pretzel into little pieces and eats them one at a time. Lately he doesn't have much of an appetite. "Heard from April?" he asks.

"Call her yourself, Oliver," Al says, eyes on the television.

Oliver sighs.

"Heard she got a dog," Al says. "Let's hope it hates men. Her kind, I mean."

"It's harmless," Oliver says with disappointment.

Al looks at him.

"There was a beautiful chocolate Lab, but no, she had to pick the scruffiest, sorriest-looking mongrel in the place." He smiles wistfully. "Sweet, though."

"Ah, so you've seen her."

"Only once."

"If you're here for absolution, you need to confess first."

"What?"

Al turns to face him. "April won't tell me what happened at the shore, so why don't you?"

Oliver sips his beer and wipes the froth from his mouth. "Nothing happened. At least not the way you mean." He glances at the television screen. The game is back on, but Al keeps his eyes on him. "We had a fight," Oliver adds. "I was an idiot. Then we sat in a rowboat and talked. That's all."

"Must have been some fight."

"I was drunk, which may be a normal Saturday night for you, but not for me."

"Okay, let's not make this personal. You already got me on Nana's shit list."

"Sorry."

Al shrugs. "I wouldn't expect anyone to think it was you." He drains his beer. "So how did you explain your bruises to Bernadette?"

"She never asked."

"Never asked?" Al whistles. "What a perfect addition to the family."

"What's that supposed to mean?"

"Does she think it odd that none of us has ever told Nana about Buddy? I mean, if Bernadette thinks that's normal, her name ought to be Night."

Oliver snaps another pretzel. "It's strange. I've tried to bring it up, but she doesn't seem interested."

"Lucky for you. Don't you know there are some things you don't tell the wife?"

Wife. The word feels strange.

Al shakes his hair like a dog and combs his hands through it. He leans closer to Oliver. "Do me a favor. Tell me Bernadette's the woman of your dreams. Tell me your heart pounds when you see her."

"For Christ's sake, Al, why do you think I'm marrying her?"

"Now, there's a question," he says, biting a pretzel. He glances back at the television.

Oliver empties his glass. He looks down the length of the bar, everyone's face fixed on the screen. "Fine," Oliver says. "Why don't you give me your theory, since you seem to have one."

"Me?" Al says. "I think April scares the shit out of you. I think you can't get married fast enough."

"That's ridiculous."

"Why don't you two just give it a go?" he says.

Oliver shakes his head. "It's an impossible relationship, Al. There's no sense even thinking about it."

"Who's talking about a relationship? Just get it out of your systems already. It's only sex, you know." He fills his mouth with popcorn. "I can't believe you two haven't done it already."

"Have you?" Oliver asks.

Al unglues his eyes from the television and looks at Oliver squarely. "Have I what?"

"You know," Oliver says gravely. "You and April." For a question that only sprang into his conscious mind this instant, the weight is immense. No, not this instant. He's been wondering for years. Suddenly everything hangs on the answer.

"Are you out of your mind?" Al says.

Oliver simply stares.

"Look, Oliver, I admit I run into a lot of women on the road, and it's true that I don't remember half their names, but I'm not a complete schmuck, either. Not the way you think."

"I see, so you're suggesting I do something that you yourself are above?"

"For God's sake, Oliver, it's not a math equation. One brother being with a particular woman does not equal another brother being with that same woman."

"I don't get what you're saying."

"That's because you've got such a goddamn thick skull."

Oliver sighs heavily. "I have an early class tomorrow. I'd better catch my train." He tosses some bills on the bar.

To Oliver's surprise, Al reaches over and gives him a quick hug, slapping his back. "Three Hail Marys and an Our Father," Al says. "And do what you have to do."

Chapter
31

THE SHRILL WHISTLE of the dog park supervisor pierces April's ears as she and Oliver approach the gate. "Grab your pets," the woman hollers at the other dog owners. "Dubious is here."

"So, he's already a fixture," Oliver says.

"Everyone knows Dubious," April says proudly. Once the dogs are secured, the supervisor opens the gate to allow them in. The other owners release their dogs to resume their play. April unleashes Dubious, but he cowers at her feet. His coat has filled in a bit since Oliver last saw him. He looks healthier, but no less shy.

"Is this always how he is?" Oliver asks.

"Only for the first five minutes. You'll see."

The field is muddy from last night's rain. Flecks of dirt soar through the air as the pack of dogs charges, bows, wrestles, and yips. Dubious only watches. He glances up at April with a questioning gaze. "It's okay," she says. "Go on." He looks back at the pack, unconvinced.

"How are the obedience classes going?" Oliver asks.

"There are a couple of real show-offs in there, a golden retriever and a standard poodle. Tough competition, but Doobie is holding his own."

Dubious ventures out from behind April's legs, sniffs a Weima-raner's butt, and as soon as the dog turns to see him takes off like lightning.

"Ah, I see," Oliver says. "He's a tease." Oliver is wearing a Mets cap pulled down low on his forehead, his face unshaven. He catches her staring at him.

She turns away abruptly. "You seem taller than you were way back when," she says. "You must have kept growing in college."

"No, it's that you wore higher heels back then."

She glances down at her ratty sneakers. Dogs zigzag around them, gleefully chasing one another. Even the Airedale can't catch Dubious. He's in his glory. "He loves to show up the purebreds," she says. "It gives him a secret thrill."

Oliver nods appreciatively. "How's it going in the barking department?"

"You know, some owners would kill for a dog who doesn't bark."

"How about a snarl? Bared teeth, perhaps?"

"I'm sure if someone were to climb in my window, Doobie would find his voice."

"Lick the thief's face is more like it," Oliver says doubtfully.

Two Labrador retrievers wrestle each other to the ground. They appear to be trying to tear each other's necks open. "It's okay," April explains. "They're brothers."

Still, she thinks Oliver looks a bit uneasy. "How's school going?" she asks.

He shrugs.

"I'm surprised you have time for something like this," she says, nodding at the dogs. "Aren't law students supposed to be overwhelmed?"

"I am." He smiles, taking some cashews from his pocket and of-fering them to her.

"Well?"

"I'm giving it one more semester. To be honest, I'm not sure if law is for me."

"Oh," she says uncertainly. "Well, you'll figure it out."

He doesn't say anything.

"Bernadette is a great sounding board, I'm sure."

He eats another cashew.

"She'll support you, whatever you decide."

He readjusts his cap in what she recognizes as an old nervous gesture of his. "You have talked to her about it, haven't you?" April asks.

"Why should I upset her if I decide to stay with it anyway?"

"She wouldn't be upset. Besides, it's what's on your mind."

"Is that what you did with T.J.?" he says. "Talk about what's on your mind?"

She bristles. "You know that wasn't the same kind of relationship."

Dubious charges back, crashing into April's knees, and sits against her, panting.

"Base," says Oliver.

"What a chicken," says April.

"So what kind of relationship was it?" Oliver asks, offering the cashews.

"You're not really supposed to bring food in here," she says. "Some dogs can be food-aggressive. Look, this one is already on to you." A dalmatian mix sits expectantly at Oliver's feet. A boxer follows, sniffing his pockets.

"Oops," Oliver says, putting the nuts away. "Shoo," he tells them. "Before you get me in trouble with the drill sergeant." But the supervisor has her back turned. The dogs give up and move away.

"So?" Oliver says.

"Hm?"

"My question."

"I don't know, Oliver. I didn't give it much thought."

"But what did you two talk about?"

"Let's just say that words were not the basis of the relationship. Doobie!" she shouts as the dog starts chewing on a pinecone. "Drop it!"

The dog dutifully drops the prize and looks up, head tilted.

"Seeing anyone now?" Oliver asks, popping another cashew into his mouth.

April puts her hand on her hip, looking up at him.

"Just curious," he says, shrugging.

"I'm on sabbatical, if you must know," she says.

He passes her some cashews. She can see he is pleased with her answer. The dalmatian returns.

"You're a troublemaker here," April tells Oliver. "Don't you have somewhere else to be?"

"Sabbatical, eh? I guess I'll have to give up on the idea of a double wedding."

She laughs. "I'm never getting married," she says, as if nothing could be more obvious.

"Ever?"

"Why should I?"

"Well, you might fall in love."

"People use that expression as if it's something that happens involuntarily, like getting clubbed by a caveman."

"Ah, you're such a romantic."

"Marriage isn't for me. Mowing a lawn, basting a turkey, I wouldn't know how to do those things."

"Not all marriages are ordinary, you know. People live in lofts in the city, cabins in the woods. It doesn't always involve lawns and turkeys."

"I'm not up for the crapshoot, which is what marriage is. Except for you and Bernadette," she adds quickly. "You two are cut out for it. You're grown-ups, I mean."

"And you're not?"

"Not if I can help it."

"April, you were grown up when you were nine years old."

"Well, maybe that's my problem. Look, you can appreciate why I don't want to have a life like my parents. Nothing against them. They did their best."

"Did they?"

"I've made my peace with them, Oliver. They had limitations, but so do we all. I just happen to be aware of mine, and that's why I'm staying single."

"So what then? A lifetime of tending bar?"

"I didn't say that, either. I haven't figured things out yet. I'm a late bloomer."

He smiles at this, and spontaneously kisses her on the cheek.

"Good-bye, then," she says, flustered.

"Same time next week?"

"No," she says. "You need to hit the books."

"Chloe!" a woman screams at her wrestling dog. "Knock it off!"

A queer sensation comes over April. Without realizing it she puts her hand on Oliver's sleeve. He pauses, watching her. "Chloe," April says. "That name was in my dream last night. A little girl on a beach. She was running away from me, giggling. She had black hair, and when she turned to look at me, her eyes were the most amazing blue." She looks up at Oliver, those clear, cerulean eyes. A feeling of recognition crosses her mind, and in the same instant fear. She withdraws her hand, folding her arms in front of her.

He looks at her, his smile fading as he tries to piece together what he's heard.

"Right, then," she says. "Good-bye, Oliver."

He nods and takes his leave. April stares curiously at the three perfect little cashews still in her hand.

Chapter

32

OLIVER'S VOICE IS HOARSE from talking above the music. The roughly hewn rafters of the Buckboard Inn are incongruous with the whirling strobe lights and amplified sound. A leather harness hangs over the bar, and a yoke for oxen on the wall near Oliver's head. Bernadette sits beside him, tapping her fingers to the beat, a hint that she wants to dance.

Oliver looks at the dance floor and decides it's too crowded. His eyes fall to one couple in particular. The beat is fast, and they dance without looking at each other, the woman twisting in place, chin raised, elbows at her sides, and the man flailing his arms and legs as if ridding himself of fleas. There is no synchronization, each dancing with an imaginary partner.

Oliver and Bernadette have spent the evening in a candlelit booth, drinking wine and dancing only occasionally. Oliver left a message on Al's machine suggesting he join them, and bring a date, but he is not surprised that his brother didn't show.

"How are you holding up?" Oliver asks.

"Fading," Bernadette says.

He reaches for the check and cracks open a peanut shell, though he isn't hungry anymore. "Look who's here," she says. "And it's only midnight."

Oliver spots Al weaving through the dance floor, April in tow. She is wearing the black dress from Buddy's funeral. Drop waist. Swingy hem above the knee. He thinks of the button he never returned.

Al spots them and comes over, his face ruddy and animated. "Look who I dragged out," he says, holding up April's hand like a prizefighter. She smiles, pulling her arm away. It was only a week ago that he saw her at the dog park, but meeting her here feels entirely different. "You guys aren't leaving, are you?" Al asks.

"We've been here all night," Oliver says.

"We can stay a little longer," Bernadette says. "Why not?"

"Order us two glasses of champagne." Al tosses a twenty on the table. "I'm feeling lucky."

April smiles. "He's been saying that all night."

Al leads her to the dance floor, his hand low on her back. Bernadette looks at Oliver and raises her eyebrow. "Someday you'll have to explain their relationship to me."

"I wouldn't mind an explanation myself," Oliver says.

Al and April move in staccato percussion. Oliver saw them dance once before, at a friend's wedding. Their presence on the floor is electrifying, the kind of couple you have to stare at. Bernadette clears her throat, fanning herself.

The new song is slow. A man taps Al's shoulder in an apparent effort to cut in. Al lets go of April and puts his arms around the man, who leaps back, cursing. April laughs. The man reaches for her hand, but Al pulls her against him, hand around her waist, and dismisses him with a shake of the head.

"Come on," Oliver says to Bernadette. "This one and we'll go."

She smiles gratefully and follows him onto the dance floor.

Al and April dance cheek-to-cheek, his leg between hers, their bodies pressed together. Her eyes are closed, his open.

"Holy smokes," Bernadette whispers, fanning herself.

Oliver draws Bernadette closer, but no matter how he positions himself, he cannot hold her as closely as Al does April.

Al moves over to where they are dancing. "Okay," he says, releasing April's hand and taking Bernadette's. "Time to spice things up." He draws Bernadette against him, her eyes startled, and sways her to the music. Bernadette looks at Oliver with alarm. She is too polite to object, Oliver thinks, but Al ought to see for himself that she isn't the type of woman who appreciates his melodrama.

"Yo, Al," Oliver says. "What do you think you're doing?"

April takes a step back toward the table. Al dips Bernadette dramatically and her bun comes undone, her hair brushing the floor. To Oliver's amazement, Bernadette shrieks, her laughter hard and bright. "Hey," Al calls. "Don't just stand there, dimwits."

Oliver's skin goes cold. He looks at April, her smile tense. *What the hell,* he offers his hand. She hesitates, then takes it. Her fingers are icy, her body wooden in his arms. He watches his brother slide his hand down Bernadette's hip as he sings to the music. They look surprisingly natural, unlike April and him, who dance with bodies apart, stiff and formal. Bernadette catches Oliver's eye and winks with a bemused smile.

The same man who tried to cut in on Al taps Oliver's shoulder. "Adele," he says. "Remember me? We met—"

Oliver responds by pulling April closer, turning her away from the man. Her hand on his shoulder feels tentative, her posture rigid. Her hair smells of his brother's cigarettes. Oliver looks for Al and Bernadette but can no longer see them.

"Doobie's home alone?" Oliver asks.

"I left the radio on for him. He likes the talk stations."

"Chewed any more slippers?"

"No, but the landlord's on to me. I had to put down an extra security deposit. See what you got me into?"

"I think you should consider agility classes for him, that is, once he masters the basic stuff."

"Sure," she says. "And when he's old enough, why not soccer and Little League?"

He meets her eye. The nearness of her smile makes him waver on his feet.

"Maybe we should sit down," she says, glancing away again.

"Right," he says, but a new song begins, "I Heard It Through the Grapevine." Without needing to discuss it they release each other and start moving to the music. His body remembers the way he used to dance with her as teenagers, the rhythm and synchronicity they shared intuitively without ever having to touch. He sees the music take possession of her down to every finger and pore. They don't touch because they don't need to. The song takes hold of them, and for a few exhilarating moments they are not their own.

The notes end. She smiles at him in a satisfied way and turns to leave.

Oliver spots Bernadette and Al in a far corner and goes over to them. "Think you can get any closer, Al?" It's the right thing to say, though Oliver is not jealous.

"All in fun," Al says, raising his hands. "Terrific dancer, your bride."

"I'm aware of that," Oliver says, putting his arm around her.

Al tips an imaginary hat. "Night, folks." He moves to the bar and sits beside a blond woman wearing polka-dot tights and a striped mini skirt. He takes out a cigarette and offers her one, gesturing toward the door.

"He's too much." Bernadette smiles, a little breathless. They walk back to the table.

"You didn't seem to mind," Oliver says, panning the room.

"He's quite a dancer." Bernadette slings her purse over her shoulder.

"I'm not sure I'd call what he was doing dancing."

"I trust you didn't suffer too much with April."

Oliver glances at her, but she does not meet his eye. He counts out the tip money. Bernadette drapes her sweater over her shoulders

and puts her arm through his. They step out the front door. April is
sitting on the steps with her jacket huddled around her.

"Isn't Al taking you home?" Oliver asks.

She smiles. "Something came up, so to speak."

"Come on," Bernadette says. "We'll drive you."

"I already called a cab."

The doors open and Al comes out with the polka-dot girl. *It didn't
take him long,* Oliver thinks.

"Oh, Rose," he says. "There you are."

April bats her eyelashes.

"Priscilla, this is my pal, Rose. Do you need a lift, sweetheart?"

"I called a cab," April says, standing up.

"Here, take my Jeep." He puts his keys in her hand. "Priscilla's
driving. In fact, why don't you stay at my place?"

"Thanks, but you know I can't sleep without trains." April returns
the keys.

Al exhales smoke and kisses her, giving the illusion that their lips
are smoldering. He steps away then comes back. "One for the Yan-
kees," he says, and kisses her again, longer this time. The blonde folds
her arms across her chest. "Old family friend," Al explains, wiping
his mouth. He takes the woman's arm and they walk off.

Oliver shakes his head.

A taxi pulls into the lot and toots its horn. "Night," April says,
slipping into the back.

In the car, Bernadette folds her hands in her lap while Oliver
drives. He keeps his eyes on the highway. The thought of Al irritates him.

"April was certainly decked out tonight, wasn't she," Bernadette
says, smoothing out her skirt.

"Hm?" he says. "Oh, I guess so."

"I take it you've danced with her before. No one moves like that
their first time out."

"Ages ago," he says. "I guess it's one of those things, like riding a bicycle."

She gazes out the window. "Is there anything else I should know about?" she says. "From ages ago?"

"No, Bernadette. It was never like that."

She nods uncertainly. "But you've thought about it, haven't you."

Oliver glances over at her. The car shudders violently as the wheels hit the rumble strip on the shoulder. Oliver rights it at once. A tractor trailer whizzes by them on the left. The car wavers in the back draft. "Sorry," Oliver says, steadying the wheel. He catches his breath.

Bernadette's hand is braced on the dashboard. She brings it back to her chest. "Should I take that as an answer?"

"The answer is no, Bernadette, and I wish you wouldn't do this."

"But you have to admit that you want to help her, don't you?"

He wants to see Bernadette's expression but tells himself to watch the road.

"The dog," she says calmly. "The money."

"I offered her money for the vet. She didn't take it."

"I'm talking about the fact that you offered."

"She's lost everything," he says. "She's still paying the bank for Buddy's funeral. Her father left her nothing but debt."

"What about the bar?"

"Knowing Quincy, there are probably liens on it."

"I know you sympathize with her. You're a good person, Oliver. I just think you should be careful."

He waits for a long moment, studying the traffic. "Careful of what?"

"The way you look at her now, it's different from when we first moved from California."

"Different how?"

"At first she was like a *Venus de Milo*, perfect in her own disfigured way, but unreal. I knew she caught your imagination, but I wasn't worried. She was only an idea carved in stone."

He swallows, unsettled by how rehearsed she sounds. "And now?"

"It appears you've become friends."

"Isn't that better?"

"Infatuation burns itself out," she says. "Friendship mixed with old chemistry—that can last a lifetime."

"No mixing," he says, "just friendship."

She smiles at him sadly.

"What can I do to convince you?"

"I'm not asking you to do anything. I'm just saying how I feel."

"Which is?"

"Scared."

He reaches over and takes her hand. "I won't go to the dog park anymore," he says. "I'll explain that I'm too busy, which is true anyway. Besides, she's doing fine now. She doesn't need me."

"I'm not asking that of you, Oliver. You do what you think is best."

"I'll tell her right away. She'll understand." He squeezes her hand. "I'm sorry, Bernadette, if I've worried you."

"I trust you," she says. "I hope you don't think otherwise."

"I know you do. I promise to make things right."

Oliver parks beside the train station and stares up at April's window. Two AM. Her light is on. There's a pain in his chest he can't account for. He looks up at the apartment, the glow of light. The logical thing would be to call her on Saturday morning and tell her he can't make it to the park. Or simply not show up. Surely she doesn't expect him. In fact there is no need to say anything at all, no less at two in the morning. The only thing he's sure of is that going up to her apartment right now is the wrong thing to do. He gets out of the car.

The front door of the building is ajar. So much for security. He goes upstairs without buzzing and knocks on her door. She opens it as far as the chain will allow. "Oliver?" she says with alarm. She is wearing a large Knicks sweatshirt atop the black brocade dress, and chewed-up slippers over her black stockings. Dubious juts his scruffy nose through the opening, sniffing enthusiastically.

"April," Oliver says, his hand on his chest.

Seeing his face, she unlatches the door. "What's happened?" she asks. "Is it Nana?"

"No, nothing like that."

She releases a breath. "I've been so worried ever since she burned that teakettle."

He nods gravely. "May I come in?"

She doesn't answer, but studies him uncertainly.

"It's not necessarily dementia," he says, entering anyway. "I've burned pots myself."

"You?" she says skeptically, pulling her sweatshirt closed.

"We're all human."

The dog sniffs his crotch. "Hey," Oliver says. Dubious flattens his ears and moves to April's feet. She remains where she is with her hand on the open door.

"I hear you're finally moving in with Nana," he says, glancing around.

April hesitates before letting the door fall shut. She folds her arms. "I wouldn't be surprised if Nana planned it this way, burned the kettle on purpose, then let me think it was my idea to move in. She's very shrewd that way. She'd do anything to advance her agenda."

He wanders into the apartment. The living room is lit with a single lamp perched over a worn easy chair. There is a blanket half on the footrest, half on the floor, an open library book facedown on the coffee table. In high school she was always reading the oddest things, horticulture, poetry, a biography of Amelia Earhart, all to the detriment of her homework. A few more steps, he thinks, and he'll be close enough to read the title of the downturned book.

"Oliver?"

"Yes." He looks up. "Her agenda?"

"You know, what Nana thinks is right for each of us. Anyway, you've got nothing to worry about. You're living the script."

"I'm not so sure. She still can't remember Bernadette's name," he says, turning to face her. "Don't you think that's a message?"

"She's proud of everything you do, Oliver. She'll be thrilled on your wedding day."

He shoves his hands in his pockets, glancing back at the book.

She cocks her head. "Do you want tea or something?"

"Sure, tea." He follows her into the kitchen. The kettle steams from recent use. He notices the stove clock is repaired. Two thirteen AM.

"So?" she says, hand on her hip. She wants to know what he's doing here.

He hesitates, balling his fingers. "I don't think it's a good idea for me to come to the dog park anymore."

"Oh," she says quietly. "Of course, I mean, you must be getting very busy with wedding plans." She lights the burner, blows out the match, and takes a mug from the cabinet.

She glances over, waiting for him to continue, but he can't think of anything else to say. She studies him, her scrutiny passing through and around him like a cool spot in a warm lake. The kettle teeters on its rack and begins to trill. "What kind?" she says. "I've got chamomile."

"That's fine."

She extinguishes the flame and pours the scalding water. She sits down at the small kitchen table and slides a steaming mug in Oliver's direction.

"April," he says. "Do you ever wonder if you're making the right decisions in your life?"

"I don't think I've made any yet," she says.

"Maybe you should consider it."

She glances at her watch. He sees he has made her nervous. She stands, wiping loose grains of sugar from the countertop. Oliver gets up and moves beside her. The windows rattle faintly. In the distance, a train whistles. "You'll be a fine lawyer, if that's what you decide," she says, dusting the sugar from her hands. "Give yourself time."

The train howls through the station, shaking the cups in the cabinets. "It's the whole package I'm not sure about," Oliver says. The apartment quiets. She looks at him.

"Sometimes I worry that I'm doing it for the wrong reasons."

"No," she says. "Don't second-guess yourself."

"It's just that I'm not as sure as I used to be."

"You're sure. You've said so many times. Besides, it's after two. It's not a good time to talk," she says. She goes to the door and opens it, their mugs of tea untouched on the table. Oliver picks up his jacket and stands in front of her.

"It's normal to feel jittery," she says, softening her tone. "Relax, Oliver. Think of the wonderful life you'll have."

He stands there, not moving.

"I'm not the person to help you with this," she says.

"Why not?"

"I really ought to get some sleep."

He feels the draft from the hallway. Tells himself to leave. The windows begin to rattle again; a local train, slowing as it pulls into the station.

He takes a small step toward her.

"Go on," she says, opening the door wider.

"Do you remember the night you first told me about Quincy?"

"No," she says firmly. "Why do you do this? Why do you drag me back to a time in my life I can't stand to think about? For God's sake, Oliver."

He puts his hand beside hers on the edge of the door. "The day I left for college, where were you?"

"How can this matter now?" She looks at her watch.

"I waited where we said we would meet," he whispers.

She closes her eyes.

"April, I know you remember."

She steps back. "Good night, Oliver."

"There's that all-night diner down the street, the one with the fish. Let's go for coffee."

"It's too late."

"I only want to talk."

"Not about this."

"Fine. Current events, then. The Mets."

She shakes her head no.

"I'll take that as a yes."

"Sometimes no means no," she says.

"Yes, sometimes," he says. "I'll wait here while you change."

She hesitates and then retreats to her room. After a minute or two, she comes back wearing jeans and a paint-splattered T-shirt. "This is crazy," she says, grabbing her purse.

Out in the hallway she locks the various bolts on her door. On the last one, the key will not come out of the tumbler.

"Shit," she says. "This has been happening lately."

"Let me try," he says, coming up behind her.

"No, I can do it."

"I used to have one like this," he insists, nudging her aside.

"If you would just leave me alone, I could do it."

She yanks it again and the key flies out. She falls back against his chest and quickly rights herself. The keys have fallen to the ground and they both bend down at once. Her elbow meets his face.

"Geez," he says, covering his eye.

"Oh, God," she says. "Are you all right?"

"I'm fine," he says, straightening. "Just Cyclopsed."

"Let me see." She lifts his hand.

He sees her blurrily. She stares worriedly into his half-closed eye, so close the hair at the back of his neck stands up. Electricity ripples across his skin.

She backs away abruptly. "You'll live," she says hastily, slinging her purse over her shoulder. "Let's go, and this better be quick."

Chapter

33

THE HIGHWAY IS SO QUIET at this hour, with one lonely pair of taillights far ahead of them. April is aware of how the car smells of Bernadette's perfume. She thinks of them, only a few hours before, sitting in these same seats. She cups her hands tightly in her lap, staring out the passenger window, her face turned away from him. They've been on the road a good forty-five minutes. "I'm pretty sure we've passed the diner." She eyes him.

"I thought we might go somewhere else," Oliver says. "It's a place you might remember. Do you mind?"

"I can't keep my eyes open."

"It's okay," he says. "Go to sleep."

She turns the radio on low, bypassing many stations before settling on one. "Ah, Horowitz," she says, leaning back.

"That could be anyone," he says stiffly. "In fact, I think it's Serkin."

"Horowitz," she repeats. "Do you know he didn't start practicing seriously until he was in his thirties?"

"He was a prodigy. He didn't need to."

"He was tortured," she says. "Then he came home."

"Left home, you mean."

"I wasn't talking literally."

When the song ends the announcer sighs, "Ah, the moonlight is audible. That was Beethoven's *Moonlight* Sonata, opus twenty-seven, number two, performed by Vladimir Horowitz." She feels Oliver glance her way but doesn't open her eyes. He *knew* it was him; of course he did.

To show his irritation, he switches to a commercial station. It's the Norah Jones song "Come Away with Me." April shields herself, telling herself it's just a pop tune, even though it cuts straight through her. She's heard it a hundred times in the bar, and every time she tries to shut the lyrics out of her mind before they crush her. She hates when a song can slice her open that way. Now, alone in the car with Oliver, she finds it excruciating. She prays not to cry. Oliver drives without speaking. The space between them feels like a living thing, with its own breath and nerve endings. She doesn't dare look at him. When the song ends, Oliver turns the radio off and they drive the rest of the way in silence.

She wakes to Oliver nudging her arm. She grumbles, turning away.

"Come on," he says. "We're here."

She glances at the dashboard to see that it's four thirty in the morning. She sits up, clutching her head. "Jesus," she says. "I don't know why I drank that champagne with Al."

They are in a gravel parking lot surrounded by trees swaying in the cool autumn air. A few leaves sail down. A state park?

"You were mumbling in your sleep," Oliver says.

"Was I?"

"You said Doobie's name."

"Oh, that," she says, rubbing her face. "I keep having this dream that he yanks the leash from my hand and runs into traffic. It's horrible. Usually I wake up just when it looks like he's about to get hit."

"You didn't wake up."

"I think he made it across this time," she says. "Skirted right between the cars." She glances at Oliver. "Why couldn't it have been that way for Buddy? Do you know how many near misses I had with that same car?"

Oliver shakes his head, looking out the window. She knows he feels the horror of it, too. She loves this quality in him, that he will let an unspeakable thing be what it is, without feeling compelled to explain or fix or analyze.

"Let's go," he says quietly. "I have something to show you."

She gets out of the car, shivering. "What happened to coffee?"

He takes his field coat from the backseat and hands it to her, then grabs a flashlight from under the passenger seat. She shoves her arms through the sleeves grudgingly and follows him up the trail.

It's a steady uphill walk until they come to a small wooden bridge spanning a stream. They stop for a moment, listening. "Now I remember," she says. "We camped here with your parents. We took this trail with Buddy and got lost."

He eyes her. "Only because you insisted on leaving the path." He turns off the flashlight to hear the water more clearly. "I've come here a few times since by myself. I don't know why. Something about the sound."

She looks up at him, his gaze intent on the dark running water.

"Each side of the bridge has its own register," he says. "The approaching water sounds like a gurgling rush, the departing water is more like a sweep."

She listens to one side and then the other. He's right, of course, though she would never have noticed on her own.

"Come on," he says. "We're not there yet."

They continue to climb, taking turns losing their footing on the growing incline. He offers his hand, and she takes it without thinking. His palm is warm against hers. They come to a broad, bare rock spread out under the thin moonlight. "Here we are," he says. "You have to lie down to really see it."

They stretch out on their backs on the cold, hard rock, their feet pointing in opposite directions, heads side by side. "Oh, my God," she says. "I never knew so many existed."

Above them the sky teems with stars. A pale crescent moon hovers over the tree line. "If you stare for a while," he says, "you can actually perceive how some stars are closer to us than others. And the colors. See how red that one is?" He points.

"I don't see the color."

"Keep staring. You will."

"Do you know constellations?" she asks.

"A few. That big trapezoid there is Pegasus, the legs go out to the right and the wings to the left. Pisces is just below it. As for your zodiac sign, it doesn't rise until next month. Taurus, that is. *The bull.*"

"Don't look at me like that, as if you're any less stubborn than I am," she says. "Gemini, right? When are you planning to let that shadowy twin of yours out from under your bed?"

"Don't worry. He's here."

She grins, looking back at the stars. "How do you know the constellations?"

"Girl I dated in college."

"Wow, why didn't you hold on to her?"

"She was a nice person, but she had no feeling for music. I once took her to a concert of Mozart divertimentos, and she fell asleep within the first half hour."

"So that was it? The poor girl didn't get another chance?"

"You don't understand. She didn't respond to any kind of music. Pop, jazz, classical, nothing. I didn't think that was humanly possible. I couldn't even think of a song that described her."

"What do you mean?"

"Everyone has a type of music that matches them somehow. Take my father, for instance, predictable, soothing, ingenious. He's a Brandenburg concerto all over."

"Really?" she says. "So you do this for everyone you know, match them to music?"

"I guess so."

"How about Bernadette?"

"Gregorian chant," he says without hesitation.

"And Al?"

"Miles Davis."

"This is amazing. How about yourself?"

"Me? I guess I am my own songs, such as they were."

"And me?"

"You?" He smiles mischievously.

"Let me guess. Some vaudeville tune."

He smirks.

"Madonna, then. Something flash-in-the-pan."

"Beethoven," he says seriously. "The second movement from Symphony Number Seven."

Her mouth opens in amazement. "Tell me it's not the one I'm thinking of, that sleepy allegretto."

"That's the one."

"You're out of your mind. That's not even close. In fact, that is probably the last song on earth that matches me."

"I didn't even have to think about it," he says. "It's always been you, since we were kids."

"Well, that proves it, Oliver. You just don't get me. You never have."

"Or maybe you're the one who doesn't get you. Have you considered that?"

"For one thing, the tempo is too slow."

"It's the beat of the human heart."

"And sad, way too sad."

"Just the opposite. It's about overcoming adversity."

"It sounds like a funeral march."

"Then you haven't heard the right rendition. Try Hélène

Grimaud's version. It's like listening to the surf. You fall in and never climb out."

"Name one thing about that song that's like me, even one."

He folds his hands under his head; she can see he is hearing the notes in his mind. "It's moving, exhilarating, transcendent. The harmony is always changing but the rhythm never does. It unfolds subtly, hypnotically, like a trance. It gives you a sense of something that was already there, like the recognition of something you always knew. It extinguishes time. It doesn't matter what came before or what will come later; each note holds everything. The music unfurls in a necessary way, like the roll of the tide. It opens out and lifts you away with it."

She is silent for a moment, barely breathing. "That's lovely, but you didn't answer my question."

"Yes I did."

She has no idea what he is talking about. "Exhilarating? Transcendent?" she says. "Do you know about my hangnail? My eczema? My PMS? Do you know that I curse myself every time my alarm clock goes off because I stay up too late for no reason and can't fall asleep except curled up with a book in the armchair, so that I wake up with the same blazing neck ache every goddamn morning? *Triumph over adversity?* Which April are you talking about?"

"That's the one." He smiles with broad satisfaction, looking back at the stars.

She feels uneasy now, the allegretto running through her mind.

"These stars," he says finally, sighing. "How can they be there every night and we don't notice?"

"Imagine," she says. "For centuries people have known them like the local landscape, and I can't name a single one."

"It's not too late."

"Let's see, that bright one there must be the North Star."

"Actually that's Vega, part of the constellation Lyra."

"Ah, Orpheus's lyre?"

"So, you were paying attention in Miss Winky's English class."

"How could I forget? His music moved everything, animate and inanimate. Even rivers turned their paths to follow him. Poor Eurydice. If only he hadn't looked back."

"Overcome by joy is how the story goes, but I never thought that made sense. It must have been a moment of doubt. He had to see if she was really there. If only he trusted the power of his playing, he might've gotten her out."

"You have to feel for him, though," she says. "He tried."

"No, he should have stayed focused. He ought to have felt her there."

She glances over at him. "Maybe she wasn't meant to be saved," April says.

"It was himself he failed to save," he says, his eyes fixed on the stars. "She wasn't just his wife, she was his soul."

She studies him.

He clears his throat. "I'm speaking metaphorically of course."

She considers this for a moment. "How did he lose her to begin with?"

"Something catastrophic happened he had no control over. She was stung by a viper and died."

"Tough break," she says.

He stares upward. They settle into silence. For a moment, April thinks she can actually feel the earth turning. It's so quiet. A few crickets hum beneath the leaves, holdouts against frost. Feathers flutter in an overhead branch.

"April," he says. "Tell me how it ended with Quincy."

"I don't want to talk about that. It's so beautiful here. I don't want to talk at all."

"Come on," he says. "If you don't tell me now, you never will."

She sighs. "Only if I can ask you something when I'm done."

"Fine."

"Anything?"

"Anything."

"Okay." She draws a breath. "After your mother died, I had nothing to do with Quincy, but I kept working there the rest of that summer, which was a mistake. Even though he stayed away like I asked, it was very uncomfortable for me. Then one night he had a fight with his girlfriend. Stupid me, I didn't even know he had one."

"Go on."

"The girlfriend, the woman he ended up marrying, was close to his age. They must have been seeing each other for a while because she basically told him to shit or get off the pot, she wanted a ring. They almost came to blows. I heard them in the parking lot. She slammed her door and told him it was over. When she was gone, Quincy came back into the bar. I was down in the stockroom, hoping he would forget I was there, but he came looking for me. I'd never seen him like that, the rage so bright you could almost see it, white and hot. I knew there would be no talking to him so I tried to run for it. He tackled me on the stairs."

She hears Oliver swallow. "And?"

She folds her arms across her chest. "After it was over it took me a long time to get to my feet. He had his back to me, lighting a cigarette. Once I got my bearings, I went up behind him and clocked him in the side of the head with my fist. I don't know what I did to his face, but I'm pretty sure I broke my finger," she says, holding it up to the sky, flexing it. "I've never been able to completely straighten it since."

Oliver reaches up, laces his fingers between hers, and brings her hand to his chest. "Where was I?" he says, his voice raw.

"I walked to your studio. I thought if only I could hear you play, everything would be okay, but you weren't there. Then I remembered that you were leaving for college the next day. I'd known that, of course, but I'd forgotten. I guess I wasn't thinking straight. Anyway, I knew where the key was hidden and let myself in. I just sat down against the piano for a while until I felt ready to go. When I finally got to my apartment, Daisy was still up, teary-eyed because you'd just left. I missed you by twenty minutes."

He squeezes her hand. "And the next day?"

"I knew we were supposed to meet, but I figured as soon as you saw me you would know something happened. Seeing you would have been as bad as looking in the mirror. I wasn't ready for either." She shivers, taking back her hand.

"*He's* the one who ought to feel shame," Oliver says, getting up on one elbow. "You see that, don't you?"

"Until that night, even though I knew the things we did were wrong, I always thought he felt something for me, not love, of course, but a kind of need that was as close to love as I was going to get."

Oliver drops his head in a gesture of defeat.

The stars are dimmer now. A faint suggestion of light spreads over the eastern horizon. "I never went back there to work, but a few weeks later he came by the new bar where I'd found a job and apologized. It wasn't a real apology. He was scared I would tell my father. I told him to get out before I called the cops."

"Why didn't you?"

"I don't know, Oliver. I just didn't want to deal with it." She sighs. One star near the horizon outshines the others. *Venus?* she wonders. *Or Mars?*

Oliver slides onto his back again, limbs spread out, staring up at the fading universe. His voice comes out small and tight. "I'd like to drive to his house right now and kill him."

She rolls onto her stomach, up on her elbows to look at him. "It was a long time ago, Oliver. I don't think about it anymore, so neither should you."

He gazes at her, cupping his hand around the side of her face. His mouth opens but he says nothing.

"Oliver," she whispers. "I put myself in that situation. There was nothing you could have done."

He draws her head down to his chest. She curls up, leaning against him, hearing the percussion of his heart. She thinks of the allegretto. She can hear it in her mind.

After a while she says, "My turn, right?"

"What?"

"I get to ask something."

"Go ahead," he says.

"You know what it is," she says.

She hears him breathe. For a long moment he says nothing. "I don't know the answer to that," he says. "One day I just stopped."

"Which day? How?"

He rakes his fingers through her hair, staring up at the draining night. Just when she thinks he is not going to answer, his voice comes out hoarsely. "That day."

She lifts her head but he won't look at her. "I did go to the studio that night before I went to see Daisy. I played something that had come to mind that day. It was dark and intense, not like anything I'd composed before. I don't know how it came to me. When I finished, I realized I was crying. I had no idea why. There was a pain in my chest that was so strong, I could hardly breathe. I had to get out of there. I never wrote the song down. I went directly to Daisy's because I wanted to forget everything, the whole summer, my mother's death. You." He brings his hand to his face, covering his eyes. "That's when it happened, wasn't it, while I was in my studio."

"I don't know. It doesn't matter. Of course you were feeling strong things; you were leaving the next day for college."

"No, it was more than that."

She closes her eyes, listening to the drum of his heart.

"That was the last time I played," he says. "After that, all I had to do was look at a piano to know it was gone."

She gathers his shirt in her fist. After few minutes, she sits up and so does he. She is unbelievably cold and stiff. She sees the same in him. They stare out to where the sky is a blend of salmon, apricot, and peach. A single fluid drop of light appears on the horizon, brilliant and gold.

"Do you feel it?" April says. "We're moving."

He glances at her.

"No," she says. "Don't look at me, look at the sun. See? It's still; we're rolling toward it. Do you feel it now?"

He stares. The drop of light bleeds quickly, growing larger until the entire orb appears clinging to the horizon by a single golden thread. Then, releasing the liquid light back to its source, the cord snaps and the earth turns freely, drifting steadily downward.

"I feel it," he says.

They continue to watch as the rock beneath them drifts forward, falling toward the light. The horizon drops steadily three, four, and then five lengths beneath the stationary sun.

"We'd better go," she says finally, "before we get clobbered by rush hour."

The sky is brighter now. He gives her a contemplative look. Frail, newborn light glows on the contour of his unshaven face. "I guess you're right," he says reluctantly.

As they start down the hill, the breeze picks up, scattering dry leaves at their feet. April's hair blows in all directions. They walk all the way down without talking. Once inside the car, everything goes abruptly quiet. Oliver stares down at his keys, not starting the engine.

"I have one more question," she says.

His eyebrows arch. He looks at her curiously, almost hopefully.

"You don't really believe what you said about my father, do you?"

He frowns suddenly and starts the ignition.

"Well?"

"If you'd read my mother's journal, you'd see why I think it's possible."

"I just don't get it, Oliver. Why would you believe something like that?"

"Of course I don't want to believe it, but I have to be realistic, too."

"Look, I know my dad did some pretty despicable things, but he did love your father. He wouldn't have gone that far."

"I'll give the diary back to you," he says, pulling onto the road. "You can decide for yourself."

"No, I don't want to read it. I already know more than she would have wanted me to."

He glances at her. "What does that mean?"

"I don't know." She looks out the window.

"You don't know?"

"I changed her bedpan, I washed the puke from her hair. I don't think she'd want her privacy invaded any more than that."

"Do you know something about the affair?"

"Enough to know it wasn't my father."

"Who then?"

She doesn't answer. He shakes his head. They drive the rest of the way home in uneasy quiet.

She doesn't mean to fall asleep again, but before she knows it she feels his fingers on her arm.

"Hey," he says softly.

She opens her eyes, sees her apartment building, and groans. Commuters stream up the stairs to the train platform, their faces stoic and worn. April glances at her watch. Eight twenty already. "I have to hurry," she says. "Doobie needs to go out."

He bites his lip, looking at a man clutching his briefcase as he darts across the street. "We never did get that cup of coffee," he says.

"Maybe next time," she says ironically; she knows there won't be any.

He doesn't smile. Instead he leans over and kisses her chastely on

the mouth. April feels Oliver's warmth flow into her. The kiss con-
sumes all of five or ten seconds, but within that interval she feels an
entire lifetime come and go. In the instant it takes the cursing man
on the platform to miss his train, a hundred years float in and out
of the car.

They lean back then, consciously distancing themselves. Oliver
smiles dolefully.

She touches her mouth self-consciously. "Oliver," she says. "You'll
be fine. You'll see. Married life will suit you."

"Right," he says, tapping the steering wheel.

"See you around then."

"Sure," he says. "See you around."

She opens her door.

"Hey," he says. "Don't think I didn't notice."

"Notice what?"

"You asked me two questions and I only asked one."

She raises her eyebrows.

"It's okay," he says. "I'm going to bank it."

"Really," she says.

"I don't know what the question is yet, but I'm holding on to
the chit."

She smiles uncertainly and closes the door behind her.

Chapter
34

OLIVER IS EARLY, THE FLORIST STILL CLOSED. He walks half a block to the dress shop. Bernadette's car is parked on the street.

Inside the door of the shop, he pauses. On the far wall, a three-way mirror faces a low pedestal. One of Bernadette's friends is being fitted for her bridesmaid's gown. He can't remember her name, though of course he should know it. On the floor, a gray-haired seamstress puts straight pins into the hem of the gown.

"Hey, Oliver," the girl says, spotting him in the mirror.

He waves sheepishly.

"Bernadette's changing. She'll be right out."

He nods and slumps into a seat.

"Pretty, isn't it?" The girl gives a twirl on the pedestal, snapping her gum between her teeth. "Organza silk, imported from Italy."

The seamstress, with a straight pin between her teeth, gives the girl an annoyed look.

"Lovely," Oliver says. He's so tired he could fall asleep in the chair.

"Oliver," Bernadette says, emerging from the dressing room. "What are you doing here?"

The pitch of her voice sends a shiver through him. "I was early for the florist."

"A minute sooner and you would have seen me in my gown!" She kisses him lightly on the cheek and tugs his earlobe. She looks rested and impeccably dressed. "Can you help me carry it out to the car?" She points to a large vinyl garment bag.

Oliver puts his sunglasses back on and lifts the bag off the rack. It is enormous, thirty pounds at least. Bernadette holds the door open for Oliver and calls so long to her friend. He carries the gown in his arms like a body.

"It'll fit better in your trunk than mine," Bernadette says. "Do you mind?"

"No. I'm parked up the street."

She opens the trunk and he lowers the garment bag inside.

"Oh." She moves her sunglasses down her nose. Her mouth opens as she recognizes the same clothes Oliver wore the night before.

He feels a softening in his chest, not remorse exactly, but sorrow; she deserves better. "Can the florist wait?" he asks gently. "I'd like to talk with you."

She closes her mouth and moves the glasses back up her nose. Her face reddens from the base of her neck to her hairline. "It was a tough appointment to get."

In the shop, Bernadette goes over the details of the flower arrangements matter-of-factly: gerbera and baby's breath on the tables, white roses for the ushers, orchid corsages for the grandmothers. She is composed, business-like, but Oliver knows her well enough to detect the thickness in her voice. He braces himself for tears in the car.

But she doesn't cry. He follows her to her apartment and carries the garment bag up three flights to her door, across the threshold. "We only have forty-five minutes until my parents get here for lunch," she says, adjusting the silverware she has already set out on the table. "Your navy blazer is in the bedroom. I can't remember if you left any ties. And don't forget to shave."

Oliver opens the coat closet and sees the futility; even empty it would not be big enough for the dress.

"Put it in the bathtub," she says. "And close the shower curtain."

He carries the cumbersome bag into the bathroom and carefully places it in the tub. When he comes back to the dining room, Bernadette is checking each crystal wineglass for fingerprint marks.

He touches her shoulders from behind. "Bernadette."

"There's a clean shirt in the closet."

"Don't you want to know why I need one?"

She covers her face with her hands.

"I did what you asked," he says. "I told her I won't be going to the dog park anymore."

"I see, and apparently it took you all night to do so."

"We went to a diner," he says. For an instant he is stunned by the swiftness and clarity of the lie. Yet it feels honest. The heart of what he's saying is true. "You were right that we had some things to work out, old stuff from childhood, but it's done now. I feel relieved, so I hope you do, too."

"I'd feel better, Oliver, if you weren't wearing yesterday's clothes."

"I'm sorry, Bernadette. Sometimes I go about things stupidly, but my intentions were sincere. I wanted to put things behind me, and I did."

"So simply," she says.

"Yes, Bernadette. I promise you."

She shakes her head dismally.

"Look, I know this has been uncomfortable for you. If you need some time . . ."

"There's no time," she says sharply. "The invitations are out. We're as good as married."

He takes a step back, stunned. "That's not what I meant."

"I made my choice the day you proposed. I thought you did, too."

"I did, Bernadette. Nothing has changed."

She stares at him for a dazed moment, a wet sheen on her cheeks. "Swear you'll never talk to her again."

He hesitates, hand on his heart. "That would be difficult, Bernadette. We may see her on holidays, my grandmother's birthday, that sort of thing."

"I mean private conversations, phone calls, the diner, the fucking dog park."

He tries not to show his shock. Never has he seen her face so knotted, a bright vein bulging on her forehead. "Fine," he says. "I agree."

She moves into his arms and starts to cry. "What an idiot you are," she says. "If only you'd changed your stupid clothes."

He puts his arms around her. "Bernadette," he says softly. "I would have confided in you anyway."

"You don't know anything about being married. Sometimes you just have to spare a person's feelings."

"I'm sorry, then. I have a lot to learn."

He holds her for a long time. She sniffles into his shirt. On the walls around them hang her children's drawings, uniformly cheerful, all rainbows and bluebirds. *What does she do,* Oliver wonders, *with the erupting volcanoes and headless monsters?*

"Oliver," she says. "I can forget everything if you just tell me you don't have feelings for her."

He caresses her back, touching the familiar curve of her spine, her small shoulders.

She steps back, looking at him for an answer.

"There's feeling," he says. "But it's grief, nostalgia, a whole tangle of things, including guilt, I suppose. But not love, not like what I have with you."

She narrows her eyes.

"Bernadette." He takes her shoulders. "I'm planning to be married to you my whole life. We'll have wonderful years and probably some hard ones, too. We will make a life with children, and it will

be good. We'll be happy. I feel it more than I've ever felt anything."
He means it now. He's completely sure.

She smiles, finally, with tender, puffy eyes. "I think of the children, too, sometimes," she says, blowing her nose. "I wonder who they'll look like."

A picture surfaces in Oliver's mind, a giggly girl with onyx hair and sapphire eyes running along a beach. In the same breath he lets the image slide away like words written in sand. "Freckly towheads," he says. "Like you."

Chapter
35

APRIL PATS NANA'S HAIR DRY with a towel and carefully combs out the silken strands. Tired from their earlier walk around the block, Nana begins to nod off.

"Try to keep your head still for just another minute or two," April says, setting out the rollers. "We're almost done."

"What do you think I'm doing?" Nana says. The radio is playing Frank Sinatra, Nana's favorite. It's a song about spring. April ought to know these titles by now.

"Nana," she ventures. "I have a question for you."

"Hm?" Nana rouses.

"After that soldier kissed you in the diner," she says tentatively. "How did you go on?"

"I told you. I didn't eat for a month. Lost twenty pounds."

"Did it feel like a rewiring of your body, every cell switched places?"

Nana turns and looks up into April's face. "Who is he?"

"No one," she says, reddening. "I'm speaking hypothetically."

"It's like this," Nana says. "All your life you're yellow. Then one day you brush up against something blue, the barest touch, and voilà, the rest of your life you're green."

April smiles curiously.

"Except that's a bad example," Nana says. "Because we're all rainbow-colored inside, each of us a different arrangement, of course. The kiss just makes all the colors more concentrated, so intense they can be hard to look at. Or feel, rather. Like a Mediterranean sunset."

April ponders this.

"But you have to feel it anyway," Nana says. "Or you shrivel up inside."

"I'm done now, Nana," she says, putting away the extra rollers. "Do you want to take a nap?"

"Remember him, April. Even when you can't picture his face anymore, you owe each other prayers. And I'm not talking about sappy, sentimental stuff. Or fantasy, either. You pray for the hardest moments in his life, years down the line, when he's in a foxhole, or his child is sick, or he finds he has cancer. No one escapes calamity, but a kiss like that can last you your whole life." She looks up at April. "I'm not saying that you think about it all the time. It just leaves you different than it found you."

April pats her shoulder and leads her toward the bedroom. "Nana," she says, tucking her in. "I know my mom and dad did their best, and I'm not saying they weren't great parents. I just want you to know that any ounce of good sense I may have picked up along the way has come from you."

She glances down for Nana's response and hears a gurgling snore. April smiles, adjusting the covers. *Naturally,* she thinks. *The last word is Nana's.*

Chapter

36

A T FIRST, OLIVER found the place disconcerting: a restored
seventeenth-century mansion-turned-restaurant, with low ceil-
ings and uneven floors. The hearth is so large, you can stand up
inside. Bernadette was in love with it, though, and helped Oliver to
see its charm. The rehearsal dinner consists of four tables of eight
with a small space cleared in the center for dancing. They have the
room to themselves.

The only ones dancing are Al and Nana. From the looks of it,
he has been a bit too generous keeping her glass filled. Al shuffles
her around like a girl, dipping and twirling. Nana protests, laughing, hitting him occasionally. Her smile could light up a city. Oliver
imagines her radiance as a young woman. She hasn't lost it. The liquor makes her movements more fluid and agile than he has seen her
in years. But also loose and unsteady. Just as she begins to lose her
balance, Al grabs her.

Sitting by herself, April watches them with a faint smile on her
face. No doubt she is the one who set Nana's hair, dressed her in
the classy gabardine outfit, orthopedic shoes, and seamed stockings. April leans on the table, fiddling with the castanets Nana was

playing earlier. They are good therapy for the hand affected by the stroke. Nana played them clumsily, but with enough occasional precision that it was obvious she was once a master.

The dessert dishes are cleared and people begin to leave, one by one kissing Oliver and Bernadette good night, wishing them luck for the morning. "My face hurts from smiling," Bernadette whispers, rubbing her cheekbones. She is wearing a high-necked lace dress, hand-tailored and soaked in tea to give it an antique tinge. Her hair is in a French braid, her earrings classic pearls.

April helps Al escort Nana to a seat. Nana appears dizzy, a little breathless; she asks for water. April kneels down, tears open the Velcro on her shoes, and massages her feet. Nana touches her hair to see if the curls are still in place, feels her earrings to make sure she hasn't lost them. Al rubs her shoulders, his hands big on her tiny frame.

Oliver stands and goes over. He pulls up a chair and sits down, taking his grandmother's hand. "Nana, you've still got the moves."

She rolls her eyes and smiles. "Oliver," she says, patting his cheek. Her face is flushed, and Oliver wonders if Al overexerted her. Nana glances across the room at Bernadette. At this distance, her hair looks nearly white, the same hue as her dress, giving her a lithe, unearthly appearance.

"Oliver," Nana says. "Are you nervous?"

"Not really." He turns to her.

"I was nervous when I married your grandfather. I thought: This is too good to be true; there's got to be a hitch."

Oliver smiles.

"He was a fine man, your grandfather. Your father turned out just like him."

"That's because you did a good job raising him," April says. She has Nana's foot on her lap, massaging her toes, unconcerned that her own dress might get dirty on the floor. It is dark red; a color you might expect of April, but one she rarely wears. The cotton knit fabric holds her shape, not clingy, but suggestive, the hem just above the knee.

"Enough," Nana says, pulling her foot away. "Do you want me to embarrass Oliver in front of his in-laws?"

April smiles a quick, easy smile, much like Nana's. She pats her grandmother's leg as she sets it down, and catches Oliver's eye. Warmth spreads in his chest. The glance is instantaneous, reflexive, yet it contains everything.

"You ought to leave your shoes off," April says to Nana. "Your feet are swollen."

"Sure," Nana says. "And walk to the parking lot in my stocking feet?"

"I'll carry you," Al says. "People will think you're my tipsy girlfriend."

Nana swats his hand. She touches her curls again as April puts on her shoes. "April, my hair's falling down."

"I'll redo it in the morning. Don't forget to set your clock. We can't be late for the wedding."

"Oliver wouldn't get married without me, right?" Nana squeezes his hand.

"Never," he says.

April gets to her feet. Oliver almost helps her up, but decides against it. As she sits down, Al squeezes into the same chair, edging her to one side, though there are plenty of empty seats. "Hear my news?" Al says.

"What's that?" Oliver says, taking a sip of Nana's water.

"Sent my résumé to the *Globe,* and they called me for an interview last week."

"The *Boston Globe*?"

"Offered me the job yesterday."

Oliver is not entirely surprised. Al went to BU and always liked the city. "Congratulations."

"And the best part," Al says, putting his arm around April, "is that Rose is coming with me."

Oliver nearly chokes on the water.

"What?" Nana says.

"Al," April says, pushing his arm off her. "I did not say that."

"But she's coming around." Al winks. "I've even scoped out an apartment for her in Nahant, right near the ocean. No one can refuse that."

Oliver brings a napkin to his mouth, clearing his throat.

"You okay?" Al asks.

"Went down the wrong pipe," he says, taking another sip.

"April?" Nana says.

"Relax," she says. "I'm not going anywhere." She gives Al an annoyed look. "We should hit the road," she says, patting Nana's hand. "It's going to be a full day tomorrow."

"Hal is taking me home," Nana says.

"Are you sure?" April says, glancing around the room.

"She's sure," Al says. "Let's you and me go for a nightcap."

"No," April says. "I'm tired."

"Just one," Al says. "Oliver, will you join us? Last night of bachelorhood, after all."

Oliver glances at Bernadette and sees she is walking in his direction.

"Come on," Al says. "It's my responsibility as best man to take you out for a drink. We'll get Rose here to pop out of a cake."

April elbows him. Bernadette appears at Oliver's side. He takes her hand. "No thanks," he says. "I'll save my energy for the morning."

Bernadette kisses Al good night. "Hope you're planning to dance with the bride tomorrow."

"Wouldn't miss it." He grins, though not convincingly.

Bernadette turns to April. Oliver searches for some sign of jealousy or resentment, but Bernadette's eyes are clear, her smile genuine. He is moved by her magnanimity. Whatever fury possessed her a few weeks ago is gone. She is all Bernadette now, graceful, kindhearted, elegant. He squeezes her hand, and she returns the pressure.

"Come on over to my parents' house in the morning if you want to get dressed together," Bernadette says to April. "We'll have a hair-dresser and makeup artist."

"Thanks," April says, "but I'll be getting Nana together. We'll meet you at the church, if that's okay."

Oliver is aware of Bernadette's effort to be kind. It humbles him. Eventually they will likely move to California, and except for occasional trips, April will return to being someone from his past. He reminds himself that years went by in his life when he barely thought of her at all. He was perfectly happy during that time. Perfectly. It's normal to feel sadness; marriage is as much letting go of the past as it is embracing the future. Everyone knows that.

He watches April and Al leave. As soon as they pass through the door, Al slings his arm gruffly around April's shoulder. He wonders about Boston, and what might happen now that Oliver is getting married. He tells himself it doesn't matter.

"I think it went well," Bernadette says when everyone is gone.

Oliver nods.

They walk to their cars. The parking lot is empty except for a few vehicles, including two at the far end, shrouded in darkness. He can barely see them.

"You're quiet," she says.

"I'm fine," he says. "How about you? Any jitters?"

"I just hope my hair comes out okay."

"Bernadette, if there's anything certain, it's that you'll look perfect."

She smiles, though not happily, he thinks. He opens her door.

"You know I love you, don't you?" he says.

"Of course." She laughs, kissing him once more.

"You look beautiful tonight."

"You told me that already." She pats his cheek. "I can't wait for my kids to see my dress tomorrow. They'll get such a kick. I can already picture them playing with the train."

"You're their princess," he says.

"Just don't expect it to be a quiet ceremony," she says. "I wouldn't put it past some of them to do cartwheels in the aisle."

He smiles. "I may do a few myself."

She smiles sadly, then looks down, covering her eyes. "I only wish my sister could be there."

He takes her in his arms.

"I'm fine," she says. "And if I ruin my makeup with tears tomorrow, you can shoot me."

"Don't wear makeup," he says. "You don't need it. You're so beautiful. I don't know how I got so lucky. What are you doing with me, anyway?"

Her smile fades. She looks at him. "It won't all be easy, Oliver. The first year usually isn't. But we'll do fine. We're going to have a good marriage."

He nods. There are tears in his eyes but he has no idea how they got there. She cups her hands around his face and kisses each eyelid. "Geez, look at *me*." He laughs, wiping his eyes.

"You're a good man, Oliver. Whatever we have to work through, we will."

He nods, brushing drops from his chin.

She studies him for a long moment.

"Bernadette," he says solemnly. "I just hope I'm all you deserve."

"You are," she says without hesitation, "and more." She kisses him once more and gets into her car. "See you at the church."

Oliver waves, watching her drive off.

He stands alone in the empty lot, riveted by the crush of stars overhead, the tattering of leaves along asphalt. He raises his hands over his head and closes his eyes, feeling the coolness of the air against his skin, the sweet, merciless touch of the breeze.

He hears movement down by the other cars. His eyes have adjusted to the darkness, and for a moment he imagines he sees a white sedan and a red Jeep. If April and Al were still around, would he join them? Why would he even consider it?

The cars are not theirs. Two teenage employees amble from the restaurant, laughing and bumping hips. The boy takes the girl's hand. He presses her against the brick wall of the building, her hair framed in ivy, and kisses her until Oliver feels his knees go weak. He starts his car and shifts into reverse.

He's not going to deceive himself. Of course Bernadette deserves better, but he will do his best to make it up to her. Over time, perhaps, he can become the man she thinks he is.

Just as he is about to pull away he notices another car in the lot. A rather tall man is loading cartons into the back of an old station wagon. He looks familiar. A queer sensation comes over Oliver. He pulls back into his spot and watches the man. He gets out and walks over. The man, bending over, jerks up with surprise. "Hey, Oliver," he says. "You scared the life out of me."

"Quincy," he says, dazed.

"Didn't your father tell you? He asked me to provide the liquor tonight. Apparently, I brought too much. Better that than running out, I figure." He grins that gentle, benign smile. "So, son, you all set for tomorrow?"

The odd feeling is getting worse. Oliver stares at him. "Uh, sure," he says. "Ready as I'll ever be."

"Better go on home and get some sleep, then. Good luck tomorrow."

Oliver gets back in his car, watches Quincy pull away. Only then does he think of his mother's journal, the back room of the bar, April's insistence that it was not her father. "Oh, God," Oliver says, watching the car swing out of the lot. "It was him."

Chapter
37

OLIVER PARKS ACROSS THE STREET and watches Quincy enter his house. He wonders if he noticed Oliver following him. The lot grades down from the curb so that the rust-colored ranch sits below street level. Someone has raked a staggering pile of leaves beside the driveway and then left them to blow. At the edge sits a child's pink bicycle.

A short, fortyish woman answers the door. She is Asian looking, with a tidy haircut that sweeps beneath her chin. "Can I help you?" she asks warily. It's midnight, after all. Her eyes move from Oliver's suit up to his face. "Were you in an accident?"

It occurs to him only then that he is soaking wet, his hair stuck to his forehead, suit dripping. When had it started raining?

The door opens farther and Quincy appears behind her. His mouth opens in what Oliver takes for fright. "Oliver," he says. "Good Lord. Pam, this is Hal's son, the party I worked tonight."

"Ah," she says. "Aren't you getting married in a few hours?" She looks at her watch.

Oliver knows he should answer, but nothing comes. He turns to Quincy. "Can we talk for a minute?"

Quincy's eyes widen. "Of course," he says without stepping aside. "Let me think. We can go to the den."

"Why not here?" asks his wife, gesturing to the couch. She is attractive, tired looking, older, perhaps, than Oliver first thought. "I'll make tea."

"The den is better," Quincy says. "To keep from waking the kids. Pam was just getting ready for bed herself."

"Tea won't be necessary," Oliver says. "Thank you."

She scrutinizes Quincy for a moment. "Fine," she says. "I'll say good night then."

In the den, Quincy does not offer to take Oliver's jacket. He closes the door behind them, hesitates, and then opens it again. "I'd better kiss the girls good night in case they've waited up for me."

Alone, Oliver appraises the room. It feels lived-in, with a bowl of half-eaten popcorn on the coffee table and LEGOs scattered on the worn carpet. Beside the window stands a piano with a child's practice book open on the ledge. Above the piano are family photos: the girls, roughly five and eight, both resembling their mother, and grandparents from both sides. Beside these is a much older, sepia-colored picture, cracked but carefully framed, of an elderly Chinese woman wearing a high-collared jacket. She is diminutive but elegant. The proportions in the photo are off somehow. Oliver leans closer, his fingers grazing the piano, and sees that the woman's feet are the size of lemons. He gives a jolt, accidentally banging the keys. The dissonance rings through the room.

Quincy comes in, closes the door, and circles the couch without sitting down. "Yes, Oliver," he says quietly. "Was something wrong with the liquor?"

Oliver realizes now how drenched he is, shivering inside his clothes. "I want to talk about my mother."

"Your mother?"

"My mother and you."

Quincy looks behind him to see that the door is closed. "What are you talking about, son?"

"You don't seem to have any qualms about doing business with my father, taking his money."

"Should I?"

Oliver raises his eyebrows. "I see. Why should screwing a man's wife deter a good business relationship."

He winces. "I don't know what you're—"

"I have my mother's journal. I have proof."

"Good Lord, Oliver. You're talking twenty years ago. I've long since done my penance."

"I'd like to know how it started."

"No, son, there's no point. You need to leave."

Oliver sits down. "Shall we call your wife in? She might be interested."

"I've got nothing to hide. I wasn't married back then."

"But my mother was."

Quincy frowns. "What happened was between us. It doesn't involve you."

"You're right," he says, standing. "It's my father you should explain things to. Let's call him up."

"Hold on," he says with irritation. "Fine. What do you want to know?"

"From the beginning."

Quincy sighs miserably. "We'd dated before she met your father. I was her accompaniment at a place in the city called Viva's."

"Accompaniment?"

"You know, on the piano. She should have kept singing. You know what a voice she had. Anyway, people give things up for their own reasons."

Oliver glances at the piano.

"She nicknamed me Silver because of my touch. Corny, I know, but it was a different world back then."

S, Oliver thinks, remembering the diary. He raises a brow. He doesn't like the fact that Quincy plays; it's a rude coincidence.

"Anyway, she met your father, and I was history. The affair was years later. Neither of us meant for it to happen. It was nostalgia, I guess. We still had feelings for each other. Look," he says. "You should go now. You're getting married in the morning."

"What about April?"

Quincy's face goes white. He sits down, looking older than his fifty-some years. "What about her?"

Oliver stares.

"She was a nice girl, April. Hard worker. Fond of you, I remember."

"I know about the molestation."

His face drains of color. "That's not how it was."

"Three years of sexual abuse of a minor. You could do time for that."

Quincy reddens. "It wasn't the way you make it sound. She . . . No, I'm not going to get into this."

"But it happened, right?"

"No, I don't know what you're talking about."

Oliver waits.

"We all do things we're not proud of, son."

Oliver gets up to leave. "What blows my mind is that you've had the gall to stay in touch with my family all these years, picnics and business deals, just like old friends. And the way you greeted April at my father's house last summer. I don't know why she didn't spit in your face."

A vein on Quincy's forehead becomes visible. "Cut me some slack, Oliver. You remember how she was back then, the mini skirts and the tits."

Oliver pictures himself landing a blow, imagines the thud as Quincy falls, sprawled in a sea of popcorn, holding his nose to stop the blood. But Oliver resists. It's not what his father would do.

"What I remember," Oliver says, "is that she was a sweet kid with no mother around to tell her how to dress. She had the bad luck to have a crush on someone she thought was nice, but turned out to be a pervert."

Quincy looks only slightly alarmed. "You ought to know her part in things before you say any more."

"She was fourteen!" Oliver pounds his fist on the coffee table. "Oh, but excuse me. You waited until she was seventeen to actually fuck her. A real gentleman."

"I'm not admitting to any of this. You have to leave now."

"Why don't you tell me about that time, Quincy, on the stairs in the stockroom? What was her part then?"

Quincy moves to open the door of the den, but Oliver puts his hand on the doorknob. "The statute of limitations isn't up. Rape of a minor is a felony."

Finally Quincy looks frightened. "I'm married now," he says hoarsely. "I got kids of my own. I'm not that person anymore."

Oliver frowns. "I want you to give my father everything you owe him and then quietly get out of his life. I'll give you till the end of the month. And if you ever have contact with April again, you can be sure you'll hear from me."

Quincy turns grimly and leads Oliver to the front door. "Look," he says. "I don't know why this is all so urgent for you. For the rest of us, it was over a long time ago."

"Really, I'm impressed that you could make things right so easily after ruining a girl's life."

Quincy glances nervously behind him. "Look, Oliver. We both know that with or without me, April would have been the same girl she was. I didn't create her."

"You used her and you damaged her, and if someone did the same to one of your daughters, you'd be hard-pressed not to kill him."

Quincy takes a nervous step back. Oliver walks up the drive, through the blowing leaves, feeling the chill breeze through his damp clothes. He knows he ought to get some sleep before morning, but it feels impossible now.

Chapter
38

THE CHURCH IS CHILLY, with thick stone walls cool to the touch and a remote, vaulted ceiling. The green-gray swirl of the marble altar matches the color of the sky, overcast and low. It is more like a November day than mid-October. Without sunlight, the stained-glass windows are muted, each pane depicting a scene Oliver cannot decipher. The pews begin to fill, as they did one year ago. Perhaps it is just Oliver's imagination, but a collective memory seems to hang over the congregation, as if assembled in commemoration, not celebration. Buddy is everywhere. Oliver retreats to the sacristy to wait.

"Best man not here yet?" the priest says, pulling his alb over his street clothes.

"He's never on time." Oliver manages a smile. He has known the old priest for years, the same man who married his high school friends and buried his mother and Buddy. He is gray-haired, overweight, with a sad, kindly smile.

"You're looking a little green around the gills," the priest says.

"Didn't sleep," Oliver says.

"The grooms never do." He smiles, smoothing his chasuble over his shoulders. "Your mother would have loved to be here, Oliver."

"Yes, I've been thinking of her."

"What a lady she was. So much grace. Not unlike your Bernadette."

Oliver smiles, looking into his hands, his stomach a cement mixer. *Jitters are normal,* he thinks. "I'd better look for my brother."

He walks down the side aisle of the church. People catch his eye: his high school soccer coach, piano teacher, his college roommate; people he has not seen in years, his whole life represented. The agitation eats at his stomach. He is aware that his smile is stiff and tells himself to relax. The pigtailed child from the engagement party frowns up at him from a pew, unhappy perhaps that his hair is still not blond. He tries to smile at her, but she'll have none of it. It seems a bad omen not to have her approval.

In the back vestibule, Nana is sitting in a chair, wearing an embroidered pale blue suit and a pillbox hat. Beside her Hal is down on one knee, fanning her. On the other side stands April with her hand on Nana's shoulder.

"Is she okay?" Oliver asks.

"I'm fine," Nana says. "I was just thinking about a dream I had this morning. I was on a hilly trail I used to hike as a child and Buddy was there up ahead. He held out his hand to help me over some rocks."

"She's a little under the weather," Hal says. "Too much excitement last night, I think."

Oliver kneels down, his tails brushing the floor, and takes Nana's hand. Her face looks pale, her eyes not quite focused. Hung over, Oliver thinks. "April." Nana winks. "Doesn't he look snappy?"

"A handsome groom if I ever saw one," she says.

Oliver stands to face her. April is wearing a cheerful pale yellow dress, her hair pulled back. He thinks she looks relaxed. He glances at the chain around her neck and recognizes it as Nana's. She must have polished it for the occasion; Oliver has never seen it so bright.

"Break a leg," April says and kisses his cheek. There is a scent on her skin, like the sea, but the moment she pulls back it is gone. "Now get out of here," she says. "It's bad luck to see the bride."

Out front, a white limousine pulls up. Oliver's muscles tense, his breathing ragged.

"April," he whispers. "I need to ask you something."

Her eyebrows fly up.

"I'm serious," he says. "It will only take a second."

"It can wait," she says firmly, glancing out at the limousine.

He takes her wrist and leads her toward a narrow stairwell leading down to the bathroom. She pulls back. A bridesmaid glances over at them, then away again as she helps an usher pin on his rose. Oliver pulls April into the stairwell and down the narrow steps.

Inside the bathroom, she covers her mouth in horror. "What are you doing?" she hisses. "People saw that."

"I found out," he says, "about my mother and Quincy."

"Oh, my God, Oliver, don't you see this isn't the time?"

"You never told me," he says, his hand still tight around her wrist.

"Bernadette is on her way into the church!"

"You could have said something, but you didn't."

"Are you having a breakdown? Get a grip, Oliver."

"I don't see why you kept it from me."

"Look, what you need to do right now is run up those stairs and get to the altar."

"April, I'll never forgive you for this." He releases her wrist and pushes back out the door.

At the top of the stairs he sees a flowing glacier of white, hears the rustle of silk and taffeta. The back of Bernadette's hair is meticulously French-braided and adorned with flowers. A little girl in a wheelchair and a boy with wide-set eyes giggle as they touch the dress, tossing up the lace and watching it float down. Their mothers gently coax them into the church. Bernadette touches the boy's cheek as he goes. The great white dress bristles as she turns to see Oliver.

Al grips Oliver's shoulder and turns him around. "This way," he says. The two walk up the aisle. Oliver's heel scuffs the white runner.

He nearly trips. The damn rented shoes. At the top of the aisle, near the altar, he and Al turn around to face the congregation.

"Have you flipped?" Al says quietly, smiling out at the crowd.

"Hm?" Oliver says.

"I'm taking attendance. Are you here?"

"Present," Oliver says.

"Aren't you going to ask me if I remembered the rings?"

Oliver does not answer. People wave to him and he waves back vacantly. The organist plays a hushed version of the Pachelbel canon. Bernadette's mother comes down the aisle accompanied by Brad. Next comes Oliver's father escorting Nana. She moves awkwardly without her walker, feet snagging the white cloth, a different woman from the one he saw dancing the night before.

Oliver scans the crowd. In the back vestibule he catches a glimpse of white, a dress like an icecap. He closes his eyes and prays, for what?

His father is having trouble getting Nana up the aisle. Oliver goes to help, but realizes halfway down that this is not the right protocol; the groom is supposed to keep his post. But what's more important here? He takes his grandmother's other elbow.

"Oliver." She beams at him, patting his arm.

He glances into the vestibule where ushers and bridesmaids are finding their places in the lineup. He hears giggles and whispers, a tone of happy excitement. No sign of April. Suddenly he realizes that Bernadette is looking at him, her mouth fixed in a dreadful, panicky smile. He looks away.

Back at the altar Oliver stands squarely and awaits the organ music. Through a side door entrance April slips in quietly and slides into the pew beside Nana. A strand of hair has fallen from her clip and cascades in a frail arc down her cheek. On her wrist he sees pink marks, the impression of his hand.

The music begins. He watches the flower girl, a relative of Bernadette's, meander up the aisle. People coo adoringly. The girl in the

wheelchair claps. Next begins a string of bridesmaids wearing char-
treuse strapless gowns. The music pauses. People stand. The wedding
march, a tune Oliver has always disliked, pipes through the organ.
Bernadette walks slowly up the aisle, face veiled, clasping her father's
arm. When he lifts her veil to kiss her, Oliver sees that she is crying.
Her father gives Oliver an uneasy look and hands her over.

Oliver smiles at her but she doesn't meet his eye. He takes her
arm and faces the priest. Bernadette signals the bridesmaids for a tissue. Oliver squeezes her hand, but she does not return the pressure.
Because he looked too soon? He thinks of Orpheus. The priest is
speaking but Oliver hardly hears.

"As we begin, we call to mind those loved ones who have gone
before us, whom we know are present in spirit to share the great
happiness of this day," the priest says. "Especially Bernadette's sister,
Jenny, and grandfather Lawrence; Oliver's grandfather Spencer, his
mother, Avila, and his cousin Buddy. God rest their souls."

Oliver shifts his weight, gripping Bernadette's hand. All he wants
now is to say *I do* and have it over with. He tries to think of his honeymoon. At this time tomorrow, they'll be on a plane.

There are whispers behind him. He hears someone say "Buddy?"
It's his grandmother's voice. Oliver turns to look though he knows
he shouldn't. Pale and weak, Nana stands and steps into the aisle.
"Buddy?" she says again, her voice oddly slurred.

The priest raises his eyebrows but continues to read as Hal tries to
usher Nana back to her seat.

"What on earth does he mean?" Nana says more loudly now.
"God rest his soul?"

"Sh, it's okay, Mom," Hal says soothingly. "Let's let them get
married."

"Oliver wouldn't get married without Buddy," she says, her voice
growing even stranger than before. "Where is he?"

An altar boy with squeaky sneakers crosses the marble floor of the
altar holding a paper cup of water.

"Sit, Mom," Hal says softly. "You're not looking so good."

She sits suddenly and awkwardly, crashing down on the pew. A collective gasp rises from the congregation. The girl with the pigtails says loudly, "What happened, Mommy?" Hal gestures to Al, putting an imaginary phone to his ear, and Al disappears off the altar into the sacristy. When Hal holds the paper cup up to Nana's lips, water dribbles from the side of her mouth. Oliver sees fear cross his father's face.

The priest announces a hymn, number 47, though everyone knows it's not the usual time for a song. There is a moment's pause as the flustered organist rifles through his book.

The priest goes to Hal, who lifts Nana in his arms and eases out of the pew. April follows. The congregation murmurs, straining for a view.

At the same moment, Oliver and Bernadette look at each other, each holding a lit candle in their hands, which they were about to join in lighting the nuptial candle. Wax drips to the floor. Just as Oliver wonders if they should still go over to the big candle, Bernadette blows hers out. A crushing feeling comes over him.

The congregation continues to sing, tentatively and off key. After a moment, flashing lights appear through the stained-glass windows. No sirens, thank God. Bernadette turns and goes into the sacristy. With what feels like his last breath, Oliver blows out his candle and heads for the door.

Outside he finds his father, brother, and the priest. "They took her to Saint Claire's," Hal says. "April's with her."

"It should never have gotten to this point," Al says. "We should have taken her this morning."

"We tried," Hal said. "She was determined."

"You ought to be with her, Dad," Oliver says. "Go on if you need to."

Hal looks at the church hopelessly. "I couldn't."

"Just go," Oliver says.

"All right, then. If everything's okay, I'll try to join you at the reception. I'm so sorry, Oliver."

"Call with news," Oliver yells after him.

Some members of the congregation have drifted out to the lawn. "Okay," the priest says gravely. "We'll gather everyone up as soon as you're ready."

Oliver finds Bernadette in the sacristy alone, her train spreading over half the floor. She moves her finger around the rim of a chalice. The sun begins to break through clouds, and swatches of color from a small rose window fall across the white of her dress.

"Bernadette," he says, moving toward her.

She holds out her hand to halt him. "How is your grandmother?"

"They took her to the hospital."

She cups her hands around the chalice, studying it with a troubled expression.

Oliver stands stock-still, to keep things from falling apart. He opens his mouth to speak, but she puts out her hand again to silence him, the heavy gown rustling.

"Talk to me," he says finally. "Is it because I saw you?"

"No, Oliver," she says. "It's because you didn't."

He puts his hand on his heart.

"Whatever was going on down there in the stairwell, I don't want to know about it. I asked you never to talk to her again, and you couldn't even make it to the wedding."

"Bernadette, there's an explanation."

"I've been praying to God for a sign," she says, "something to tell me this is the right thing to do. I'd say I got more than I bargained for."

"No, I'll make everything up to you."

She stares at her engagement ring.

"Yo, Oliver," Al calls from the doorway. "Time to move. He's got another wedding at noon."

"Not now," Oliver shouts. "Give us a minute."

"This is fate, Oliver. We can tell people we're postponing on account of your grandmother."

He looks bewildered.

She slips the diamond off her finger.

Oliver's chest constricts, an enormous weight sitting on him.

Bernadette's eyes redden. She drops the ring into the chalice. He moves toward her.

"Don't," she says.

He puts his hand on his chest; he feels he is dying. "Okay, we don't have to get married today, but give me another chance. We can talk things through."

"You looked right through me, Oliver. There I was about to walk up the aisle, and you didn't even see me."

"How stupid of me, Bernadette. I'm sorry."

She rubs her forehead in small circles, the way she does when there's a headache coming on. She looks up at the stained glass, the jaws of a whale closing upon the horrified Jonah. Oliver sinks to his knees.

"I knew from the moment we moved here, the way you looked at her. I have myself to blame."

"Bernadette, you're wrong. Please, let me prove it to you."

"Oliver," she says. "You just did."

Chapter
39

MONITORS BEEP. The room smells of medication. April holds Nana's hand, bruised by the IV, and looks into her stark, pale face. An oxygen tube runs into her nose; another sucks fluid from her lungs with a faint, gurgling noise. Nana winces and coughs. April holds her hand more tightly. She is only allowed five minutes. Hal was in just before her. Nana looks small in the bed, like a child. One side of her lip is turned down; the limbs on half of her body are motionless.

Why didn't April do something earlier? She knew from the moment she arrived at Nana's apartment this morning that she wasn't well. April found her sitting in an armchair in her alcove, already dressed for Oliver's wedding, clutching her purse and saying the rosary. She was tired and drawn, not quite lucid, but April attributed it to the rehearsal dinner.

Nana's eyes move beneath their lids, her forehead tense. April hopes she is not in pain. "Nana," she whispers, but she doesn't hear.

April bows her head, stroking Nana's hand. Suddenly Nana jolts, eyes riveted on the ceiling in an expression of fright, seeing something April does not.

"Nana," she says. "It's okay."

Nana turns and for an instant sees April. She shakes her head to say no, then looks back at the ceiling, beyond the ceiling, to the wall behind the bed, her head thrown back like a corpse, or child tasting rain. April tries not to look at her gaping mouth. She hears the long wheeze of each breath. Nana raises her good hand, wavering, and feels blindly around her neck, dislodging her oxygen tube. April presses it back, then moves to the head of the bed, bending low so Nana can see her cross around April's neck. "Is this what you're looking for?" April says.

Nana's lips, bared over her teeth, cannot close into a kiss, so April presses the cool metal to Nana's cheek. Her breath has a singed, metallic aroma; death has already found its root. Her expression is hollow-eyed, alert and resolved. April wants last words, a hug, a reassuring glance, but all she has is a look in Nana's eye that says this is the part she must do alone.

Hal enters the room. April does not want to leave, but Nana nods slightly, telling her it is okay to go. April kisses Nana's forehead and squeezes her hand, then kisses the cross and slips it inside her dress.

Chapter
40

B Y THE TIME OLIVER ARRIVES at his father's house, it is early
evening. He has spent the day working out a nightmare of
details: canceling hotel reservations and plane tickets, building a
mental list of things to worry about later, such as returning gifts and
retrieving possessions from Bernadette's apartment. The reception,
which could not be canceled, went on without them.

In the church parking lot, Bernadette's father and brother grabbed
Oliver by the arms and promised a lawsuit, forty thousand dollars
for nonrefundable wedding expenses, and another ten for pain and
suffering. Impressive, Oliver thought, that they had already worked
out the numbers. He didn't bother to explain it was Bernadette who
backed out. He had caught a glimpse of her in the rectory courtyard,
weeping in her mother's arms. His first instinct was to rush to her; it
felt so strange not to be the one comforting her. Al's Jeep is parked in
his father's driveway. Oliver noticed on his way home that April's car
was still in the church parking lot, untouched since morning.

The house is quiet. Flowers cover the small table in the front foyer,
a bridesmaid's bouquet, a rose from Al's lapel, and Nana's orchid
wristband. The scent overpowers him.

He finds them in the family room, a Giants game on the television, which only Al appears to watch. Hal dozes in a chair, newspaper spread on his lap. No one speaks. They are still dressed in their wedding garb, but with shoes off, ties undone. Dirty paper plates and disposable cutlery litter the coffee table. In the center sits a partially eaten layer of wedding cake, the plastic bride and groom still intact.

Oliver clears his throat. "How's Nana?"

His father and brother look up. Al bites his lip. Hal rubs his eyes and folds his newspaper. Neither answers. On the table beside the wedding cake, Oliver notices Nana's pillbox hat. On the floor, her leg brace. He thinks he ought to feel something awful. His father rises, comes wearily across the room, and puts his hand on Oliver's shoulder.

Oliver slips off his ascot and tosses it on an end table. He taps his fist against his forehead, trying to jar his brain, his heart, back into operation.

"It was a massive stroke," his father says. "There was nothing anyone could have done."

Oliver runs his hands through his hair. Al clicks off the television and stands. He punches Oliver's arm lightly. "You okay?"

"I'm fine." Oliver tries to think. Nana had another stroke, is that what they're saying? He can't fit anything more in his brain. "Is there more cake?" he asks stupidly.

"Enough for an army," his father says. "We had it for dinner."

"I have to get going." Al gives Oliver a quick hug, slapping his back. Oliver feels ill at ease. He does not react. Al kisses his father good-bye. "Call me tomorrow about the wake," he says, squeezing his father's shoulder.

Hal nods, staring at the rug. *Just lost his mother,* Oliver thinks. He ought to console his father, too. Offer some small gesture, but Oliver is at a loss.

Al slings on his rented jacket, small for his shoulders. "Can someone give April a lift back to her car?"

"We'll take care of it," his father says. "Let her sleep for now."

Al leaves. Oliver turns the game back on. Nana's dead, he thinks; the words might make the reality sink in. He eats a piece of wedding cake and washes it down with beer. Then another piece and another until he feels sick.

During a commercial, his father lowers the volume. "Oliver," he says. "Do you want to talk about it?"

He takes a swallow. "She changed her mind," he says and raises the volume.

"Oliver," he persists. "When was the last time you slept?"

Oliver considers this. Not last night. Not the night before. What does that make, seventy-two hours? "I'm not sure," he says.

"Close your eyes," his father says, "before you start to hallucinate."

What if this whole day was a hallucination? Oliver thinks, sliding back in the chair. In fact, it must be.

He supposes his father is right, he should close his eyes, but instead he manages to engage his mind, at least minimally, on the football game, a kind of mental gum chewing.

His father keeps glancing over at him. "When you feel like talking, let me know," he says finally.

"Maybe tomorrow," Oliver says.

When the game is over, he goes upstairs to see if there are any clothes in his old bedroom he can change into. As he walks up the steps, his thighs ache, every muscle exhausted. He begins to wonder if he will ever be able to sleep again, or if his body has forgotten how. He finds nothing in his closet that would fit. He ought to head home anyway. It's getting late, and Nana is dead.

The door to Al's room is closed, and he knows April has to be in there. It irritates him that she chose to sleep in Al's bed. At the same time, he does not want her anywhere near him.

He opens the door. The primrose-yellow dress is draped over the back of a chair. She is curled up, hugging a pillow, her satin slip taut across her backside. Oliver kicks the metal wastebasket. April bolts upright, hand to her chest.

"If you need a ride I'm leaving in five minutes," he says, and leaves the room.

In the family room he puts on his jacket, the damn tails that get in the way of everything. He stuffs his ascot in his pocket, reminding himself to return everything by noon tomorrow. He says good night to his father. Five minutes have not passed but he leaves anyway.

He gets into his car, covered with streamers and shaving cream. JUST MARRIED is written across the back window. Earlier in the day, he almost yanked off his tailpipe trying to get rid of the beer cans. The night has turned cold. Days getting shorter. He rolls up his window and turns over the engine.

April comes out of the house wearing the yellow dress and Hal's suit coat, which he no doubt insisted she borrow. The sleeves fall to her knuckles. One shoe is on her foot and the other in her hand. She opens the door, gets in, and slams it shut.

Her hair is half fallen from its bun, makeup lightly smeared beneath her eyes. "I could have used an extra minute for the bathroom," she says, slipping on the other heel.

He pulls out of the driveway. She takes a tissue from her purse, wets it with her tongue, and runs it under her eyes, which are raw and puffy. She lets down her hair and rakes her hands through it, buttons Hal's suit jacket and turns the collar up. Then she folds her arms across her chest. He could turn on the heat for her, but doesn't.

"I still haven't called Mr. Bergfalk," she says. "How am I supposed to do that?"

He drives over the limit, accelerating through yellow lights. "Aren't you going to ask me what happened?" he says hoarsely.

She looks at him with surprise. "Your father just told me a little while ago. I'm so sorry, Oliver, but I'm sure she'll change her mind. It's just the confusion of the day."

"No," he says, tightening his hands on the wheel. "She's not taking me back." He feels throbbing in his head like a drug wearing off.

"Give her time. Talk to her. Surely there's hope."

"We spoke three times today," he says. "Each time she was more furious than before."

"That's a start."

Oliver tastes beer and cake, the sickening blend. He turns hard into the deserted church lot. People in passing cars honk and shout, presuming they are newlyweds. He pulls up next to April's car and lurches to a halt. His headache is excruciating. He leans back on the headrest for a minute. The instant he closes his eyes, the boat begins to shift and sway. A wave hits them broadside, and his head smacks against the driver's-side window. His eyes fly open.

"Oliver, you're falling asleep," she says. "Let me drive you home."

"I just need some fresh air," he says, getting out. He wanders down to the trunk, puts one arm around his middle, and covers his eyes with the other. He hears her beside him. "You caused this, you know," he says.

April rakes her hands through her hair. "I knew as soon as I got to her house," she says. "She didn't look well. I pleaded with her to let me take her to the hospital. She said if she still didn't feel well after the ceremony, we could go. How stupid of me!"

"That's not what I'm taking about," Oliver says, drawing his hand down over his mouth, meeting her eye.

"Oh, God," she says. "I'm sorry, Oliver. If that's true, I am absolutely sorry. But I know she'll take you back. And I did try to warn you. You have to admit that you acted like a complete ass. What were you thinking?"

"I have no idea," he says. "I wasn't thinking."

He moves back to the driver's-side door, leaning on the car as he goes.

"You're not driving," she says. "You're half asleep."

"I'm better now."

She steers him toward the passenger seat instead.

"Bernadette asked me not to talk to you again, and I didn't last."

"It's not too late," April says, opening his door. "We'll stop talking now."

"I think we should, out of respect for Bernadette, even though she'll never know."

"Don't be a pessimist," she says, helping him into the car. "You'll be married by Tuesday. Elope somewhere. Now put on your seat belt."

"How long?" he says, slumping back in the seat.

"Till Tuesday?"

"The not talking."

"I don't know. The rest of our lives? Give me your keys."

He pulls them out of his pocket. "Six months, for starters," he says. "That's how long it takes to quit smoking."

She goes around to the driver's-side door and gets in. It must be true, what his father said about hallucinating, because he thinks he hears the rustle of taffeta.

"Nana would want us to use Franklin's Funeral Parlor. That's where Spencer was. Hey, you're not buckled," she says.

He's not sleeping; he just wants to close his eyes for a moment. She reaches across him for the belt. He feels her hair against his cheek, smells pine needles near the tree line, and hears the crunch of their sneakers on snow. Outside the church, a bride and groom duck under a shower of rice and into a waiting limousine. Bernadette's laughter is hard and bright in the crisp autumn air. She pulls her train in after her. It is miles long. The groom waves ecstatically to his family and dips in behind her. His blond hair and white tuxedo catch the afternoon light. Oliver rakes his fingers through the hair at the base of her neck, touches his cheek to hers until he feels her ear against his lips. "April," he whispers. "I blame you for everything."

She pats his knee. "Sh," she says, turning over the engine. "Six months, remember?"

It's three in the morning when Oliver wakes up in his driveway, still strapped in. The doors are locked and he finds the keys in his pocket. Once inside his apartment, he paces from one room to the next. He knows he ought to do something, change his clothes, eat,

get to bed, but he can't. Twice he picks up the phone to call Bernadette only to remember the time. Something enormous has run over
his chest, pulverizing everything.

The apartment is filled with wedding gifts. Those from his side of
the family and friends had been left here while Bernadette's went to
her parents' house. He sees a rather large, flat box with FRAGILE written in many directions. It takes him a moment to recognize April's
handwriting.

He tells himself he doesn't care what's inside, but tears it open
anyway. It's a large, antique mirror with an elaborate, carved trim.
Odd, he thinks. What does she mean by this? As he leans it atop the
mantel and steps back, a reflection appears, a bedraggled man in a
wrinkled black tuxedo with ashen skin and the saddest eyes Oliver
has ever seen. It's happened, he thinks. He's burned his life to the
ground.

Absently he sits down on the piano bench. An emotion he cannot name thickens in his throat. He thinks of the woman from the
photograph with the bound feet, her queer, self-satisfied expression.
Why didn't he sell the piano long ago? What was the point of keeping it now, after so many years? He imagines the woman, the pain
she must have felt as hour by hour, year by year, the natural force of
her growth pressed against its confinement; the tension that must
have permeated her entire being—all set against the conviction she
was doing what had to be done.

SPRING

Chapter
41

T HE LATE-MARCH AIR IS COOL AND DAMP, the swift clouds so
low they appear within reach. As the road dips and rises along
the rocky Massachusetts coastline, the car passes through fog and
emerges again. April is on her way home to study. She has a midterm
tomorrow and another on Thursday, followed by a two-week break.
She has an urge to pick up and leave town for a few days, to go someplace she's never been.

"I think you should." Al called her at work earlier in the day. "In
fact, I've got a game in Vegas next week. Why don't you come? I can
give you the miles."

"Why? So we can gamble away my riches?" she said.

"No," Al said. "So we can eat sushi and get married."

"Right," she said, laughing.

"When are you going to take me seriously?" he said.

"Good-bye, Al," she said.

"I mean it about the miles," he said. "I'll never use them all. Go
ahead and get out of town. It doesn't have to be with me. You've got
a passport, right?"

"Yes, but I was only thinking of Maine."

"Expand your horizons, darling. I'll even mind the Doobster for you."

"Thanks," she said. "I'll think about it."

The car is hesitant, stalling now and then. The engine sounds rougher than usual, or maybe it's just the rain striking the roof. After a winter by the sea, the car is in worse shape, fenders rusting, wires corroded. Buddy would not be pleased. The registration is in April's name; she pays for the insurance, but she still feels it is on extended loan.

The car is April's reminder of everything she did, or allowed. The chain of cause and effect stretches back not only days before Buddy's death, the neglected brake job, but years, decades. April wonders if she had lived differently, if Buddy would still be alive, or if Oliver might have his life back.

Her own loneliness does not concern her. She thinks of it as fertile ground, an oasis that has been with her all these years but that she ignored until now. Her car radio died shortly after she moved to Nahant, and the first time she drove without it she felt anxious and alone, the pressure of her own thoughts inflating like a balloon, empty and ready to burst. She could not name how she felt about even the simplest things, like Oliver's leaving. She was lost.

Now, although the radio is fixed, she drives without it. Her thoughts move not in a linear, directed way, but circuitously, like the tide. She has learned to mark the currents in the cove near her apartment by noticing a boulder in the surf, dry at the lowest ebb, submerged at the highest.

She turns onto the causeway. The surf is choppy, the salt air sharp in her nostrils. The car sways in the wind, and she struggles to keep it in lane. She parks in front of her apartment and tucks her library books inside her jacket, Elizabeth Bishop, Willa Cather, and *Do-It-Yourself Auto Repair*. The gale is so strong she can't open the car door. Nahant is vulnerable to squalls because of its location, a tiny peninsula jutting out into the North Atlantic, connected to the mainland by a narrow, two-mile isthmus. April chose the place for its sound. After living by the station for so long, she cannot sleep in silence. The surf echoes in her apartment, plangent as trains.

The apartments, set apart on the southernmost tip of the island, are the only rentals. Surrounded by ocean on three sides, the Point is rocky and austere, a place of perpetual wind. With one church, one general store, and no bars, Nahant is not a location anyone would have expected her to choose.

She tries again to shove open the car door, but the wind is too strong. With her wipers off, the hood appears to liquefy, a blurry river of milk. She shifts over to the passenger seat where a gust nearly takes the door off its hinges.

As she opens her apartment door, Dubious's scruffy snout sticks out. She hears his tail rapping against the furniture. "Doobie." She laughs, kneeling down. He rushes away and returns with a slipper.

"No," she says gently.

He dashes off again, this time returning with a dish towel.

"Eh, eh." She shakes her head.

Once more he darts away, racing back to her with a stringy, gnawed rope toy. "Well, thank you," she says, returning it to him. "You're very thoughtful."

He picks up his ball and runs hopefully to the door. "Tomorrow," she says. "It's raining."

His ears flatten back.

"We'll do business, though," she says, taking the leash. "Just don't blow away."

He dances around her twice, and then sits for the leash.

After they return, she dries off his paws and goes out onto the balcony. The wind tangles the curtains behind her. Pictures rattle against the walls. The sea is gray, the color of the sky, both in motion, barely distinguishable. Waves extend in frothy lines from one horizon to the other, rolling inland. The rock is underwater, buffeted by invisible currents.

She goes indoors, makes tea, and flips through her mail, stopping when she sees Hal's handwriting. Oliver has been writing to his father once a month describing the places he encounters, and each time Hal mails photocopies to her and Al, surely without Oliver's knowledge. April takes the envelope, the fifth in five months, and puts it aside. Sometimes it takes her days to open one. It's not the content she braces herself for, but the familiarity of his handwriting.

The previous letters, now stacked on her desk, are long, sumptuous narratives worthy of a travel writer. He was smitten by Europe, her castles, catacombs, and ruins. He wandered through them, searching for something that would open his mind to the past. He filled pages with Krakow and Budapest, cities that embody their history. April pictures him moving across the continent like a kid just out of college, with nothing but backpack and maps, his face unshaven and tanned. Before leaving, he sold his car and gave up his apartment. His last act was to sell his piano and use the money for a plane ticket.

When April heard through Hal that Oliver was selling the piano, she found the ad in the newspaper and asked a friend to call about it for her. When the piano movers came to take it, Oliver had no idea it was April who bought it. She can't play, but sometimes at night she sits with her back to its side.

She spreads her class notes on the small desk in her bedroom. Dubious makes three circles at her feet and settles down. Two more months in a drafty lecture hall with runny-nosed teenagers and she will be done with her first semester. She turns the pages of her textbook. *The History of Western Civilization,* chapter 27, the Weimar Republic.

She ought to sell the car, she thinks. The thought comes to her just like that. School is the place to advertise it. Some nineteen-year-old will claim the car, and April will find herself something new to drive.

Chapter

42

THE GROUND IS SPONGY beneath Oliver's hiking boots, the boggy turf green even in March. Island fog makes it hard for Oliver to get his bearings, but the boom of ocean against rock below tells him he is nearing the bluffs. The island is wedge-shaped, with one side sloping down to small, sandy beaches, and the other ending abruptly at hundred-foot cliffs.

He didn't expect to come to Ireland, but after five months in seven countries, he found himself in Le Havre, France, where a ferry was embarking for Rosslare. Two days on the Irish Sea seemed reason enough to board. It turned out to be a rough voyage. Oliver spent day and night on deck, staring out at towering waves.

He crossed the lush Irish countryside by train and landed in Galway, where he saw a posting for a ferry to the Aran Islands. Traveling alone, he has begun to remember how to move by instinct. He is like a boy in the woods, choosing trails by impulse without worrying about how to get back, driven by the need to get lost. As the ferry chugged out of Galway Bay and into the choppy Atlantic, he had no doubt this was where he had been headed all along. The mainland faded and disappeared, and the three small islands rose up in a dare to the sea.

Inishmore is grassy, rocky, and nearly treeless. Since arriving over two weeks ago, Oliver has walked the circumference, first the tranquil, sloping side, where water laps the beaches and pony traps pull the random tourist, and now the cliff side, which faces nothing but ocean and, beyond the earth's curve, North America. As far as he can tell, Oliver is standing on Europe's westernmost landfall.

There are no paths or guardrails. This side of the island is all grass, divided into parcels by mortarless walls that appear as old as the island itself. The stones separate one man's sheep from another's.

He hears the cawing of terns below and sees he is only feet from the edge. He crab-walks to the rim, where he hangs his feet over the bottomless drop. The cliff is wildly uneven; pastures have fallen into the sea at random. He is on the edge of a jagged point; to his right and left the sea has chewed thirty or forty feet deeper into land. The tops of the cliffs cantilever out over the ocean while it quarries below. Into these caves glide waves and cormorants. The slosh of water against rock is intoxicating. Oliver is the stone, cleansed and carved.

He recalls April's voice from childhood, over the sound of the surf one summer. "Come on," she called. "The tide's going out. We can make it."

Oliver stared at the mountain of rock emerging from the sea about a hundred feet offshore, just at the edge of a cove. To him, it had the shape of a gigantic wolf curled in sleep. Even if they reached it, how could they possibly scale it, especially with a four-year-old in tow?

"Do you have any idea how fast the tide comes in here?" he called.

But April had already hoisted Buddy up on her shoulders and was making her way gingerly across the slick, rounded boulders. It didn't matter that she had rolled up her shorts. They were instantly doused by waves moving in turbulent sheets across the bed of stones. Oliver knew better than to try to stop her.

They were twelve. Oliver's parents had invited April and Buddy on a camping trip. Buddy liked to wake April and Oliver every morning to go exploring before breakfast. Al, then fourteen, was dead asleep at that hour, and refused to be roused for anything short of the tent catching fire.

"Wait up," Oliver called. He had on sturdier sandals than April, but still it was hard to find his footing on the slick, ribbon-like seaweed. The ocean smell was strong here. In the fleeting moments when the water stilled between surges, it was surreally clear. Rocks of all colors glistened beneath the surface. He saw a sea urchin, and then, to his amazement, a starfish with long, graceful fingers and a spiny, salmon-ocher back. It appeared only for an instant before being obliterated by the next influx of water.

"How can you see where you're going?" Oliver asked. April's hands were cupped around Buddy's ankles while her hair flew wildly about her face.

"Do me a favor," she said. "Tie it in a knot."

He had done this before, so he knew to grasp the hair at the base of her skull, twist it snugly into a rope down to the tip, then tie the whole thing in a slip knot.

Was the water deeper now because they were getting closer to the sleeping wolf, or was the tide coming in? Looking back over the rocks they had already crossed, it was impossible to tell. The closer they got to the huge rock, the more the boulders were encrusted with sharp, gnarly barnacles.

"The barnacles are closed," Oliver said, bending to look at them. "Doesn't that mean they've been out of water for a while?"

"Does it?" she said.

"Low tide's over," he said. "We don't have much time."

"We've gotten this far, Oliver," she said. "Let's at least see the view from the top."

"How are we supposed to get up there?"

They hoisted themselves up on a ledge, the back paw of the wolf. "I'll go first," she said. "You pass Buddy up to me." She began to climb. The rock was a creamy pink with crystalline specks that sparkled in the morning sun. When she reached the next level spot, she lay on her stomach and reached her hands down for Buddy. Oliver held the boy over his head until April had grabbed hold. They heard a thunderous boom as a wave struck the rock from the opposite side. Fine spray came down on them from over the rise. "Here comes the tide," Oliver shouted.

"Hurry up," Buddy called down to him. "We're almost at the top."

As they approached the crest, they each took one of the boy's hands. As soon as they stepped over the rise, a burst of wind almost knocked them off their feet. They grabbed each other, Buddy between them, and went to their knees. It was like being in a wind tunnel. April's hair came undone and whipped behind her like a tattered flag. Oliver's sweatshirt nearly flew clear off his body. Buddy howled laughter, raising his arms. April and Oliver held him tightly. The wind was so strong it was hard to breathe, but somehow they were smiling. The expanse of ocean before them was more than Oliver's eyes could take in. He had never seen so much sea at once. Rows of whitecaps extended out to the horizon. With the vast, glinting ocean before them and the strident wind in their faces, Oliver wondered: *If this moment were a song, what would it sound like?*

He doesn't know how long he has been sitting there when he smells the musky aroma of burning peat and realizes he is hungry. He left the B&B at dawn, so he guesses it must be close to nine by now, four in the morning back home, though he's not inclined to think that way anymore. The fog has thinned and he begins walking, passing black-faced sheep and a lone horse switching its tail as it watches him. He sees a white building and moves toward it, hoping to find a road he can follow. It turns out to be a church, simple and small, with stone walls and a slate roof that probably replaced the thatch.

Without thinking, he goes inside. Frail light filters onto the pews.

It is empty. He has not been inside a church since his wedding day. Through blood-red glass, the tabernacle flame shimmers, indicating the presence of the Eucharist. Oliver genuflects, though he's not sure why, and when he stands, he notices beside the altar a modest, upright piano.

At the same moment Oliver stands frozen in the church, April awakens to the sound of wind. A dream swims in her mind, and she quiets herself to remember it clearly. She is lying in the back of a canoe, her arm draped over the side, fingertips raking the cool water. Fly fishing, Buddy stands in front, reeling in his line. He turns to look at her over his shoulder, his grin wide and confident. "This is it," he says. "I'm going for broke." As he throws his arm back to cast, the endless swerve of the line slicing across the sky, the latch on his wristwatch opens. April reaches over the side of the boat and snatches the watch an instant before it hits the water. When she looks up, Buddy is gone. The boat is still, the water undisturbed. He has vanished, and in his place on the forward bench of the canoe lies a glistening rainbow trout.

April sits up in bed. She looks for her watch atop the library books on the night table, but finds it has fallen to the floor. She reaches for it. Four twelve AM. She shivers. The dream felt so real.

If Oliver takes a single step farther into the church, he will lose his bearings. Something here wants him, the way fire does wood. He pictures the stove at the B&B where he brews himself tea. Each night he tosses a brick of peat into the flames and watches, transfixed, as the peat is gradually inhabited, consumed, obliterated into light and heat. The fire ravages the peat, the peat fueling the fire, transformed as one into fragrance and ash.

He tells himself he only wants to see if the piano is tuned. Fragments of memories shower his mind, like the time he waded into the ocean at night and dove toward the lane of moonlight lilting on the rhythmic sea. The memory glints and vanishes like a knife through water, ephemeral as fingers shaping a chord.

Shaken by the dream, April pulls on her robe. Dubious stands abruptly and shakes, his eyes sleepy and dazed. "It's okay," she says. "Go back to sleep."

In her pocket is Oliver's letter. She stares at it, remembering hide-and-seek, how good he was at keeping still. When she found him, it was because he summoned her. Even now she can almost hear the pause between his breaths, the silence around each heartbeat. At the same time, he is infinitely far, like someone she never knew.

In the living room, the sliding glass door is wet with spray sucked from the crests of waves. April opens it a few inches and feels the burst of cool salt air lift her hair off her shoulders. The sky is remarkably clear now. She recognizes Vega and the constellation Orion. The sea has never sounded so close. The dog circles her nervously. With her eyes on the darkened window, she slides down against the piano and listens.

He tests a note. The piano feels like a stranger, cold and stiff. He remembers lying in the rowboat with April, water lapping the wood. It was true what she said about setting fire to everyone she touched.

The cold, damp church has swollen the wood of the piano. The keys are a fraction late springing back, but it's in tune. He plays Bach's Minuet in G Sharp, one of the first he practiced as a boy, and the piano rises to it.

The sea is turbulent outside. Dubious rests his head in April's lap. She moves her grandmother's cross between her fingers, opens the letter, and reads. *Dear Dad,* it begins. She feels voyeuristic, reading someone else's mail, but Hal seems determined to share it. As she reads, she learns that Oliver is in Ireland now, on an island called Inishmore where he plans to stay through April. After that, he's not sure if he will return to California, go back to law school, or some third option he hasn't thought of yet. He's leaning toward something impractical. April folds the letter, smiling, and strokes the dog's back.

She notices a second envelope within the first. She takes it out and sees *Please forward to April* written in Oliver's pen. She gives a start. Dubious looks up at her curiously. Until now Oliver has not so much as mentioned her. She opens it to find only a postcard, an aerial shot of an island off Galway Bay, breathtaking and bleak. She stares at the image without flipping it over, afraid of what he has written. Looking at the island, she imagines it some five thousand miles due east, skirting the opposite shore. She wonders about the people who live there, how one learns to survive the presence of so much beauty. Bracing herself, she turns the postcard over. In the upper-left corner the faintly typeset address of a B&B has been circled in the same blue pen as her name on the envelope. Below that, nothing is written. Not a word.